A Place To Stand

A Place To Stand
A Tale of the Peace River Country

J. W. Secrist

Bloomington, IN  Milton Keynes, UK

AuthorHouse™
1663 Liberty Drive, Suite 200
Bloomington, IN 47403
www.authorhouse.com
Phone: 1-800-839-8640

AuthorHouse™ UK Ltd.
500 Avebury Boulevard
Central Milton Keynes, MK9 2BE
www.authorhouse.co.uk
Phone: 08001974150

© 2006 J. W. Secrist. All rights reserved.

No part of this book may be reproduced, stored in a retrieval system, or transmitted by any means without the written permission of the author.

First published by AuthorHouse 6/2/2006

ISBN: 1-4259-0742-3 (e)
ISBN: 1-4259-0741-5 (sc)

Library of Congress Control Number: 2005911253

Printed in the United States of America
Bloomington, Indiana

This book is printed on acid-free paper.

Cover illustration courtesy of Beth Ardill

Contents

Preface	~	*vii*
1971	~	*1*
1929	~	*6*
1914	~	*17*
1937	~	*62*
1944	~	*87*
1963	~	*169*

Preface

This book is a work of fiction; however, I have drawn somewhat on the lives of people I have known personally and many I have only known about. While no attempt was made to duplicate the lives of real persons, I must admit to borrowing ideas from episodes of those people whose interesting lives impressed me. Any resemblance of characters in this novel with anyone, living or dead, is coincidental.

The North American pioneer epic is behind us now, but only just. British Columbia's Peace River Country was among the last places on this hemisphere, perhaps the whole earth, to see its lands come under the influence and the plow of the pioneer homesteader, coming into the scope of settlement at a time when the world was changing from the technology of the horse to the combustion engine. People are still living here, as elsewhere, who have seen and lived through this change. This is their collective story.

A Place To Stand

1971

On a stunningly beautiful May afternoon in the old hamlet of Hudson's Hope, Tassy Brennan became Mrs. Loren Rutmar. The bride was radiant in a long white gown, her jet-black hair pushed up high on her head, a long plait of it hanging down her back. The light brown of her face was set off nicely by the pink flush of her cheeks and her flawless white teeth. Her young cousins scurried about like excited chipmunks, one of them proudly carrying her long taffeta train.

Tassy (Patricia) was given in marriage by her grandfather, Liam Brennan, his angular, slightly-stooped figure clad in a dark grey suit, obviously out of his element in these surroundings, but making a valiant effort to be gracious. Liam's clean-shaven, weather-beaten and deeply-lined face was testament to a life spent outdoors. His hair, almost white now, was still thick and full. He stood with his hands clasped over one another at his waist. Those hands caught the eye, for though Liam was not of anything more than ordinary size, his scarred hands were thick and powerful looking. Some of the fingers looked odd, slightly misshapen even. He wore no rings or adornment of any kind.

Just now, the marriage ceremony completed, he stood outside the church door, Tassy and her solemn young husband at her side, shaking hands and conversing with the small crowd of acquaintances, friends and relatives in attendance. By Loren's side stood his parents, his father a somewhat larger and stouter replica of Liam, his mother short, round and smiling and behind them a gaggle of Loren's siblings, all of them very formal, the parents struggling with their English, speaking when they had to in heavy German accents. But taken all in all, it was a happy and festive occasion, made all the more so, Liam thought, because the sun shone today out of a cloudless, windless blue sky, an anomaly in a near two week spate of rain and overcast.

From time to time Tassy took and squeezed Liam's hand.

"Grampa, thank you so much…I'm so very happy today. Thank you for everything, for all of this, for the beautiful gift…for just being here." She put her arm on his shoulder, pulled him down slightly and kissed him on a weather-blasted cheek.

"If only Gramma could have been here today."

"Yes," said Liam, "she would surely have enjoyed this."

Joanna's young daughters scampered about now, throwing rice and frolicking on the edge of the adults.

"Amelia! Stop that!" Joanna commanded. "Get back over here! And you, too, Nancy!"

The children complied but their energy and enthusiasm for the moment guaranteed that they would not retain decorum for very long.

On the periphery of the group, well out of the swirl of the social vortex, stood a very tall young man also clad in a new suit, looking, like Liam, a bit out of place and not making any more effort than he had to be garrulous. At his side, holding his hand and wiping her smiling face from time to time with a handkerchief stood a pretty young woman. Presently he came forward and in the midst of the group of chattering well-wishers, he leaned down and whispered something in Liam's ear. Liam stood up a bit straighter and turned to his right. A few yards away, on the grass next to the graveled parking lot, stood three native men, clad in cowboy hats, jeans and bright western shirts. They were an interesting trio, two of the men much younger than the shrunken, bent-over old man they supported on either elbow. The thickset, passive-faced man on the left contrasted sharply with the one on the right. This one was slender-hipped, broad-shouldered and had a very handsome hawk-like visage. He was nattily attired in a new black hat, stripped purple and white shirt with a string of pearly buttons on each wrist; his boots were black and obviously expensive. At Liam's recognition he ground out his cigarette and strode forward jauntily, though with a noticeable limp, a dazzling smile on his handsome face, speaking loudly as he grasped Liam's hand.

"Hey, Liam! Good to see you, man. Sorry to be so late, but Noah ain't that easy to get goin' anymore. Fact is, I think he mighta forgot till we went to get him."

"Royce, I'm glad you and Noah could make it, and him too." He nodded at the other young man.

"Yeah, that's Alex, my brother who lives at Chetwynd. Hey, you sure got a nice setup here, and, wow, is Tassy a knockout! Who's the lucky guy anyways? He from around here?"

"Her husband's name is Loren, Loren Rutmar. And, yes, his family's from Beryl Prairie, they farm out there." Liam turned, his hand on Royce's elbow. "I guess you know Tassy," he said, "and this is Loren." Royce gave the slightly startled Tassy a hug and a buss on the cheek, extending his hand to Loren, and Loren taking it solemnly.

"Hey, man, good to see you. So now we're gonna have you in the family," he said loudly. "Tassy here's one of my favorite relatives. Right, Tassy?" That they had met only once before seemed of little consequence to Royce. He spoke as though they were old and intimate acquaintances. "So you two gonna be livin' round here now?"

"Yes," Loren responded. "We'll be living in Fort St. John. I'll be working at McCoy Brothers; Tassy's got a job with the city as a clerk."

"Hey, man, that's great. Probably be seein' you pretty often then. Not right away though. My leg's almost healed up now; I'll be back ridin' in a few weeks. Maybe even in time for the Stampede." Royce blathered on, for the moment stealing the limelight and enjoying it immensely, Tassy and Loren slightly startled but conversing politely with him.

Liam turned to old Noah standing nearly forgotten at the edge of the group, leaning heavily on a stout walking stick. Liam observed him carefully. He seemed much smaller than he remembered. But then, Liam thought, who knows how old he'd be by now. Noah wore a cowboy hat like the other two and jeans and a wide western belt, but instead of the brassy western shirt, he was clad in a fringed jacket of deer or elk skin, beautifully embroidered on the front with beads and porcupine quills. He, alone of those gathered there, wore moccasins sheathed in low rubbers. He was stooped over, much more so even than Liam, his face looking down, partially hiding his features. He still wore his hair long, the snow-white braids hanging down over the front of his jacket.

"Noah, I'm glad you came," said Liam, now at his side and looking slightly down at him. "I wasn't even sure if you got the invitation we sent."

Noah raised his head slightly and looked up. His features had undergone the remorseless winnowing of time: cheeks sunken and fantastically lined, chin and nose closer together now, aided by the loss of teeth, head held low on a thin neck. And yet, Liam thought, it's easy to recognize him. The nose is still the same and the eyes, sunk deep into their gnarly sockets, black as obsidian and still piercing when he looks in your face.

"Well, Noah, it's been a long time since we last saw each other," said Liam, grasping as he always did with this old man to find a line of conversation. "How you been getting along?"

Noah made no response.

"Sure good to have some nice weather for a change," said Liam, trying another tack. "I was gettin' pretty sick of rain."

"Royce rides good them horses, wins money lots."

"I've heard that," said Liam, thinking to have found a topic. "Heard he was gonna ride again in Calgary this year. Guess he did okay there last year," said Liam. "I hadn't heard about his accident though. Where'd he get his leg broke?"

Noah made no response to this nor to any other comment Liam made for the next couple of minutes, seeming to have fallen back into some other reality that he had left but briefly. "Noah," Liam finally said, "come over and see Tassy and Loren, they'll be so happy you're here." He wondered to himself if that were really true. He led Noah carefully over to stand in front of Tassy, the old man taking short, hesitant steps leaning heavily on his walking stick and Liam's arm. When he stood in front of Tassy, Liam spoke, "Noah, this is Tassy now and her new husband Loren." He started to say more, then checked himself. Tassy stood looking down at Noah, a mixture of perplexity, compassion, perhaps even a tinge of fright, playing across her beautiful face.

"Noah...," she said. "I'm glad that you could come here today." For what seemed an eternity, old Noah stood, his face angled down, staring at something in another world.

"Noah, say hi to Tassy!" It was Royce speaking loudly into Noah's ear. The old man raised his head and for a short moment his piercing black eyes held hers, then he raised his withered right hand and placed it on Tassy's cheek. She smiled down rigidly at him, waiting for him to speak, but he did not. He dropped his hand, slowly pivoted on his cane and started to shuffle away. "We go now," he said.

As the last of the marriage party left, Loren and Tassy having departed half an hour earlier, crepe paper fluttering from their small car, strings of tin cans rattling behind it, Carson moved to Liam's side, Jennifer still holding his hand.

"Well, what do you think? Turned out pretty good I thought."

"It was wonderful," said Jennifer still dabbing at her eyes, "just a beautiful wedding!"

"Couldn't have asked for better," said Liam, watching the last cars leave the church parking lot. "Sure was glad to see us get a break with the weather."

"Too bad Gramma couldn't have been here," Carson said uncharacteristically. "She sure would have liked this."

Liam made no answer to this, but he nodded his assent, his eyes looking past the other two, seemingly lost in thoughts of his own.

Later as he drove alone back to the home place, Liam found his mind kept circling back to other times far removed from the festiveness of the occasion he'd just presided over. The river road undulated and twisted sharply from time to time and the vernal beauty of the river valley, clad in its late spring greenery slid by the windows of the car nearly unnoticed; Liam paid only cursory attention. His thoughts flickered far back to another time, seemingly now, almost another world.

1929

Wolf-haunted and murky in the grey light of late afternoon, the prominent ridges on the north, cloven by deep brush-choked draws, drew back several hundred yards from the river. Patches of brush and clumps of coarse grass lay exposed and free of snow on the eroded bluffs, testament to the power of wind and sun even in the depths of a northern winter. The river flowed eastward in great serpentine S's. Except for various side channels of the river itself, which were pocked with piles of driftwood, the flats on its left, once part of the river channel itself, were a jumble of burnt-over timber, shot through with new growth. The great river lay buried under several feet of snow and half as much ice.

To the right, beginning on the south bank and extending into greyish oblivion, tremendous stands of virgin timber, some of portentous girth, lay like an immense blanket over everything. On the river the snow lay in various depths, drifted and crusted by wind, but under the timber the sea of intertwined conifers reduced the snow cover to a mere dusting of the ground, their boughs and limbs supporting potential avalanches. This shield, this canopy, lay monotonously, everlastingly over all. Nothing interrupted its domain, only the rise and decline of hills that quickly lost themselves in the grey gloom. There was no fog on this day, but the steady fall of tiny granular snowflakes propelled by the relentless wind reduced visibility to a few hundred yards and dulled the edge of every sound, even the low moan of the wind in the timber.

It was an ordinary enough scene to the man: featureless riverbanks, ceaseless snow, gloomy indistinguishable sky, gnawing cold, silence. Hadn't it been like this for him a hundred times? A thousand? What was it about the way light blended surface and sky together, made it sometimes dreamlike, unreal, even faintly menacing, as though a person could just pass out of sight like a river island or the bluffs that appeared and as quickly were erased by the ceaseless snow and by the moving sled.

The remembrance of the sled, of his icy mittened hands clutching the handles, pulled Liam back into his world of reality—a world of cold, of objective, of responsibility. The looming promontory barely visible though only a few hundred feet away became not just another object to get past but a goal, a need. On the south facing bank of a low hill which looked over a large tributary of the river upon which the sled now moved was a crumbling, decrepit hut of spruce logs built sometime years before by a trapper who had plied his trade up and down the tributary. The trapper, though himself long since vanished, had built well. Despite mudslides, the ravages of pests and scavengers and the unrelenting hand of time, the hut remained. Partly roofless, vermin-ridden, sagging, it nevertheless offered some shelter, the only human-made shelter in the immediate area. Liam hated the thought of the pack rat stench, the morose look of the place, but his practical brain told him that it offered some relief, no matter how marginal, from the aching cold. He knew he could duplicate, even improve on the situation, but it would take precious time, time which he clearly knew he did not have.

Rounding the slow curve of the hill, Liam stopped the dogs and peered speculatively upstream from the mouth of the frozen stream. From where the sled sat, he could not see the hut but saw plainly the heavy stand of spruce in which it stood. He urged the tired dogs into the stiff breeze that blew down the ice-sheathed stream, and minutes later they strained up the steep bank to the hut, almost obscured in the dense timber. Liam had stopped here before, always when forced by need to do so. He did not relish the darkness of the place, its poorly thought-out arrangement and also because no one had ever taken time to clear a proper trail to the river. Apparently, its architect had paid scant attention to any of this; for him the hut had served only as temporary shelter and storage for traps and other paraphernalia of his livelihood. Once the hut had contained a bunk built against the north wall and a table-like bench and stool. These, along with the door, its shreds of leather hinges still spiked to the frame, were long vanished, likely burned for warmth by other itinerants. The roof, which had been a haphazard affair of small spruce rails covered over with mud, moss and other flotsam, had collapsed over one end of the hut and appeared about to disintegrate altogether. Some recent interloper had propped up the rotten rails up sticks and there it remained, nothing more than a windbreak and snow deflector.

Liam's eyes darted around the interior of sagging logs. He paused, exhaled deeply, and set to work. First, he tied the five famished dogs to separate trees and proceeded to cut a few small branches to shore up what remained of the roof. With the economy of movement characteristic of men who have spent much of their lives in the open, Liam found a small dry snag, hewed it down, cut it to short lengths and piled them just inside the hut. Next he tramped the snow which had sifted inside and spread a heavy canvas tarp in the corner. When he had a fire going, most of the smoke blowing through the gap in the roof, he finally turned his attention to the bundled figure still wrapped in a snow-covered skin robe on the sled.

"Warm enough?"

"Yes, I think so, Liam, but I got to stand up for a while. This seat is so hard and cold."

"Of course, Marta. Why didn't you say something? I could have taken time to help you up."

"It's all right. Help me with the snowshoes."

"You won't need those. I'll carry you inside."

"I can do it myself, you needn't bother."

Even as she objected, Liam picked her up in his arms, though she was not a small woman, and carried her into the hut, pausing to step out of snowshoes at the door.

"Sit on the tarp by the fire. I'll boil some tea."

"Please, Liam, I've got to stand and move a little. My back is hurting so much." She stood lumpishly, wrapped in a dirty Hudson Bay blanket, her hands hanging like mallets at the ends of her rigid arms. A couple of times she started to move, to help her husband, but her extreme discomfort and awkwardness stopped her before she started. Her face was ashen and her teeth were clenched tightly. She needed to move, to do something, for she felt a compulsion to do her part as she had always done, but a heavy torpor seemed to possess her. She willed to act, to move, but her wretchedly cold and painful body betrayed her. For a few minutes she just stood at the edge of the slow growing fire, moving only to avoid the pitchy smoke, the fact of her advanced pregnancy apparent even in the voluminous clothes and blankets.

Finally, her face puckered up and for a moment she nearly lost the iron resolve that she had clung to through the previous hours.

"Oh, Lord, will this awful winter never end? My God, Liam, it's nearly April and look at it! Still five feet of snow out in the open, everything frozen and lifeless, the stock almost out of feed, turned out to try and forage and for what? Can a cow eat willows or trees? The crust on the snow will cut their legs to pieces if they try to move far. That is if the wolves don't kill them all first! If only there was something green and alive, something besides these endless trees! Something to tell us this winter is going to end, that something is still alive and warm. And look at us! Freezing the life out of us in this miserable place. Liam, by this time in Amsterdam, there were blooming flowers everywhere, the trees were leafed out, there were green fields, the cattle fed and contented. Oh, Liam, why are we here? Why do we stay? And our sons alone at home except for that worthless Wallace that is supposed to be a hand! And what of this one inside me? The time is past, I am sure of it. Something is terribly wrong. I know it! Oh, God, Liam, what can we do? It should have been born by now and yet—it lives. Several times today I felt it move inside me. What can we do if there is no doctor at Dawson Creek?" She flung her arm back in a gesture of helplessness, very near the hysteria she had been suppressing for weeks. "And look at this place! Who would want it but us? We must be the greatest fools in the world! We..."

She stopped. Liam stood across the fire from her looking deeply into her eyes. She started to say something again, checked herself, took a deep gasp and buried her face in her sleeve. She sobbed, deep wrenching shudders that rocked her back and forth.

Placing his mittened hands carefully around her, Liam sat her down on the tarp and pulled the heavy cowhide around and under her. She did not resist. Her swollen body made her clumsy and the bulky clothing made her incapable of any but the most basic movement. He took his mitt off and placed his hand gently on her cheek. For a few moments, the deep sobs continued and then they stopped abruptly.

"Liam, I'm sorry. I don't know what came over me. Liam, I'm so sorry. Please...I didn't mean the things I said. It's just that, for a minute.... I won't do it again—ever."

"Marta, listen to me. I know there must be some problem with the baby, but there is a doctor at Dawson Creek, I'm sure of it. Ed Wallace was treated by him for blood poisoning last fall. They say he stays at Dawson Creek all the time now, not just visits now and then like before. Marta, it's just one more day. By this time tomorrow, we'll be there. I know how this has been, how it is now for you, but you mustn't give in. You've got to trust me to get you there. I will, you know I will. I'd have you there tonight but these dogs are finished until they can rest. Anyway, you couldn't stand another hour on that sled right now. Let's make you as warm and comfortable as we can. I'll build a fire on both sides of us and in a few hours we'll get up and by the time it's dark again, I'll have you there. All right? Marta, we've done a lot of things, been through a lot together. We'll come through this one, too, I know."

As the northern night closed around them, the wind died down, first to a faint murmur in the trees, then finally to a deep stillness. The sky cleared and, though moonless, the aurora flashed boldly in faint blues, pinks and yellows. They started in the northwest but presently slashed the sky from one end to the other with their strange phantasms. It was strange, mused Liam, how the lights never seemed quite real, as though you were seeing them in a dream. The great sweep of the river valley and its eroded hills lay like a slumbering animal, completely, utterly still. Far in the west, the upthrust peaks of the Ominecas would have been visible had the heavy timber not blocked the view of them. They would have looked, for all the world, like the teeth in a giant saw, those peaks whose summits were clothed everlastingly in a white shroud, ranges some of whose slopes and clefts had rarely if ever yet felt the foot of man.

None of this, save the stars and aurora flashing through the dense conifers, was visible to the two figures huddled together for warmth in woolen blankets and cowhides with the hair side in. A thick mat of spruce boughs kept them off the surface of the snow, but the cold, not intense at first, gradually worked into them like water into hard clay.

Liam held the sleeping Marta close to him throughout the long night, but he himself slept little. The nagging apprehension that possessed him and which he had carefully concealed from Marta now took full play in his sleepless imaginings. His mind returned again and again to their two small sons left in a cabin seventy miles away upriver, of their vulnerability to disaster in the absence of adult supervision. He thought of nine year old Jack, a grey-eyed facsimile of his mother, who, though only a child, bore the enormous responsibility of minding the five year old Wilson and forking what little hay remained to the small herd of cattle, carefully husbanded to their present number of twenty. The boys were not alone; they might have been better off if they had been. Ostensibly watching over them was the adolescent son of another pioneer family a few miles distant from the Brennans. Wilkie Wallace was, on the surface, a witless misfit whose total lack of social acumen and inability to perform any task without constant adult intervention caused most people to dismiss him as hopeless. That there was some retardation in Wilkie's thinking processes could hardly be denied, but for the past two summers and all of the present winter, he had worked for Liam precisely because there was no one else available—no one else who could be considered remotely employable. The few native families that moved hither and yon up and down the Peace did not consider farm work respectable for a man. Tasks requiring horsemanship or a fine-tuned trigger finger attracted them in numbers; feeding cattle, curing hay, making fences, working the land did not interest them. Wilkie found a place at the Brennan's simply because he was available, if not competent; he asked for and received no pay, save food and shelter, and he exhibited no desire to do anything else.

Wilkie's family was quite content with the arrangement. The fact is they dreaded the day when they would have to take him back. So Wilkie now sat vacantly in the kitchen of the Brennan cabin, looking out the window occasionally but mostly just staring around the room. He ritualistically filled the wood box when the last stick was burned, stoked the fire when the room began to grow cold and helped feed the livestock. Wilkie's imagination was not developed enough for him to be fearful of much. He was quite at ease with Liam and Marta's absence except that it necessitated his pulling together something for the three of them to eat. In truth, young Jack was looking after that; Wilkie watched blankly.

If Liam feared for his sons' safety while he and Marta were gone, it was not because any danger threatened them from outside the place. In summer, marauding bears commonly passed through their land and while they mostly avoided humans, they posed a potential menace whenever encountered, even if accidentally. In winter though, they dozed the months away in hibernation. In country such as that inhabited by the Brennans and their far-flung neighbors, winter temperatures could fall to almost 60 degrees below zero. That necessitated keeping stoves blazing and produced a hazard common to everyone. The distinct possibility of a house fire was a reality that lived in the imagination of all because a fire in winter would destroy everything: shelter from the fierce cold, clothing and foodstuffs necessary to survive until spring. Once a fire started, it was next to impossible to contain it. Dry tindery logs often chinked with moss were a combination that could turn a spark into an inferno in minutes. Water, other than the meager amounts melted from snow for domestic uses, was unavailable in winter. Any accidental fire was a menace that everyone feared and scrupulously sought to avoid.

Throughout the long hours of night, the vulnerability of his sons and the present problem with Marta's pregnancy was a maggot that ate away in Liam's mind. When the stars began to fade in the bone-chilling pre-dawn, Liam rose, rustled some firewood, boiled tea, fed the dogs a few scraps, got Marta settled on the sled, and they struck off again down river on the ice. They soon struck the winter road from Fort St. John across the winter ice of the Peace and on to Dawson Creek. In truth, the road was little more than a trace that wound through poplar-covered hills and along the edge of a few stump farms. Crude though it was and little used in winter except for freighters and RCMP patrols, it struck a spark of new hope in both of them. It was a sign that they were not alone as they so often felt, that others lived in this difficult land, knew their hardships, their trials, their needs. Others knew the bite of winter cold, the scourge of summer insects and the loneliness, the sometimes terrible loneliness.

The dogs seemed to gain a new surge of energy and pulled with purpose if not enthusiasm. As she had on the previous day, Marta experienced sensations that told her child was trying to be born. Late in the afternoon she began to have excruciating labor pains. Liam wanted to stop, to try and help her, but she made him push on, sensing that she needed the help of a doctor.

Long after dark had settled in again, Liam carried Marta into the tarpaper-covered building that served as a hospital. The German immigrant doctor there delivered her caesarean of twins, so identical in every way except their sex that not even their mother could tell them apart at first. The doctor impressed on Liam that his wife had suffered a severe ordeal and needed bed rest, perhaps for several weeks.

Liam left Marta in the care of a local midwife and struck for home in the afternoon of the following day. He encountered neither man nor beast once he started upstream on the ice of the great river. He was forced intermittently to stop and let the dogs rest, but he never made a camp nor really rested himself. Late into the second day he reckoned he was within 15 miles of home when he first heard the pack, but it was a long time before he saw any of them. The dogs knew of their presence before he did.

Liam was intent on staying in the tracks they had made going downriver, though in many places they had vanished, blown in by the wind, and he did not look behind him until the dogs grew extremely nervous and unsteady. Finally he swung around, looking back downriver and squinting in the blinding light of the setting sun. Several hundred yards behind him he saw some dark specks on the river surface moving boldly in his direction. Liam halted the cowering dogs and counted more than twenty wolves strung out the width of the river. He knew that in a long winter like this the packs became ravenous and aggressive though he expected no real trouble from them. When they were still a considerable distance away, the wolves stopped. Instinctively, Liam ran his hand over the stock of his winchester lashed to the sled inside a wool blanket. Reassured, he turned his back on the wolves, surveyed the panting dogs, seized the handles and started the dogs again upriver. They traveled more swiftly now, the wretchedly tired dogs urged on by their dread of the terror only a few hundred feet behind them. Liam disdained to even look behind him though he felt the presence of the pack in the electric nervousness of his dogs. When he finally did turn and peer behind him, he saw that the wolves were keeping pace but were only a little closer, except for one long lean grey one that had pulled far ahead of the others and now ran almost parallel to the sled far on the right near the edge of the wooded banks. For a few moments Liam watched this magnificent traveling machine as it ran on the crusted snow, its long legs moving smoothly almost effortlessly in an undulating lope. Powerful predators, capable of covering forty miles or more in a single night of hunting, wolves are beautifully adapted to their purpose. The long shaggy winter coat partially conceals legs that are extremely long and sinewy, ending in huge dog-like paws that keep the animals on crusted snow instead of plunging through at each step like their hapless ungulate prey.

On an impulse, Liam pulled the rifle, halted the dogs and fired a snap shot at the flowing shape of the nearest wolf. At the sound of the shot, the animal leaped into the air as though avoiding something under itself, spun to the right and tore pell mell into the bank timber. The wolves behind the sled did the same and before the shot stopped echoing up the valley not a wolf remained on the river or in Liam's sight at all. He was astonished to find the sled dogs had not torn off upriver without him, but were cowering in their tracks.

As they neared the home place in the quasi-light of a quarter moon, Liam was perplexed at the numbers of wolf tracks up, down, and across the river surface. It looked like a really big pack had been hunting hereabouts. Liam idly wondered how they were finding anything to eat; in the past two winters the wolves had grown so numerous that all game was scarce, especially the larger animals like the elk and mule deer, indigenous to the area. Twenty years or so earlier wood bison, too, had been present but mysteriously seemed to have vanished from the land. None had been killed or even sighted for several years. Until the wolf-plagued recent winters, moose, an animal unknown in these parts, had begun to filter into the country from the north and east. But Liam had not seen a single animal in the whole of the winter, and only occasionally any tracks. It was as though the wolves had swept the country clean of game. Not even porcupines were immune. Quill piles scattered through the woods made Liam wonder at the fate of creatures that would have had to absorb some of those quills to make the kill.

He was not slow to make the connection. As the exhausted dogs hauled at the sled across the wide opening that led to the buildings of the home place, Liam felt alarm bells going off in his head, for he saw none of the livestock in the near fields or as yet not even near the buildings. Usually, they hung around, hoping for a few shreds of the now virtually exhausted hay or tried to rustle a few blades of dry grass. As the sled drew along side a thicket only a couple of hundred yards from the buildings, Liam stood on the brake and stopped the dogs. The remains of something lay scattered off on a slight side hill to his left. In an instant he recognized it as one of his heifers. The bones and skin of the animal were scattered over half an acre of ground. Even the large sockets of the legs and pelvis had been torn apart. A gnawed and eyeless skull stared sightlessly.

Apprehension, fear, anger, struck Liam at the same instant. He left the sled and rushed on foot through the narrow brush trail and into the opening of the poplars where the cabin stood, only to be brought up short again. Cattle carcasses seemed to be scattered everywhere, some only partially consumed, some gnawed to bare bones. Liam unconsciously checked off what he saw, easily recognizing each animal. Then he saw that at least one of them was still alive. An old cow, hind legs splayed grotesquely apart, lay on her brisket, her eyes rolling and her soundless mouth agape. The snow around her torn flanks was a crimson wallow. Great pieces of flesh had been torn from those living flanks, eaten to the bone at the hinds and loin. The poor beast's tormentors had not bothered to kill her before they feasted on her flesh. She made no effort to move as Liam crept past her, past the hay shed and into the small yard between the cattle shelter and cabin. Another cow lay in an entrails-encircled heap, another wretchedly maimed but still on its feet. Then he saw the first wolf carcass and then another a few yards away, a third lay against the railing of the stock shelter and a great black one sprawled amidst the hide and bones of a yearling steer; the last one lay not twenty yards from the cabin door.

The shot so stunned and surprised Liam that for an instant he didn't fathom its meaning though the angry buzz of bullets was not a sound with which he was altogether unfamiliar. The second shot, following instantly behind the first, snapped close to his head with a malicious crack, Liam hearing the shot and literally feeling the bullet brush past his temple. With a shriek of terror, he rocketed himself behind a near woodpile. A third shot routed the quaking dogs and they retreated in a roiling mass of tangled lines and snapping, struggling fur.

"Wilkie! Wilkie, for God's sake, stop! It's me, Liam! Don't shoot anymore! The wolves are gone! Don't shoot! I'm coming. Now, goddamnit, don't shoot!"

And then the night, which had been so full of chaos, was silent. Silent as death. No light shone anywhere in the cabin. Liam slowly got to his feet, his vulnerability and the abject terror of his near miss not yet registering in his consciousness.

"Now don't shoot any more! It's me, Liam! The wolves are gone. If you're pointing the gun this way, put it down! And, Wilkie, put the hammer down and keep it pointed at the floor!"

An eternity later, Liam lifted the door latch. It was locked from the inside.

"Open up, Wilkie! It's all right now."

Nothing stirred. The house remained deathly quiet.

"Wilkie! Open the door. Now!"

A low sound came from inside; it sounded at first like a puppy whimpering. It was a child crying. At the same time, the bolt of the door rustled. Liam flung open the door and stepped inside the blackened interior, his heart pounding in his throat. He felt small hands clutch his waist; his own hand clasp a shock of hair. Jack. Liam found the coal oil lantern and lit it. In the sputtering light it gave he saw five year old Wilson in the arms of the terrified Wilkie, long past speech and peering at him with dilated eyes. Jack clung to Liam's coat, finally breaking the silence with wracking sobs. At his feet lay a pile of expended cartridges, the rifle resting on the low sill of the open window, the hammer still cocked.

1914

Spring was a long time coming. The frontier town of Edmonton sprawled like a dirty sheepskin on both sides of the North Saskatchewan River, the streets a chaos of melting snow piles, ankle-deep mud and horse droppings. There was an optimism and a sense of purpose in the air. The rails of the Grande Trunk Railway had only recently reached there, bringing with it the hope of prosperity and development, a sense of belonging to something larger than itself. Travel "down East" could now be a reality for the scant few able to afford it, but nevertheless a dream that all could share even if but few realized it. The railroad also encouraged the development of lands heretofore thought only useful for grazing because of their remoteness from agricultural markets. Land would soon be put to the plow that had, until then, been virgin sod.

Northwest of the sprawl of Edmonton lay a country as yet little developed, in fact little known. Most of it lay as it had since time immemorial, a vastness of rolling poplar-covered hills, festooned with sluggish muskeg streams and spattered with shallow lakes. Cutting through the land, flowing always northeast ran great rivers which drained the mountain passes to the south and west. In time, these rivers, the Athabasca, the Smokey, the Little Smokey would become famous for the hunting of big game exceeded nowhere else in all of North America for its quality and diversity. Further northeast, all of these rivers merged with another mighty stream flowing from the west. This river also carried an immense volume of water. And because it was comparatively placid once it freed itself from the cordilleran barrier, it had been much used as a route into the lands which it drained. From the time when Alexander McKenzie and his expedition had struggled up its vast reaches on their voyage to the Pacific, the Peace had been a highway for those seeking their fortunes in the immense country that formed its drainage. Fur traders opened trading posts along its banks and under the auspices of the Hudson Bay and Northwest Fur Companies did a loose commerce with the native bands thinly strewn through the country. Most of the posts did not prosper and were eventually abandoned; the ones that did, McLeod Lake, Hudson's Hope, Fort St. John and Grouard, provided the toehold that would later nurture settlement.

In reality, the Peace River country was one of the last great frontiers, begun centuries earlier when the first whites had thrust inland from the Atlantic Coast. For more than 100 years, white men had come and gone up and down the calm waters of the lower Peace, but only a mere handful had come to stay. Though the occupation by the Beaver, Sikanni, Woodland Cree and other indigenous peoples extended back into the mists of time, in the year 1914 the country was little changed from the way it was in the beginning

One of the first tasks that had to be done to lend any encouragement to those who would wrest the land from wilderness was a survey. And so as the last of the snow dissolved into the matted grass of the previous summer and the river shook off its ice, a paddle wheeler set out from Peace River Landing and turned upstream. It was into May and the old craft was breasting a current already swelling with run-off from the ice-locked summits that fed the river far to the west. Among the eight seasoned hands of the survey crew on board was a well-knit young Irishman who had joined the crew the summer before. In the company of his more experienced companions, he had proven that he could stand the rigors of living in the open under every climatic whim, and he had shown that he possessed a quick intelligence by learning to use the demanding instruments of the surveyor's profession. The crew was one of several commissioned to divide and survey the immense tracts of land that lay in what is now northwestern Alberta and northeastern British Columbia, formerly known as New Caledonia. All the previous summer, the crew had labored in the lower reaches of what came to be known as the Peace River Block. The things that this crew and others found and recorded, later helped set in motion the great influx of settlers who came to take up the land.

It was a land to set the mind of an ambitious man to turning. True, it lay far north of most anything thought to be farmable in North America; travel was difficult and virtually impossible away from the rivers except on foot or horseback. No axe had ever hewn the seemingly endless tracts of mixed forest. The forests were pocked with that bane of northern travel, the muskeg swamp. Winter was the dominant season at these latitudes; they were invariably long and cold. The summer months wrought a wonderful change on the country after the deathlike grip of winter, but it brought other trials as well. The swamps and the vegetation that grew everywhere spawned clouds of mosquitoes and flies that could, and did, make life miserable for the uninitiated. And there was the endless isolation. The few white women living in the country at this time well understood this fact of life. Often years elapsed between visits with others of their kind. But there was a subdued optimism that infected people who saw this land, could not forget it, and returned to claim a piece of it.

As Liam embarked on his second summer on the survey, he did so with the strength of his youth and the vitality drawn from the life he led. The toils, discomfort and often outright hardships of the previous summer had receded in his consciousness and he longed to be back on the land. The crew whiled away the hours as the paddle wheeler wheezed its way up the swollen waters of the Peace. From horizon to horizon the earth was turning a pale green as great rolling expanses of poplar and birch were leafing out. Here and there in shaded places patches of ice remained, remnants of drifts and a poignant memory of the past winter.

But spring was in the air everywhere. Great skeins of waterfowl filled the skies with rush of their wings, their haunting calls. The boat stopped at designated points along the way to take on wood to stoke the boilers. Everyone, even passengers, were expected to turn out and lend a hand with the heavy work. It was not particularly looked forward to but it did punctuate the monotony and provided passengers such as Liam with an outlet for pent up energy. The pilot skillfully negotiated the plethora of snags, gravel bars, floating trees and occasional rough water with the confidence born of long experience. Small streams with deeply eroded beds far below the surrounding plateau continually kept their tryst with the main river. At their confluences were often found hazards such as logjams and shallow water. The boat generally stayed well out from the steep banks, for to come near the shore was to place the craft in peril from protruding sweepers.

On the fourth day, after fog and drizzle had cut visibility all day, the sky cleared in the late afternoon and suddenly a dramatic scene hushed the passengers. Far away, perhaps a hundred miles or more, the receding sunlight caught the summits of a jagged line of peaks. In the red incandescence of the western sky, they appeared as great ivory teeth, beautiful, pristine and possibly forbidding. Liam knew instantly where they were for the memory of this place was etched into his mind.

The crew disembarked next day at the old Hudson Bay post of Fort St. John. Horses were procured and a crew of Beaver Indians hired to carry the prodigious baggage of the crew around the area they had been engaged to survey. This land lay directly upstream from the Fort and extended for many miles to the north. In the following weeks the crew chained their way across great expanses of land, some of it dense muskeg and windfall-clotted ravines, but much of it parkland comprised of scattered pockets of birch and aspen interspersed with waist high native grasses and wild pea vine. Survey stakes were driven at the corners of mile square sections whose exact location was meticulously fixed with the use of sextant and transit. Some of these markers would never be found again; others would remain untouched for decades before their whereabouts would be of interest. But a rough survey was done, and land that had lain for millennia, carved, pounded and shaped by only the unknowing elements, now came within the frame of reference of civilized man, if not yet under his control. The clear unblemished beauty of the country moved Liam Brennan, as it had others who had seen it before him. A seed took root inside his consciousness: the desire to possess a part of this place, to put his mark on it, to live upon it and make a home there. These were only imaginings and fleeting images in his mind, nothing that he spoke of to others.

The days were long and the nearly total daylight allowed the surveyors to complete a remarkable amount of work. At times they were so harassed by hordes of mosquitoes and black flies that any activity away from a smudge fire was agony. These spells usually were terminated by wind or storm, but the insect torment was never held at bay for long.

Occasionally the crew encountered others who had reason to be about the country, people such as the Hudson Bay Factor from Fort St. John, a few white trappers, prospectors, and family groups of natives. It was from avid conversation with some of these that the news-starved men heard bits and pieces of the Great War that was raging in Europe. Any news that made its way to this remote corner of the world was fragmentary, often inaccurate and sometimes months behind the actual events. Nevertheless, young men hungry for diversion from the toil and monotony of their days listened and sometimes read accounts of great battles won and lost with rising ardor. So it happened that fall, at the end of the survey work for that season, Liam found himself in the company of several other young men at the Canadian Army recruiting station in Edmonton.

Mud in the trenches was nearly over the tops of their shoes and stank everlastingly of oil and human waste. A viscous black-brown stew punctuated with puddles of scum-covered water stretched up and down the trench in either direction until visibility was cut off by a slight change of direction. All the trenches were deeper than a man's height and every few yards were bunkers cut back into the front facing walls. These bunkers were walled with heavy wood ties or logs and had a low roof of the same material. For a while it had been possible to keep the water out of the bunkers, but with frequent rains, the water gradually rose higher, finally settling into the bunkers and creating the inevitable sludge that found its way into everything. And now the rats had returned with a vengeance, fattened from feeding on the abundant corpses. At first only a few were noticeable, but during the preceding days they had become numerous to the point of being pestilential. No foodstuffs were safe from them anywhere, even on one's person. They scurried about the reeking trenches, over equipment, over clothing and food, over the miserable huddled men, over the wounded and the dead.

The shelling had gone on for more than 24 straight hours. The wretched humanity pressing into the sides of the trenches were drunk with weariness, with shell shock, their filthy vacuous faces and blood-rimmed eyes an amalgamation of horror, exhaustion, hopelessness. In more than two years at the front, Liam had not experienced anything like it. He felt too tired to move, almost indifferent now to the deafening crescendo around him. Then, as the long night began to lighten into gray dawn, the shelling abruptly stopped. For a time the mud-encrusted figures huddled against the walls of the trench remained in a deathlike suspension of movement. As they began to ease up over the tops of the trenches to stare out in front of them, it came. First a few brief rattle of machine gun fire that increased to a sustained hail, a storm of flying steel that tore at the sandbags along the top of the trench and nearly took the head off the man at Liam's elbow. The man grasped his face spasmodically, then fell backwards into the reeking trench. Liam turned to look and automatically stepped down into the trench to his fallen comrade. As soon as he raised the shattered face from the muck, he realized the futility of trying to help him; he started to lift himself up the sloping side of the trench, working the bolt of his rifle as he did so. Immediately something spun him around and sent him flying sideways back into the trench. In what seemed to him only a millisecond, forms came over the top of the trench. He found himself looking straight into the bore of a German rifle, the bayonet fixed to the end of it inches from his face.

In the early fall the Belgian rains fell incessantly, seemingly everlasting, until the quarter mile square inside the barbwire was an ocean of mud. Prisoners and guards alike slogged to and fro in the wasteland between the shacks that housed the POW's. These stretched the entire length of the wire-enclosed compound on two sides. Every few meters a raised platform covered over by a tiny V-shaped roof sheltered a guard who peered out miserably at the human flotsam moving beneath him. Some of the platforms contained a tripod upon which a water-cooled machine gun was perched, belts of ammunition falling from the breech into buckets beneath them. All of the guards carried rifles. Several months had now passed since any of the prisoners had made any overt attempt at escape, the horrible diet and numbing boredom having robbed most of them of the energy or the will. The misery of the place was only partly shared by the German guards: they endured the fits of bad weather, the mind-numbing sameness, the horrible stench and the ubiquitous mud, but they at least got food on a semi-regular basis. The diet of the prisoners incarcerated in the camp had never been good; lately, it had descended to near starvation level. A thin slop of potato peels, cabbage and sometimes ground corncobs made up the bulk of their diet and even this was becoming scarcer.

The countryside around, had any of the prisoners been able to see it, was composed of deep, black fertile soil, but the disruptions of the endless war had put production of any type of foodstuffs to a fraction of its pre-occupation level. The civilian residents still remaining in the area, seemingly composed mostly of women, children and old men, were not much in evidence, and when they were seen they appeared cowed by their German overlords; they moved about as unobtrusively as possible.

Liam Brennan had survived nineteen months in the POW camp. In the long months spent there, he had seen the prisoner population constantly in flux. The dead went out the back gate of the compound and new prisoners came in the front. Many, like himself, arrived with terrible wounds. At the beginning he had seemed a sure candidate for one of the unmarked graves in a field behind the back gate. He had even thought that himself at first, for a time maybe even wished for it. His wound ran pus for weeks, and a high fever had kept him hovering near death for many days. A bullet had passed completely through his upper right chest and out the back, missing his clavicle and tearing a hole through the shoulder blade. But his twenty four year old body would not give in so easily. After being taken prisoner, he had been treated briefly at a German field dressing station, spent two nights in the "hospital" there and had been loaded on a cattle car with others and moved to the POW camp in central Belgium. That he even survived the journey there was testament to the vitality and resilience of his toughened body. He had been laid on a cot of slabs and a straw-stuffed tick to presumably await his exit out the back gate. Through the weeks following his arrival, he floated in and out of a haze of delirium punctuated with short periods of lucidity. The lice-infected tick on which he lay became encrusted with his own body fluids and the constant excretion from his wound. Those with whom he was imprisoned brought him cups of thin gruel when it was available and tepid water from a communal bucket. All used the fetid and reeking slit trench at the back of the huts. Liam was fortunate in this respect for at least he was capable of walking which was more than could be said for some of his fellows.

The winter of 1917-18 was not a noticeably cold one, but the rains fell for weeks on end, turning the already wretched POW compound into a sea of muck. So many prisoners perished that winter of the accumulated effects of malnutrition, dysentery, common disease and perhaps just hopelessness that the prison guards were hard pressed to find enough able-bodied prisoners to keep up with the grave digging. Somehow Liam's emaciated body clung to life. While after a long time his wound had partially healed, his weight had dropped so much that he, like most of the others, appeared almost skeletal. He dragged his half-alive body around, not noticeably different from the small number of wounded prisoners who still survived. At this point had it not been for small amounts of food now voluntarily brought to the camp by nearby civilians, moved by what they saw happening, perhaps none of the prisoners would have lived into the spring. The German guards were faring only slightly better, the rigor of their watchfulness was melting away.

In the beginning, several organized attempts at escape were carried out by the stronger members of the prison population; a handful had even managed to get away into the countryside, but most attempts ended in abject failure. The participants were marched outside the compound and unceremoniously shot. Liam had not been part of any of these ill-fated enterprises simply because he was not strong enough.

During the summer of the following year, aircraft became increasingly evident in the skies over the immediate countryside and on occasion the prisoners and guards alike watched with interest as German and Allied planes engaged extended dogfights overhead. Once a badly wounded Canadian pilot was captured when his plane was shot down. He was brought to the camp but died in his first night there.

The prisoners now noticed a gradual but increasing lack of vigilance by the German guards. Most of the prisoners in the sordid camp were too weak and indifferent to make trouble or try to escape, and it was becoming increasingly evident that the Great German War Machine had faltered. The trickle of new prisoners brought news that the Germans were now falling back on all fronts. And one day in mid-November, the guards were simply gone.

As the import of this gradually dawned on the prisoners, they moved out into the immediate countryside, foraging for food in a land swept clean as by a locust invasion. It was moving into late fall now and the meager harvest was long gone. Liam and several of the other prisoners walked well out into the farm country that lay all around.

In one of the farmyards, Liam saw a person digging carrots and potatoes from what presumably had been the family garden. He approached the shabbily clad figure. He gestured that he was hungry. The figure stood upright and turned to look at him with suspicious guarded eyes. Liam found himself looking into the face of a slender girl. At first, she held her spade in front of her defensively, obviously intimidated by his emaciated, filthy appearance. For a moment she stood uncertain, then she beckoned him to follow her to the door of the household kitchen. There was a long exchange between the girl and someone inside. Finally she ushered him into a tiny high-ceilinged room where a cast iron stove radiated a weak heat, a coal bucket sitting on the floor beside it. An older woman, presumably the girl's mother, appeared and began a heated discussion with her daughter, in what Liam took to be Dutch. Finally, the elder lady beckoned Liam to sit on a high-backed wooden chair. She prepared and began boiling a pot of vegetables. At first the three of them sat in silence. When Liam finally spoke to them the girl answered him back in a broken but understandable English. Her name was Marta Vandermere; her mother's name was Madeline. They had been living here alone at the farm since the departure sometime early in the War of Marta's father to serve in the Belgian Army. Nothing had been heard of him in over a year. When the occupying Germans had established a POW camp in the area, most of the native Belgians had attempted to keep their distance. Although generally they were ignored, sometimes the Germans came and took farm produce.

The tiny farmhouse was clean and sparsely furnished. Its plain wooden floors looked scrubbed and there was a faint smell of lye soap. A shed of some kind was attached to the back of the house with two small buildings that appeared to be animal shelters in the back yard. The wooden fence around the yard looked dilapidated; some of it was missing altogether.

When the vegetables had cooked, Madeline spooned a portion into a large pewter bowl and set it on the table in front of Liam. She also set a bowl for Marta and herself.

Liam waited for them to begin eating but both sat watching him. He picked up his spoon and began to eat, trying hard to keep enough control that he did not bolt his food as his starved body compelled him to do. The two women began to eat only after he did. They ate slowly and gravely, carefully observing Liam's every move. Marta eventually apologized for the lack of bread; there had been no flour in the household for many months. After several bowls of vegetables, Liam sat back in his chair and considered his hosts more carefully. Both of the women were dressed in shabby, shapeless dresses that fell nearly to the ground; both were quite thin. Marta said in her slow halting English that since the past winter the only food they had was what they had grown.

Both of the women had square even features. The family resemblance was evident though the older woman, Madeline, had a deeply lined face. Both had large strong-looking peasant hands, roughed by manual work. Marta's hair was a bit darker than her mother's, a sort of light brown. It was tied so that it fell along the side of her neck. She observed Liam with clear grey eyes that betrayed neither hostility nor friendliness.

They fell into a discussion of what the disappearance of the Germans might mean. Liam felt sure that the war must have ended, though neither of the women proffered any sure opinion. They were simply relieved that the Germans were gone. The early winter evening came on and it was clear to Liam, perhaps to his hosts as well, that he had little strength to move on that night and look for shelter. Liam finally summoned the courage to ask if he might stay the night; he would stay in one of the out buildings if they would allow it. The women considered privately in the next room, and the conversation seemed to Liam to last a long time. Liam was told he could sleep in the shed at the back of the house. He was given a bundle of coarse blankets and a bucket of warm water with which to wash himself. He slept on the floor of the shed.

Liam did not leave next morning as he had thought to do. In fact, he remained at the Vandermere's for the next seven weeks. At the end of that time, a British infantry unit appeared on the road and the surviving POW's from the camp who still remained in the area were picked up. Among them was Liam Brennan, still pitifully thin but now generally recovered from his wounds.

With the armistice signed at Versailles, most of the Canadian units were discharged and returned home. Liam stayed in Europe for a time. He had originally immigrated to Canada from Northern Ireland and most of his family remained there. He spent some weeks visiting his brothers and sisters and their families, his parents both being deceased by that time.

Liam also corresponded with Marta through short letters that he sent almost daily. During the weeks spent at the Vandermere place, a relationship had kindled between the two young people, and though it had progressed no further than holding hands through long, late night conversations, Liam had persuaded Marta to return to Canada with him. Marta was hardly out of her teens, but the circumstances of war had matured her beyond her years. As Liam came to observe, to know her better, he saw not just a tall slender girl, nearly as tall as he, but her clear grey eyes, direct gaze and clear skin. While plain of feature, she was attractive in her manner and in the way she presented herself. She listened carefully when Liam spoke to her and she looked directly into his eyes when she spoke to him. There seemed no guile in her.

Marta was apprehensive about leaving her mother alone and when Liam saw this he suggested that Madeline come with them. They spent many hours attempting to persuade her that she should come to Canada and make a new life there with them. At last Madeline seemed settled on that idea and when Liam left with the British Army unit, it had been agreed that he would be back to take them to Canada with him in a few weeks. Never once, even at the parting, did Marta betray any sign that she felt that Liam might not really keep his word to her. Her trust in him was almost childlike.

It was during his time in Ireland that Liam remembered why he had left it in the first place. Though the land had a haunting beauty, there was widespread poverty and human misery there. The countryside was cut up into tiny holdings, divided and divided again by subsequent generations until few people could wrestle a living off the land at all. And in the cities men worked long hours in factories for meager wages, wages that could hardly support the large families, even if, as often as not, they were not squandered in the pubs on payday. There was a hopelessness hung like a pall over everyone. Added to the despair concerning employment was the religious tension. Clashes between Catholics and Protestants had become so common that it was much like a war, but a war that went on without end. People did not look forward to the future or even try to plan for it; they seemed bent only on surviving the present. Liam had carried those attitudes with him when he had first gone to Canada at 17 years of age. But after his arrival in the New World he came to the gradual realization that a working man could own something there, that he could progress and make something of himself. In Ireland, indeed in all of Europe, ownership of land was left only to the wealthy or high born, but in the vastness of North America, a person could find a place for himself, a place where he could own as much of the earth as his own enterprise, intelligence and ambition allowed. And so it was that when Liam departed Ireland for the second time he did so in the conviction that he would make a better life in far away Canada, and that it was unlikely he would ever see the country of his birth again.

He met Marta in Amsterdam and two days later they were married in a simple ceremony, only the magistrate, Madeline and themselves being present. Though she had originally consented to emigration with Marta and Liam, in the end Madeline could not be persuaded to leave her native land. Marta tried over and over to change her mind, but it was not to be. Madeline returned to her home in the Belgian countryside. She was adamant that she would keep in touch by letter. Marta and Madeline's parting was a sad and tearful one, both of them sensing perhaps that their separation might be final.

Their first days of marriage were spent in rented rooms and later in the tiny stuffy passenger hold of the ship taking them to America, but Liam and Marta quickly fell into the rhythm of all young people in love. Their lovemaking was often done in the few frantic moments of privacy they could find, but they quickly became accustomed to each other's body, and the novelty of this new life was a whirlwind that carried them along through the first weeks of their marriage. As they lay together under the coarse bedding, they talked of the life they would build together, of the children they hoped to have, of their hopes, their aspirations for the future life that neither of them could as yet clearly envision. Even as Liam tried to explain to Marta the place he remembered along the banks of the great river, he was sure she really could not comprehend the reality of the life he was taking her into. From his previous work on the survey, seemingly so far behind him now, Liam knew exactly the place he wanted to settle, but he also understood that a young woman, raised in the placid Belgian countryside replete with the accouterments of civilization as it was known then, could scarcely be expected to envision the life of a settler in a new and totally raw country. Liam knew that no matter how he described it to her, she would not really be emotionally prepared for this new life so totally alien to anything she had known before. He also sensed in her a deep commitment to him and to a new beginning. He already knew she could stand hardship and privation and that her strong will would be her greatest asset. He only hoped that he would be able to create the life for them that he had so glowingly described over and over.

Twelve weeks after leaving Liverpool, the Brennans arrived at the hamlet of Peace River, Alberta, Canada. Their journey had spanned half the circumference of the earth and had taken them across the Atlantic to Halifax, where they traveled by rail to Toronto, through the lake and river country of the shield to Winnipeg and finally across the prairie lands of Manitoba, Saskatchewan and Alberta to Edmonton.

After a few days there, Liam put into motion the plan he had harbored in his mind for so long. He bought a team of horses, a few basic household items, tarps, and an assortment of hand tools. They set out for Peace River town on a well-traveled road and luckily managed to hit one of the dry spells which had shrunk the mud holes, making travel easier. They spent several nights camping beside the road, sometimes in the company of others bound for the same place. It was now mid-May and mosquitoes, which had hatched by the billions in the sloughs,and low country, became a torment. At night the animals as well as the human travelers huddled close to smoke smudges kindled to retard the pestilential mosquitoes. As they got further from Edmonton, except for the area right along the road, the land was a primeval forest that undulated away to the horizon in every direction. Streams cut through the landscape and these had to be forded at the known safe crossings. Waterfowl of every description inhabited the route. Some of them found their way onto the menu of the travelers.

When they finally reached it, Peace River town was something of a disappointment. The community was spread on both sides of the sluggishly flowing river from which it took its name. It seemed to Marta to be anything but the beautiful stream Liam had described. The hamlet appeared to be built perilously near the river, apparently on an ancient floodplain. The town itself seemed mostly a collection of shacks and unpainted buildings with business operations thrown in willy nilly.

To get to the town it was necessary to drop down off the low plateau to the deeply eroded valley of the river. There was a substantial dock where the riverboats could be moored to take on passengers, freight and fuel. It was the riverboats which had drawn Liam to Peace River town. He knew enough of the country to realize that the only real passable route into the upper reaches of the Peace River Block, which he had helped survey in the years before the war, lay by water.

Liam and Marta spent the three days of waiting for the next boat upriver by making a few final purchases. They bought a well-used horse-drawn hay mower, a one bottom breaking plough, and a harrow. The cost of their fare and the transportation of their team of horses and equipment nearly used up the substantial money Liam had been paid when he left the army in Europe. A few more acquisitions, consisting of cooking equipment, flour, salt and a little tea and sugar, completed their entire grubstake with which to start their new life as pioneer homesteaders.

On a sunlit, mosquito-marred morning in late May, the Brennans began the last leg of their long voyage. The smoke-spewing old steamer pulled away from the dock and headed upstream, and Liam and Marta bid the shantytown a last goodbye. Neither of them could have known it then, but long years would pass before they again saw anything as close to civilization as that remote little river town.

There were a few other passengers on board, but none looked to be homesteaders. Most of them were either trappers or miners heading to the Omineca gold fields. One young couple had some provisions they intended to use to open a store at one of the tiny hamlets upriver. The boat's destination was the old Hudson Bay post town of Hudson's Hope which lay at the head of navigable water on the Peace River. Upriver from there, the waters constricted into a series of terrifying rapids through which no steamboat could hope to negotiate.

The captain of the boat was an amicable sort, used to his job and well versed in the nuances of the river. To keep the steam turbines turning, plenty of fuel was needed to stoke the furnace. This was supplied every few miles by fuel depots, which amounted to green poplar logs cut by crews of men engaged for that purpose. Much time was consumed taking on logs and this became a routine that the passengers became accustomed to.

On the second day out, the sunlit skies of the previous week gradually darkened and a light drizzle turned to a driving rain by late afternoon. Marta had, up until that time, spent most of her time topside watching the constantly changing panorama of the river slide by. Now she was forced to take shelter below deck. The darkening day took its toll on her as the adventure of the previous days was eclipsed by the downpour. It was not so easy to feel optimistic now; the rain-darkened timber on the banks seemed somehow more ominous, perhaps even sinister. Marta knew she was completely out of her element, her realm of understanding. The farmlands of Western Europe had done little to prepare her for what she now saw. She was almost completely dependent on the knowledge of her husband until such time as she was able to get some experience in these new and raw surroundings. She was made more than a little apprehensive by the almost total lack of evidence of human habitation along the riverbanks. There were small clearings where woodcutters plied the steamer with more firewood, but of actual permanent-appearing homes or cultured farmland she saw virtually none. And the mosquitoes! No matter where she located herself they were always present to torment with their biting and continual drone. Even the heavy rainfall did not give total relief from them.

Strangely, the following day brought a complete reversal of the dreary overcast of the previous one. The Brennans had spent an uncomfortable night in the tiny room they shared below deck. Coming up topside in the dawn light, Marta saw a sky that was completely clear of clouds and a vivid blue. The sun had not yet risen high enough for its light to penetrate the river channel running deep down between high timbered banks, but it shone in beautiful relief on the mosaic of undulating forest slopes that stretched away in every direction. On the right bank she saw groups of animals that Liam said were mule deer, an indigenous and plentiful species found all over the area. Twice that morning they spotted black bears foraging at the water's edge. The animals bolted into the undergrowth at the approach of the steamer.

Some of the gnawing apprehension that Marta had experienced since leaving the landing at Peace River town began to ebb as she looked upon the pristine beauty of the country through which they passed. It amazed her how different it looked in the clear light of a peaceful summer morning. She began to look at the shoreline more closely. She noticed, in the hours she spent topside that day and the one following, how smaller streams ran into the broader river on which they traveled. These streams always seemed to emerge from deeply eroded ravines and tree-choked canyons. The terrain on the north bank had open park-like slopes covered in grass and often littered with burned snags and stumps. There were pockets of heavy timber near the water's edge. It was easy to see that animals used the slopes continuously, for trails were visible across them even from the river. The slopes of the south bank, deprived of direct light from the sun low on the horizon, were nearly always heavily timbered with little open space among the trees. Nowhere was there any indication of the hand of man; it was as though she saw the earth in its pre-human state, before man emerged to change its face.

Waterfowl became increasingly abundant. Ducks and various shore birds were seen at the edge of the river and several pairs of majestic black and grey geese as well. The day seemed a fortunate one, for a stiff breeze blew along the water giving relief, even if only temporary, from the insect torment.

Two days later in the blue of another glorious summer morning, a startling vista that Liam remembered so well appeared between the low slopes extending to the west. A ragged saw-toothed range of mountains arose on the western horizon. Even at the great distance they obviously were from the steamboat, they seemed majestic, their peaks still clothed in snow. They seemed to rise up out of the plateau like a protective rampart to whatever might lie behind them. They soon vanished as the river made a wide turn and then, hours later, turned up again. As the old paddle wheeler steamed further upriver, the mountains became visible only to vanish and then reappear again as the topography permitted. There was something mesmerizing about them, certainly Marta had never seen anything like them in the low lands of Western Europe. They seemed to her a promise of positive things to come. Marta could not have said of exactly what, but their pristine beauty inspired hope.

Late in the afternoon of the following day under low overcast skies, Liam and Marta Brennan put down all their earthly belongings on a gravel bar on a turn of the great river and set out to seek their lives in a land they would come to know well. It was then a land that had only lightly felt the hand of civilized man. It had been traveled by explorers, trappers, and gold seekers for a few decades, by native Indian groups since time immemorial. The long arm of Canadian law now sat ensconced in the form of an RCMP detachment at Hudson's Hope a few miles upstream and another at Fort St. John two days journey downstream, but as yet only a handful of hardy souls had come to put down roots on the land. There was good reason for this: virtually no roads were then in existence, and the few that were, were little more than traces along streams that led to the trading posts. Summer travel was confined to these rough, hole-pocked trails where a team in the hands of a skilled driver might get through if his equipment wasn't jolted to pieces on the ruts and tree roots along the way. Most things moved on the backs of men and packhorses. The exception to this was travel by boat on the big river and a few of its tributaries. But unless it could be hauled upstream by one of the paddle wheelers still plying the Peace, goods had to be "frogged" upstream by the dangerous and back-breaking method of pulling boats or rafts by long ropes attached to men toiling along the edge of the water.

Winter was the only season when moving very far was even remotely feasible. The deep cold froze the streams over under thick ice and then the ice was covered by layers of snow. A dog team could travel far in a day under the right conditions. The summer trails through the bush could still be used by horse or dog team and were free of the quagmires that plagued them in the temperate months. At this time, immediately after World War I, a tiny fraction of the land, and this only on the river flats, had ever felt the plow, but this was destined to change soon. A series of forest fires had denuded much of the land in the area of the dense timber that had covered it since the retreat of the Wisconsin Ice. True, great portions of the land were untouched by the fires, but many square miles were left with only "islands" of old growth timber with areas of grass growing between the charred stumps. Into this milieu came the first homesteaders, refugees from the wind blown prairies of Saskatchewan, Alberta and the Dakotas. They left their drought-ridden farms in the south in the hope of a better life in a new land. Liam and Marta came in the vanguard of a wave of settlers that would trickle into the Peace River Block for the next fifty years.

For Marta, this adventure was into a land, a situation, a lifestyle totally alien to her, but her husband was not going into this venture blind. Five years earlier, Liam had been on the very land on which they now stood, had helped survey much of the surrounding area and had vowed that here was a place he would come back to. As he stood with his young bride, a team of gentle draft horses, a few bits and pieces of equipment and bundles of personal effects, this on a rocky gravel bar miles from the nearest settlement and half a world from the land that gave him birth, Liam Brennan must have had some doubts as to the sense of that vow. He was still a young man, though seasoned beyond his years by a terrible war, brutal prison camp conditions and even by the hardscrabble life he had led before the war. He had no illusions about the hardships awaiting them as they set out to carve out a life for themselves in a remote and virtually unknown corner of the world. He knew, above all, that the hope of this moment and the dream of the quest on which they now embarked had sustained him through those dark days in war-torn Europe. Whatever difficulties must be faced, whatever hardships endured in this raw place would be nothing compared to what he had already lived through. His will would be tested again and again in the years ahead as he and Marta struggled to make something of their tiny place in the sun.

34 J. W. Secrist

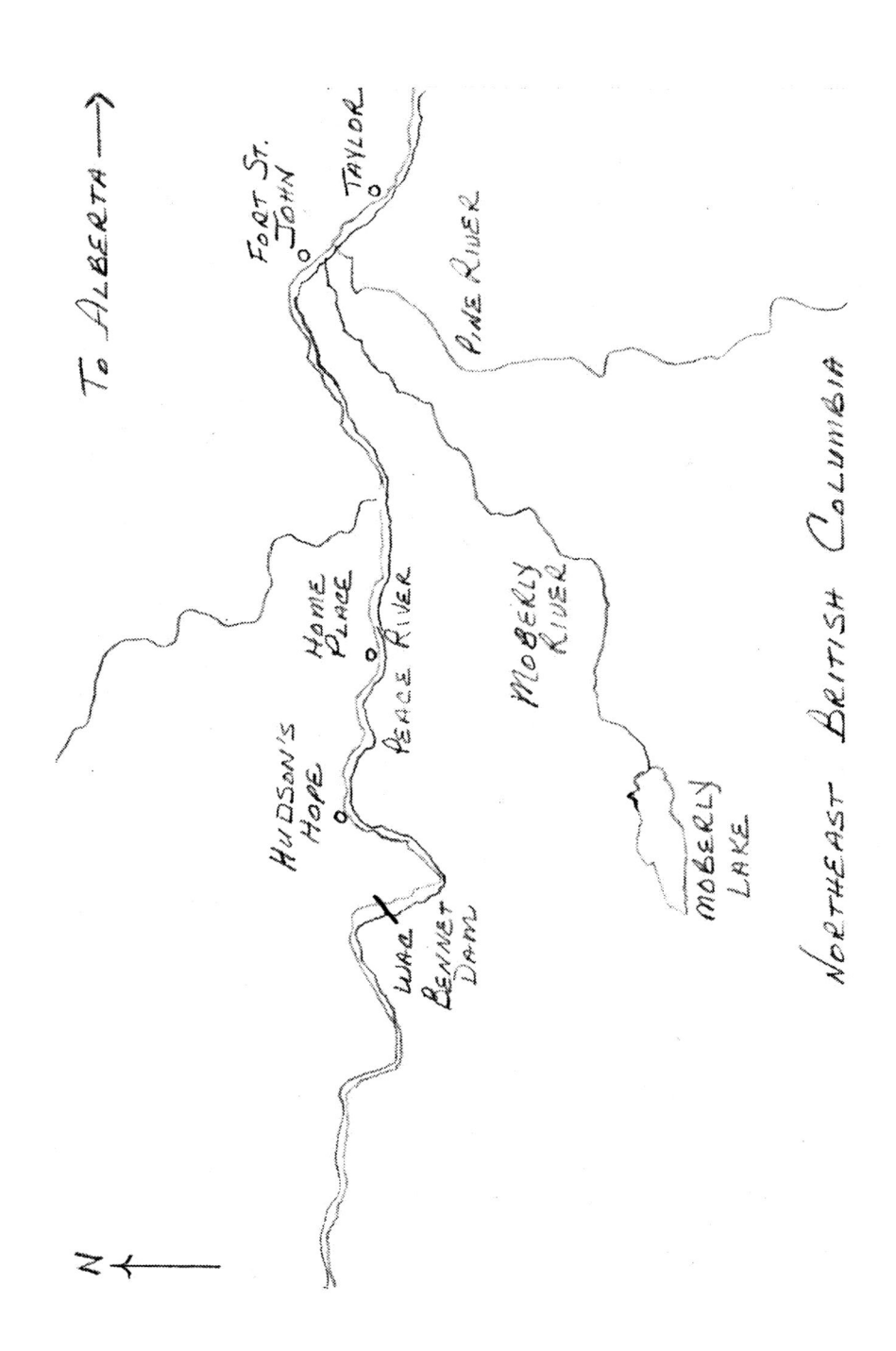

After Liam constructed a travois of rough poles onto which he lashed their belongings, the team dragged it up a steep incline and onto the bench land directly adjacent to the river. Even this was not easy as brush and small trees had to be hacked out of the way. Marta followed the team up onto the bench as the last load was taken up. When the horses stopped, she gazed about her; a tiny shudder of apprehension passed through her. Was this what they had traveled half the distance around the world for? Extending to the north, on their immediate right if they were looking upriver, was an extensive flat, a meadow apparently for high grass and pea vine grew profusely. Marta took a few steps into the meadow and immediately fell headfirst over a charred log partially concealed in the grass. Liam helped her to her feet.

"Be careful, Marta. This flat is criss-crossed with these downed trees. They're what remains of the forest that stood here a few years ago. We have to be careful now. God only knows how far away the nearest doctor is."

Beyond the flat lay a long steep ridge with open hillsides of sparse grass, deeply eroded in places by water and wind. To the east the flat extended a few hundred yards to where the meadow grass gradually morphed into islands of dead, blackened trees and finally to where the living forest took over again. Looking west the scene was much the same except the land had a distinct roll to it.

"Somewhere very close to here there is a spring. I remember it from before. I've got to find it as it is one of the main reasons I wanted to come back here to settle. Good water, except for the river itself, is hard to find. I only saw a few good springs in all the time I spent in this area when we surveyed."

"But, Liam, we can get all the water we want from the river."

"Marta, the river is at least fifty feet below this flat. We don't want to spend half our lives hauling water up here. We need to find that spring; it's still here someplace. It's got to be close to here unless I've got myself confused. I'm going to walk along this flat for a ways and see if I can find it. Why don't you make a fire and fix something to eat. I'm turning the horses loose to graze; try to keep them in sight."

As Liam moved off up river, Marta continued to gaze about her. From where she stood she could still hear the murmur of the great river. She also heard bird noises and felt a warm breeze on her back blowing downriver. Far off toward the base of the steep ridge, she thought she saw an animal of some kind. She stared at it for a moment, but it seemed gradually to blend into the timber and then disappeared altogether. Liam had told her that wild animals were common here and not to be surprised by them, but the sighting made her nervous. She was unaccustomed to seeing any kind of animal except domestic ones. She began to gather dry sticks that were strewn about everywhere but found herself stopping to look around nervously. She saw no more of whatever it was against the far hillside. She started a small fire and heated water in an iron pot into which she dropped a few small potatoes. As she was rummaging through their belongings, she saw Liam far up the flat walking back toward her.

"Found it," he said as he walked up to the fire. "The flow's only half as much as I remember, but it's there. It trickles into a gully and down into the river. We'll probably want to move our things over there, but we won't worry about it today."

In the days that followed, Liam and Marta set up a crude tent shelter out of tarps propped up with green poles anchored with rope. They were fortunate in that none of the extended soaking rains so common to the area in summer occurred. They were hit a few times by squalls but were able to keep their belongings relatively dry. They moved their things to the area alongside the spring. The water from it really only oozed out but Liam was confident he could increase the flow as soon as he could get a sandpoint. For the time being, the river supplied their water requirements. They cleared a few square yards of blowdown and fire debris. After spading up the soddy dirt and breaking the clods, they planted it with the precious hoard of garden seeds they had brought with them. Into the virgin soil went potatoes, carrot and pea seeds. Despite the frequent squalls, the ground remained quite dry; Marta spent a part of each morning carrying buckets of water from the river to the tiny garden. Amazingly, the plants sprouted and flourished.

Liam was obsessed with the need to put up some kind of shelter which they could use to survive the long winter that he knew was not so far away. He also knew that what he wanted to build was out of the question before the cold weather set it. He began to fall fire-killed trees with his axe, using the team to drag them to the area he and Marta had selected for a cabin site. It was to be twelve feet square, a pitifully small structure, but Liam realized he had no time this summer for anything bigger.

It was an agonizingly slow procedure. The logs had to be adzed flat on the bottoms and tops, or at least as flat as possible. Then the ends had to be dovetailed together and the logs fitted together one at a time. Liam did not bother to smooth or flatten the inside faces of the logs, as he was certain that this building was only a temporary shelter, not their real home. Two small openings were left for windows and a door space had to be cut out to provide for the future door. Gradually the walls grew and poles were put in place for roof rafters. Then the real work began. Liam had had the vision to bring a large whip saw for making boards, but it was soon apparent that cutting boards for a roof was out of the question for the present. There simply was not enough time before cold weather. They settled on a dubious compromise. In place of the boards, a tight mat of partially woven willows was painstakingly constructed over the pole rafters. They dug moss from a nearby muskeg and stuffed it into the maze of willows. Over top of this was added a thick layer of soddy dirt. Neither of them had any real confidence that it would hold back extended rain, but it was all they could think of with their limited time and resources. Many long hours were consumed with this work, leaving both of them exhausted at the end of the long days.

Another problem had to be confronted: what to do with the horses when winter came? If snowfall was light, they could paw enough grass from the snow to survive. But what if the snowfall became so deep that they couldn't paw through it? Liam knew they could not afford to lose the team. Finally they settled on a solution. Marta would take the scythe and cut as much of the long grass close by as possible. It would be allowed to dry and then collected into a stook of hay to be closely guarded until it became absolutely necessary to feed in the ensuing winter. In theory, it was a simple task; in practice, it was something quite different.

Charred blowdown trees lay thickly intertwined in the tall grass. At first Marta toiled to move them but the futility of this soon drove her to scythe over the tops of the downed trees and then try to pick out the cut grass with a wooden pitchfork. It was slow, exasperating work. Marta's European farming upbringing had introduced her to physical labor early in life, but it took all of her resources of patience and perseverance to keep going. The insects remained a torment, mosquitoes rising by the millions from the tall damp grass. Both Marta and Liam's faces were red and swollen, so were their exposed hands and wrists. Smudge fires could keep the bugs at bay as long as a person stood right in the smoke; as soon as he moved away a few feet the tormentors returned in force.

Marta made small piles of the grass as soon as it dried, and these in turn were converted into larger ones. Using the team and travois, Liam eventually got most of the hay together into a larger stack that was to be the backup food supply for the team in the winter.

Liam killed a small doe a few days after their arrival and they had a temporary supply of fresh meat. He tried to smoke some of the meat in long thin strips but the result was not appetizing. The dried meat was tough and stringy, though a little salt made it more palatable. Deer were numerous around the flat so meat was not an immediate concern.

Clearing a small area of blowdown near the shelter became Liam's focus when he dared free himself from the labor of building the cabin. The days were long and generally warm. Only a few hours of darkness prevailed in these summer months, which was both a blessing and a curse. Both of them felt compelled to labor on as long as there was light to see. They fell exhausted into their bed for a few hours only to rise up at first light and repeat the process over again.

One late summer morning Marta awoke and peered out of their tarpaulin shelter. A bit of movement very close by caught her eye. She recoiled in fright from what she saw. A few yards away, a large black bear was digging among their growing vegetables. Marta was frozen with fear for an instant, and then she shook Liam awake. She was so frightened that she could only point. Liam got up, saw the bear, and picked up his rifle that was lying beside him. He levered a round into the chamber; the noise alerted the bear who turned his head to stare at them. As the shot resounded across the flat, the bear dropped and raced pell mell away from them across the blowdown flat and out of sight into an island of standing timber.

"You must have missed," whispered Marta.

"No, I couldn't have. It was so close and I was holding right in the middle of him. He's got to be hit. I'll see if I can find him."

"Don't go! He was so big and he could still be alive!"

"I'll wait a bit. He can't have gone far. I'll just give him some time to stiffen and die. I know he's hit."

Liam drank a cup of tea, Marta staying very close to him, the fear still in her eyes. An hour later when Liam followed the heavy blood trail into the timber, he found the bear in a pool of congealed blood, already stiffening in death. He skinned the animal and cut out the hams and loins. He knew the meat was edible from previous experience. The flesh of this bear was encased in a thick layer of white fat, almost like a pig. In pieces, Liam carried the whole of the carcass into their camp and they spent a day rendering the fat into a thick white lard.

The vegetable patch was a success, far more than could have been expected with the soil so rough and with no way to weed the rows except to pull weeds and grass. They had no hoe, only a heavy shovel. Rain was not so prevalent as it had been, so Marta put in many laborious hours carrying water to the plants.

Long days of hard labor left them weary at night, but they were young and in the prime of their physical lives. They clung to each other through the short nights in their bed and were content with their lives. In the late summer Marta confirmed to Liam what he already suspected: that she was with child and they could expect it to be born the next spring. This knowledge drove Liam ever harder, for he saw how much had to be done before the birth of their child.

Sunlight hours began almost imperceptibly to shorten. They had brought no calendar but reckoned that it was late August. Since their arrival nearly three months earlier, they had seen no other people. There were times though when the breeze was blowing downriver that they thought they detected the smell of someone's fire. Twice more that summer the old paddle wheel steamer passed on its way upstream to Hudson's Hope and then passed again a few days later headed downstream. When they waved from the high bank the pilot sounded his whistle. Just seeing the boat helped to raise their spirits. But that was all. They saw no other humans.

This changed abruptly one day when Liam was chipping away with his adze on a log for the cabin, so deeply engrossed in his work that he did not see the three figures on horseback until they were nearly beside him. He stood up abruptly and stared at the riders who had reined up a few feet away. For a second he felt a shiver run down his spine. This was due in part to his amazement that these three could have come all the way across the meadow unnoticed. The other part had to do with their appearance.

All three were natives. Two women sat their mounts a few feet behind a formidable-looking man. The women wore long dresses of material that at one time were probably bright colors of red, purple and green, now faded with time and use. Both wore high moccasins. The women's faces were impassive; neither of them spoke or made any gestures at all. The man in front, closest to Liam, was a figure to rivet the eye. He sat a tall bay horse and was the only one of the three who rode a white man's saddle. It was scuffed and battered, all the leather thongs normally attached had been cut off. Behind the pommel running perpendicular to his body rested a much-used lever action rifle of some sort. He was attired in a hodgepodge of native and white apparel. He wore high beaded moccasins, trousers of some sort of serge material, a beaded leather shirt with porcupine quills forming a design across the chest, and a long bandana of red cloth wrapped several times around his neck. Around both arms just above the wrist, he wore wide bracelets of what might have been copper. On his head rested a battered derby hat with many holes burned in it.

His face commanded attention. He stared at Liam out of deeply recessed, piercing black eyes under thick brows. His nose, long and aquiline, was badly bent to one side, his cheeks prominently lined. His hair was pulled back in a bun behind his head, long stands of it shot with grey hung down past his ears and onto his shoulders. It was nearly impossible to guess at his age, for he looked neither young nor old. His carriage was of a man still in the active years of his life.

He stepped lightly off his horse and said, "You got tobacca?"

Liam pulled a sack of rollings and paper from his shirt pocket and handed them over. The tall native took them and saying nothing rolled himself a smoke expertly. He reached into a pile of smoldering rubbish Marta had been burning, picked up a coal in his fingers, lit the cigarette, and drew deeply. He looked directly into Liam's eyes and it was impossible to say whether his look was hostile or not; certainly his ambience betrayed no real happiness at seeing Liam before him. Liam started to say something in greeting but the man cut him off.

"This my land and my people's land. We hunt here. Lots of deer. Bear too. Good place for camp."

"This is a good place," said Liam. "We stay here now. As you say, a good place to hunt, to camp."

"Too much white man here. This land intian hunt place. Not good for white. Too much white man now. You go. This place intian place. You go from here."

"Well," said Liam, struggling to keep his voice from ratcheting upward with nervousness, "I'm sure we'll be no bother to you here. You hunt, it doesn't bother us. We will not interfere with you." Liam stood up a little straighter and said what he felt he must. "My wife and I have come to live here now; we will not be leaving. We have filed on this land with the Canadian government and they have assured us that it is permissible to be here." Liam paused. He wondered if any of this meant anything to the man in front of him. He wondered how the government had figured the natives into the equation. Liam changed his tack. "My name is Liam Brennan and my wife is Marta." He stuck out his hand and as he did so, he said, "And may I ask your name?"

The native stood impassively, he made no effort to take Liam's hand. He took another long drag on the cigarette, dropped it, ground it with his heel and swung back up effortlessly onto his horse.

"My name Noah. This intian land."

For a moment he sat in front of Liam, then he put his heels to the horse, reined him 180 degrees and rode between the two women, back the way they had come. The women fell in behind him without ever having spoken or been acknowledged. Back across the meadow they rode, the horses picking their way through the blowdown. Liam watched them until they faded into the timber.

"Are they going to make trouble?"

Liam felt Marta's hand on his arm. He hadn't even realized that she had come up beside him during the conversation.

"I don't know. I hope it won't come to that. They obviously don't want us here. They want us to believe we are on their land and are here at their askance. I can't decide if it means any more than that. But they're going to have to accept it. I guess we can't expect them to be happy about us being here. The only thing I'm sure of is that we've got to try to be friendly and accommodating, but we must never let them believe that they can intimidate us. I'm not sure how things are going to fit with them once we start to break ground. Right now I think it's best not to worry about it."

"Those women," said Marta, "they didn't say anything, not one word. I am not sure what they felt, their faces revealed nothing."

The Brennans realized that they needed to replenish their depleted supply of staples before the onset of winter. Another nagging question was what to do about a stove? Liam had no illusions about being able to survive the deep cold without a good stove. A fireplace, even if they had had one, was really nothing more than a decoration; the heat basically went up the chimney, and a fire left burning at night invariably went out and then sucked all of the remaining heat out of a house. The problem of the stove was many sided: Where could they get one? What would it cost? Their supply of cash was very low. And how could they transport it back here? True, they had the reliable old team of percherons but as yet no wagon or sleigh with which to haul anything the many miles back from the trading post.

On a crisp morning sometime in early September, Liam and Marta closed the flaps of the makeshift tent in which they had lived for the past months and set out across the flat to pick up the trail that would take them to Hudson's Hope, which Liam believed was about twenty miles distant. Each of them rode one of the gentle old work horses, which in addition to its rider also carried its harness. Liam hoped somehow to acquire a wagon or cart which they could hitch the team to for transporting their purchases back to the flat. The trail did not look promising. It was very narrow, extremely rough and, even as dry as the weather now was, was pocked with mud holes, some of them very ominous looking. As well, the trail intersected and crossed several small creeks that flowed into the big river a few hundred yards to their left. Liam brought the axe tied by a leather carrying case to the harness. He would need to use it if they attempted to get a wagon back.

About an hour up the trail on another river flat, they encountered a homestead, or what passed for one. A very roughly built log hut squatted a few yards left of the trail, only a few feet from a tiny creek flowing toward the river. So this explained the smoke they had smelled now and then since their arrival. A mongrel dog barked loudly at them while straining at a leather thong connected to a stake driven into the earth near the door. A woman appeared in the doorway but neither spoke nor came forward. At that instant a man walked from the timber just back of the hut.

"Hello," said Liam in a loud voice. The man nodded his head and came forward.

"Must be the folks from downriver, eh? We heard in the Hope that somebody had taken up somewhere downstream of us. Name's Wallace, Edmond Wallace. This here's my wife, Bella."

Bella came out of the house a few steps and stopped, looking shyly at the Brennans. It was easy to see her native ancestry in her straight black hair and dark eyes. She looked at the mounted couple and there seemed a glint of friendliness in her eyes, but she did not speak.

"Headed for the Hope, eh? Probably needin' to trade up some things 'fore winter sets in, I'd guess. If so, you picked as good a time as any. The road's in good shape and the tradin' post's got more things now than it used to have. They don't give no credit though. They deals in cash money, fur or gold dust, and everthing's plenty expensive."

The man talked on, monopolizing the conversation as though he needed to talk to someone. In the quarter hour they spoke with him, the Brennans learned that they had come here a few years earlier from Manitoba, that his wife was a Metis from the Red River country, that they had three children, all of whom were down at the river fishing. He had tried some gold panning on the local creeks, had found a few colors but nothing of any consequence. They supported themselves through trapping, which hadn't been good lately, and by occasional work for the Factor of the Hudson Bay Company at the Hope. In deed, judging from the tattered condition of their clothes and the poor appearance of their place, they had not prospered here.

Liam and Marta did not go all the way to Hudson's Hope that day but camped on the edge of the big river several hours upstream from their place. There was a startling vista here; they could look straight up the smooth flowing river and over the top of several islands near its center. In the background they saw a mountain range running what looked to be perpendicular to the river. There was a great notch in the mountains, and through it, they could see, stretching away into the hazy mist of the western horizon, range after range of purplish, snow-capped mountains. It was a startling sight for people accustomed to flat country. To Marta, they were a thrilling sight but also inspired in her a spasm of fear. They look wild and forbidding, as though humankind had never penetrated them nor set his hand to them. It was as if the known world ended at their feet. The river itself rolled on languidly and majestically below as they sat near their tiny campfire. The river dominated the landscape as far as they could see up river or down. The waters sighed as though the river had always been here, as though this valley was its domain and the puniness of human intervention was not even a consideration. There was a great calm about the river, but there was also a sense of leviathan power. A great whirlpool sucked and gurgled in the lee of a rock island directly below them, and they marvelled at the blue-green depths. Pieces of driftwood spun round and round in the vortex of the pool, seemingly caught forever. The sun sank below the horizon but the light lingered. Far upstream an animal swam the whole width of the river and emerged on the right bank. The creature was very dark, but Liam thought it must not be a bear because its legs looked long. The animal vanished into the timber, and after a while the couple sat silently looking up the great river valley.

As night fell they sat around their fire, which had burned down to embers. It was one of the few times they had actually been able to sit and relax without the cares of daily pioneer life interrupting. They sat for a long time gazing at the darkening horizon, not even bothering with conversation. Of late Marta had been experiencing a deep spate of homesickness; at times it was so intense as to feel to her like a physical ailment. It came most intensely during those few moments when she had the time away from the daily cares of her life for introspection. It had been many months since she had had any contact with her mother. Of her father nothing had been heard from him since his regiment had gone to the front nearly two years ago now. Marta had a deep sense of loss; she clearly felt that her father was gone, one of the millions of fatalities of a terrible war. She wondered how her mother was getting by and wished again for the hundredth time that Madeline had come with her and Liam to Canada.

The twilight faded into darkness and the sky became lit with the light of millions of stars. And again as she had seen on nights before, the aurora began to flicker, first on the northeastern edge of the sky and then began to stretch almost directly overhead. The colors were pink and a pale shade of green; the colors kept changing, as did their location. Marta glanced about her and realized how clear the night sky was; it was not really dark at all. From across the river, in the deep abyss of black timber came a low moan, which scaled up and up and then was joined by other voices. The howl of the wolves echoed up and down the valley and it seemed to pervade everything.

"They're on the other side of the river, Marta. They won't be any bother to us. They're hunting tonight. I'm glad we've got the horses with us. Wolves are a terrible threat to livestock, but I don't think they ever bother humans. At least I've never heard of it."

"Will they stay over there? I am afraid they'll come over here tonight. Their cries are frightening. It's almost—otherworldly."

"Actually, at times I like hearing it," said Liam. "But then on other occasions their howling seems like a threat—a threat to everything living, in winter especially. Wolves always work together and they are remorseless once they get onto the track of some poor animal. But they're a fact of life here, Marta. We're never going to be without them, so we just have to resign ourselves to that and accept it."

They sat listening as a single wolf voice started again with a low wailing moan. Other voices joined, until it was almost a crescendo of howling. The wolf talk continued for nearly an hour, then it abruptly ended. The northern lights flickered and flashed, but everything seemed still. The great river below them moved past with a faint hum that they felt as much as heard. Marta and Liam pulled their wool blankets about them and lay down near the embers of the fire. Sleep came to Liam quickly. Marta pressed close to him for warmth and comfort but remained awake for a long time going over in her mind the events that had brought her from the settled predictability of her Belgian homeland to a tiny pin prick of human occupation in the wilderness of western Canada. She wondered if this was a fated union or just a toss of the dice on the table of chance. She knew she loved Liam and wanted to be with him. It would have been easier if they had settled somewhere closer to civilization, someplace where they could interact with other people and take comfort in some kind of existence where there was a pattern, some kind of order and predictability. At times, she felt terribly inadequate to come to such a raw land and be the type of companion and wife she felt compelled to be. There was so little for her to look to in the way of a guide as to what a woman in a place like this should emulate. She was terribly intimidated by the rawness of the country. There seemed almost no place to begin to build their lives into the only pattern she knew, the one of her European childhood: a life with order, with a rhythm to the seasons and a place where things such as planting and harvesting, taking meals, socializing, marrying, dying, happened in some kind of order and predictability. As she thought of their place with its charred stumps, canvas lean-to and seemingly total disorder, she shuddered a little. Could anything such as this ever be converted into the type of life that she had always known? Known, that is, before the War changed everything. She finally drifted into sleep pressed tightly into the small of her husband's back with the aurora fading and the first light of dawn beginning to paint the eastern sky with crimson.

Hudson's Hope was another disappointment. It consisted of a police barracks, a smithy, a ramshackle general store and a few log buildings. The backdrop to the hamlet was certainly spectacular. It was built on a bench high above the great river on a table land underlaid with great stone slabs and boulders. From its eastern edge one could look miles down the valley and see several loops of the river before it vanished into the distance. Below, right to the edge of the river, were a few log buildings, the only real signs that could be seen of human habitation from this vantage point.

The hamlet seemed to have a plentiful supply of dogs, some of which raced out at them aggressively as they rode up to the store. From the general store was procured the flour, salt, tea, and other staples needed for wintering at their place. They also bought a heavy cast iron stove, a few hand tools, shells for the rifle, and some trapping paraphernalia. Later in the morning Liam spent the last of their cash for an iron-wheeled wagon in dubious condition and a mongrel bitch. The dog was an unfriendly animal of medium size and uncertain lineage, a mottled brown and black, and in very poor condition. The half-breed from whom she was purchased assured Liam that the dog was pregnant and would whelp in a few weeks. Liam was unimpressed with the dog but since he had got it for next to nothing and knew that they would later need dogs, he tethered it behind the wagon with a leather thong for the trip back. Liam and Marta had wanted to buy a milk cow but soon found they had absolutely no cash left and anyway, no one seemed to have an animal that was suitable or that they would part with.

Late in the afternoon of the day of their arrival, they started back. For the first few hours, things went relatively well. The old team, well-broke to harness, pulled the high wagon willingly and the small load inside it. The dog trailed sullenly at the rear, securely tied to the wagon box. Marta and Liam sat on the wooden seat which had an iron spring under it, though it did little to take out the jolts of the rough track. They camped again in the same place as they had the previous night. As they started out again the next morning, they could see that they were in for a weather change. The sky, already a slate grey, seemed to grow darker as they set out downriver. Within half an hour the first raindrops fell. Liam again pulled the tarpaulin cover as tight as he could around the perishables that were in the wagon. Neither Liam nor Marta had any type of rain clothing, so they too wrapped themselves as best they could into a canvas tarp. It proved to be only a moderate protection from the rain, for as it increased gradually in volume, it ran down their necks and soaked into their clothing. The road quickly changed from just rough and lumpy to a slippery quagmire. Puddles formed quickly in the viscous clay soil, and as the horses strained to keep their footing, clots of mud were hurled back into Marta and Liam's faces.

The wagon seemed never to move straight now; the back end was continually sliding off the track and into the brush and trees. When a small tree lodged against the wheel, Liam was obliged to get down, cut out and move the pieces before they could continue. The rain fell steadily. Clouds of water vapor rose from the backs of the horses as they strained in their harnesses. The creeks they had to cross were rising steadily now. As they came to the largest of these creeks, they were alarmed to see that it had risen several feet and small pieces of trees and other flotsam rushed by. Liam did not want to cross here now, but quickly saw that there was no other alternative. There was not even room on the narrow tree-hugged road to turn the team and wagon around.

"Hold on, Marta, we've got to do it."

The horses plunged into the creek, and for a moment, it seemed it would push them downstream, but the team set their huge feet, leaned into the current, and lurched ahead. The wagon was lifted completely off the ground by the current and threatened to pull the team downstream with it.

"Hip! Agnes! Pearl! Hip!" Liam screamed at the team and hit them with the loose end of the lines. The upstream left wheel caught on something beneath the surface and for an instant the wagon dipped dangerously on that side, nearly swamped by the rushing current. The horses squatted down to get a purchase with their powerful back legs and with a jerk that nearly unseated Liam and Marta, they lunged through the middle of the stream and up the steep bank on the other side. Marta was frozen with fear, but she clung with a death grip to the sides of the wooden seat as the wagon slipped and lurched up the far bank. Liam stopped the loyal old team for a moment to let them catch their wind and to calm them. He and Marta looked at each other.

"You got mud on your face," he said as he wiped a glob off her cheek.

"So have you."

Liam swiped his face and his hand came away smeared with mud. He looked into her eyes and when she returned his look, he kissed her quickly on the mouth.

"Ready for the next one?" he inquired through a forced smile.

Marta hesitated, looked back at him, let out a deep breath, and said softly, "Yes."

It was many hours later when they finally got to the homestead. The rain was still falling steadily and the horses were stumbling with exhaustion. Neither of them had a stitch of dry clothing on; water was even sloshing in their shoes from running down their trouser legs. Liam helped Marta down, got a fire started in their shelter, tied up the tired horses and fed them some of the precious hay. They stripped off their sopping clothes and put on dry ones. Marta was so cold it was all she could do to force herself to put together a meal. Liam was sick with worry about their supplies in the wagon. He brought in the heavy bags of flour, which was all they would have to last them through the long winter. The top of one bag was definitely damp so they tore open the top and set the whole thing near the fire in hopes that it would dry and not spoil the rest of the bag. They ate a meal of meat and rice, and although the food warmed them some, they both were chilled with cold until they rolled into the wool blankets of their bed. Marta was amazed at how cold it could be even in summer when there was no snow.

Rain fell steadily for the next three days, then it stopped as abruptly as it had begun. The wind came up from the southwest and the clouds began to shred. A brilliant sun came out and the soaked grass and foliage began to dry. Liam now knew they had to get their log house finished as quickly as possible. He and Marta worked endlessly to get a covering of sod on the roof and get the stove installed. Then a supply of firewood had to be brought in. Firewood was the one thing they had in abundance. Liam used the team to drag in fire-killed trees that stood on the edge of the flat in three directions. Cutting these trees down with an axe was backbreaking work. Nearly all the trees on the ground were charred and half rotted, so they were poor material for fuel, but they lay on the ground and blocked passage in every direction. When he wasn't dragging in trees for fuel, Liam spent endless hours piling these snags for burning. He dared not light any fires at this time of year for fear of losing control of it. He planned to wait until snow fell then burn the piles.

Marta continued to tend the garden, scythe the long grass where it could be reached. The pile of hay they had made for the horses' winter use was still pitifully small so this remained a priority. They set about making a snake fence around the hay pile and building a small corral. They constructed a rough lean-to that would do no more than provide the horses with shelter from the wind.

Long hours of sunlight and abundant moisture had combined to make the garden more of a success than they could have hoped for. They feasted on peas and potatoes when they came on; it was a welcome respite from their diet of meat, rice and white flour. In addition to the cultivated plants, wild serviceberries and rose hips were abundant. Marta picked pails full of the saskatoons as the serviceberries were called. She spread them in the sun to dry, later to be stored for winter use. The rose hips would provide needed vitamins in the months when no fresh food would be available.

On the path up from the river to the flat, in a clay bank, Liam dug a cave, or root cellar as he called it, where the produce they gathered from their garden and from the wild could be stored without being destroyed by the cold. He spent days shoring up the sides and top with logs and constructing the rough doors to the entrance.

Both Liam and Marta now worked with a heightened sense of urgency. The days were clearly growing shorter and the nights longer. In mid-September, the nights became frosty, and by the end of that month heavy frost was occurring nearly every night. The potatoes and carrots were dug and piled inside the cellar; the cabbages were cut into strips and layered in a crock and salted down to make kraut.

They moved their possessions out of the lean-to and into their tiny cabin. They had intended to put in a floor of split logs but the time to saw the logs had never been found. They would try to make do by packing down the earth floor with clay dug from the riverbanks. They would put in a floor in the spring. The stove they had bought was a great comfort as it heated the cabin delightfully. But Liam was uneasy about the chimney, which was only a metal pipe thrust up through the rafters and dirt of the roof. He had packed wet clay around the pipe to dry and hopefully provide enough insulation to keep the roof from catching fire. Liam set up a frame onto which he could lay large logs and then use the cross-buck saw to cut them into stove lengths. Many hours of hard labor were put into this enterprise. A huge woodpile grew beside the cabin as the woodcutting continued.

The horses were allowed to graze on the flat during the daylight hours, but they were brought in and put inside the small corral at night. They seemed content to stay on the grassy flat except when they trudged down the trail to the river for water.

Fall came on with the frosty nights. Deer were still plentiful around the homestead; Liam shot two of them and he and Marta dried the meat over a smoky fire. Neither of them was particularly fond of the dried meat, but having conversed with those who had wintered in the area before, Liam knew that game could vanish altogether for long periods when winter descended. The deer hides were carefully scraped and dried. Neither of them had any real idea how to render them into coats or clothing, but as they had little in the way of winter clothes, it was a hope that the hides would be of use. The leaves on the trees turned a beautiful gold and for a few days the surrounding country was a panorama of gold-leafed deciduous aspen mixed with the green of the pine and spruce. The days were shortening noticeably now but the weather remained clear and stunningly beautiful. In a morning in mid-October they awoke to a stiff north wind and the air filled with clouds of leaves showering off the trees. By nightfall the land had taken on a new, more barren look, as the majority of the trees were naked of their leaves. This was followed by a cold drenching rain, which gradually turned to sleet and then to wind-driven wet snow.

Marta and Liam were forced inside their cabin for the better part of three days. Liam noted with some apprehension that water oozed through the ceiling in a couple of places near the stove pipe, but it was amazing, given the materials of which it was constructed, how weatherproof the roof was. The harnesses were brought into the cabin, as there was no waterproof place to leave them outside. The last of the garden produce was gathered in and stored.

A few dazzlingly clear days followed the end of the storm and the wet snow melted away. The days were cool and bracing. Great flocks of ducks and geese flew overhead for several days, filling the air with their music. There was a sense of expectation in the air, as though the earth was waiting for something. Marta felt this and when a few days later, the skies greyed and snow began to filter down, it was almost anti-climatic. They had prepared for winter with such intensity and for so long, it was almost a relief when it actually began to happen.

By late November there were a few inches of snow on the ground, and though the temperatures had stayed mostly below freezing, there had been little sign of the intense cold that Liam had described. Marta began to relax a bit and even to enjoy the cessation of labor that cold weather brought. She turned more of her thoughts to the welfare of her unborn child as her body began to change shape. She had not really thought too deeply about giving birth out here, but now she began to wonder if there would be any doctor or skilled mid-wife to help. She and Liam spoke of it often, but nothing as yet had been decided.

On a day, late in November, Marta got her first taste of what real winter might be like. Liam had gone off very early in the morning to inspect some of the country that lay north of their place. He had been mulling over in his mind how they could lay their hands on some cash and the only thing he could come up with was trapping. He was not actually experienced with this, but he knew something about the type of country where fur-bearing animals might be found. He had set out just after daylight with a promise to be back before nightfall. He just wanted to look over some of the timberland and swamps where he could set traps for lynx and marten. He took a few scraps of food, his rifle, and was fairly lightly dressed, as the exertion of plodding through the snow and brush would keep him more than warm enough.

Before noon, a stiff north breeze sprang up. Marta could feel the air growing colder by the minute. By early afternoon the cabin thermometer was in freefall. As agreed, Marta went into the meadow flat and caught the old team, brought them in and locked them in the corral. She had on a heavy wool coat and mittens but by the time she had finished, she was stiff and shaking with cold. As she fled to the cabin, she glanced at the thermometer, which read minus 25 Fahrenheit, where earlier that morning it had only been minus 2. Despite the plunging temperature, a dry wind-driven snow began to fall; the wind increased. Standing outside the door of the cabin Marta could not clearly see the north edge of the flat, which she knew was only a few hundred yards away. By late afternoon the temperature was still falling and Marta was growing apprehensive. Did Liam have on enough clothing to stay warm? Had the wind-blown snow confused him so that he had lost his way? Could he have injured himself some way? She continually walked outside and peered across the rapidly darkening flat. The logs of the cabin creaked and popped as the blanket of cold fell on the earth. She heard several loud reports that startled her and each time she went to the door and peered out. She did not realize that what she was hearing were trees exploding in the cold. It grew darker and she lit the lantern. Just as her apprehension was growing almost to panic, she heard something outside, and the door was flung open. Liam and the dog both came into the cabin; his face was very pale and his beard clotted with ice.

"Never seen the temperature drop this fast. My hands and feet are damn near frozen. Kept reasonably warm until the last couple of hours, then no matter how hard I walked I couldn't keep the cold out. Should have dressed warmer, I guess."

They ate a warm meal and Liam felt better but wondered if the tips of some of his fingers were frostbitten. They sat listening to the groaning of the cabin walls. Liam got up and went out to feed the horses a bit of hay. Snow was falling lightly and was whipped by a vicious wind. When they finally went to bed, the thermometer stood at minus 40 and was still inching lower.

Despite her nervousness, Marta slept soundly. When she woke, Liam was lighting the lantern and putting more wood in the stove. The thermometer outside read minus 46 but the wind had died away. Tiny particles of snow still filtered down. A heavy ice fog hung like a shroud over the whole flat. Liam went out and let the horses out to paw for grass. He was concerned about using any of the precious hay so early in the winter.

The deep cold lasted nearly a week, then it gradually began to subside, and when it did, Liam again journeyed to the plateau north of the flat and took with him the few small animal traps they had and some heavy wire snares. He left at first light and did not get back until hours after dark in a state of near exhaustion.

Tip, the mongrel dog Liam had got in Hudson's Hope, was nearing her time. She did not like to come into the cabin even when urged to do so, so a crude box filled with hay was made for her just outside the cabin door. On a moderately warm December morning Tip gave birth to seven puppies. One of them did not live out the day, and Liam took the two remaining females and killed them, leaving four of the original litter, all males. Tip had improved her condition since joining the Brennans, so she was able to nourish her pups and they grew rapidly. They had no reservations about coming into the cabin and tottered over everything and got underfoot if allowed in.

In the middle of the month a small group of woodland caribou turned up one day on the flat. They seemed mesmerized by the two horses and stared at them, ran off, but returned inquisitively. Liam took his rifle and circled around in front of them through the thick timber. The herd started back across the flat, then crossed directly in front of him and he killed two of them with as many shots. Both were young bulls whose white and buff coats were impressive. Liam skinned and quartered them. A thick layer of fat covered the carcasses, and the meat Liam hoped would be a welcome change from mule deer. With the dogs to feed, more meat was needed.

Marta, with Liam's help, set about trying to make something of the dried deerskins. The heavily haired hides would, they hoped, make warm coats if they could just figure out how to make them. Neither of them had any idea how to tan a hide, so they ended up cutting the hides up with the hair on and attempting to sew the pieces together to make coats. The result was a pullover garment without any buttons whatsoever, with holes cut for the arms and long enough in the body to hang nearly to the knees. Only a small opening was left for the head to go through, so a heavy scarf could seal off cold air from coming in around the neck. Unlikely as it appeared, this heavy cloak-like coat put on over the wool clothing they had already, provided the protection from deep cold that they had lacked before.

There seemed to be a plentiful supply of fur-bearing animals around, but Liam had little immediate success with trapping. Most of the traps were found sprung and the bait gone. Liam rehearsed in his mind the few tips he had picked up about trapping. He brought all of the traps back to the cabin and boiled them in water filled with spruce needles. On resetting them, he was careful not to touch them with anything but leather gloves. He tried different types of sets, especially for lynx, and shortly after Christmas, he finally was rewarded. In one week he caught two lynx which looked to be in prime condition. As the winter progressed he caught several more and a few marten as well.

In late January, there was another spate of deep cold, even colder than the first one. It subsided quickly, but on its heels came a series of heavy snowstorms. Where early on, less than a foot of powdery snow was on the ground, after this last snowfall, the depth was above the knees. Just getting out to check his traps became exhausting work. Liam knew about snowshoes and had even used them but had only a rudimentary idea of how to construct them. He cut some willows that were still supple enough to bend when heated in the cabin and set to work attaching strips of deer hide across the willows to hold them in a bow shape. He coated this with bear grease. The resulting snowshoes were clumsy and very difficult to use, but only allowed Liam to sink a few inches into the snow as he walked across it. Keeping them attached to his shoes was a never-ending trial. Liam's near daily trips to his trapline consumed most of his time and nearly all of his energy. His already lean body grew leaner and whipcord tough. His face and hands suffered in the cold. The tips of a couple of his fingers had turned black and the nails came out. This was not surprising as nearly everything he touched was frozen rock hard, and there were some tasks, such as getting animals out of snares, that he could not do in mitts. His beard protected his face somewhat, but his nose and cheekbones were touched with frost.

As the days began to lengthen with late winter, Marta became more and more preoccupied with the nearing birth of their child. Finally Liam snowshoed the five miles or more to the Wallace's homestead. Edmond had just returned from Hudson's Hope. He confirmed that there was no doctor there, though once or twice a year a person came out from Fort St. John to pull teeth and take care of other dental problems. Liam learned that Bella had acted as midwife a few times in Manitoba, and on learning of this, he asked if she would come to the Brennans' place when Marta's time came, which she consented to do. She was also convinced to come with her husband and at least become familiar with Marta before the birth. It was decided that the Wallaces would come to Liam and Marta's place in a week or so, bring the children and make a social day of it. It would also give Marta a chance to learn something of Bella. Liam could not really make much of her. She was laconic at the best of times, but she seemed competent in her role of wife and mother. After taking a meal with the Wallaces, Liam returned after dark to Marta and their place. Marta seemed a bit uneasy about having Bella and the family come, but Liam convinced her that it would be good to have an experienced person at the birth.

A few days later, Noah appeared again; this time he was by himself, still riding the same bay horse. Because it was so cold, Liam invited him into the cabin, where he and Liam drank tea and smoked. It was learned that Noah was part of a large band of Beaver Indians, that they were wintering somewhere east of there, that hunting had been poor in the last few weeks. Indeed, it had been some time since Liam had seen any of the deer that had been so numerous on the flat in the fall and summer. Noah said that he had recently killed a moose, the first one seen all winter though several sets of tracks had been spotted. Noah claimed to know how to trap lynx and marten and gave Liam several tips on sets and locations.

During Noah's visit, Marta sat quietly with the men at the table but took little part in the conversation. She found Noah interesting but his presence was somehow intimidating to her. He had a dark, deeply-lined face, black eyes, thick grey-black hair and reeked of wood smoke. She learned from the conversation that the two women with him on the previous visit were both wives and that he had several children. When he had drunk his fill of tea, he abruptly rose to his feet, walked to the door, nodded at them and departed. He had not seemed overly friendly but had made no threatening statements about their presence. Noah rode off across the flat, picked up the trail toward Hudson's Hope and vanished into the trees. Marta wondered how he could stand to ride a horse on such a cold day, especially when he had not appeared to be that warmly dressed. Liam was of the opinion that it would be to their advantage to maintain amicable relations with the natives, and Noah in particular, if possible. He knew some of the natives had a bad reputation for drink but thus far, he had seen none of it.

In February another phenomenon occurred that was, according to Liam, indicative of the Peace River country. On an overcast morning they awoke as usual to cold many degrees below zero. Liam was preparing to go to the trapline but had not made the early start he had thought about the day before. As he forked over a few bits of hay to the significantly thinner team, he thought it felt a bit warmer, even than it had been minutes earlier. A soft breeze wafted across the flat.

"Marta, come out and feel this. I think we're starting a Chinook."

"A Chinook? What is a Chinook?"

"A wind that blows the cold away for a while. A warm wind. Sometimes it warms up so much it actually thaws."

Within an hour the cold had decreased so much they could stand to be outside in shirtsleeves; in another hour water began dripping from the roof. The clouds in the west lifted and seemed to hold just over the mountains with some pinkish sky in between.

The Chinook blew for five days. The snow level dropped by half as the powdery snow compressed into a heavy white blanket. The leaks in the cabin began again; the horses pawed industriously for dry grass under the snow.

"Liam," Marta spoke sharply. "Liam."

Liam looked up from the stool he sat upon, a fresh coyote hide across his knees and a fleshing knife in his hand. Something in the tone of her voice caused him to pause.

"Liam, I think it might be coming. I just felt something—a pain." As she spoke she winced visibly, "And there it is again." Her hands gripped the sides of the plank table so hard her knuckles were white.

It was a bitterly cold night in early March and both had sat up late, Liam with his never-ending work from his trapline, Marta uncharacteristically animated moving around the tiny cabin nervously tinkering with their few possessions. The stove was burning as hot as Liam dared allow against another period of bone-chilling cold that had set in a few days previously.

Liam laid down the skin, got to his feet, moved to where Marta now sat, hunched in a chair. He took her hand in his and placed his other on her swollen abdomen.

"Marta, what do you think? Are you sure? From what we've figured it seems a bit early." He sat in a chair beside her and they conversed quietly for a few minutes. Some of the tension in Marta's body seemed to relax momentarily. A week earlier Marta had had some pains she thought might be the start of her labor, but they had subsided. Not, however, before Liam had taken the two horses and gone as fast as he could for Wallaces. Upon his frantic return with Bella, they found Marta as he had left her and the pains she had been feeling gone. Marta was deeply embarrassed, but Bella comforted her with the information that such things often happened, especially with the first child.

Suddenly Marta's body went rigid and her hand gripped Liam's like a vise. "No, it's not like last time," she gasped. "I know it is starting."

Liam rose quickly, picked up Marta and put her on their bed. "I'll be back as fast as those horses can travel." He pulled on some heavy clothing.

As he stood in the doorway for an instant, Marta said, "Please, Liam, hurry. It's coming fast!"

The horses stood passively as Liam mounted one of them, the lead rope for the other in his hand. He wished they owned a saddle, though the size of these draft animals was not conducive to any regular sized saddle anyway. Liam rode bareback as they jogged out of the yard. Once on the trail, Liam goaded the animal out of its spine-jarring trot into a rocking gallop, clenching his thighs and knees tightly to stay astride the broad lunging back. Liam hardly noticed the cold as he and the two horses breasted a stiff wind while plowing along the rugged trace of a trail. Once Liam's mount stumbled over an unseen obstacle and nearly went down. Liam caught a handful of the coarse mane as he was pitched forward, just narrowly avoiding being hurled over the horse's head and under its feet. The horses began first to breathe deeply then to gasp spasmodically as they tired. The gallop was gone, and they were in a labored trot when they lurched into the clearing where the Wallace cabin stood. The sound of the horses' hooves had alerted the Wallaces, as the whole family stood outlined in the light of the door.

"The baby's coming now for certain," gasped Liam. "Please come now, Bella. This time it's for sure."

Bella disappeared into the cabin for a couple of minutes, then she reappeared bundled in a heavy coat and leather leggings. Her husband helped her up onto the panting horse, its sides wet with lather, but Bella never winced. She sat on the great heaving back like a small bird.

They started back. Liam noticed, as he had on their first trip, that Bella sat her horse much easier than he did. She did not seem to rock around on its back despite having no saddle. She held the halter rope, which was the only equipment on the horse, in her right hand and twisted the fingers of her other into the long strands of the mane. She queried Liam a bit on how severe Marta's pains were and how often they were coming. When Liam told her they had only been minutes apart when he left, she scolded him for waiting so long.

The horses were staggering with fatigue when Bella and Liam pounded them into the yard. Liam leapt down, pulled Bella from her horse, and they rushed to the door. Just before Liam flung open the door, he heard crying. It was not Marta. As he stood framed in the doorway, he saw Marta by the flickering light of their oil lantern. She lay propped on her side in the bed. At her breast was a tiny wizened face wailing mightily.

"Too late," said an ashen-faced Marta, but she smiled weakly as she looked up. "We have a son."

A warm day in mid-May, a gentle breeze blew across the home flat, a bit stiffer as one got closer to the river. Liam could hear geese squawking, but at the moment he could not see any of them. In the previous weeks great clouds of ducks and geese had been winging up and down the valley, the air full of their raucous mating calls. A few days earlier the ice had broken up in the river in a spectacular display of natural power. In the hours before the ice gave way, the river groaned and creaked; some of the noises it made were awesome, even frightening. At times it had sounded almost like thunder and these noises continued all of one night. About an hour after first light Liam, Marta, and Jack—they had named him Jack because they liked the name and given him the middle name of Marta's father, Medgar, who lay somewhere in northern France in a soldier's grave—stood on the high level bank several meters above the creaking ice and watched an event that would become an icon in their calendar year. The river ice was covered with slush and tiny rivulets of water. The grey ice began to shudder and vibrate like some great living organism, which indeed, it was. As they gazed across the pulsating ice toward the far bank, a massive wedge of ice thrust itself up out of the depths of the river. There was a ripping explosive sound as the ice in front of the block gave way under it. In the matter of a few seconds, what had been solid ice, became a seething cauldron of great chunks of ice which seemed to break apart and tip back on itself. Suddenly the whole center of the river was moving, the cracking of the ice rising to a crescendo. The eerie noise continued for several hours into the afternoon, the channel in the middle gradually widening as more and more of the ice gave way on the sides. Had the channel of the river not been cut so deeply into the valley through which it flowed, it might have threatened to inundate the flat as great jams kept forming in mid-river, and several times the water rose quickly above them for several meters. But the gargantuan power of the water behind the ice jams broke them loose and the water level subsided quickly. In addition to the creaking and cracking, there was the hiss of smaller particles rushing past as the great river shook off its winter cloak. Marta and Liam stood on the bank for hours mesmerized by the awesome display, looking at one another from time to time but speaking little, struck into silence by the feelings they felt inadequate to express.

It was a warm day in late May. Liam and Marta had been planting potatoes. Liam had taken the team and plowed the plot they had planted the previous summer. The earth was not so rough as it had been; the deep brown-black furrows glistened in the sun and a slight cloud of vapor rose from them. After the plowing, they had taken up hand tools and worked the sod of the furrows into a finer bed of loam into which they dropped the potato cuttings. The soil still contained much of the root systems and sod that had held it together for eons; the work was strenuous but satisfying. Marta felt a kind of partnership with the earth as she covered over the cuttings, knowing that with the human effort added to the growing capacity of the land, a reward would be reaped. She had felt this kinship with the land as she worked in the fields of her native Belgium long before she came to Canada. The baby lay on a bundle of blankets under the wagon bed to keep him out of the sun. He was not a fussy baby; he lay looking up at the trees out of eyes the color of the sky. A fuzz of brownish hair was just forming over his pink scalp. He nursed at his mother's breast every couple of hours, and it agreed with him. His cheeks had a healthy rose tinge to them and he was alert and mostly happy. His doting parents sometimes sat looking at him and at each other in wonderment of this masterpiece they had created. Just now he had a wooden serving spoon clutched in his fat fingers and kept waving and sucking it alternately.

The only negative to their bucolic afternoon was the return of the insect plague which had bedeviled them so a year earlier. Mosquito bites had become so commonplace that all of them, even baby Jack, had red welts on every exposed part of their bodies. By mid-afternoon Liam had built a smudge from old dry stumps and green popular saplings. The smoke was sometimes almost overwhelming, but it did repel the mosquitoes and black flies. Even the horses and the dogs edged closer to it as the morning breeze fell still in the long afternoon.

Near the end of the long spring day, Marta, now too tired to work much more, looked up and down the valley at the evidence of spring all around. The popular and cottonwood trees in the bottom of the valley had begun to leaf out a week earlier, their color a vivid, lush green. As the hills rose on either side of the river, the color changed to a delicate lime green as the elevation increased. On Liam's trapline, which had now been shut down for the season, many of the trees in the dense swamp areas had only just begun to bud out and had no leaves at all as yet. Marta was feeling a little more secure about the whole enterprise now. There had been moments during the long, cold, dark months when she wondered how life could ever come back again. She had never experienced anything like the terrible cold of the past winter, but she had to admit the country had its pristine beauty, too. Some of the nights when the aurora was flashing and pulsating, the sky lit with the constellations, and the ever-changing phases of the moon, the earth seemed like a fairy land, a bitter cold one, but beautiful beyond words. Sometimes at night she had stood outside the cabin door and gazed across the moonlit flat and wondered how the world could be so beautiful and so potentially deadly at the same time. Their lives here at times still seemed part of a dream, for in truth, she still lived inside her European psyche. Little that she had ever done in her previous existence, with the exception of her feel for the land and for growing things, had prepared her for the life in which she found herself. It was amazing to her what a change in feelings she could have on a day so stunningly beautiful as this. It was true she hungered for human contact even though Liam worked hard to make her part of his world. During late winter Liam was only at home half the time at best. When he was home, he was deeply engrossed in preparing the hides that he took and keeping trapline equipment repaired. Liam was far from illiterate or unread, but his current life left him little room for mental effort beyond the ordinary cares of the day. In her girlhood days, which now seemed light years behind her, Marta had always had a small circle of friends both adult and adolescent whom she saw and interacted with on a regular basis. She had attempted to strike up a friendship with Bella Wallace, but so far, little had come of it. They were from totally different worlds.

Bella's life in the Manitoba Metis settlements had not been markedly different from what she was living now. The trapline, crude agriculture, poverty, long winters and sometimes catastrophe were all part of her life. Her husband was not an ambitious man, though most of the time he managed to provide for Bella and their growing brood of children. He was not very interested in individual industry such as trapping, but mostly hung about the settlement of Hudson's Hope, taking odd jobs and day work where he could get it. In the few times when Marta and Bella had been together, Marta found conversation with her difficult partly because Bella was taciturn to begin with and secondly, because her frame of reference did not go beyond her current life situation.

Liam, Marta, and baby Jack had made a couple of trips to the Hope fairly recently before the frost went out of the ground and turned the trail impassable for a time, and she had met a few people, but their time there was only transient. Liam always had things that required his immediate attention at home. There was a core of families living there such as the Beatties, the Pecks, the Starks, the Parsons and others who had put down roots a few years earlier, but as yet their paths had not crossed with Liam and Marta except perhaps a word exchanged at the trading post-store. There was also an RCMP detachment there as well as a log Anglican Church but the personnel changed periodically while the rest of the community was more static. In truth, despite the presence of families, men still outnumbered women. This was because many trappers made the hamlet their headquarters though they were only seen with any regularity during the warmer months. There was some coal mining being done in the Peace Canyon but as yet it was a small enterprise handled by only a few. The town had dogs and scenery in abundance. In all, though Marta had met a few people, she had yet to make what she felt was a special friend, which was something she longed for.

1937

Mud flew in every direction as the driver gunned the spattered truck westward along the pitted, hole-pocked road. There was so much mud on the windshield that it seemed impossible that anyone could see out of it. The truck, which was relatively new, looked anything but, as it dripped mud everywhere and the tires were so encased in it that there was barely room for them beneath the rattling fenders. Young Willie Brennan watched entranced as the wildly careening vehicle drew nearer.

Willie had been born four years after his brother Jack. In between, Marta had suffered several miscarriages and for a time she and Liam agonized over whether they would have any more children. It was decided upon the birth of their second son to name him Louis Wilson. In truth, Liam did not really favor the name, but it was done in deference to Marta, who named him Louis after her maternal grandfather. No one seemed to know how it happened, but by the time the child was a few months old, his parents had fallen into the habit of calling him Willie. Willie he remained.

Willie had been sent that morning by his father to fix the fence along the part of their land that bordered the road. Willie had been methodically tightening wires and driving in staples when the truck appeared. It was not unusual to see mechanized traffic on the Hope Road these days, though travel on the scantily maintained road was mostly limited to times of dry weather or for a few weeks in the late fall after the ground froze and before the snow got too deep. To see someone on the road after a rain was a rarity for good reason: usually the enterprise ended in being struck in one of the myriad mud holes, or even worse, sliding completely off the road and into the brush. That very thing was happening just as the truck roared by Willie. The left front of the truck dipped wildly, pulling the back around so that the vehicle was actually moving sideways. The driver compensated for this by pressing the accelerator to the floor, hoping to power out of the skid. Instead of gaining control, the truck swapped ends like a treacherous bronco and skidded off the road through the water-filled ditch, through the fence Willie had just finished repairing, and came to a stop with its back end on the Brennans' pasture and the front end deep in the ditch mud.

"Hey!" yelled Willie. "Hey, you've wrecked our fence."

"Hey, yourself," replied a male voice from inside the truck. "Can't get this goddamned door open. I told the old man he should have bought a Chev." A young fellow only a little older than Willie was extricating himself through the driver side window. He stepped out into the mud and clomped up to the firmer footing of the field, stepping over the flattened wire absentmindedly.

"You made a mess of our fence. You'll have to fix it or Dad's gonna be mighty mad."

"The hell with your fence. If you Brennans hadn't built it so close to the road, nothing woulda happened."

"Except you'd still be stuck," said Willie. "It's gonna take some doin' to drag you outa there."

"You guys got a tractor around here? That'll pull me outa there sure."

"Yeah, we got a tractor but it's way down on the south field. Jack's using it to plow wheat stubble."

"Shit! You must have a team here someplace. I'm always seeing those plugs of yours in the field when I pass by here."

"What about our fence?" retorted Willie. "I just spent half the morning putting it back together."

"Worry about finding something to pull me out with, then we'll see about the fence."

"Ain't you Lindsay Garner?" said Willie. "My Dad says your family chews up this road worse than anyone else who uses it."

"Hell, he does. Well, the road's public property. We put in our days working on it just like everybody else. Not my fault you Brennans built your damn fence so close to the road."

Lindsay was the only son of a family who had moved into the Hope a few years earlier. They obviously had arrived with some means, because

Court Garner, Lindsay's father, had bought a small business and also established the town's first tavern. They had been one of the first families to own an automobile, and Lindsay, while still only a teenager, was a veteran of traveling the road from the Hope to Fort St. John. Lindsay loved anything with an engine and spent every leisure moment fiddling with mechanics. Willie himself was much attracted to mechanical gadgets, and when Liam had purchased the tractor a couple of years back, he and his brother Jack had quickly learned to operate it. As yet, the Brennans owned no automobile, but Liam's sons were pestering him about it continually. Liam still had a team of massive Percherons, descended from the mares he and Marta had brought with them years earlier. The boys were competent with horses in all aspects of their use, but their real interest was anything mechanical, especially engines. Liam himself saw clearly that machines were poised to replace horsepower, but he somehow held back.

Later in the morning when the Garner truck had been dragged up onto the Brennans' field and put on the driveway and hence back onto the road to the Hope, Willie and Liam stood beside the team as Lindsay gunned the engine and sent the truck tearing back up the road again, going out of sight in the same mud-flinging chaos in which he had appeared.

"That kid'll have that truck in the ditch before he goes another mile," muttered Liam. "I don't see why Court lets him drive, the way he handles that truck. And look at what he's done to the road again." Both of them surveyed the skid marks that snaked back and forth across the mud road. "If people would use some sense and just wait a day or two before using the road, we wouldn't have to spend half the summer every year trying to make it passable." It was clear from his demeanor that Liam found the Garners in general, and Lindsay in particular, hard to tolerate. They had an arrogance about everything they did that grated on him.

Liam and his family had now been living on the flat for eighteen years. The changes wrought on the land, though seemingly slow to Liam, were immense. Liam had proved-up on the original quarter section, had filed on another and had bought the rights to another half section from a neighbor immediately downriver who several years previously had grown disenchanted with the rigors of pioneering, sold his land to Liam for a song and departed. Year by year, acre by acre, Liam, Marta, and later their sons had brought the wilderness land under the plow. The backbreaking labor required to accomplish this had taken its toll on all of them though their pride in its continued accomplishment was deeply ingrained in them.

Except for his steel gray hair and lined face, Liam looked much the same. His arms were knots of braided muscle, his hands especially the fingers slightly deformed from years of frostbite on their tips. He had quickly mastered the art of trapping fur-bearing animals and the cash from this had fueled the endless needs of the family farm. Years earlier he and Marta had bought a handful of mixed breed cattle and through careful husbandry and despite regular losses to wolves, they had now a herd of nearly fifty. In the summer following their first winter, Liam and Marta had worked themselves nearly to exhaustion to erect a good log building for their home. Unlike its sod-roofed predecessor, the new house had a roof of split pine shingles, a wooden floor, and was composed of three rooms on the ground floor and two bedrooms in the loft. The labor to construct and finish that house had been scattered over half a dozen years, but they had built well. The now weathered logs of the house had taken on a grey-brown color and stood sturdily on the cleared acres that composed the home place, which was the name by which all of them referred to the original quarter. With the backdrop of the great river, a visitor would have been struck by the beauty of the place. Unlike many of his neighbors, Liam took an interest in the appearance of the home place. Many outbuildings now stood on the land, but all of them were kept well back from the house itself. A profusion of stock corrals stood along with a log barn, but they were well back away from the house.

The original house, in which Liam and Marta endured their first winter, had been moved with horsepower to take on a new life as an equipment shed. Actually, the logs were still as tightly dovetailed together as when Liam had built the cabin, though the bottom round of logs was now going rotten and it had twice been re-roofed.

The yard around the new house did not have a true lawn, but the family kept the grass scythed down in the summer months, and Marta had constructed two flower beds on the south side of the house to the amazement of the neighbors. Although they grew some grain crops, it was so difficult to get grain to market that nearly all of it was fed to animals. In addition to the cattle herd, the Brennans owned a half-wild herd of pigs that, though they could always be converted into ready cash, were a constant challenge to keep under control.

The sedimentary soil of the flat had proved wonderfully productive; Marta's garden flourished and she now had rows of raspberries and strawberries in addition to the profusion of root vegetables. In most ways they were self sufficient; but more out of social needs than anything else, they took several trips each year to one or the other of the two equidistant settlements, Hudson's Hope and Fort St. John. Fort St. John, which had begun as a Hudson's Bay post more than a century earlier, had remained until recently an obscure blot in a sea of wilderness. In the previous decade settlers had begun to trickle in from the drought-stricken prairie provinces and the U.S. to take up the rich lands of which explorers and travelers had so glowingly written. Like the Brennans, they often found unspeakable hardship, privation, and isolation, but the hardiest of them now had a toe-hold and were bringing the plow and the whipsaw to play against primeval forces. Fort St. John now had several business establishments, a bank, Hudson's Bay post and the ubiquitous RCMP barracks. It also had streets so heavy in viscous mud that it could bog a good team. Several cars and trucks were now in evidence, though their use, except under exceptionally favorable conditions was limited. The town also had a doctor and a school, though several one-room log schools dotted the far-flung reaches.

The education of their children had long been a priority of Liam and Marta. There was no way for the children to attend any schools unless they boarded with other families. Neither parent wanted to part with the children for a greater part of any year and the children did not want to live with strangers. So, beginning when Jack was about six years old, Marta had taken it upon herself to teach her own children. She sent out for small reading primers and later texts of various kinds. Marta had much to learn herself about English, though considering the little chance she had to interact with others except her immediate family, she was reasonably well spoken. The reading of English had been a problem for her, but through the repetitive hours of teaching her kids their letters, she became a much better reader herself. Her native Dutch was not spoken in the home, though many times Marta longed to hear it and express herself in it. As for the kids, they learned to love reading and ciphering. Reading was their only window into a world they knew and saw nothing of. Even a trip to Fort St. John with its mostly unpainted buildings, hitching rails and unrelieved banality was an adventure to them.

Jack, being the eldest, had an older sibling's mental perspective. He was usually serious, and the responsibility of being the oldest child sat heavily on him. He was an adequate learner of the skills of reading and writing, but he showed early on that he shared his parents', particularly his father's, love of the pragmatic. Before he was ten years old, he was actively involved with Liam on the trapline. He learned to respect winter and isolation but not to fear it. He became adept at trapping and easily picked up the nuances of lynx and beaver sets. Skinning animals and caring for the fur became skills at which he excelled. In his teenage years, he traveled far up the Peace to the great canyon where it broke through the Rockies and into the valley where his family lived. As others did before and after him, he marvelled at the tracks of great reptiles preserved forever in the stone of the river canyon. The roar of the cascading water mesmerized him as the constricted water surged in roaring maelstroms around the boulders and escarpments that blocked its path.

In Jack's sixteenth summer, Liam reluctantly allowed him to hire on with a big game outfitter operating out of Hudson's Hope. The man's business involved taking hunters, mostly wealthy industrialists, hunting in the pristine wilderness of the Prophet River country lying to the northwest. The heavy work of cutting trail, packing and managing horses agreed with Jack, as it was much like the pioneer farming he had been raised to. Liam was reluctant to let him go, not because he feared that it was too hard for Jack, but first, because he missed Jack's help and second, because he vaguely feared the worldliness his son knew nothing of and would surely encounter in trafficking with others beyond his microcosm of a world.

The first trip Jack took into the mountain vastness lasted seven weeks. His employer, who had been several times into the region before, took Jack, as a wrangler and trail cutter, a cook, three native guides, two American hunters plus twenty five horses into country that had seen little of modern man. Though it had been lightly traversed by native Sikanni Indians for centuries, it bore few marks of any of humankind. The object of the hunter's efforts was the bountiful big game found in the mountain vastness of the upper Prophet and Muskwa ranges. Jack saw for the first time bands of stone sheep, the most sought-after of any of the trophies the hunters pursued. In the beginning, he had little chance to get near any of the hunting, as his job of wrangler kept him close to the main camp. During the last two weeks, Jack went with a native guide and an American hunter looking to take a good specimen of a stone sheep. It was the first time Jack had ever been on top of a mountain; the scene from the top ridges of the sheep range was breathtaking. The hunter took a beautiful ram with long, heavily broomed horns. He gave his Indian guide a fine rifle and Jack an excellent pair of binoculars. Jack, who had never expected anything but his meager wages and the experience, was flabbergasted. It opened in his imagination the possibilities of a job like this.

The next year and the next, the outfitter hired him back through the hunting season, and Jack quickly rose from wrangler to assistant guide to full-fledged guide. He learned to ride and handle difficult horses, to pack a horse with nearly any kind of load and, most important of all, he learned the lure of high mountain hunting. Jack was by nature a respectful young man of those older than himself, but he learned to handle himself with older men and assert himself if the situation demanded it. Most of the men he guided were very impressed with his skills, despite his being many years their junior. By the end of his third year, Jack knew what he was going to do with his life. He would get his own hunting outfit as soon as he could and be his own boss. He had already begun to form the nucleus of a plan. He realized it would be necessary for him to borrow money to get started; his father was the object of his first attempts to persuade others to help him materially and financially to begin his business. Jack clearly saw, that in addition to living the kind of outdoor life that he had been raised to and loved, it was an enterprise that could also be very lucrative. Liam had always envisioned Jack as the natural successor to himself on the farm but was eventually persuaded to aid his son, by helping him buy some unbroken horses and later after they had been broken to the rigors of the trail, to winter them at the farm. Liam, while proud of his son's ambition and independence, was troubled. Many, many times through the tough years as he and Marta had poured their lives into creating a frontier ranch from what had been wilderness, they dreamed and planned for the better lives they could start their children into. He saw his boys, Jack, Wilson and Paul, as willing participants in the family enterprise of raising crops and livestock. That they might make other plans had really never occurred to him. Liam even envisioned Joanna marrying and then staying with her future husband to become part of the family enterprise.

Marta, while as focused on their lives as Liam, saw their children sometimes in a more objective light than he. She sensed that the ranch was not going to hold Jack. He had already seen a possibility for himself that made the routine of ranch life pale by comparison. Jack intended to stay connected to the ranch, but actually making it his full-time focus was already fading quickly. Marta also saw that Willie, their second son, would be doing something besides farming. He had already learned the basics of combustion engines, by tearing down and re-assembling the family tractor several times and lately by working on the truck that Liam had bought. Willie was intrigued with any kind of machinery and loved to take things apart ostensibly to repair them, but also to discover how they worked. He had already had an offer by a Fort St. John truck dealership, but Liam wouldn't hear of it. Willie was bitterly disappointed and vowed to himself that as soon as he was of legal age, he would pursue his own interests, which did not include plowing, pitching hay or pulling calves.

Paul, the twin brother of Joanna and youngest son, was by his early teenage years, the tallest of the family. He was already taller than Liam by age fourteen. By virtue of being younger, Paul often evaded the chores that had always been expected of Jack and Willie. He did the farm tasks given him but usually with little enthusiasm. He was mostly mild mannered but had a stubborn temper when he felt put upon. He had a well-knit athletic body but he was not really given to wild, rough play, as were his other siblings. Paul, more than any of Liam and Marta's children, loved to read and daydream. In the minutes that he could steal from the unremitting work around the place, Paul would lose himself in books. He had an insatiable curiosity about many things, but they were not usually hands-on interests such as Willie was drawn to. Paul liked to read about other times and places. He was a superb reader and sometimes took the effort to find words in the dictionary that he had come across in his reading but did not know the meaning of. His brothers were fond of him but also a bit contemptuous of his bookishness. They, particularly Willie, often teased and tormented him about his physical laziness and his lack of interest in what they considered manly pursuits.

By their early adolescent years, both Jack and Willie had learned to use guns and often took game animals for the family larder. Paul had learned to shoot, but he took no pleasure in hunting or killing animals. He did not even like fishing despite the fact that the great river just below their buildings offered superb fishing for several species of game fish. Paul was taller and blonder than any of the others. He resembled his mother's side of the family and sometimes Marta caught remembered images of her father in Paul's looks and actions. Marta sensed, far more clearly than Liam, that Paul's world would never be a frontier ranch on the Peace River; she did not know what Paul would pursue, but it was clear to her already that it would be far from here.

Paul's twin sister Joanna was also tall and blonde. She had a passel of pets around the place. This included dogs, cats, rabbits, and even a tame pig. She was forever bringing lost or injured animals or birds into the house to save them from whatever predicament she had found them in. Her current protege was an injured red-tailed hawk she had found somewhere. Over her parent's objections and her brothers' scoffing, she had ensconced the bird in the woodhouse and had induced it to eat from her fingers and even sit on her gloved hand. When anyone else approached it, the raptor shrieked, hissed and threatened with its talons. Joanna was constantly setting traps for mice to keep the bird fed.

It was clear to anyone who saw her gawky coltish figure that some day she would be a woman to turn men's heads. She had the same habit of looking people directly in the eye when she spoke to them, as did her mother. At fourteen she had not taken any particular interest in boys yet, though her close friend Lila Wallace one year older than her, talked of nothing else. They had been close friends all of their short lives but Joanna Brennan possessed a streak of independence of mind that her friend lacked. As small children, they had played together as only best friends can, but with the onset of adolescence things began to change. Lila's near total focus on boys began to bore Joanna. Joanna was interested in everything, boys included. She grew closer to her mother as she began to mature and the two spent many hours together working and confiding in one another. Joanna asked endless questions about the old country, her grandparents, social customs, and she listened over and over to the story of her parents' unlikely meeting, their marriage and their life together. Joanna idolized her father, though it did not always show as she was very apt to disagree with him on issues that had to do with her headstrong behavior. Liam was often puzzled and even angered by her strong-willed demeanor but was also secretly proud of her independence. Her habit was to question the reason for everything including her parents' rules of behavior for her.

"Why can't you just do what you're asked like your brothers, instead of always arguing?" asked Liam. "You'd think your mother and I know nothing."

"Well, if you say I can't go down to Hudson Hope with Lila, I want to know why. I know my way there and back blindfolded. Besides, Willie has promised to drive us there Saturday in the truck; we can stay with the Harpers and come back Sunday afternoon. I don't see what is so bad about that," chided Joanna. "You'd let the boys do it without batting an eye. Why is it so different when a girl wants to do the same things?"

"You know it's not the same," said Marta. "Your father has been over that with you several times before. This is definitely a 'no.' When you go to town to spend the night, it will be with your family."

Later, as she sat in the loft of the barn with her cats, Joanna grudgingly admitted to herself that her parents had the right to censure her behavior and that they did it out of concern for her. She secretly wished she had not been so sharp or out of sorts with them. It just always seemed to happen that way. The truth was she had only been moderately interested in the trip anyway, it was just an opportunity to test her parents' will. She wondered why Lila's parents regulated her life so little. Even at her age she could see the total difference in her parents' view of child rearing and that of the Wallaces. Lila did pretty much as she pleased; it seemed at times that her parents hardly noticed. There were six other children in the family besides Lila by this time, so Joanna figured their hardscrabble lives left little time for regimenting by the parents.

Wallace was often without work for extended periods of time and their eldest son Wilkie showed little capacity for independent employment despite the fact that he was now in his middle twenties. Although Wilkie could drive the family truck, albeit haphazardly, it was becoming apparent to all who knew him that it was unlikely that he would ever be totally independent of his parents. None of the Wallace children had pursued education beyond the lower grades and now the two eldest daughters had married local men and begun their own families.

Jack and Willie had both finished their grade 8 year by correspondence, but neither was inclined to pursue education any further. Because of their mother's persistence, both of them were strong readers and competent at mathematics, though their understanding of the world outside the ranch was not extensive. The twins had both persisted with their correspondence studies and were actually ahead of students their own age who attended public school. Paul and Joanna were clearly more interested in book learning than either of their older brothers. There was an undercurrent of competition between the two of them to see who could attain the better marks in their studies. This served both well as they spurred each other to excellence though either was likely to pout if the other exceeded him.

In the spring of 1940 two events occurred which altered the course of the Brennan family. The first was Jack's marriage to Anne Curry, the daughter of Thomas Curry, his outfitter employer for the past three years. Their romance was the outcome of Jack working out of Tom's hunting camps while Tom's young daughter, Anne, filled in from time to time as camp cook. Not surprisingly, she could wrangle horses almost as well as her father and certainly as well as Jack. By the end of the third season the romance between the two had become painfully obvious to Anne's parents, though Liam and Marta knew little of it. They were thunderstruck when Jack announced to them in March that he and Anne were going to marry immediately. Liam and Marta argued with Jack strenuously about his marriage to such a young girl; she had only recently turned sixteen years of age. But when they learned that Anne was at least two months pregnant, their objections were muted. The Currys, for their part, were not terribly upset, for they had seen it coming and besides they were both fond of Jack. His membership in their family would be welcome. This was doubly so because Tom saw in young Jack a valuable employee, if not yet full-fledged partner for his flourishing outfitting business. The previous fall Jack had guided several wealthy American hunting clients for Tom and already some of them were inquiring if Jack would be available to guide them in the upcoming hunting season.

So a rather hastily put together ceremony united in marriage nineteen year old Jack Brennan and sixteen year old Anne Curry in mid-April of that year. The whole affair had happened so quickly that Liam and Marta were stunned by the swiftness of it but put their reservations aside and resolved to do what they could to help the young couple get started. Jack and Anne rented a house for the summer in Hudson's Hope, Jack realizing he would be spending precious little time there until late fall.

The second event was set in motion in late May as Tom and Jack set about breaking and shoeing horses and getting set to pack in the supplies they would need for the pending hunting season. Tom's hunting territory lay more than a hundred miles away from the Hope, most of it over trails that had been hacked out of a pristine wilderness. The trails passed over country that few white men had seen, over treacherous stretches of bog and muskeg, through narrow canyons and heavily timbered valleys. The trail traversed major mountain passes and crossed dozens of small creeks. Also three major rivers lay directly in its path.

In early June, Tom, Jack, two Indian guides, and thirty horses pulled out of Hudson's Hope, the pack horses laden with the food, equipment, tents and every sort of paraphernalia needed for the season's hunting, the beginning of which was only a few weeks in the future. They would have to pack this mountain of gear into Tom's base camp, build holding corrals, semi-permanent tent shelters, and a rough storage cabin plus cut trails into the two or three drainages that Tom planned to hunt that year. Near the end of July, Tom and one of the guides would take some of the horses, return to the Hope and bring in the first of three hunting parties he had lined up, each about three weeks apart.

The previous days had been strenuous ones, what with having to break and shoe twenty head of unbroken colts and at least get them to the point where they would tolerate a pack on their backs and could be led by a man on horseback. Most of the colts could now be handled and packed without extreme danger to their handlers, though the greenest of them still required tying up a hind foot during this operation. Many of the horses had had to be thrown and tied to put shoes on them. Jack's body ached yet from the punishment he had given it, but he was full of enthusiasm and looked forward to the coming days despite his knowledge of the hardships ahead. With three seasons already behind him, Jack felt ready to cope with whatever lay ahead. No matter how hard it got, in Jack's mind, it was infinitely more interesting and certainly more exciting that sitting behind a team of plow horses or raking hay in the flat meadows of the home place. He also knew that this job paid something in cash money, a rare commodity at home. Chronologically, Jack was still an adolescent but was years older in experience and trail savvy. He sat a horse now like one born to it, though until he had left the farm, he had had little experience with saddle horses. Of course, the rudiments of packing a horse had been taught to him by Liam in early childhood. He had a healthy respect of horses' power to injure men, having been kicked and bitten many times, but he handled horses with boldness and competence. Jack was not above medium height but his 175 pounds were set on a solid frame. He had the large corded hands so useful in handling ropes and knots.

This day, Jack was clad in red and green Mackinaw shirt, light wool trousers, leather mukluks under robber galoshes, and topped with a black felt hat much stained with sweat and dirt. Jack had tried to keep the hat's original cowboy shape, but continual soaking, being stepped on by horses and Jack's incessant tugging at it had made of it something different. Marta said the hat now had "character."

Tom, Jack and the Indian guides all sat horses that would not find favor on the parade grounds but were infinitely suited to their environment. Most of them were the offspring of drafty mares mated with blooded stallions. Bays, duns, blacks and sorrels were part of the string, all of them showing their draft blood in their hairy fetlocks and large feet. Each cowboy rode an association saddle with saddlebags attached and carried a lever action rifle that rode muzzle forward under their right legs. The horses they rode were all veterans of wilderness travel, all shod on the front feet with the cowboys riding in long stirrups. Tom carried a lariat attached to the swell of his saddle, as did one of the natives. Each man led a packhorse with four or five other packhorses "tailed-up" behind. A few of the gentler, more predictable horses were let loose with their halter ropes tied up so that they could move freely without stepping on the rope.

As the long caravan snaked up out of the boggy flats west of Beryl Prairie, Jack wondered why this year was so different from the previous ones. Last year and the year before, they had left the Hope at approximately the same time to dry solid trail conditions, and if the swamps were no different, at least the few snatches of road had been relatively dry and easy going. This year, so far, every step was a muddy morass. Creeks crossing the trails that in the previous years held little or no running water were now swollen with runoff. The first few days there were endless interruptions with green horses balking or "blowing up" and bucking off their loads. It was only when some of the broncy ones became nearly exhausted with resisting that things began to level out. In one of the melees at a crossing, a packhorse had slammed a pannier against Tom's leg so hard that at first he feared it was broken. Two days later it was still so swollen that he had to hobble about painfully whenever he was afoot. The weather remained a patchwork of sunny skies in the morning giving way to cloud and wind in the afternoon. No rain fell at first.

Signs of northern summer were unfolding everywhere. Moose and deer now had their young and many were sighted every day. The woodlands, so often silent in winter, were atwitter in birdsong. The trail they followed wound around continual swamps and shallow ponds; beaver were at work refurbishing their dams and the explosive slaps of their tails was a common sound as they dove beneath the surface of the water at the approach of the pack train. The deciduous trees were now fully leafed out and mixed with the ubiquitous black spruce and pine; they walled off any visibility except when crossing higher ground. Jack felt, as he always did in the summer woods, a faint claustrophobia from the closeness of the woven and interlaced sticks, trees and bushes. There was a closeness here that made him faintly uneasy, as though the forest, stretching away to infinity on every side, could just ingest a person, swallow him up.

Today it was still and clammy, the humidity high though the temperature was really only moderately warm. From this wet, warm milieu, mosquitoes rose in untold multitudes tormenting man and beast alike. All the men rode with the top buttons of their shirts done up, their hats pulled down low on their heads, and kept a steady swatting and rubbing of exposed parts to fight off the insect scourge. The horses switched their tails furiously, stomped their feet, threw their heads, and took every opportunity to rub their heads and necks on something, usually the rear end of the horse in front of them. And if this was not sufficient misery, great blue-green horseflies rose up out of the brush to bite man or horse if given the opportunity. After hours of this, some of the horses were nearly uncontrollable in their attempts to evade the insect torment. Jack longed to get up out of the lowland sauna and onto the higher ridges that he knew lay just ahead.

The string was traveling a fairly well marked trail at the moment, known as the old RCMP trail. It snaked north along the eastern edge of the first mountains, crossing many tributaries of the Halfway River and eventually crossing and re-crossing the Halfway itself. Jack recognized some of the tree blazes he himself had made and many familiar to him that were grey and indistinct with time. This trail had been used lightly for many years though little improved with age. They constantly had to cut snags and fallen trees where they blocked forward progress. In theory, the trail was just wide enough for a man on horseback or a packhorse to pass, but the cowboys were continually fighting limbs and brush away from their faces and being careful not to bark their knees on trees that protruded into the trail.

Late in the evening of the fourth day out, the string found itself on a raised flat on the north side of the Halfway. They had crossed and re-crossed the stream many times in the last two days, but Jack recognized the place immediately as the final crossing before leaving the Halfway watershed behind. He, like the others, was soaked from his waist down from high water crossings where the horses had had to swim to make the far bank. This did not bode well with Tom.

"Never seen the Halfway this high before. The first time we've ever had to swim on any of these crossings was today. If it stays hot the snowmelt in the mountains will keep them rivers up for weeks. Damn country! Never know what to expect!"

"I hope we get lucky with the Besa," said Jack. "That crossing by big spruce camp is bad sometimes even in low water. Remember last spring? We had a jackpot there and you said it wasn't even particularly high water."

"No use worryin' over it," Tom said. "We got to get across and get set up no matter what. We've barely got enough time to get everything done as it is."

"Sure is high water," said Charlie, one of the native guides. "No use tryna cross them rivers if water too high. Best to wait a while."

"Well, that's easy for you to say," said Tom, "but we're just gonna have to tough it out no matter what. The first hunt is only about a month away, and there's no way I'm gonna cut those hunters loose. We got to be ready to go."

After the packs had been pulled, the horses hobbled and eating grass, and a good fire built, Jack took his rifle and walked along the edge of the flat. In only a few minutes he had shot a yearling mule deer buck in prime condition. He and the two natives slung the small carcass over one of the few gentle packhorses and hauled it into camp. While Tom set a decent cooking fire and boiled the ubiquitous rice and coffee, the other three set about skinning the buck and taking it apart. With guts, hide and legs removed, it was remarkable how small the carcass was. The natives expertly removed the tiny tenderloins, cut out the backstraps, then removed the hind quarters at the ball joint; they set one side of the rib cage on a spit of green willows, well back from the fire. They cut the front quarters from the spine and neck and set to cutting the meat into long thin strips.

After days of a diet of rice and canned tomatoes, all of them felt ravenous as the tenderloins fried in lard on a bed of hot coals. These served really as no more than appetizers, and while they were being consumed, Tom cut steaks from the backstraps, rolled them in flour and set them sizzling in the hot pan. Everyone ate a helping of rice and drank cup after cup of hot sugar-laden coffee.

"Amazin' how much meat a man can eat when he's really hungry," Tom said. "I'll wager we'll clean up these backstraps and put a pretty good dent in one of the hinds tonight. In the morning we can work on them ribs if we don't let 'em get burnt."

"Sure is good meat," Charlie said. "Best time of year for deer."

Joey Deschutes, the other native, said little but he kept his plate and coffee cup full. Joey came from the native settlement of Moberly Lake, and if the facts had been known, was actually less than half native. His father was a white man from that community who had been but one of his half-breed mother's many liaisons. Joey was only fifteen years old, but already had a year of wrangling and a short lifetime of handling dangerous horses behind him. Life on the trail or in the bush suited him; he got constantly into trouble when he hung around home. He was short and slight, but surprisingly strong for what little meat he had on his bones. Joey had attended the community school sporadically and could read and write, but only just barely.

Charlie, three times Joey's age, had been knocking around in the mountains with various outfitters for over a decade. He was wonderfully proficient with horses, could rope and ride with the best of them and had a happy, sunny disposition. Charlie read or wrote not a word, but his grasp of natural lore was extensive. He possessed an uncanny sense of direction, and his ability to foretell coming weather bordered on the mystical. He knew many plants to eat or use as medicines and he knew more about hunting large ungulates than the combined knowledge of his companions. He had been working with Tom since he had started up his outfitting string a few years earlier.

As they sat around the fire into the elongated twilight, Charlie said offhandedly, "She comes rain pretty soon, I think."

"What!" Tom retorted. "There ain't a cloud in the sky anywhere. Goddamnit, don't even think about rain. It'll only mess us up worse. We got no time to dick around with all the slowdowns rain causes."

"Pretty soon, sometime it rains," replied Charlie. "Maybe starts tomorrow." The two younger ones were so intent on filling themselves with the delicious meat that they did not even comment. Right then, with the evening calm and quiet, the horses contently chomping grass and the insects held at bay by the smoky fire, it was difficult to expend much energy worrying about tomorrow, especially something as mundane as rain.

An hour before it became really dark, which would only last a couple of hours, Jack and Joey caught up the horse leaders, removed their rope hobbles, and tied them high and short in a clump of trees a couple of hundred yards from camp. Jack stopped to gaze at the mountain peaks now clearly visible along the whole of the northwestern horizon. The ranges, all of them, still seemed deep in snow. The snowline extended far down into the timbered slopes anywhere he looked. Just above the rim of the mountain horizon was a light pink band which faded gradually into the dark blue of the western sky. The prominent constellations were already visible, and by habit Jack located the big dipper and the north star which the end of the dipper pointed more or less at. Where they would be traveling for the next couple of days would take them nearly exactly northwest. After they crossed the Besa they would be in the real mountains, thought Jack.

Those were mountains already making a name for themselves as prime habitat for stone sheep. For some reason, not yet entirely clear to Jack, the hunters they brought into the country were greatly enamored of the heavy swept-up horns of the stone rams. The hunters they guided wanted lots of different game, among them moose, grizzly bear, caribou, and goat, but none of these were sought after with the same zeal as the great stone rams. It was quickly becoming apparent in the hunting fraternity, composed nearly exclusively of moneyed American industrialists, that the great sweep of country lying between the Prophet and Muskwa Rivers was one of the greatest areas for stone sheep anywhere. A handful of years earlier, a mighty ram had been taken in these very mountains that some felt could never be duplicated. As things stood then, only those with deep wallets and plenty of time on their hands could really afford the resources required just to get into prime stone sheep country. This is where men like Tom saw their opportunity. If a man had some knowledge of the country, had put together a string of reliable horses and the rigging required to sustain a hunt for long periods of time, he could expect to find himself employed every year and in a time when any other paying job was nearly non-existent. A handful of resourceful men and their retainers were poised at the start of an industry that would grow for the next half century.

Every piece of vegetation dripped water. The rain had descended on the little caravan of men and animals just as Charlie had predicted. They had now had no respite from it for forty eight hours. The rain did not fall in sheets nor even seemed to fall heavily, but it was relentless. Though each of the riders was equipped with a heavy oil-impregnated rain poncho, the water gradually got into every piece of clothing they wore. Just now, Jack could feel water seeping into his heavy woolen socks. He had not been off his horse more than momentarily for hours, but his leather moccasins were saturated, even under the rubber overshoes that he wore. The water had now saturated his underwear and was "wicking" into his socks. Rain dripped off his wide slouch hat onto his poncho, but some inevitably ran down his neck and into his lower clothing. In a soaker rain like this, Jack already knew from previous experience, there was no way to stay dry unless you stopped, got under a grove of heavy spruce trees, and kept a fire blazing; and even then, you usually got soaked trying to find firewood. All in all, it was just as well to keep traveling, but it required mental effort to keep your mind off how really cold and miserable you felt.

They were now going gradually downhill, following a very rocky creek. They had crossed into this, the Besa watershed, earlier in the day as they came up out of the Nevis Valley and crossed a low pass to the headwaters of the stream they now followed, which ran almost due north. The previous day they had crossed the Sikanni River, having found it necessary to find a crossing other than the one they usually used. The volume of water in the Sikanni was truly awesome, and if one worried about large trees and other flotsam borne on the roily chocolate waters, frightening. The Sikanni ran through a fairly wide valley and was not closely hemmed in by its banks in most places. The group had reconnoitered both up and downstream until they found the conditions they sought. They choose a gravely shoreline that moved into deep water only gradually and where the current did not run over any large submerged boulders. On the opposite bank a hundred yards downstream was another shoreline that closely duplicated the first. Under ordinary conditions their horses would not have had to swim but could simply ford the river, staying on the gravel bars where the water was rarely more than stirrup high. On this crossing, that was out of the question. Tom knew they'd have to swim, so he tried to pick fairly calm deep water with an easy exit on the other side. In that, they were successful; no incidents or problems were encountered and the pack string swam the river without incident. All the riders were soaked to their chests but it was the best they could do. Most of the horses in the string had been raised in the primitive ranching country along the Peace River, so they were not overly concerned about deep water. A few of the pack horses had tried to turn back and had needed to be driven into deep water, but once lined out, they swam lustily for the far bank. That lay behind them now and they were moving toward a crossing of another large river. Jack knew that this crossing could be different. The Besa is the main tributary of a torrent of water flowing northeast, called the Prophet. At this time, only a few white men had seen the Prophet River or even the Besa for that matter. These rivers drained an enormous tract of wilderness that ran from the eastern edge of the Rocky Mountains to the tiny hamlet of Fort Nelson far to the northeast. Here the Prophet flowed into its sister river, the Muskwa. These waters formed part of the headwaters of the mighty MacKenzie River system which drained into the Arctic Ocean many hundreds of miles to the north.

Tom did not concern himself with any of this; he was trying to focus himself on what they would face when confronted with the intimidating Besa. As with all of these northern rivers, the Besa was not a great impediment to crossing when the waters were at normal depth. Near what they called big spruce camp, they had routinely crossed the grey-green waters of the Besa in previous years, even on the occasions when the water was higher than usual. They had made a habit of camping on the north bank, as behind it lay a small meadow created by some forest fire of the past. Today, however, Tom had no intention of stopping at the camp other than to secure loads and tighten cinches.

When they were still more than a mile from the crossing, Jack began to feel or hear the roar of the river, he couldn't decide which. By now they were in the lower end of the tributary creek they followed and even the water in it was very high and running extremely fast. The trail had kept to the left side most of the way down, now due to projecting walls of rock that pushed out right into the stream itself, it became necessary to keep crossing the creek back and forth. Normally, the water in the creek was crystal clear and relatively placid, but today the creek snarled and pounded, its water silty and carrying all manner of flotsam. The horses clattered through the rocks now nearly invisible in the clouded water. They became jumpy and irritable as the noise of the big river far below grew from a whisper to an audible roar as they gradually drew closer. There was a tension, an expectation that affected all, man and beast alike. A heaviness, almost like something physical, set in Jack's stomach and it seemed to have transferred itself to the horses, as they were becoming jumpy and more intractable.

Jack glanced up at the leaden skies overhead as if searching for a shaft of blue, something to break the heavy apprehension that he was increasingly feeling. Jack brought up the rear, the two natives rode ahead of him seemingly impassive, though Jack knew they must be as cold and wretched as he. Tom rode lead, picking his way along the trail and trying by his own bearing to dispel the apprehension he knew his companions behind him felt. Tom felt a sense of foreboding himself, but put it down to the wet cheerless surroundings and the unsettling roar coming up at them from the river they could not yet even see. Hadn't they always succeeded in getting through no matter how threatening the situation seemed? If a man wanted to succeed in this country he had to push himself, always. Only the relentless and the fearless succeeded here, Tom believed. If a person was turned back by hard work, exasperation or physical danger, he had no business in this country. Tom was reinforcing himself with these notions gathered from a life spent in wilderness settings. He also spurred himself on with the sure knowledge of the monetary rewards to be won by faithful adherence to a plan of action.

A plan. Tom knew deep in his being that they had no business crossing this river under the present conditions. He knew that and he hadn't even caught sight of the river yet. He knew that Charlie would advise waiting until the storm subsided and the waters dropped before they attempted the crossing and he would be right. But he also knew the short tether of time their late departure had put them on. Every day had to count for something now. They had to cross this river now, push on to their hunting area, and establish the base he knew they needed for their hunting operations; and he himself had to come back and collect the first party of hunters and bring them in. He knew he was short-handed and short of time, but if this business was to pay it couldn't be otherwise. He thought of how much he needed Anne in camp to help organize and cook, but her pregnancy cancelled all of that out. Tom had been exasperated with Jack getting her pregnant, in fact, at first really angry. But he secretly admired the way Jack had stood up to him, had confessed what they had done, and told Tom he wanted to marry her. Tom and Jack had been working together for three hunting seasons by then and Tom was not blind to the advantages of having Jack not only as an employee but a member of the family. Still,

Tom wished that Anne had been available to help with the camps. She was better than anyone he could hope to hire to replace her.

As the horses with their sodden loads threaded a way through the final stand of climax spruce which guarded the banks of the river, the riders got their first glimpses through the timber. What they saw did not inspire confidence. The greyish waters were rushing past with such speed that the center of the river appeared, and was, higher even than at its banks. Large trees, torn out of the banks by their roots, rushed by, their needle-covered boughs turning menacingly in the hissing current. The long island that had always stood adjacent to the near bank separated only by a knee deep current, was now completely under the water. The small trees that had grown up on the island since its creation sometime in the past by conditions similar to the present, were bent into the current, their branches full of all manner of water-borne debris. The gravel bar they had always got out on on the far side had disappeared altogether under the rushing waters. Two hundred yards downstream just in front of where the river made an abrupt turn left caused by the projection of a giant bank of granite, lay another startling change. A massive logjam stuck out from the left bank almost completely across the river, only open just in front of the rock wall where the tortured water sucked and roared around the corner. From where they stopped on the banks under the canopy of giant spruce, the jam appeared to be at least ten feet high above the water, possibly even more.

The pack string stopped as they neared the water itself; everyone dismounted, horses were tied to trees and the men came together in a little knot, the river rushing by at their feet.

"Sheez too high," said Charlie. "We got to wait. I think she drops couple a days. Too high now." No one else made any remark, but Tom looked sourly up and down river, muttering under his breath and shaking his head. The rain could not now be heard above the din of the river, but it fell with an implacable steadiness that was unnerving. Water trickled off hats and ran down ponchos. Tom soon began to pick his way up the bank against the current of the river. All of them watched him intently at first but gradually were distracted. An immense spruce tore by, borne on the current as though it were a piece of bark. The huge roots raked the bank next to them, pirouetted and spun back away and into the current. Jack watched the tree as it moved toward the huge jam. He began to follow it along the bank as it hurtled downstream. He had to see what would happen when it struck the jam. At first it looked as though the tree might slide around the jam and be pulled through the great sucking whirlpool against the boulders of the right bank. But as it closed on the jam, the tree seemed to pull back to the left straight into the jam itself. Jack wondered if the tree would take part of the jam out or just stick in it. He didn't have long to wonder. The tree struck the jam with a splintering of branches, rolled partway over, spun, as though by some great invisible hand, the great root system perpendicular for an instant and then was pulled completely under the jam, accompanied by the snaps of breaking limbs. In a millisecond, it had disappeared altogether. A shudder involuntarily ran down Jack's spine. He knew and understood the power of running water; he had seen it many times at home on the great river, but here in this closed-in canyon with the suffocating timber all around and the relentless rain falling, he felt that power more keenly than he ever had before.

Tom spent hours trudging up and down the river in both directions, hoping for some plausible crossing to present itself and finding none. In the late afternoon, they gave up, pulled all the saddles and packs and tied most of the horses to trees, leaving only a few at a time to forage for the few blades of grass or sedge among the clotted timber. They made a sodden camp in the flattest place they could find and erected one of the canvas tents. The saddles and packs were put into two great heaps and covered with canvass top tarps. Joey minded and changed off the horses, Jack cooked over a smoky fire in the overhang of the tent, Charlie gathered firewood and Tom sulked. Night came on with no noticeable change in the rainfall. They drove some sticks into the bank to make some measurement overnight as to whether the river was rising or falling. Certainly it did not appear to be falling.

Morning brought no change that anyone could see. The rain continued to fall all into the next day and into the second night. Sometime in the night, the rain stopped, for when Tom poked his head out of the tent at first light there was none falling.

When they had eaten a light breakfast of coffee and bacon, Tom saddled Bearcat. Bearcat was a tall grey gelding twelve years of age. Tom had taken him on a trade with a neighbor when the horse was eight years old. Until then he had never felt the touch of leather. At first the horse had appeared to be a hopeless outlaw. He nearly tore apart an eight-foot-high breaking corral, had to be thrown to get a halter on, and had bucked furiously the first half dozen times Tom rode him. Tom was almost ready to give up and shoot him when the first progress finally became apparent. Though up to then, no one but Tom had ever ridden him, he proved to be unusual. First, he cared not a whit about leaving other horses, and second, once Tom got him past the bronc stage, there was nothing he would not cross. Where other horses reared and plunged to evade muskeg, Bearcat had only to be pointed at it and he plowed through. It was the same thing with water; fast-running, deep water did not deter him, he would plunge in and swim powerfully wherever he was pointed.

Tom mounted Bearcat and rode off upstream. About two hundred yards from the camp, Tom forced the horse out into the current and in an instant they struck out for the opposite shore. The current of the river was awesome, so powerful that despite the strength of Bearcat, the two were only about two-thirds of the way across when they came abreast of the intently watching crew on the south bank. Tom now angled the horse into the current and they progressed laboriously toward the far shore. About ten feet from the bank, Bearcat struck the invisible gravel bar and from there he pulled easily out of the current and onto the far bank. Tom whooped and waved; the crew waved back. Half an hour later Tom walked Bearcat up the far bank even further upstream than he had on the opposite bank, plunged in and swam the river back toward the little knot of men standing on the bank. As the horse drew abreast of them about fifteen feet out, again he struck rock and gravel and pulled up out of the river almost at Jack's feet. The water was deeper here than it had been at the far bank, but the powerful horse lunged up the near-perpendicular bank, Tom leaning far ahead, nearly on his thick neck. The horse stood shaking water off him; Tom sat him with a mirthless smile on his face.

"I knew this river wouldn't stop me. We'll eat something, pack up and cross this son of a bitch," he said.

"I don't know, Tom. Looks too hard for pack string," Charlie intoned. "Best I think if we wait awhile. Too much current."

"Charlie, we can't sit here any longer. I just showed you it can be done. We just got to bite the bullet and do it. If we put in up there where I did, we'll make it sure. We just got to be sure the packs are all on good and that none of them cayuses turn back."

It took more than three hours to break camp, saddle and pack all the horses. This time the entire pack string set off up the bank as Tom had done earlier. All of the riders were mounted on horses that were proven swimmers.

"Suck er up!" yelled Tom, and he plunged into the river exactly where he had before. He led one of the pack horse leaders with four others tailed up behind. Behind him in a tight snorting group came several more horses, their lead ropes tied to their packs; Joey whooped and yelled to keep them moving. Behind that set came another knot of packhorses driven by Charlie. Jack brought up the rear. His instructions had been to prevent any of the packhorses from turning back once the crossing was started. Jack felt the power of the current, far more powerful than anything he had ever experienced, but his saddle horse swam strongly, only his eyes and nostrils above water. Some of the green packhorses were wild-eyed and pawing each other but the string stayed in formation until after they passed center of the river. Then, inexplicably, one of the packhorses, a large bay that heretofore had caused no problems, broke from the pack and turned to swim back the way he had come. Three other packhorses followed him.

"Head that son of a bitch!" shrieked Tom.

Jack was already swinging his horse to try and cut the packhorses off. His saddle horse fought the reins and for an instant it appeared Jack couldn't turn him. Finally the horse gave to the reins and Jack rode alongside the leader of the break, screaming and whipping the horse across the face to turn him back. Two trailing packhorses hesitated for an instant then turned back to continue the crossing, but the other two were white-eyed and struggled frantically to push past Jack and his mount and return back to the bank they had just left.

"Let em go, Jack! Let em go!" Tom screamed. "You're too close to the jam."

Jack glanced up and knew real fear for the first time in his life. He abandoned the crazed packhorses and turned his blowing mount back toward the bank that Tom and the first knot of packhorses were just clamoring up onto. For a few seconds, it looked like Jack's saddle horse would be able to make it, but the current now was so powerful that he could make little headway. Jack had only seconds to ponder his next move: the two packhorses just ahead of him struck the jam, tried frantically for a second to climb on it, were upended and pulled under the logs. Jack's horse hit the jam only seconds behind them. It looked to Tom and the others like Jack reached up to the logs and tried to get off his horse. In a heartbeat the monstrous current pulled the horse over sideways and both rider and horse disappeared into the whirlpool under the jam.

For an instant, the other three riders who were just emerging from the crossing upstream were paralyzed with horror. Tom dropped the lead rope of his packhorse and drove Bearcat through the small trees that lined the shore between himself and the logjam. It didn't look to Charlie like there was room for a mounted horse to pass through, but horse and rider caromed off the trees and struggled forward. As they broke out of the small trees, Tom pushed along the bank until he was alongside the jam and he could see its true proportions for the first time. He was numbed by what he saw. Not only did the jam extend three quarters of the way across the river but also it looked to be about fifty yards deep. Tom dismounted not even bothering to tie his horse and leapt out onto the jam itself. He nearly fell through it several times but struggled far out past the center and toward the downstream side. The river spewed and boiled as it freed itself from the logs, but Tom could see nothing of Jack or the three horses.

They spent panicky hours all the rest of the day searching the banks on both sides of the river below the logjam. On the second day, Joey found a lash rope and Jack's hat washed upon a spit of gravel bar miles below the jam. They continued for another nightmarish day, but not a single article was found. The next morning Tom struck out on the back trail with heavy heart. He knew he had to notify the RCMP at the Hope and then the part he dreaded most: informing the families. Charlie and Joey continued on with the half-starved horses for their main camp several days and another major river crossing ahead of them.

Later that summer an RCMP detachment came in, searched the river downstream for three days and found nothing. That fall more than fifty miles downstream, the bloated, rotting carcass of a horse was found washed into a shallow back channel of the river, saddle still intact. The saddle belonged to Jack Brennan. No trace of Jack or the other two horses was ever found.

1944

The farm on the edge of the great river looked much different now from the way it had almost a quarter century earlier. It had the air of settled country now. The fields both east and west of the house and yards were now mostly cleared of timber. Many of the fields had been brought under cultivation and the relatively rich soil of the flats produced superb crops of oats and barley. Some of the fields still produced a mix of grass hay and the newly seeded alfalfas. It was evident that the Brennans' cattle herd had increased. Heavy pole corrals and various log buildings sat just west of the house and the barbwire fencing that ran along the Hope Road on both sides extended for miles in both directions.

A powerful caterpillar tractor sat near the shop building, one track off, the rollers exposed and the heavy cowling pulled from the front of the radiator. Willie Brennan sat cross-legged on a canvas tarp to the side of the tractor, wrenches and tools strung about with tractor parts, his hands covered in blackened grease.

"Willie, Ma's got dinner ready. Come and eat, and hurry up before things get cold. Tell Dad." Willie got up off the tarp in the easy movement of the young. He began to wipe at his hands with some grease-covered rags that were strewn about, walking absentmindedly toward the cavernous shop.

"Dad, Ma says to come and eat now." On hearing no reply, Willie strode out of the brilliant sunshine and into the darkened interior. He walked a few more steps and stopped. "Dad?"

"I'm here, Willie."

Willie looked carefully, and as his eyes adjusted to the darkened interior, he could see Liam, now seated on the edge of a workbench, his legs extending to the floor on both sides of its 90-degree corner.

"Dad, Ma wants us to come to dinner right now."

"Willie, are you sure about this Army thing? Really sure? The war'll be over probably in a year or so. Your joining in won't really change anything, and we're getting so much accomplished here now."

"Dad, we've been over this and over it. I want to do my part in the war effort, the same as you did yours. I'm old enough now to go or will be in a few months. Dad, it's what I want. I want you to sign with me so I can join up. I just want to do my part, the way you did yours and the way Jack didn't get a chance to. When the war ends, I'll be back here and we'll build this into the place you've always wanted. It won't be long and my army service will help us get more land."

"Willie, I really don't care so much about the land, I just want what's right for all of us. You think you know what you're getting into, but you don't. There's nothing glorious about it. It's dirty and miserable and dangerous. Men die or are crippled because of stupid decisions made by men who won't share in those dangers. Soldiers are just cannon-fodder, Willie. They often die for no good reason except some fine officer's ego. Willie, I know what I'm talking about. At the Somme, thousands of Canadians died for nothing, Willie, for nothing." Liam was now off the bench and standing looking into Willie's face, his hands clenched and his lined face set in a grimace.

"Are you coming to dinner or not?" They both turned to face the tall, slim figure of Joanna, standing in the double doorway. "Honestly, Ma's about to give up and throw your dinner out. Please come right now."

She turned on her heel and strode back to the house. Liam watched her, for an instant, struck as he often was by her self-assurance and presence. She was already one of the tallest members of the family. Her dark blonde hair was pulled into a bun at the back of her head. She had sharp facial features, that looked as if they needed filling in, and clear light skin. There was something about the way she carried herself that demanded attention. She seemed to have no doubts about herself in the way that young girls often did. She did not behave like a teenager, and the way in which she interacted with adults compelled them to respond to her in a way they might not have to another adolescent. She gave the impression of never having had a doubt about anything.

Liam slowly relaxed the set of his rigid body, delayed for a second, and began to follow Willie to the house. Liam was still clearly a vigorous and strong man. His wiry figure had changed only a little in the years he had spent at the home place. He still had the heavily corded forearms and powerful work-worn hands and still carried himself well, if one discounted a slight stoop when he walked. The greatest change lay in his face. His cheeks and neck were now etched in deep lines; the corners of his eyes were crow-footed back into the hairline of his temples. His forehead was much lighter than the rest of his face, shielded from the sunlight by the wide-brimmed hat he never left the house without.

His hair had never thinned or receded, but instead of a dark brown was now greyed to a near frost white. His light eyes seemed receded back into their sockets and had prominent dark pouches beneath them. Dark sunspots splotched the sides of his cheeks, nose, and neck. Liam was not a bad looking man when, on those rare occasions he took any time with himself, or at least that was Marta's summation. Dressed as he was today and carrying several days' growth of beard, it combined to give him the appearance of an aging ranch hand, which in fact he was.

The four of them sat down at the long trestle table that ran across what passed for a dining room, but was really only an extension of the kitchen. The interior of their log home showed everywhere the thoughtful touch of a woman's hand. The logs that lined the interior walls had been hand-sanded until they were smooth, then painted over with a thin clear lacquer that made the logs shine. The chinking on the interior walls had been meticulously done in a kind of white plaster. This required constant attention in peeling out the cracked portions and resealing them with new plaster. Two large windows on either side of the kitchen provided light in daytime. At night, kerosene lanterns still held forth, but even then, Liam was at work with a plan to wire the house and provide it with electricity by means of a diesel light plant.

The ground floor continued beyond the kitchen, dominated by a massive wood cook stove, and into a sort of spacious sitting room. A lacquered wood stairway at one side spiraled up into the bedrooms that comprised the second floor. The sitting room had another smaller wood burner at the far end which had been set back into a massive stone wall. When Liam built the house, he already knew the futility of fireplaces for heating and had not built one. The ceiling was fully eight feet high and the upper floor rested on huge adzed pine beams that ran across the ceiling at four-foot intervals, the bottom sides left round. Homemade furniture sat randomly about the sitting room—several beautiful rockers, some straight-backed willow chairs and even a homemade chesterfield covered over in tanned cowhide. Marta usually covered the seat with coyote hides tanned with the hair still on. On the walls were deer and sheep horns bolted to plaques, which hung from the logs. A few painted pictures were interspersed between them. The whole south wall was dominated by the awards the Brennan children had earned from correspondence and ribbons and trophies won with their animals at the local fair. A large black and white photograph of Jack sitting on a horse in the front yard sat on a half round table at the side of the south window.

The entire floor of both the main and upstairs was constructed of milled tamarack boards. Liam had spent the better part of one winter cutting down and hauling them to a nearby neighbor for sawing. Endless hours had been spent fitting those boards into a near-seamless floor. Marta kept the floors cleaned and polished. Oval-shaped rag rugs of various sizes lay upon the floors. As yet the house had no indoor plumbing; a two-seater outhouse set 30 yards from the house into a clump of trees still served. The large double enamel sink of the kitchen drained through the wall into a deep gravel-filled trench that tapered away, growing deeper as it got further from the house. It had been there long enough by now as to be nearly invisible because dirt and grass had covered over the top of the gravel. The system had worked flawlessly since the construction of the house.

The four of them sat down at the table after Marta and Joanna had brought steaming bowls of potatoes and rutabagas, sliced fresh carrots and an aromatic roast of some sort of game. This was backed by a large pitcher of very hot dark gravy. All of them sat with folded arms and bowed heads as Liam said a brief grace.

"Doesn't look like things are moving so fast with the cat," said Joanna. "There's just as much stuff scattered around as there has been for the last week. I thought you were gonna fix it, Willie."

"I am fixin' it," retorted Willie. "I made lots of progress on that clutch this morning. It's just that you, Joanna, don't realize how much time it takes to fix one of those things. And, Dad, we're gonna need some gaskets and hoses from town before I can finish that rad. Could we get that stuff today? If we wait, it'll be the weekend and half the time that parts house isn't even open on Saturday." At the mention of town, Joanna sat up and looked at Liam.

"Dad, I could drive into Fort St. John and get that stuff. I'm pretty good with that truck now. The last time Ma and I went in, I drove all the way back, and the road is pretty dry right now."

The banter of conversation went back and forth between the family members, and, as usual, Joanna ended up having her way. She and Marta would leave right after dinner, drive the 25 or so miles into the Fort, gather the parts, and, owing to the long hours of daylight, still reasonably expect to be back before dark. And Joanna was actually right about being able to handle the truck. She drove it at any excuse, had mastered the gear shifting, and as with everything she did, proceeded to earn the grudging respect of her siblings with her natural ability. She already had much more confidence with machinery than did Marta. Her twin bother Paul squabbled with her constantly about who got to drive, but currently Paul had a summer job with a local rancher and only came home now and then. Actually Paul hated cows and cowshit, the things his job kept him in, but he hoped to get enough money saved to start college in a few months, no more correspondence. At fifteen Paul already had his high school equivalency. What Paul dreamed of doing was going to Edmonton and starting on a University course. Actually, Paul as yet had no idea of what to study, but he felt that anything was better than picking rocks and shoveling cowshit, as he colorfully characterized ranch life. Paul was a tall, country-confident, young man, able to handle horses or machines and the heaviest and dirtiest of ranch work, but his heart had never been in that life. Even as a small child he had dreamed and fantasized about town life. How he envied some of his friends whose fathers ran stores or other such small businesses! He envied their lives of what seemed to him to be ease and dirt-free work. He longed to be free of what he considered the chains of ranch life: getting up all hours of the night with sick or injured animals, pulling calves out of ungrateful cows, the repetitious sameness of planting, cultivating and harvesting, and most of all, the numbing isolation that made the normal pleasures of town living impossibly out of reach. Paul had a quick mind for facts and figures. On those few occasions when he had a little free time, he usually had his nose in a book.

Joanna and Marta set off. Willie went back to his work on the cat. It was a fairly warm, late summer afternoon, with a slight breeze blowing out of the east upriver. Liam saddled a horse and rode out into the far west corner of the place, ostensibly to look in on some of the yearling stock pastured there. There was no pressing reason to do this; only the day before yesterday Liam had done the same thing and found all well.

There were times, many times, when Liam felt the need of solitude. As the horse walked leisurely along the north bank of the river, Liam's mind flickered into recollection, as it seemed to do so often now.

The news of Jack's death had been a numbing blow to Liam, as it had to all the family. Somehow, perhaps because no trace of Jack had ever been found, closure had been elusive. Perhaps more so for Liam. Marta had grieved as only a mother can, for many months tears never far from the surface. Liam had been paralyzed with grief that whole summer after the news, but somehow he could not let it work out of him as it had done with Marta and the other children. That first summer, hardly anything got done or finished on the place. Liam moved as if in a haze, the grief for his lost son sitting on him like a heavy shroud. For a time, he became uncommunicative and withdrawn. He found himself so many times, just as today, making a conscious effort to be alone, certainly avoiding anyone outside the immediate family. His mind came back to Jack over and over. Jack, the one of Liam's children who really shared Liam's feeling for the land, the child who could take his place when Liam and Marta grew old, and nurture it into the dreams Liam had always fostered.

Jack's face and form seemed to come into Liam's consciousness so much, even in daytime. In the first year, nights had been hell. Liam interacted over and over with Jack in his dreams. But for some reason, in those dreams, Jack was always a small child; they hunted together and ran the trapline; they worked together in the garden; they built fences and rode in the wagon. For a time Liam's frame became almost skeletal, his clothes hung on him like bags. Liam sought no refuge in alcohol and neither had he any interest in food. It had only been in the last year or so that Liam regained a measure of his former weight.

As the horse moved out from the river and into the long fields, Liam attempted to force his mind into focus. He was deeply anxious about Willie's infatuation with joining the military. Like father, like son. It was hard for Liam to remember the ardor that he himself had felt when he and so many other boys had joined up in Edmonton. Those days seemed like a fading dream now; sometimes he wondered if they had ever existed. But Liam had never forgotten the reality of the life in the trenches either; it was an old brand burned into his memory. He had willed himself to wall off those prison camp days in Belgium from the rest of his memory and, until recently, had been fairly successful. It was so amazing and so terrible how things seemed to repeat themselves. It wasn't that he felt Willie incompetent. Far from it. He knew Willie to be his equal already in handling ranch tasks and far his superior in the understanding and handling of mechanical things. Two years previous, when the Alaska Highway was being constructed, Willie had quickly hired on as an operator and persuaded Liam to come, too. They worked together through that electrifying winter when the U.S. Army Corps of Engineers rammed a road through to Fairbanks, Alaska. In many ways those bitter cold months and ever-taxing problems had given Liam a reason to live again. Liam had marveled at Willie's aptitude in mastering the use of the great machines used to tear through the swamps and silent frozen boreal forests that lay everlastingly in the way. Liam and Willie both stayed on to the finish of the project in Fairbanks and had returned home in the spring with more money than Liam had ever seen in his life. They had purchased a massive caterpillar tractor from the Army and had used it to clear, in a few weeks, tracts of land that would have taken decades to change with horsepower. It was this same machine that Willie was rebuilding at the home place. The money had gone quickly, but now the Brennans had title and government leases on vast tracts of land, as yet mostly untouched. If only Jack were here to help them develop it. Liam tore these thoughts angrily from his mind; it was a place he knew he did not want to go today.

The yearlings were shortly going to need moving; Liam saw this as he rode through the fenced fields and timber where the cattle were quickly cropping the grass to the ground. Liam tried to focus on this immediate problem, but his mind kept drifting off.

A nagging concern of both Liam and Marta had to do with Anne, Jack's widow. In the winter, following Jack's death, Anne had given birth to their son, Carson. For another year, Anne had continued to work with her father in his guiding business but then had met a young man from Alberta who was working briefly in Dawson Creek. She had married this fellow and moved back to Edmonton with him. For a time she kept up a correspondence with Marta, but this had gradually faded; it had been many months since the Brennans had heard anything from her or anything about her and Jack's son. Marta spoke to Tom and Sylvia every time she was at the Hope, but the last couple of visits the Currys had seemed a bit evasive about Anne's life in Alberta. Finally, a few weeks earlier, Tom had told Marta that from the little they had been told, Anne had another child and had split-up with her second husband. She apparently had some sort of job and was trying to provide for her two small children on her own. She seemed reticent to communicate much even with her parents. Neither the Brennans nor the Currys had seen young Carson since Anne had left British Columbia.

Liam rode steadily along the north fence and then headed back in a roundabout way toward the flats. Twice he dismounted to drive staples back into sections of the fence where the wires had been pulled off the posts. Once he spent half an hour splicing a broken wire back together.

Liam needed no enlightenment on what had caused the problem with the fences. When he had first seen this country in 1912, he had not even seen a moose track, much less a moose. After he and Marta took up their lives on the home place just after the Great War, a moose sighting was rare. By the late 1920's, moose were becoming more numerous and began to be an important part of the homesteader's meat larder. By the 1940's moose had become so numerous as to be reaching plague proportions, especially for ranchers like the Brennans, who were forced to put up stacks of hay for their animals. It was next to impossible to fence a moose away from a haystack and losses to moose were monumental. And fences! Moose couldn't be bothered with wire fences. If a moose saw the fence, he might jump over it, which was not hard for him, but as often as not, especially if something had spooked him, he simply ran through it. Liam marvelled at this, because many times he had seen blood trails meandering off into the timber after a moose-fence collision. But he had never actually seen a moose obviously crippled by barbed wire. If a horse tangled with wire, it nearly always resulted in crippling or even fatal wounds.

If moose were increasing, the great herds of mule deer that had been on the Peace breaks in the early years of the Brennans' tenure were in obvious decline. The reasons for this were clear to nearly anyone who paid any attention. As the ranchers' cattle herds increased, the river breaks, which had always been a traditional wintering area for the deer, were becoming badly overgrazed by cattle. Deer also seemed far more susceptible to deep snow and extended cold than moose. Liam worried about this overgrazing, had even discussed it with his rancher neighbors, but no positive steps had been taken to change anything. The dichotomy of the livestock-wildlife question did not elude Liam. He felt a sense of loss with the declining wildlife, and sometimes pondered how ranchers like himself could develop the potential of their holdings and avoid so much destruction of the natural world. It was an old problem, he knew. Modern man inevitably seemed to destroy even as he built.

Today, as he rode along in the warm sunlight, the problem did not seem so pressing. The panorama of the sun-drenched river valley stretched ahead of him, the dark green of the coniferous south bank contrasting with the poplar-pocked open slopes of the north. The great island-studded river flowed serenely through the middle of the picture, the green of its central waters semi-reflected in the deep blue of a summer sky. Only a breath of wind rustled up the river today; it was a scene that had been repeated many times in Liam's life, but one which always helped him regain his sense of equilibrium. It was the sense of being part of the life of this valley that helped dissolve some of the care Liam felt within.

In the late summer, after most of the harvesting was done, Louis Wilson Brennan enlisted in the Canadian Army with an armored division out of Calgary. He was immediately sent into training in Ontario and kept his family entertained with his lively and upbeat letters. Willie was trained as an armored personnel operator, a job at which he excelled and enjoyed. No one seemed to know when, but the rumor mill had it that Willie's unit would be in the European Theater before Christmas. By then, the Allied landings in Normandy had put the Nazi war machine into retreat across all of Western Europe. Most people seemed to believe that the war could not last much longer, some even predicted a German surrender before the first of the new year.

That same fall, Paul and Joanna both enrolled in the University of Alberta at Edmonton. Just getting to Edmonton was no small feat. Liam had taken them by truck from the home place to Fort St. John and from there via the newly created, but far from completed, Alaska Highway to Dawson Creek. From there it was a long journey by rail to the growing city of Edmonton.

It had now been nearly twenty five years since Liam and Marta had passed through Edmonton on their journey to a new life. Liam would have scarcely recognized it now. It had morphed from a frontier jumping off spot for gold seekers, homesteaders, and adventurers at the start of the twentieth century, replete with muddy streets and horse rails, to something a bit different. The old frontier ethic had not entirely abandoned it, but it was boasting a growing population of people who had come to stay. Nucleus neighborhoods of look-alike houses and working class people had sprung up in many places at the edge of the old town, and the establishment of a university lent Edmonton an obvious aura of permanence and stability.

The departure of the twins for the mysteries of higher learning had been foreseen by Liam and Marta since Paul and Joanna had been small children. But it didn't make it any easier. Liam knew that the ranch was slowly turning into the monetary success he had always hoped for, but without his children around him, it seemed empty. Liam now had no illusions about Paul: he would not ever be coming back to stay. As yet, Liam and Marta were unsure where Joanna's personality would take her. In many ways, Liam missed Joanna even more than the boys. The two of them had maintained an uneasy relationship since the onset of Joanna's teenaged years: she had never been totally and openly rebellious but she challenged every decision her parents made in her regards. They marvelled at her obvious intelligence, juxtaposed at times with the headstrong silliness of adolescence. Joanna had never shown any real interest in the plentiful supply of local young males who were attracted to her. While her childhood playmates paired off quickly, some of them already married and starting families, Joanna stayed basically aloof. Her parents conjectured about what kind of boys she might meet at school, but they did not worry about her in that regard. Whomever Joanna choose for herself, Liam knew he would have to be as independent and headstrong as she.

The letters that the twins sent home were a source of wonderment for their parents, who read and reread them avidly. Courses such as sociology, chemistry and classical literature were subjects Liam and Marta could only guess at.

"Looks like a few days yet 'til breakup," said Liam. "Guess it's a good thing, too. We'd never have made it in if the ice were melting."

"There were a couple of times I thought we might not make it anyway," replied Marta. "Those switchbacks coming up off Bear Flats have got to be fixed. As soon as breakup gets here, they'll be totally impassable as usual."

"Well, yes," replied Liam, "there's always talk every spring, then everybody gets busy and nothing much gets done." Marta and Liam had engaged in small talk since leaving home an hour before, but neither of them was really very intent on the conversation.

Liam braked the truck to a halt at the bus station. Apparently the bus from Edmonton had already arrived as there were a few loiterers standing outside smoking and spitting. There didn't look to be a lot of people inside. They both got out and walked tentatively to the door of the station. Before they could open it, Willie barged out the door and into his mother's arms. Liam stood awkwardly to their side patting Willie's back and saying over and over, "Willie, son, I'm so glad you're home."

Marta at first could do nothing but cling to her son, the tears falling from her cheeks and onto the icy sidewalk. She hugged and kissed Willie again and again.

"Easy, Mom, you'll tip me over. I'm not too solid on these crutches."

Both Liam and Marta tried not to stare at the shortened right trouser leg, pinned together at what appeared to be about 10 inches below the knee. Liam moved to put his arm around his son, but Willie edged away and said, "Well, let's get out of here. Dad, can you grab my duffel bag? It's just inside the door."

Liam retrieved the heavy green canvas bag with 'Corporal L.W. Brennan' painted in black letters on the side. He pitched it into the back of the pickup. He wondered how Willie had managed his heavy bag at all the stops between here and the east coast when he was on crutches and on the only leg he now had.

As they started the steep descent into the river valley, Liam stopped the truck and put back on the heavy tire chains he had taken off earlier. As he tightened them, his mind was on the conversation he and Marta had been having with their son, or more precisely, the lack of it. As the truck had lumbered out of town, Liam had taken sideways glances at Willie who rode on the passenger door side, Marta wedged between them. He saw a young man that seemed to have aged years and yet he had been away from them less than a year. Willie's face was very gaunt, his skin pale and waxy-looking, and his eyes had dark smudges under them and what appeared to be lines across his cleanly shaven cheeks. In a way, he almost looked middle-aged. Willie had never carried much flesh, but now he looked almost skeletal.

It took quite a bit of prompting to get him to talk, but once started, the words poured out of him. He told of his armored personnel carrier being hit by artillery fire, which had blown one of the tracks off. As he and his fellows had leaped from the crippled vehicle, there had been a terrific explosion. Willie said he still didn't know if the carrier had exploded or it had taken another hit. When he regained consciousness, he was lying in a burning field with wounded and dying all around him. He knew he had been very fortunate, for a medic had dragged him out of the patches of burning oil, tourniqueted his shattered right leg just below his knee where his life blood was pumping out of him. Most of the others had not been so lucky. Willie was one of only two who survived in the carrier. The fighting around him had been intense, or at least he had been told so; he had little memory of the next few days. He was treated at a makeshift field hospital, so close to the fighting that they were nearly overrun several times. Because he was at this station for over six days and had not been moved back from the front, he had been reported missing in action. That was what had prompted the terrifying telegram Liam and Marta had received. Liam's heart came up into his throat just remembering it. After they received the telegram from Ottawa, it had been eighteen days before they received a second, which told them their son lived. A third, actually it was a letter by Willie himself, told them the numbing truth: his right leg had been amputated between the knee and ankle. He was being sent home to Canada.

Willie found it challenging to keep the self-pity and bitterness out of his voice. "So what am I good for now, I can't work, can't carry anything. God, I won't even be able to run machinery. Sometimes I think I'd have been better off like the rest of them—dead and gone."

"Please, don't," said Marta.

" Hell, I won't be able to do much of anything; it's even hard just to get into a car much less try to drive it. If those medics had only got me out of there sooner, they might have saved my leg."

"But you said they did so much for you," replied Marta.

"Yeah, and a fat lot of good it's done for me. Can you see me even trying to run something as simple as a cat? I won't even be able to brake it around. Jesus, what am I gonna be good for now?"

"Don't talk like that," wept Marta. "Willie, please don't."

"And can you see me trying to socialize at the dances. Hey, here's a two-step for one-legged Willie."

"Don't, Willie!" Liam was surprised by the tone of his own voice. He leaned over Marta and grasped Willie's arm with his right hand. "Son, we'll figure things out. You've got a long life to live yet; we'll work this out. Just try to give things a chance. I know things look very dark to you now, I know they do. Sometimes what happens to us seems so hard, sometimes seems to be impossible. But life will get better, Son. Please, give life a chance to get better. We'll help. I know, to some degree from personal experience, what you've been through. Try to let all the pain and hurt of the past weeks seep out of you. We'll create some things at home for you that you will be able to do. Willie, don't forget that you have your family on your side. We will do everything in our power to try to make things right, better, but you have to help us."

It was a long speech for Liam, something totally unrehearsed but spoken out of a deep love and concern for his son.

The rest of the way to the home place, Willie mostly just sat, teeth clenched, gazing fiercely through the windshield, hardly noticing anything outside. Marta clung to his arm and laid her head on his shoulder.

"Willie," she said. "I'm so very thankful that you were able to come back to us. For a few weeks, I wondered if it would ever happen. Thank God, you've come home."

Late winter wore into spring, with all its accompanying annoyances. At first, great ponds, small lakes actually, stood everywhere only to give way to viscous mud as the ground thawed and the water sank into it. As always, the road and yards around the home place swam in mud. Just walking from the house to the numerous outbuildings was a trial. At this time of year it was a challenge just to keep the mud and slop outside. Boots clotted with mud and manure lay in a pile on the porch just outside the kitchen door. Outer clothing, sometimes not much cleaner, hung on pegs inside the door. No matter how they had planned differently, these conditions conspired to keep the deeply troubled Willie indoors most of the time. He took to sitting at the kitchen table, smoking cigarettes, one after another, and staring with self pity nearly dripping off him at the fields that lay outside. He struggled to be civil to his always-attending parents. Whenever it was possible, Liam tried to get Willie to ride with him in the truck, on the tractor, even on the horse-drawn feed wagons that ferried hay to the livestock. Most of the time Willie thought of reasons not to go and on the few times he did go, he was sullen and belligerent to the point that it was hard for Liam to keep his temper in check. Sometimes, Liam was able to keep him occupied fixing some implement or piece of machinery where he could work sitting down or leaning on one crutch. Willie would try to get into the task, sometimes succeeding for short periods of time, but always falling back quickly into the deep well of resentment and self pity. His appetite was poor and though Marta cooked foods constantly that she knew he had loved in times past, he put only a little flesh on his spare frame.

One Saturday afternoon a few weeks after his return home, Hart McKenna, a young man from the Hope, whom Willie had known since childhood, drove into the yard. He and Willie engaged in a long conversation as they sat on the front steps. After a bit, Willie came into the house, put on his coat and told Marta he was riding into Fort St. John with Hart; they'd be back tomorrow. Nothing was asked about the purpose of the trip and Willie did not breach the subject. That evening as Liam and Marta sat at the supper table, Liam expressed his misgivings.

"I've always felt like Hart McKenna wasn't worth a pinch of dog shit. He never has kept a job at anything for long and you remember those summers when he was a kid and I hired him at Willie's urging. He never could be trusted to finish anything without being checked up on continually. Every job I ever gave him I had to send him back to do it over and half the time ended up doing it myself."

"But, Liam, he's grown up now. I'm sure he must have changed, become more reliable, learned responsibility."

"Well, if he has, nobody seems to have noticed. The word I get is he spends most of his time in the beer parlor down at the Hope, playing pool and cadging drinks. Hell, he's quit so many jobs or been run off that nobody wants to hire him anymore. I also hear the RCMP have had a few talks with him. He's old enough—even older than Willie—to have been in the service by now, but maybe they won't even take him. I doubt he's made any effort to enlist anyway."

"Willie's old enough," put in Marta, "to take care of himself now, Liam. There's little use in our trying to choose his associates. In a few months, hopefully, he'll come to grips with himself and begin to settle into something. I know he's been through a terrible experience and I know that right now he's having an awful time dealing with his disability."

"I know that, Marta, but there's lots of things he'll be able to do. And you know that rehabilitation person told us when he was here about Willie being able to be fitted with a false...a prosthesis for his leg. Nobody anymore has to go around on crutches if he doesn't want to. Willie didn't want to even consider it, but I'm hoping when he gets through this current spate of blues that he'll relent and get it done. The sooner he stops mooning around and wallowing in self pity the better."

Things did not look much better, when two days later, Willie arrived back at the ranch sick and obviously in the throes of an awful hangover. He lurched into the house, refused any help from his mother, went into his bedroom, closed the door, and did not come out until the following day. He was surly and uncooperative the rest of the week; and to add to his parents' deep consternation, a few days later another event occurred that they were completely unprepared for.

Shortly after the long May twilight was beginning to darken into the rose-purple tinge of a brief summer night, and Marta was just laying down her weeding hoe, she saw a smallish figure walking toward her, down the long lane from the road. As visitors were rare anytime and people coming on foot nearly non-existent, Marta stood where she was for a long time, watching the child, for that's what it was, drawing slowly nearer. As he grew closer, Marta noticed his blondish hair and very dirty clothing; he carried no coat nor did he have on a hat. As he approached, Marta finally recognized him.

"Carson?"

"Yes."

"What are you doing here, Carson? I thought you were at Gramma Curry's." She rushed to meet him, dropped to her knees and swept him into her arms. The child did not reciprocate the hug but stood limply while Marta interrogated him.

"Carson, how did you get clear over here from the Hope? Did someone drop you off? Surely you didn't walk clear over here?"

"Caught a ride with the people up the road. I walked from there."

"You mean the Wallaces?"

"I guess so," said Carson. "They let me ride in the back of their truck."

"And they let you walk by yourself all the way from their place? Did they know who you are?"

"Guess so."

"Did Gramma Curry say you could come?"

"Not exactly."

"Not exactly? Do they even know you came over here?" retorted Marta. Her voice had taken on a mix of concern and exasperation.

"No," said Carson.

"Then why, for Pete's sake, did you leave?"

"Tired of it there. It's no fun."

Marta stood and stared down at her grandson. He had the same blonde hair and blue eyes that Jack had had. Looking at him sent a sharp tremor through her. A few weeks ago when she was in Hudson's Hope, she had visited the Currys at their home. She had been told the unsettling news that Anne had another man now and there was trouble between him and the children of her previous marriages. There were now three of them, two younger than Carson. Apparently Carson had run away from home a couple of times. Anne had been beside herself as to what to do with him, so the Currys had Carson sent to their place for the summer. Tom and Sylvia had stopped briefly on their way back from picking him up in Fort St. John. It was one of the few times since Anne had moved to Alberta that the Brennans had even seen their grandson. The child they met with the Currys had seemed withdrawn and unresponsive. He was almost like a miniature version of Willie in some ways, for despite being a child, there was a distinct edge of belligerency, even insolence in his demeanor. It was so clear that he was Jack's child in appearance, but in behavior and attitude the Jack Marta and Liam remembered was totally the opposite of this unresponsive, unfriendly boy. The Currys had only stayed a couple of hours and after the three of them departed for the Hope, Liam and Marta pondered the life Carson might have been leading in his mother's home, wondered apprehensively about Anne's men and the influences her children might be receiving.

That was two weeks ago and now here was Carson, apparently having left the Currys without their knowledge or consent. Marta got Carson to the house and fed him. After, he had fallen asleep. She and Liam wondered what they should do. The next day Liam drove to the Hope to counsel with the Currys. Since Tom was going to be away in the mountains most of the summer, it was decided that Carson should stay at the Brennans until further notice.

It soon became apparent, especially to Liam, what a challenge Carson was going to be. The child was obviously not used to much adult supervision and quickly bridled when confronted by authority. It was not that he was lazy, but Carson seemed to have a time schedule all his own. Because Liam was of the school that believed children needed work and responsibility, Carson was assigned chores and sometimes repetitive tasks. Usually he seemed to like doing something for the first time or until the novelty wore off, then Liam found that unless he was checked on and supervised, things went uncompleted. There were angry confrontations sometimes and Carson threatened to run away, but Liam persisted in demanding obedience and responsibility.

When, in late summer, Carson returned to his mother's home in Edmonton, Liam wondered what, if anything, had been accomplished with him. The child seemed so cold, so unloving, and edged always with an air of defiance. Thus began a cycle, a routine that repeated itself over and over each summer, when Carson couldn't or wouldn't be tolerated anymore at home. Each summer he would arrive, always noticeably changed physically, though his character and attitudes seemed, at least to his grandparents, mainly unchanged.

The relationship that developed between Willie and Carson was one that was hard for Liam and Marta to grasp. Both of them had a sullenness that made conflict between them inevitable.

"Hey, sprout, who told you it was okay to go into my room and go through my stuff? Eh? And I never said you could start my car and drive it around. And another thing, you're not old enough to smoke and I know you been taking my tobacco. You leave my things alone, goddamnit!"

"Yeah, yeah."

"Don't yeah, yeah me! I catch you in my things again, you're gonna get your ass kicked up between your eyes, you hear me!"

"And you're gonna do it on one leg, right?"

"Don't mess with me, Carson. I can handle the likes of you on one leg, with one arm, too, if I have to."

Sometimes they worked peaceably together for short periods. Willie now had discarded his crutches for a prosthesis, an imitation leg and foot made of light wood. When he wanted to be, he was fairly light on his feet. His love of things mechanical kept him occupied at times. He kept the machinery and vehicles in reasonable shape on the place, but the steadiness of his pre-war personality, which his parents remembered, seemed to have evaporated. His moods changed swiftly, often for the worst, and these were the times when conflict with Carson, or even Liam, occurred.

"Can't you hold that bolt from turning like I told you? Is that too big a job for you?"

"Might help if you gave me the right wrench instead of this knuckle buster." Carson hurled the crescent wrench to the ground and stared defiantly at Willie.

"Look, if you'd just concentrate on what you're doing instead of daydreaming all the time, we'd get this thing back together. 'Course, I know that life out here in the sticks doesn't compare to what a big time city guy like yourself is used to, right, Big Timer?"

"Up your ass! Put this piece of shit together yourself. I don't have to take any crap from you!" Carson stalked off toward the barn.

"Yeah, well, don't be expecting any favors out of me then, Kid, like anymore trips with me down to the Hope."

The next day, things would be smoothed over temporarily, but only until Willie's short patience wore off again.

And yet—there were days when Willie and Carson would repair to the river to fish or fix a fence or work some livestock, moments when they seemed to revel in each other's company—for a while. Willie's wildly vacillating moods usually dictated how things went. He took to leaving the place for days at a time; by then he had stopped giving his parents any excuses for his absences, which often stretched for a week or more, usually after receiving his veteran's stipend which came in the mail monthly. It made little difference how long he was gone, and it was nearly always to Fort St. John. Willie usually returned sick from booze and more depressed than when he had left. When Marta and Liam suggested he get some professional help for his increasingly heavy drinking, Willie refused to admit that a problem existed.

"Hell, in the army everybody drank. A little alcohol allows a guy to let off some steam. God knows a few days around this place, anybody needs a break."

"Don't use language like that around here," retorted Liam. "You know better. Your mother and I have taught you better. Willie, it's time you got on with your life. You have to let go of things that have happened in the past and start living in the present. Your mother and I want you to stay here if you want, Willie, and your mechanical work is appreciated; but, Willie, you got to pull up your socks and be more reliable, more steady—the way you used to be"

"Look, Dad. I'm not anything like the way I used to be. The war changed all of that. I dunno. I...I just don't know."

"Willie, why don't you try to meet some nice girls." Marta said, "Someone you could bring out here and meet us and....and maybe even think of settling down with."

"Right and lots of nice girls are gonna be excited about settling in with a one-legged guy, the better to do the farm work and be the life of every dance!"

"Willie! Damnit, quit it! What's done is done, nothing is gonna change it! You don't want to hear this, but it's got to be said!" Liam took a deep breath, rapped the table heavily with his clenched hand. "Willie, you have spent the last five years drowning yourself in self-pity. You've got to stop feeling hard done by and pull yourself together. The war's long over and what happened in it is over, too. And don't give me this crap about honest girls not being interested in a man just because he has some kind of disability. Lay off those chippies that you're hanging around with in town. Yes, I know more about that than you think I do. Stop hanging around beer parlor floozies and then I guarantee decent girls will take an interest."

Marta opened her mouth to speak but was silenced by the sound of Willie's chair scraping on the floor as he stood up from his untouched dinner. He darted for the door, grabbed his coat and slammed the front door behind him and bolted into the yard. He moved to his battered car, dove into the seat, fired it up, and sped out of the yard on gravel-churning wheels. Liam and Marta sat stiffly at the table, large tears forming in Marta's eyes and finally rolling down her cheeks. Liam closed his eyes and sat with his elbows on the table, his hands at his temples.

The first real winds of change in decades were blowing through the lives of the families living within the scope of the great river. After the construction of the Alaska Highway, connecting the Peace country with the rest of Canada in 1942, there was a lull lasting into the late 40's, and then things began to change rapidly. Leduc #1, the first big oil find in western Canada, spurred major oil exploration that extended all the way up the east slope of the Rockies from Edmonton to the hamlet of Fort Nelson and beyond. Suddenly, sleepy little burgs like Fort St. John came awake with a jolt. Drilling rigs sprang up around the country like oversized Christmas trees. Farm boys, who usually considered themselves lucky to find a job tending cows through the long winters, suddenly found themselves in demand as laborers, rig hands, cat skinners, and truck drivers. Sleepy hamlets boomed overnight. Weekends found rig hands in town, many of them with money in their pockets for the first time in their lives, anxious for excitement and diversion from their labors and the numbing cold as oil exploration was a winter scheme. Sordid beer parlors sprang up replete with loud music and steely-eyed bouncers to keep some semblance of order. The search for underground riches brought new people and a new pace of life to the Peace country. Anyone wanting a job and possessing the wherewithal to keep it need not look far. Towns like Fort St. John, that had started their existence with the fur trade and then later agriculture brought by the fleeing victims of the dust bowl, changed quickly into what became known as oil towns.

The rapid influx of oil workers brought demands for housing, new schools, hospitals, stores, restaurants and entertainment. With more people and more money came new problems. For the first time in living memory, people began to find it necessary to lock their houses. Petty crime became frequent and booze-fueled violence around the downtown core of noisy beer joints became the norm day or night. Some of the first and most noticeable to suffer from the boom times were fringes of the aboriginal community who found themselves swept up by the easy availability of alcohol. Drunken, staggering, often beaten up, natives became a common sight in town. They were often seen even in the coldest weather, poorly clad, wandering aimlessly around town, waiting for the beer parlors to open. Some of them died under the wheels of trucks and automobiles or froze to death in doorways. The influx of oil exploration brought a huge improvement in living for many people, but for others, it brought much misery.

Willie was gone nearly a month. When he returned to the home place, he appeared to try harder than he had since the debacle of the war to fit himself into the daily life of the ranch. He offered no information on his absence, and for his parents none was required, for they knew through comments from neighbors that he had spent days and nights in a drunken haze around the town's drinking establishments often in the company of the lowest sort of humanity. Of the women in his life, they could only guess.

Willie persevered at the ranch well into early winter of 1953, and his parents, Marta in particular, began to be hopeful for him again. Then just after the first big freeze-up in mid-November, he disappeared again. A week, then ten days passed and no word of him.

The previous September had brought other concerns into the Brennan household. In the past, Carson had always returned to Edmonton and the family of his mother in the fall, ostensibly to return to school. Liam suspected Carson took little interest in school and being left on his own most of the time failed to apply himself or chronically played hooky. This year Carson simply refused to return to Edmonton. Liam had even taken him into town, paid for his bus ticket and sent him off only to have him turn up back at the home place a few days later. Liam and Marta were furious with him but eventually relented and allowed Carson to stay on his promise to take his school subjects by correspondence.

At thirteen years of age, Carson had a tall, spare frame that one day would fill out into that of a powerful man. Now his face was blotched with adolescent pimples and a light fuzz was already noticeable on his cheeks. His face haunted Marta at times because it was such a close facsimile of Jack's, with his brownish, blonde hair and blue eyes. In the past few summers, the sharp edge of Carson's ingrained defiance and lack of deference for authority had smoothed over somewhat but had not disappeared. In truth, though Carson felt a deep bond with his grandparents, his taciturn personality made overt demonstrations of love difficult for him. He still was given to spats of sulkiness usually over adult insistence of authority and sometimes retreated into uncommunicative obtusity that could last for days. Carson admired Willie's abilities with all things mechanical and showed some of the same aptitudes himself as he and Willie collaborated on various projects.

Each time Carson returned to the ranch from Edmonton, all the facets of his nature which his grandparents abhorred seemed to have strengthened again, but by the end of summer, he had slipped back into a muted semi-cooperativeness that made his life in the Brennan household bearable. He never seemed to willingly give any information about the part of his life spent with Anne and his other siblings. That he did not get on with his current stepfather was about all he would commit. It was now clear that Carson's magnet was the home place and while from time to time in spats of anger he complained bitterly about the repetitiveness and drudgery of farm life, even threatening to leave forever, it was apparent that the valley of the great river had sunk into his bones. Though Carson had never used the word 'love,' it probably came the closest to defining his inner feelings for life at the home place. He only communicated these feelings to his grandparents through his actions.

Carson had never acquired Liam's love of animals and horses in particular, though he had become tolerable at handling the team of gentle draft horses, using the saddle horses where it was required and working with the ever-growing herd of cattle. The dogs on the ranch loved Carson and accompanied him with tails wagging in enthusiasm wherever he went. Where he really shined was in the operation of the various machines that the ranch had acquired over time. His greatest pleasure was operating the huge caterpillar tractor which was in constant use in land clearing, digging stock water dugouts, road and culvert building and a thousand other tasks that in the not very distant past had only been possible with horse power. Liam had been reluctant at first to even allow Carson to move the rumbling monster about the yard, but little by little he became convinced that Carson could handle the cat as well as he and almost as well as Willie. In the coming summer, Liam had contracted with a local logging operator to use the cat in the construction of a five-mile or more stretch of road into a patch of virgin spruce the logger wished to exploit. It was the first good opportunity Liam had had to make some serious money since his and Willie's employment on the Alaska Highway several years earlier. Carson knew of this and it was his dream to run the huge dozer that would be the main thrust of the road building. He also knew that Willie would undoubtedly figure into the equation but even he could see that Willie's inconstancy would be a factor in him getting his chance, too.

Marta sat listening to Message Time after the eight o'clock news. Message Time was an event peculiar to the BC Peace region, something that occurred twice daily nearly every day of the year. After delivering the national and local news, messages could be sent by radio to individuals in the far-flung reaches of the area, which was much faster than any other communication method of the day. The voice on the radio was droning on now, "To Sally and Mike on the Cameron, the Co-op has your tractor parts in. To Big Nine Outfitters, pick up the hunters in the morning at eight o'clock. To the Brennan family on the Hope Road, contact the Fort St. John RCMP regarding a serious family matter..." While the radio voice repeated the message, Marta rushed from the house and in an alarmed voice informed her husband of what she had heard.

A short time later, the two of them sped over the snowless frozen ruts of the Hudson Hope road to Fort St. John. Both of them prepared themselves for another episode with Willie's downward spiralling life. They had made previous trips under much the same conditions, trips that culminated in bailing Willie out of the local lockup for public drunkenness and nuisance. Earlier, Willie had spent two days in jail for his part in a drunken brawl in one of the local watering holes and for assaulting the police officers sent to break it up. Those episodes had been terrible humiliations for both parents and Willie too. This had led to the greatest family crisis since Jack's death. Each time Willie had sworn that it could never happen again, but it had. And now...what? With sinking heart the Brennans entered the RCMP detachment, told the clerk at the desk who they were. A moment later a solemn-looking officer ushered them into an office, closed the door and seated them in straight-backed wooden chairs. With the briefest of introductions, the man said, "It is my unpleasant duty to inform you that Louis Brennan was found this morning at the back of a local business establishment, frozen to death in a doorway."

Willie Brennan was laid to rest on a mid-November day with full military honors. The small chapel overflowed with friends, acquaintances and family members. So much so that the crowd extended out into the brightly sunlit yard, dusted now with an inch of new snow. The heavily clad mourners in the yard strained to hear the services, which were conducted by the local Anglican Minister. Along with Willie's younger brother Paul, Carson served as one of the six pallbearers that bore the coffin into the chapel and later to interment. The tragedy of the moment was deeply ingrained into the minds of all in attendance: the death of a young man in the prime years of his life brought on by his inexplicable choices.

That winter was the darkest ever in the lives of the Brennan family, even worse than the aftermath of Jack's death. Worse, because they had been so powerless to do anything to prevent it. Jack's death had been an accident, a fatal stroke dealt by forces of nature, forces totally outside human control. But this—a death almost foreseeable before it happened—like an animal standing in the tracks of a speeding train, a train composed of enigmatic choices and repeated mistakes. And the decline and death of Willie had been so utterly beyond the power of parents or family to prevent. And so useless!

Over and over through the long night of that winter these emotions seared the minds of Marta and Liam. They sat together for hours, sometimes holding hands and staring through the window into the snow-covered fields, but seeing nothing. Days, nights, mealtimes came and went with scarce attention paid to any of it. At night, as they lay together, it was as though the spark of life was nearly extinguished, their bodies wooden and empty and exhausted. The death of a child sometimes drives a wedge between spouses and opens wounds that do not heal. In Marta and Liam's case, it drove them together as nothing had since their beginnings. Liam held Marta and comforted her even when his own heart was pierced with a pain he did not know existed until then. They spent days, weeks, hardly out of sight of each other, hardly speaking, but clinging emotionally to each other as drowning men will to a raft. They found it impossible to even think about the future for they were hardly alive in the present.

The life of the ranch during those black days really turned in the hands of Carson. He fed and tended the animals, even made and carried out decisions concerning the numerous livestock that had always been the ken of Liam. He cut the wood, stoked the stove, cooked a few rudimentary meals, and though he said little, he tried to comfort his grandparents with his attendance to their needs. Often he just stayed out of the house for the day, for he felt himself an intruder when he moved among the ashen-faced couple.

Christmas came and went. There were gifts and loving letters especially from old friends and neighbors. Paul and Joanna came home for a few days, Joanna bringing with her a husky, black-haired, bespectacled fellow whom she introduced as her fiancé, Russel Grove. They had met at University. Ordinarily this would have been an event of great portent, and Joanna's young man a figure of intense parental scrutiny, but in the grey aftermath of Willie's death, the energy for any of this could not be summoned by either Liam or Marta. They were cordial and formal with the young pair and tried to construct a facade of family togetherness, but that veil was thin and transparent. It was just too early to communicate much yet.

With the twins returned to their lives far away, the January cold intensified. The temperature rarely came above minus 20 even in mid-day and at night, the logs of the house creaked and groaned with the crushing cold.

Liam gradually emerged from his grey pall of grief and was forced back outside with Carson to battle the never-ending problems caused by the intense cold. They were forced to try to keep water holes open in the dugouts for the bawling cattle and everlastingly fork out hay from the horse-drawn wagon. There was now a tractor for that purpose, but no engine on the whole place could be started in weather such as this. Throughout January and into February the cold continued without any real interruption, and the dry grainy snow fell continually. The powerful horses needed all their strength to drag the heavily laden hay sled through the snow-clogged feed lots. Moose and deer materialized out of the surrounding country and plundered haystacks set aside to keep the cattle alive through the winter. No matter how much energy Liam and Carson expended, they could never chase them away for very long. They tried to erect wood fences of sorts around the haystacks, but even these were mostly ineffectual. The starving moose pushed into them or simply jumped over them. Famished herds of deer swarmed around the haystacks, loaded their systems with it, and then died by the dozens when the compacted hay would not pass through them. Rings of dead deer lay around every stack of hay they could reach.

And the wolves. In daylight they were virtually never seen, but with the falling of darkness the weird primeval chorus of their howling went on and on. They skulked about the near fields and consumed the carcasses of the dead around the haystacks. They began to encroach into the yard themselves, their tracks going everywhere until the cowed and terrified dogs had to be locked up in the wood shed at night to keep the wolves from killing them. Next they killed a yearling heifer within three hundred yards of the house; they spent only two or three nights consuming it. Even the skull and bones were dragged off.

At first Carson and Liam sat up in the darkened outbuildings and tried to kill the wolves with their rifles, but it was maddeningly and brutally cold work. The wolves seemed to sense when they were there and hung back in the timber. When they did get a shot it was only at dark blurs that moved like shadowy insects against the white backdrop. Sometimes Liam just opened the kitchen door at intervals and fired into the air and it kept the packs at bay but never for long. As the monthly full moon faded and finally was not seen at all for a few nights, the starving packs grew ever bolder. Even the great draft horses were shut up at night as a precaution against them. Liam had been through episodes with wolf predation before, and he knew it had never been this intense or lasted so long.

On a moonless but starlit night in early February, young Carson sat burrowed deeply into the side of a haystack overlooking a small field where he and Liam had put out hay for the cattle that afternoon. Carson was clad in heavy wool clothing covered over with leather and sheepskin outer garments. Over that was a heavy tanned cowhide with the hair still on, turned hair inward and wrapped around his torso. He clutched Liam's winchester in mittened hands, trying to decide how he could use it even if he had the chance. The thermometer stood at minus 51 Fahrenheit. He knew that because he had read it on the thermometer on the side of the porch when he had left at midnight to take his 2-hour shift and spell off his grandfather. During Liam's shift before midnight things had been uneventful. Loud, eerie howling had issued from the heavy timber north of the house and had gone on and on, but Liam did not see a single wolf.

The cattle, only a few yards away, continued to munch their hay but were nervous and flighty. Just before Carson came to relieve him, Liam noticed the ice fog begin to lift up off the river again and slowly waft across the adjacent field toward the buildings.

Carson came, they exchanged a few words, and Liam trudged to the house, grateful for even a brief respite from the fearful cold. Now Carson huddled into the hay, pulled the heavy cowskin around him. He already felt his feet tingling with the cold, though they were encased in wool and leather.

Time crawled by. Carson tried to distract himself by thinking of something else, but his mind was a blank. He tried to stay as still as he could but the cold seemed to search out openings to get at him. The ice fog hung over the whole flat now, but at least thirty feet above the surface. It finally occurred to him that the howling had stopped. How long had it been since he last heard it? Maybe they've moved off, he thought, and on the heels of that, he wondered should he even be bothering to stay out here now? He was thinking now about being warm by the stove, of eating something hot....what's? Out of the corner of his eye he saw them—half a dozen great gaunt shapes moving past his left side very close to the stack. It appeared their attention was riveted on a group of cows only a few yards in front of them. The cattle milled about, their feet crunching loudly on the packed snow; one of them lowed nervously. Carson watched the pack, mesmerized by their gliding silence, then he threw back the cowhide, raised the rifle and cocked the hammer. At the loud clink of the metal, the wolves froze for an instant, then broke for the timber. Carson fired into their tightly grouped bodies as they swung past him. He heard an agonized shriek. He cocked the rifle and fired again and again at the fleeing specks. At the last shot he heard another animal scream and then they were gone. The cattle stampeded toward the corrals and shelters. Carson stood up and fumbled to reload the rifle. His fingers felt as though he was touching hot metal and he realized he had shucked off his mitt and was holding the rifle in his bare hand. He thrust his mitt back on, grimacing from the frightful pain. And then Liam was there.

"Grampa, I got one for sure, it's right there, and I must of hit another one." They walked out to the still form only a few feet in front of them. Liam bent and examined it, Carson holding a heavy flashlight. "It's just a young one," Liam said, "probably this year's pup." They grabbed the back legs and together dragged the blood-seeping carcass into the barn. Carson ran his hand along the hair of the silver-grey side and felt the ribs jutting up against the skin like a washboard.

"Pretty poor shape, I'd say," Carson said.

"Starving," Liam said. "Nothing but bones and skin."

In the grey daylight of the following morning, they walked out through the deep snow following the tracks of last night's fleeing wolves. A few yards into the dark spruce timber, they encountered the second wolf. This one was a great black-white specked male with deep yellow eyes. They were blinking. The animal, though shot through the pelvis, still lived. Liam shot it behind the ear. It had survived the night wounded as it was and in horrific cold.

"I could almost admire these things if they weren't such nuisances," Liam muttered. "The poor buggers are suffering this winter like everything else. Help me drag him back, the skin's prime and will be worth something."

Later, as the skinless carcass dangled on the rope they had hung it on to skin, Carson was astonished at its size.

"This animal would weigh more than two hundred pounds if it were in good flesh," said Liam. "It's got to be a pack leader. Maybe they'll back off for a while."

As though Liam's words were a prophecy, a chinook wind began to blow later the same day. By the following morning, the temperature had risen to the point where water was beginning to drip off the eaves of the house. The wolves seemed to have vanished; they were not even heard for the next several nights. The following cold spat lasted another two weeks, and though howling was heard far off down river, no more wolves were seen that winter.

In early October of the following fall, the weather turned snowy and cold, stayed that way for a few days, then a warm chinook wind abruptly warmed the valley turning the mud roads into quagmires. On the heels of this came another cold snap that turned everything to iron again. On a snowy morning in mid-month Liam set out for his trapline with a saddle horse and three pack horses loaded heavily with traps, canned food, nails, and the supplies needed to sustain the trapline through the coming winter months. The main line cabin was only a few hours from the home place and Liam expected to go there, unload the supplies, stay the night and possibly return the next day. If the work he had to do at the cabin, which consisted mainly of cutting stove wood, took him longer than expected, he would stay another night and return the following day. These were not unusual trips; Liam had followed this routine in much the same way during all the years the family had lived at the home place. Marta was used to the routine of it, but Liam's absence from home always kept her nervous and fretful. Marta watched Liam out of the yard, across the near fields, around the prominent butte to the northeast and out of sight as he entered the heavy timber which cloaked the deep gully running through the cleft between two grazed off hills. In the early years there had been more clumps of coarse grass growing on the hills, but today they looked smooth under three or four inches of new fallen snow. Liam noted with concern the multiple tiny creases under the snow where the hill was visibly eroding in rainy periods because the grass was being clipped to the ground by livestock. None of the cattle were visible here now; they were in the fields around the house picking through the remnants of this year's grain harvest. The sight of the eroding hills again raised alarms in Liam's mind, but he pressed the thought away, unwilling to worry about it today.

The sky was a mix of low-lying grey clouds and unusual-looking spots where the blue above seemed semi-visible through the murk. It was not viciously cold, but the temperature was low enough that Liam had set forth in light woolen long johns, wool pants and shirt with moose leather coat and homemade chaps. On his feet he wore thick socks inside ankle length moccasins covered over with low rubber boots. He wore thick hide mitts. A toque of lamb's wool made by Marta completed his ensemble. His stirrups were the wide wooden type banded with metal. These were wide enough to allow him to get his heavily covered feet into them.

All of the horses were the part-Percheron descendents of the team Liam had brought with him originally, lightened considerably by the introduction of thoroughbred blood. None of the horses was young, all of them veterans of the trail Liam now traversed along the edge of the steep, timber-choked gully. A few hundred yards up the gully, the trail began to veer away from it, gradually easing into the side of the hill as the slope lessened and the terrain slowly blended into the plateau above the river valley out of which they were ascending. The horses managed the slope with little slipping, as all of them were sharp-shod on the front feet. Liam was obliged to continually fend away from his face the high undergrowth, which stretched out on both sides of the narrow trail. In a few places Liam stopped, dismounted and hacked away some of the brush with a homemade machete which he carried suspended from his saddle in a leather scabbard. The trail they traveled had originally been only a game trail, but through regular use and periodic brush cutting, Liam had turned it into a passable route.

As they reached the height of land, Liam stopped the horses to let them catch their breath. He gazed back at the panoramic valley. It never failed to touch him with its grandeur, though today the colors were mostly grey-green and white. Most of the river was still open but fenders of snow-covered ice reached out from the banks where the current was weak. He could not see the house, but he could see the smoke haze from its chimney, saw some of the outbuildings and many of his foraging cattle. From where he sat his horse, he could see no other evidence of habitation in the valley, which, of course, was only an illusion now. Homesteads had been taken up since the Brennans' arrival, both up and down river. But on a grey, poor visibility day like this, it was easy to remember the valley as he had first seen it not so very long ago. He marveled that so much toil, so much sweat and effort for so long could produce so little visible change on the vastness of this valley. Again he knew this to be a facade; the whole river valley was greatly changed. There was ten times the population that had existed here in the Brennans' first years and more coming all the time. On a day like this though, one could feel in his marrow the isolation that had everlastingly surrounded the Brennans in their early years here.

There had been moments then when it seemed they were the only people on this side of the planet, cut off by an ocean of timber and mountains. There were times, especially in deep snow winters, when it had almost amounted to a claustrophobic pain, times when even Liam wondered why they had chosen to pursue their lives along the banks of this remote nearly unknown river.

When a person left the valley in the direction in which Liam now traveled, it seemed as though he could vanish into the blur of brush and timber, like he had never existed at all. But here was a place to stand, something he would never have known in the crowded Ireland of his youth. This was a place where a person could make his mark, carve out something for himself and his offspring if he had a mind to do it and had some ambition and staying power. Liam sat up and started his horse; these were only imaginings. He knew this country and most of it for thirty or forty miles in any direction as well as some men knew a city. Had he not trapped and hunted over it for more than a quarter century?

Once on the rolling plateau, the pack string fell into a slow but steady walk, Liam stopping them occasionally to rest. The snow seemed heavier here; it built up under the horses' shoes to be knocked off and then rebuilt again. It made riding more bumpy and uneven than it would have been otherwise. It was a small inconvenience compared to the way Liam had done it in the first few winters: by carrying his supplies in on his back. He was still a powerful man, toughened by the years of frontier labor, but he also knew he could not approach the endurance that he had possessed then. His old war wound seemed to bother him lately but only in wet or very cold weather. Today was neither of those, but he still felt a slight tinge in his back, like something rough being rubbed against the inside of his upper rib cage.

During the next couple of hours Liam saw several of the now common moose, a couple of deer, and once a pine marten shot up into a tree directly in front of him. This was good; marten were an important part of the fur species he trapped. The animal jumped quickly through the boughs of a tight bunch of timber and disappeared.

When he was only half an hour or so from his main line cabin, he was jolted out of his daydreams by a large animal form that crashed off the trail and into the surrounding timber. His saddle horse snorted and shied abruptly to the side, the pack horses followed suit, snorting alarmingly while Liam fought the tree branches away from his face. The animal was gone in an instant, but Liam had seen enough of it to recognize its grizzly bear form, and if he needed any convincing, there were the great paw tracks directly in the trail in front of him. As the horses calmed, Liam considered this unusual phenomenon. It wasn't unusual to see grizzly, but it was uncommon to see them out of their dens so late in the year, especially once the snow piled up to any depth. This was nothing to concern himself about. Liam knew that grizzlies might leave their dens for short periods at any time during hibernation, though this usually was an animal that had not stored enough fat to keep it drowsy through the winter. As the string moved out again, Liam quickly put the bear in the back of his mind as he pondered the work that lay ahead. The only thing that was cause for concern was the proximity of this sighting to his line cabins and trapline.

As the horses plodded into the miniscule clearing where the main cabin sat, Liam looked at it with familiar eyes. Everything seemed as he had left it. This crude structure, built by his own hand, had afforded him periodic shelter through most of the previous thirty winters. It was built of small diameter logs laid up to a height of about seven and a half feet at the main pole then tapering a foot both ways from center to the outer walls. It was only about ten feet by twelve but contained all the accouterments of trapper necessity. A narrow bunk lay against the south wall close to a small drum-type wood burner. On the opposite wall sat a bench nailed into the logs and supported on the dirt floor by legs cut from tree limbs. These stuck out in a triangle from the juncture of the floor and walls to the outer edge of the rough bench. The bench was gouged and scarred from hundreds of animal skinnings, the stain of grease ground into the rough boards. On the walls higher up were two shelves containing a mish-mash of equipment: a dish pan, a heavy iron frying pan, some pots and a few knives, forks, and spoons. No food of any kind was ever left in the cabin during the non-trapping season, so usually the cabin went unmolested by scavengers. In the horse packs lay the flour, sugar, rice, coffee and canned goods that would be needed in the coming season. The door, constructed of planks and hung on cowhide hinges, fitted fairly well into the door space. A tiny window left in the top of the door was roughly covered over with a piece of glass held in place with bent horseshoe nails. Hanging from every available space were steel leg-hold traps of various sizes with the accumulated rust of years of use. A heavy, slightly rusted axe sat in the corner; one of the first tasks was to sharpen it. The cabin would probably have looked spooky to the uninitiated, but to Liam it was home away from home. There were few creature comforts here, but a man could work or get a few hours of sleep in a warm environment, something that men like Liam knew would be in short supply in the paralyzing cold that lay just ahead.

Liam tied the horses to the hitching rail outside, which was composed of a tree nailed horizontally to two vertical ones. He unloaded the packhorses with little wasted effort. In minutes he had carried all six pack boxes into the cabin where he could remove the contents at his leisure. First, he unsaddled all the horses, fed each of them a large coffee can of oats, a bag of which had come on the top packs; then he looked about him.

As he remembered, the woodpile, which sat next to the door under the overhanging roof, was nearly used up. Liam had been killing trees for years in a clump a few yards away, this by hacking off the bark in a ring around the tree trunk and leaving it for a couple of years at which time it could be felled, cut into lengths and split for stove wood. Securing firewood was a year-round chore both here and at the home place. There never seemed to be enough wood for the next expected onslaught of cold. This was a job that Liam, like most settlers, was efficient at. At least, in this type of weather, a person could stay warm cutting wood.

He set to work. After sharpening the axe with a file and then short-tying the horses, heaping the saddles and blankets on the ground under a canvas tarp, he walked into the trees a hundred yards or so from the cabin and began to fall trees with the axe. Layer by layer, his outer clothing was removed as he warmed to the task.

Within an hour he had four good-sized trees on the ground and began limbing them in preparation for dragging them to the cabin with the horses. Suddenly he heard the horses snort loudly and stomp their feet. He stopped and listened intently but heard nothing more at first. The memory of the grizzly flickered in the back of his mind, but he fell back into his work, and for a few minutes heard nothing from the horses. Suddenly, almost simultaneously, he heard the horses snorting and then the crash of timber breaking. He clutched his axe and took several rapid strides toward the cabin and the tethered horses. He just glimpsed the horses through the trees as they tore loose from the tie pole and bolted past him in terror, one of them dragging the pole beneath its flailing hooves. It was when he moved to cut them off that he saw it. The great shaggy shape of the grizzly lurched in the timber between him and the fleeing terrified horses. Liam changed direction and moved toward the cabin in great strides. His loaded rifle lay propped against the wall just inside the door. For an instant the bear seemed not to see him, then it turned and without a sound cut off his move to the cabin. For just a second the bear stood facing him, only twenty feet away, its black porcine eyes boring into Liam's, the long hair of its neck standing like a picket fence. In an instant Liam realized why the animal was out of its den so late, for despite its large frame the bear was emaciated. A huge suppurating wound covered the right side of its back just behind the humped shoulders, and even from where he stood, Liam could smell the stench, the nauseating odor of rotting flesh. The bear sounded a low rumbling growl and hurled itself toward him.

Liam stepped so that a tree separated him, but the creature was around it and on him in an instant. Liam raised his axe and as the bear lunged at him, he swung with every fiber of his strength. He felt the axe hit and then it was torn out of his grasp in the same milisecond. The bear collided with him and sent him sprawling on his back. He had only time enough to raise his hands to his face and turn onto his side before the enraged animal was upon him. He felt the hot rotten breath of the bear as it tried to grasp his face. He fended the slavering jaws away with his hands and he heard his wrist crunch amid the enraged roar of the bear. He rolled and struggled to keep away from it and heard himself screaming. The bear raked him the full length of his left rib cage with grappling hook claws, all the time keeping up a terrifying roar. Again it went for his face and as Liam fended it off, the bear grabbed his entire left shoulder in its mouth and lifted him off the ground, shaking him as a dog shakes a rat. Then, as Liam was blacking out, or perhaps he thought, dying, the bear abruptly stopped its attack and tore into the woods.

Liam knew not how long he lay there, perhaps only a few seconds, perhaps much longer, he wasn't sure. The world spun and rocked. He gave up trying to stand, pain shot through his back and legs. He knew he had to get off the ground and to the cabin which was only a few yards away. He started on hands and knees, but even that proved impossible. He crawled, digging his right elbow into the frozen earth and pushing with his feet. The earth spun and reeled; vomit and blood covered his whole upper torso. Halfway to the cabin, he heard, only a little way off, the bawling roar of the great bear. He heard it again and it seemed close. Using every ounce of strength he could summon, he crawled to the cabin door, pulled it open and was just dragging his tortured body through it when he heard the bear again, very close. He rolled, pushed the door shut with his feet, grabbed the rifle and with it pulled down the latch, holding the door shut. An instant later the entire wall and door of the cabin shook as the bear hurled into it. Holding the bottom of the door with his feet, Liam was shoved backward on the floor as a huge arm and claw reached around it almost touching his foot. Lying on his side, Liam fired the rifle, once, twice, three times through the planking of the door. The horrible roaring increased in tempo, and as the bear raged against the door in tormented frenzy, Liam fired once more.

He had no idea how much time had passed when his tormented body dragged him back into semi-consciousness. The cabin lay in deep blackness. The stillness was only broken by his tortured breathing. The rifle lay on the floor between his legs; his feet still wedged into the door. It was extremely cold; his body shook. Where was the bear? Would it come back again? Was it dead? Alive? For long seconds he felt himself in a terrible nightmare, afraid to move, afraid to make any sound.

.....The German guard was standing over him, speaking loudly and dragging off the stinking bedding that covered him. "Aufstehen, aufstehen!" he said over and over in a guttural tone, though there was no emotion in it. The guard began to pull on his arm, dragging him off the straw mat that covered the low bed on which he lay. Liam's feet felt the icy floor, but the rest of his body felt as though it were on fire, sweat was pouring out of his matted hair and down into his eyes. Another arm went around his waist or he would have fallen on his face.

"C'mon," said Sam. "C'mon we got to move you a bit or you're gonna die where you are. We gotta wash that wound."

Yes, it was Sam, wasn't it? Sam, his friend, who had tried to help him survive in the camp. Sam, the only other person Liam recognized from his old company. The pain in his chest was so sharp that when he was hauled upright he shrieked in pain.

"God, leave me be! Let me die here. I can't take anymore!"

"C'mon, Liam, don't quit now. We're gonna beat this place yet."

Liam felt himself half-carried, half dragged out of the stench of the building and into the open. He felt the mud squish through his socks. What had happened to his boots? A man needs his boots! Rain spattered his face; grey figures moved around him. Why did they haul him out here? Why couldn't he just be left to die in peace...

When he woke the next time, his body was convulsed in a wracking trembling. The interior of the cabin still deep night. He reached again for the rifle and felt the congealed blood on his hand; the other hand seemed not to work at all. He tried to listen outside, but his chattering teeth drowned out everything else. Liam knew he had never been in pain like this, not even in Belgium, and for a fleeting instant he thought of using the rifle a last time. No! I want to live! I want to live! And if I do live, will I be able to do anything...a cripple? His attempts to even sit upright resulted in numbing torment; he cried out in pain and frustration. He knew now what he had to do to live out the night, get onto the bunk and cover himself with something before he froze to death on the floor. Two heavy wool blankets lay on top of the packs only a foot or so away from his outstretched hand. He began to inch his way toward the bunk; his entire torso felt wet. He knew he was swathed in his own blood, though he could really see nothing. With the power of one arm and his numbed legs, he scrabbled to the side of the crude bunk. With supreme effort he rolled to his right and felt his fingers on the blankets. He pulled both of them over him...

Thin light came through the window opening when he woke again. The glass window had somehow disappeared, probably broken on the floor around him. He knew not what time it was; but he did know he could not stay on the floor many more hours and live. He had somehow to haul himself into that bunk just above his prostrate body. The world reeled and spun, but if he didn't make it this time, he knew he'd never wake again. He gritted his chattering teeth and sat up abruptly and heard a piercing scream come from deep within himself. He slung his right arm over the top of the bunk grasping for something to hold onto. Driving with his legs, he tore himself loose from the blood-clotted blankets and onto the straw tick of the bunk. He had only time to reach down and drag one of the blankets over himself before the black void settled over him again.

***

It looks almost unreal, thought Marta. She stood at the kitchen window looking east across the near field, covered now in a few inches of new snow. Fence posts stuck up out of the brilliant white in long straight rows that disappeared into the timber beyond the fields. Somehow, she thought, early winter always makes things look so orderly, so organized, hiding the unsightly excrescence that always covers a frontier homestead: the tools and machinery which often seem strung about so haphazardly, the corrals, the assorted and often ill-matched buildings, the woodpiles, and fuel tanks. Most of all it is wonderful to have the everlasting mud frozen and covered up for a while. When it was clear and blue after a new snowfall, the valley seemed so picturesque in its serene beauty, enchanted even. The sky, while still mainly grey, seemed trying to open up some patches of blue.

The end of the warm summer months that meandered into fall and were often so brief was a difficult time for Marta. The days grew noticeably shorter and the land seemed to be gathering itself for something. There was a stillness, a suspension of life, an expectation as though...as though the land waited.

And, of course, Marta mused, it waited only for the weight of the great silent winter.

"Winter," Liam always said, "is a fame of mind. You just adapt to it, do different things, winter things. Don't fight it; let it carry you on, think of the everyday present. Plan for spring and summer but don't mourn for it. Accept things as they are. Everything changes in its own time. Even winter. Accept things."

Accept things, thought Marta, like some of the work I need to do today. Like going to the root cellar and getting some potatoes and onions.

Marta put on a light coat, stepped into her man's boots and emerged out the back door. The dog plunged happily over to her in expectation of some morsel of food. Marta didn't disappoint. She tossed him a few scraps from the previous meal. The dog waved his tail joyously and gobbled loudly. Marta began to walk to the root house door which emerged from a man-made mound of earth only a few yards from her house. At first, she didn't notice the horse standing under the hayshed eating out of the haystack. Marta finally noticed him and stopped.

"Those blasted creatures are out again!" She set down her bucket and started for the horse intending to catch him and put him back into the field where he belonged. Then she stopped. The grey gelding wore a halter and the lead rope dragged beneath his feet. The end of the rope still had a loop in it. Marta stared at it and a little shiver of apprehension ran down her back. The horse was Calaban, one of the horses Liam had taken yesterday out to the line cabin. Marta walked to the tall grey and picked up the lead rope while he placidly munched hay. Pondering what this could mean, she led the horse past the hayshed to turn him loose in the pasture. As they passed the back of the hayshed, the part she couldn't see before, she was brought up with a gasp. Three more horses, all with halter and trailing lead ropes, stood quietly eating hay. Marta dropped the rope and ran toward the barn where Carson should be feeding hay to the yearling calves.

"Carson! Carson!"

"I'm over here," came the return voice.

"Carson, something's wrong. Liam's horses have come home without him. I just hope he hasn't had some kind of a problem. An accident maybe."

"Well, maybe he just let the horses go after he hauled that stuff up to the cabin."

"Carson, he wouldn't do that. He needed them to bring back the saddles and blankets and he needed something to ride. Those horses are here, all four of them, with none of their tack. I don't like this. I want to go to look for him. I've been there lots of times; I know the way."

"But, Gramma, it's pretty cool now with the snow. Why don't I go? I've been there too, only a couple of weeks ago. I'll catch up another horse to ride and lead Liam's saddle horse. They most likely just pulled away from where he tied them while he was doing something and came home. I don't think Liam would get into trouble. It's pretty late in the day; maybe I should go in the morning."

"No, I don't like this. Liam knows how to tie horses. There is something wrong, I think. Please, if you are going, I want you to go now. If you don't want to do that, I'm going myself."

"Okay, okay," mumbled Carson. He moved off to the corral to catch another horse, while Marta brought Calaban to the tack shed after turning out the other three.

Thirty minutes later Carson was leaving the yard with Marta's admonition in his ears. "Don't waste any time, Carson. It takes at least four hours to get over there and that's about all the daylight you have. Stay on the trail and go straight to the cabin. Liam will be around there someplace. If the two of you are not back by this time tomorrow, I'm coming myself."

The trail to the cabin was not difficult to follow though very light snow was falling. The loose horses had obviously followed the trail home and it was well marked. After an hour on the trail, Carson realized he should have listened to Marta and put on more clothing. He began to dismount and walk every so often to try and stay warm. Carson knew he was not yet fully at ease in this new environment, so different from the city life he knew in Edmonton. In the past few weeks some of the surly edge had come off him. He still found accepting authority difficult, even from his grandparents.

"Shit," he said out loud. "Why can't we have some roads in this goddamn place instead of riding these damn horses everywhere? Everything here takes so damn long to do. Hell, if we had a car up here, I'd get over there in minutes." He glanced up at the dark ravine-strewn forest through which he rode and felt the stupidity of his words sink in. Roads might be put in here sometime, but for now a wheeled vehicle couldn't move ten feet. The somber forest stretched around him in every direction, quiet, unchanging. Another person of his age and limited experience might have been cowed by its dark immensity but Carson, by nature a loner, liked the ambience. If he did not exactly feel confident, he liked the sense of being on his own, no one to criticize or instruct or demand. By nature and by experience, he strove against anyone attempting to control the direction of his energy. Flashes of his unhappy family life, his school futility, his total lack of direction meandered through his consciousness. The horses plodded on, stolid in their effort, making no move to turn back or to move faster. Carson had only limited experience with horses, but he and Liam had ridden this same pair over the trail only a few days earlier. Carson had no particular feeling about horses; they were simply a way to get someplace. He had little understanding of the countless hours spent by humans, mainly his grandfather, in getting these gentle, well-broken horses to the stage they were at now. Had he been mounted on a fractious inexperienced colt, his appreciation of the horses he now traveled with would have been greater. Carson merely sat his saddle, which was now beginning to grate on his backside, held the reins and directed the horses along the trail. He tried getting the horses to trot, which they did, but he quickly realized he was better off letting them walk, so he could keep the limbs and brush out of his face.

Nothing seemed to move in the forest, even the birds which he had noticed last trip seemed missing. The afternoon wore on, the sun, fast sinking behind a smudge of cloud, gave little light. Carson couldn't exactly remember how far he had come or how much he had to go, but it was obviously getting colder. He got off to walk a ways, leading the plodding horses behind him. His hands and feet were getting very cold. He wore only light clothing and a coat. The fact that Marta had advised him, even pleaded a bit, to dress warmer, came back to him. "Shit, at least if I was in Edmonton, I could go in a building and warm up. Up here everything is hard." Again a glance at the implacable forest showed this outburst for the silliness it was.

Shortly after he got back on his saddle horse, he could feel a change in it. The horse was hanging back now and Carson kept kicking his sides to keep him moving. Both horses began to blow a little, lifting their heads and walking sideways. This increased until finally Carson's saddle horse lunged sideways, scratching his face and very nearly throwing him. He looked up to find himself at the edge of the clearing, the cabin itself only a few yards away, indistinct now in the falling darkness. Both horses shied sideways again, snorting loudly and refusing to move forward. Carson slid off, pulled the lead rope from his saddle and tied his horse to a tree, then did the same for the other. He turned again to look at the cabin. Something was not right here. The door. What was wrong with the door? The horses continued to snort loudly and walk around their trees. The one he had been leading reared up and tried to pull loose, but the knot held. Carson edged closer. He thought for the first time that he wished he had a gun. A large dark object seemed to extend out from the cabin door. He stopped again and peered intently through the quasi-darkness. What was it? An animal? God, it looked huge! Carson backed away, then edged closer. The thing did not move. He picked up a light pole lying under the overhang and prodded it. Nothing. He pushed at it with the pole, smelled a powerful nauseating stench and as he did so the thing fell over sideways and he found himself staring into the lifeless eyes of a great shaggy animal. He backed up so quickly he tripped and fell backward into the snow. His heart beat like a trip hammer, but he rose to his feet still grasping the pole. Only when he looked at the great yellow teeth hanging from the black jaw did he recognize that here was a great bear of some kind. As he peered more closely, he saw that it lay half-frozen in a black pool of congealed blood. The stench that arose from it was overwhelming. He saw a great swatch of pus-matted hair on its back and a deep rent in the side of its neck. He could not open the door of the cabin until he managed to push the horrible head and shoulders to the side. The animal had died leaning against the door and was now semi-frozen into place against it. At first, he was loath even to touch the carcass but found he could only move it by grasping the massive head, prying and pushing it to the side. Then he saw the four holes in the shattered planking. He stood, unsure of what to do next. The horses fonched and blew.

"Liam! Liam!" Somehow he feared to open the door. He tried it and it held fast. Locked from the inside. "Liam!" Then he heard a low frightening groan. For a second he felt real terror. He jumped back from the door. "Liam! Grampa!" Again he heard something. It sounded more like a deep breath. He pried on the door with the pole but to no advantage. He walked out through the clearing looking for something he could use to pry off the door. He tripped over it before he saw it. It was almost dark now, but he looked down, saw a wood handle, picked it up and realized he had what he needed. He grasped the axe and strode to the door, attempting to pry it loose, but there was nothing to get a purchase on. Finally he knew what he had to do. He stood parallel to the door and began to hack at it with the axe. Between stokes he heard something inside again. The planks of the door were two inches thick and held together by two other planks nailed perpendicular to them. He chopped and hacked and stopped to catch his breath.

"Carson?"

"It's me, Grampa. I can't get the door open. Can you open it from the inside?"

No answer. Carson struck again now with greater volition. Finally he felt one of the planks loosen. He hit it with the blunt side of the axe. The door was partly slashed open. Carson reached through the rent and grasped the inner latch, forced it up and pulled open the door.

He could not see at first into the blackened interior. As his eyes adjusted he stepped carefully inside. He could see a blanket-shrouded figure on the bunk. He picked up the blood-encrusted rifle from the floor and as he leaned it into the wall, he saw the blankets move slightly and heard a weak voice.

"Carson, is it you? I'm hurt.... Start the stove."

"Liam…Grampa, are you....What happened?"

"Bear," rasped Liam. "Start the stove." Carson recovered his senses and quickly stuffed kindling into the wood burner. He tossed in a splash of kerosene and touched a match to it. As the flames lit the room, he stared at the figure on the bunk. The blankets in places were soaked through completely with blood. Dried blood clung to the pole legs of the bunk and lay in a stiff pool on the floor next to the door. After bumping his head on it several times, Carson lit the lantern suspended from the low roof pole. He kept up a steady one-sided conversation with his Grandfather, but only occasionally did Liam respond, and then in gasps and whispers. Carson looked at the shattered door and knew it was useless to try to close it, so he hung a canvass tarp over the doorway and pinned it against the logs with splinters from the door.

Carson wondered what he should do. Could Liam ride? But it was already too dark to return to the home place tonight. What should I do, he thought?

"Carson, I need a drink...find some...water."

Carson looked around, found a pan of some sort, filled it with snow, and set it on the stove, which was now getting very hot. After it melted, he cooled it outside, poured it into a tin cup. He lifted Liam's head and held the cup for him while he sucked greedily at the water. Liam could not seem to get enough water; Carson repeated the procedure again.

Liam seemed to be passing in and out of consciousness. As the room heated, Carson tried to settle the blankets more comfortably around Liam. When he tried to lift the blood-soaked blanket from his chest, Liam moaned in pain. Carson could now see the shattered left arm and hand. It was near impossible to get the blankets off without hurting him. The congealed blood stuck to the blankets, to his long woolen underwear and to the hair of his chest and shoulders. At first Carson could only see the matted blood, but as he picked the blanket away as carefully as he could, he was stunned by what he saw. Liam's left shoulder was a swollen purplish blob, with puncture marks oozing blackened blood. The left side of his back was a series of terrible tears where the outer tissue had been ripped loose to expose the muscles and tendons beneath; in one place two of the ribs were clearly exposed. Carson did not know, did not have the means to do very much. He got the blankets loose from the wounds, spread them back over Liam as best he could. Liam twitched and groaned and kept tangling in the blankets. Sometimes for a few seconds Liam's head cleared and he would speak. Once he said, "Carson, when it gets light we have to leave here and go home....no matter what. I don't know how we're gonna do it but... you have to help me."

Through the long night Carson never stirred from the bedside except to keep the stove going and melt more snow into water. Liam alternately shook with chills and then sweat until it ran down his forehead and cheeks. He continued to thrash and cry out. Sometimes his breath rattled in his throat, which was the scariest part for Carson.

As night greyed into dawn, Carson went outside, finally remembering the tied horses. He had heard them shuffling and stomping around the trees they were tethered to in the night; they were still there at dawn.

Amazingly, with Carson pulling on his good arm, Liam was able to get out of the bunk and stand. His knees shook and his whole body trembled spasmodically, but he remained on his feet. Getting Liam on the saddle horse looked impossible at first. The gentle old horse stood quietly as Carson got Liam's right hand on the saddle horn and his left foot in the stirrup. Carson got his shoulder under Liam's buttocks and lifted with all his strength while Liam pulled with his right arm and drove upward into the stirrup with his leg. The rasping screams torn from Liam's mouth frightened the old horse, but he stood while Liam mounted. It was impossible to get any of Liam's heavy outer clothing on him, so Carson climbed up behind him and folded both crusted blankets around his shoulders.

They started off. Liam was only semi-conscious most of the time. Carson realized that Liam would never be able to stay in the saddle by himself. He sat behind him, holding the reins and blankets. He cut the knotted lead rope of the second horse and it followed behind. The horse on which they rode was old but still a powerful animal. Carson got off sometimes and stood or walked by its side, but for the most of the four hours it carried both riders. Both horses were ravenously hungry and tried constantly to pick something to eat from the brush as they passed. Carson could feel Liam's body trembling against his chest and he marveled at his stoicism though he would not have known to call it that.

When they began the sharp descent into the river valley, it was all Carson could do to keep both of them on and keep control of the horse at the same time. He was terrified that the now tired horse would lose his footing and fall with them. As it neared home, the horse began to forge ahead faster and this was some of the roughest ground. When they broke out of the steep ravine and into the south field, Marta, who had been watching for them from the kitchen window since daylight, rushed to meet them. As the horse came abreast of her, Carson stepped off the sweating horse. Marta grabbed him by the arm, put her hand on Liam's knee.

"Liam, what happened!? For God's sake, what has happened to him?" She addressed this last question to Carson.

"A bear, Gramma. By the cabin. Grampa killed it."

Liam gasped a bit, leaned forward in the saddle and muttered something they did not catch. Marta led the tired horse to the front door, Carson walking beside his now semi-comatose grandfather. As they eased him to the ground, a shuddering shriek came out of Liam, but he stayed on his feet. In the house they laid him on a bed and Marta began the wrenching task of cutting off his blood-soaked outer clothing and woolen underwear.

"Carson, you must go to the hospital at the Hope. Bring Doctor Holmes back. He must come now! Do not let him delay." As the tired Carson stared dumbly at her, she went on. "Take the truck, I know you can drive it. Try to keep out of the deep ruts on the road. If you can get to Hudson's Hope early enough, you can get the doctor back here by tonight. He must come now! Go. Be sure the truck is full of gas. Go now and please hurry."

Carson pulled the saddles from the tired horses, left the saddles in the snow where they fell, turned the horses out to forage in the near field with the other livestock. He started the truck fairly easily, which surprised him, filled it with fuel and gunned it down the long driveway to the main road. Carson had never driven this truck more than a few hundred yards and that in the roadless fields, but he had in idle moments sat in the truck pretending to drive it and shift the uncomplicated gears. He roared down the snow-choked lane and out onto the Hudson Hope Road. Despite his nervous exhaustion, he felt more sense of purpose than he had ever felt in his life. Something, someone depended on him. He had to make decisions, felt himself in control of a situation. His body was tired but his mind was keenly aware.

Some of the normal mud holes on the road were now full of snow and though the ground was frozen in most places, the holes still had water under the ice that sucked at the wheels if they were not avoided. The truck only had three forward gears, so shifting was not the problem it might have been otherwise. Carson constantly swerved and dodged to miss the worst holes. The truck skidded, almost sliding off the shoulder, but Carson gunned the engine and fought it back on the road. For several miles he did not encounter another vehicle. Then, abruptly, a heavy farm truck rounded the corner directly ahead of him and squarely in the middle of the narrow road. Carson had an instant of sheer panic, then cut the hurtling vehicle sharply to his left off the road and into some small trees. The oncoming truck missed him by inches but stopped as Carson and his truck spun off the road. Instantly, the pickup was high centered, both back wheels off the ground, the front end jammed down into a deep ice-covered hole.

"Where in hell do you think you're going driving like that?" yelled the other driver, now out of his vehicle and standing beside the driver door, a stunned Carson still sitting in the seat.

"To get the doctor. Liam's hurt. I got to get him back today."

"Hurt? What's the matter with him?"

"Bear got him," muttered Carson, as he climbed out of the stalled stuck truck.

"A bear? How bad?"

"Bad," said Carson.

"Get in," said the other man. "Your pickup's there for a while. I'll take you back to the Hope in this one."

Two hours later, Carson found himself sitting in the seat of a much newer truck driven by a man who seemed far too young to be a doctor. Dr. Laziuk, the man had said. Old Dr. Holmes had moved months ago and he was his replacement. In the seat between them sat two very large leather bags containing the doctor's instruments.

"So, you say your grandfather was attacked by a bear? How long ago? Has anything been done for him?"

"He's home. Gramma was cutting off his clothes."

"How did he get to where he is? Could he walk?"

"Horse," mumbled Carson. He felt himself withdrawing into himself as he always did in the company of strangers.

"Your grandfather was able to ride a horse?" queried the doctor.

"I held him on," said Carson.

Dr. Laziuk asked a few more questions, but after a few mumbled answers from Carson, they drove on in silence.

At the home place, Laziuk was appalled at what he saw. "Mrs. Brennan, your husband's wounds are very serious. First, I'm going to inject him with a powerful sedative, then I'm going to, with your permission, give him a shot of a new drug to combat the terrible infections he is developing. This drug is fairly new but was used extensively during the war to combat infections in injured soldiers. The drug is called penicillin."

"Yes, I've heard of it," said Marta. "Go ahead."

"Mrs. Brennan, the treatment that your husband will need, and very quickly, is beyond my scope as a country doctor. He will need the skill of highly trained surgeons that can only be provided in a large center. I want, with your permission, to have your husband transported to the Royal Alexander Hospital in Edmonton. There he can be worked on by surgeons of the highest order. His left wrist, arm and his shoulder plus the lacerations on his back are going to require repair that only specialists can truly provide."

"But," stammered Marta, "how on earth will we ever get him to Edmonton?"

"Mrs. Brennan, I will leave here after I have cleaned these wounds, return to Hudson's Hope and send for an ambulance to come and take your husband to Fort St. John. I'll arrange for a plane to meet him on return to Fort St. John and transport your husband by air. I know this may entail great expense and sacrifice for your family, but if your husband is to have a decent chance to recover, I know of no other way."

True to the doctor's word, late the next afternoon a heavy, tired-chained ambulance rumbled into the yard. The two attendants carefully loaded Liam into the ambulance on a stretcher for return to Fort St. John.

"Carson, please look after the stock while we're gone," said Marta. "I don't know when we'll be back. Listen to the radio every evening. I'll send you a message when I can." With that, the ambulance rocked out of the yard and up onto the main road. Fourteen-year-old Carson Brennan stared after them, sensing vaguely that this was a new beginning for him. It would be more than ten weeks before he saw his grandparents again and many days before he saw anyone at all.

In late January, on a bone-chilling but crystal clear afternoon, a chained-up truck clanked slowly off the Hudson Hope road down the long lane and into the yard. The driver got out and, with Marta, helped a pale, very thin Liam from the cab. After coffee had been brewed and consumed and the driver sent on his way, Liam and Marta sat looking across the table at their grandson. Something had changed. Carson sat up in his chair, looked at them when he spoke and proceeded to bring them up to date on the home situation, especially as it applied to the livestock that he had husbanded through the long dark weeks of their absence.

"Grampa, the heifers got out of their corrals and mixed with the old cows, but by myself I couldn't separate them. I've just fed the heifers with the cows if that's all right. It's been so cold the last month I could never start the tractor, so I've just fed with the team and wagon. Mr. Wallace came over a few times and helped me hitch the horses and showed me some about handling them. I haven't had too much trouble with the team. They seem to know what to do. The rest of the horses are still in the north field, but I've been feeding them now cause it seems like they're having trouble digging through all that snow. Your bitch dog had pups under the woodpile a few days after you left. I think she's only got four or five now, but she had more at first. I been feeding her scraps from the house when I can, but she's really thin." Carson rambled on and on as though he were starved for talk. Liam had a hard time reconciling this young man across the table with the laconic, sometimes sullen child who had arrived the previous summer.

When Liam stood up to pour more coffee, Carson could see that his left arm looked white and appeared much thinner than he remembered it, a series of purple scars ran across the top of the wrist, replacing the mangled flesh that Carson so vividly remembered.

"Doc says my left arm will never be as strong as the other, but that I'll get some strength back when I start to use it again. Shoulder's pretty stiff too, but at least I'm able to use it some now. There were times I didn't know if I'd ever get out of the hospital alive, but I know I owe anything I've got left to those army surgeons and to the rehab people—they just wouldn't let me quit. And to Marta...to Gramma. She never left me alone for more than a few hours." He put his arm around Marta. Carson was astonished to see tears streaming down both of their faces.

"Dad," said Paul, propping his elbows on the kitchen table as he spoke. "You know all this oil exploration and drilling is here to stay." He said it as though reciting a fact. "Imperial's got licenses now over half the country between here and Fort Nelson and Gulf, too. You know what you ought to do? You ought to hire out your cat and maybe even get another one, hell, maybe half a dozen. You could make more in a winter doing on-site work for drilling than you could in half a lifetime on this stump ranch."

"How many eggs are you good for today, Paul?" asked Marta brightly. "You used to eat half a dozen at a sitting when you were home."

"Oh, Mom, I don't eat like that anymore. You know they're telling us now that eating eggs all the time and drinking milk isn't the best."

"What? How can good food be bad for a person?" said Liam. "I've been eating that stuff all my life and it hasn't hurt me. How can it be bad?"

"Dad, we learned at university that that stuff can clog up your arteries and mess with your heart."

"Well, a few more won't do any harm," Marta said. She set a plate with three eggs, thick slices of bacon, fried potatoes, and homemade toast in front of Paul.

"Course it doesn't hurt if you only eat it sometimes," said Paul as he slathered ketchup over the potatoes and eggs.

"And here's some of your favorite jam," Marta said as she slid a bowl of purplish jelly to Paul.

"Saskatoon and raspberry," said Paul as he stood up and hugged his mother. "There's got to be some rewards for living out here," he said, spooning a great gob of jam onto his plate and plastering it on his toast.

"Anyway, Dad, you should think about getting in on this oil work. I'm positive it will pay off in spades and from what I've been able to garner from doing my thesis on anticlines, the oil business should be here for a long time."

"You know, Paul, I've never liked being around the confusion and noise of those oilrigs. And the stink!"

"Hell, Dad, it's the smell of money! You owe it to yourself after the way you and Mom have sacrificed to make a buck while you got a chance. This opportunity likely will never pass your way again, not like this!"

"And where's the money gonna come from to buy these dozers?" Liam said. "We have enough trouble just buying parts to keep the one we got running."

"Dad, you're just the kind of person that the banks would loan money to. You're not flush with cash but all this stuff you got around here, the cattle, the buildings, the machinery you got already to say nothing of the acres you've got title to now. You could borrow a pile against what you got here and with things moving the way they are you could look to pay off a lot of iron in a hurry."

"I've never even considered mortgaging anything we've got on the place," said Liam. "We've always just paid for things as we went, we've really never borrowed or wanted to."

"You need to think about the future, Dad. You're not going to be running traplines and raising cows forever. It would be nice when you have to give all that up to have some cash in the bank and I'm telling you this opportunity won't come along again in your lifetime, probably never. I've even got a couple of oil patch guys you could talk to, people who might be looking for cat work, hauling and the like this winter. When I went to work for Imperial, it opened my eyes in a hurry to the money to be had in the industry, and I'm not just talking about the giant companies like the one I'm working for and Gulf, Texaco, and the rest of them. The spin-off work for private operators and people with the wherewithal to do their bidding on site is huge. Hell, who better than you to make a move? You got one of the biggest cats around here and you keep it in good running order. And like I said, if you want to expand into more machines, I know it could be done. Actually, you ought to think about having two or three cats and hire someone else to run them. There's no reason for you to shake around on those things at your age and especially after that bear thing."

"Hell, I'm not that old and I doubt there's many guys around, Carson here excluded," he reached over and tousled Carson's blonde hair, "that can operate a D-8 better than me."

"That's not the point, Dad. There's lots of guys still here that worked on the Highway and that know their way around a dozer. Hire the best ones you can find. Somebody's gonna have to keep everything rolling, getting the fuel out, keeping the machines running, giving the operators their orders for the day. And, most important, somebody's got to stay on top of getting jobs and contracts. Dad, that's got to be you."

Carson listened to his uncle, nodding his head slightly in agreement as he listened. Carson finally put in, "Grampa, you know that logging road we built last year, if we hadn't bid so low we could have done good on it. Once we got into it, it wasn't hard to build that road. We had a lot of bad luck with the breakdowns at the end, but Cecil Parsons said we actually got it done ahead of schedule. If we had one of them new cats with hydraulic angle blades, it would really speed things up." Carson stopped and eyed Paul, wondering if he was seen as being out of line, too aggressive, too bold for the teenager he was. Carson knew, and rightly so, that age stood for little here, only experience really counted. And didn't he have a pile of it? Carson had spent days on end in the seat of the dozer, never bitched about conditions and long hours and had been every bit as good an operator as his grandfather by the job's end. Carson saw himself as an extension of Liam now, an integral part of the home place, and the events that had transpired in the past couple of years had powerfully reinforced that. A bond had grown between grandfather and grandson that, while completely unspoken, was a powerful current between them. Liam saw clearly that it was useless to rail at Carson about school, for the time for that had come and gone. Liam felt in his bones that here was the son he had pined for, one who had this place in his blood, one who wanted to see it continue and flourish. If Carson wanted to cast his lot here, then so be it. He and Marta had discussed this endlessly out of Carson's hearing and Marta, so concerned for Carson's future, was a long time extinguishing her doubts about his lack of formal education, but recent events had gradually salved over those doubts and she had begun to acquiesce to Carson's wish to stay.

When Paul returned to Calgary, Liam and Marta spent many evenings agonizing over the conversations they had had with him. Perhaps he was right—maybe this was the time to make a move—a change in the direction of their lives.

Marta was just coming out of the Royal Bank through the swinging glass doors that led out onto the main street. The air was hot and dusty and large trucks rumbled up and down the one real street of the town impregnating the air with the pungent smell of diesel smoke. Incongruously mixed with these portents of change were the slated wooden sidewalks and the hitching rails for the horses seen less and less in town now. Turning right to reach her truck parked a few yards away, she heard a voice behind her call out, "Mrs. Brennan." The female voice was not loud and at first Marta did not realize how close the woman was. A very young lightly built native woman, clad in jeans and moccasins, her long hair spilling over a light jacket, walked closer to Marta, who now stopped, half turned and stared.

"Mrs. Brennan?"

"Yes. I'm Mrs. Brennan," said the astonished Marta.

"Mrs. Brennan, this is Patricia. She is Willie's baby."

Marta stood thunderstruck.

"This is Willie's girl," repeated the young woman. "She is not born until after Willie he is dead. Her name is Patricia."

Marta stared at the black-eyed child she held in her arms. The child looked back at Marta impassively.

"Willie's child, you say!"

"Yes. Me and Willie used to be together sometimes."

Marta stood frozen in place on the sidewalk, her eyes wide. She moved her lips to say something but no sound came out.

"So, now you know." The woman spun on her heels and moved away in the opposite direction leaving Marta to stare after her, her mind spinning turbulently. Marta started to follow after her, stopped, and slowly turned around. She got into the truck, started it, all the while trying to think what she should do. She drove east a couple of blocks, turned around and headed back west. She drove carefully down the street where she had seen the woman walking but did not see her again.

Upon arrival at the home place, she sought out Liam who was sharpening fence posts, took him into the house and related the episode to him. For a long time they conjectured back and forth across the kitchen table as to the truth of the woman's declaration, and if it was true, what it might mean for them.

"Marta, let's look at some possibilities. If the child is Willie's, and it may or may not be, the woman may be looking at us as a way to get something, money maybe, I don't know."

"But if it is Willie's child, then it is our grandchild, Liam. If it is, we should do something. I don't know what, but something. If this is true, that child is our own flesh and blood."

"Marta, we better be careful. You say the woman was native and didn't even identify herself?"

"No, she never even mentioned a name, and I was too flustered to even think to ask."

"It might just be a plot or something—say to get who knows what. I think we better try to think this through."

"Oh, Liam, I can't get that child out of my mind. She looked so uncared for—so pathetic—and so beautiful."

On a cloudy, windy day that same summer, Marta stood at the kitchen sink, washing and snipping beans. A low-slung car suddenly pulled up in front of the house. The windows of the vehicle were partly covered over with dried mud and dust from the road, but Marta could see that there were several people inside. The back door swung open on loudly creaking hinges and a woman got out unsteadily. She bent over, reached back into the seat and lifted out a child into her arms. Marta recognized them instantly. The woman walked up the low porch steps and banged loudly on the door of the house.

Marta swept open the door and stared into the woman's face. A smell of wood smoke and stale alcohol wafted in the air. While Marta stood frozen, unable to decide what to say or whether to invite her inside, the woman extended the child forward into Marta's chest. Her arms came up automatically and she found the child in her arms.

"You take it now," said the woman; her eyes seemed glazed over and she weaved slightly as she stood. "You take now. I come back."

She turned and descended the steps, unsteadily opened the car door and got inside. The car sat for a few seconds then made a wide u-turn in the yard and rattled back down the driveway, the muffler dragging on the ground and bouncing over the bumps as the car sped up. Marta found herself standing at the bottom of the steps staring after them, too astonished for words. She finally looked down at the burden in the crook of her arm. The child looked at her with huge dark eyes. Perhaps there was fear in them, perhaps not, Marta could not say. Around her nostrils and mouth was a scaly layer of dried mucous and dirt. Her hair, jet black and filthy, seemed plastered to her head. She was clad in a greasy-looking shirt and tiny bib overalls, which, had they been clean, would have been attractive on the child, and a pair of what once had been white socks. No shoes. A very unpleasant odor emanated from her.

At first Marta could not think what to do, so she sat the child on a kitchen chair, her tiny legs hanging down over the seat.

"What is your name?" Marta said this thinking at the same time how stupid it was—the child probably wouldn't speak—and was brought up short when the child responded immediately.

"Tassy." She looked back impassively at Marta out of the deep pool of her dark eyes.

"Your mother told me your name was Patricia. That is a nice name," said Marta in an unnaturally inflected voice.

The child nodded slightly. "Tassy," she said.

At that moment the back door opened and Liam walked in.

"Who was that in the...? Liam stopped in mid-sentence and looked a long time at Marta and the child. "So, they been here already. It was predictable, I guess."

Marta spent hours the rest of that day bathing the child in the sink, throwing out her reeking clothes and digging through the remains of clothing she still kept from the time of her own children. Both she and Liam were surprised at how little resistance or fuss the child made. They quickly discovered that she could walk, speak clearly if she wanted to, and feed herself.

"I guess that isn't so amazing. If this baby was born after Willie died," Marta stated, "she could be anywhere between two and two and a half years old."

The first night, the child cried bitterly when the lights were put out and she was left in bed by herself. Marta got up and held her, rocking her as she remembered doing in the past. The child soon fell asleep, and when Marta and Liam looked in on her at first light, she was sitting up in bed staring through the open door into the kitchen.

It amazed Marta how quickly the child fell into the rhythms of a new life. Hesitant at first, the child seemed naturally loquacious for she would converse easily with Marta in short simple sentences. She hung back from Liam in the beginning, obviously afraid of his maleness or maybe it was just his deeper, more resonant voice. Carson was totally in awe of her, and said little at first, though in a few days he was vying for her attention. Occasionally, for reasons only a mother might know, the child had crying jags where she repeated over and over, "Mommy! Want Mommy!" At such times Marta sat with her on a chair or on the homemade davenport, spoke soothingly to her, and waited for the storm to pass, which inevitably it did, and the natural happy nature of the child returned. Though all three adults knew the child's name, they quickly fell into the habit of calling her Tassy. Though they didn't actually say so, both of the males looked forward to meal times and early evenings when they had opportunity to be near her.

Then about seven or eight weeks after her arrival, the very thing that Marta feared most happened. A different car, but containing the same young woman, splashed into the yard in the middle of a cold September rainstorm. Liam and Carson were away from the home place for the day, and Marta was home by herself. The woman banged loudly on the door, and before Marta could respond, she opened the door and walked into the kitchen. She was clad in moccasins inside short rubbers, jeans, some sort of leather or suede coat very stained and dirty, her disheveled black hair extending to her shoulders.

"I come now for my baby."

Marta froze for a moment then she said, "Are you sure you don't want me to keep her for a while?" She knew that it sounded stupid but could think of nothing to say.

"Where's my baby?" the woman said in a slurred voice. "I come to take her now." At that moment Tassy toddled into the kitchen, saw her mother, ran to her and was caught up into her arms. The woman kissed her and held her to her breast.

"I miss her," she said. She turned and started out the door.

"Wait," Marta stammered. "I...you...haven't even told me your name." Marta followed her down the steps. "Please. What is your name?"

"Leena," said the woman. She pushed Tassy into the back seat, closed the door, then opened the front passenger side and got in. Before she could close it, Marta put her hand on it to keep it from closing.

"When will I see you again? Please let me see Tassy again!"

The woman tugged the door out of her hand and muttered, "We go now," and slammed the door. Marta stood riveted to the ground, her mind an emotional hurricane as the driver gunned the car out of the driveway. She read 'Peace Taxi' in bold letters across the door. She stood in the driving rain, rivulets running down her face and soaking her dress, watching the car until it got to the main road. It turned left and vanished out of sight behind the timber. Marta's shoulders shook as the sobs began. She walked back through the still open door of the kitchen, closed it behind her, sat at the table, buried her face in her hands, and sobbed uncontrollably for a long time.

It was the third week of December. Marta had gone to Fort St. John for the day with Liam. Earlier that same month they had created Outlook Contracting Limited and now ostensibly were entering the business world. Liam, Marta, and Carson had been to town several times already to complete the required paperwork. They had also purchased another huge used dozer that had come onto the market through a foreclosure sale. It had been a very nerve-wracking experience for all of them. They had mortgaged their home, their land, and their animals to borrow the money. Liam agonized over whether they had done the right thing, and although Marta had expressed misgivings before the company was created, now that it existed, she spoke positively about it to Liam whatever private feelings she held. Carson was vocally optimistic as only the young and inexperienced can be. It was harder for him to understand and appreciate the kind of risk the family was putting itself into. They had already secured their first contract, the site work for a string of drilling projects with a company out of Calgary. This was to begin sometime after the first of the year and would entail having the two huge dozers trucked over a hundred miles northeast over frozen winter roads. Carson and another cat skinner Liam had hired would be living in a crude drilling camp many hours from the nearest community. From there they would be working long days and nights, keeping in contact with Liam, who would be traveling back and forth as terrain and weather permitted. If Carson felt any apprehension about the responsibility he would be assuming, it did not show. His normally laconic personality remained the same.

Carson was at the home place today while Liam and Marta took care of some business matters in town. Marta did some Christmas shopping and picked up some needed groceries; Liam met yet again with emissaries of the drilling company. As the early evening darkness descended on them, they lingered a while longer in town than they normally would have and took dinner at one of the local restaurants. Liam was trying as he had for weeks to ease the sadness out of Marta that she had not lost in the months since Tassy had gone. Since then Marta had made futile efforts to contact Leena but as yet those efforts had yielded nothing.

The night was still and cold though not of the degree possible in that time of year. As they left the restaurant, only a few doors away from two of the noisy beer parlors, it was apparent to them that some of the oil field crews were in town. As always when they descended on the town the RCMP cruisers were busy trying to break up fights and hauling the hell-raising, drunken and often comatose, to lockup in the town jail. Loud western music blared through the constantly swinging doors of the bars as a cavalcade of oil workers, town ne'er-do-wells and natives came and went. Two native women were presently engaged in a hair-pulling, eye-gouging catfight just outside the doors of the building adjacent to their truck, which stood idling next to the street. Just before they reached the truck someone came up behind them and grabbed Marta's coat. Both of them turned around in astonishment. For a second Liam thought someone was trying to pick a fight with him; but as he and Marta turned around, they found themselves staring into the face of a stout, middle-aged native woman. As before, a child was thrust into Marta's arms. The woman simply muttered, "Leena says you take now." The woman turned, crossed the street without looking in either direction, and disappeared into the bar. Marta stood and gazed down at the sleeping child in her arms. As was the case before, the child and her clothing were caked in filth, but there was no question that it was Tassy.

For the first time in all the winters at the home place, Liam did not operate his trapline. He and Carson had packed in the traps and supplies in October, as Liam had always done, but this year that was the end of it. He had not even been back to his line cabin. He simply had not had the time. He was constantly on the go to help Carson and the other skinner keep their machines operating in the fearful cold. There were constant delays: hoses ruptured or were torn off, water-polluted fuel had to be drained from the tanks, cleats had to be welded on to the worn tracks for adequate traction, hydraulics malfunctioned and there were never-ending problems starting the machines if they were turned off at night. Finally, reluctantly, Liam was forced to adopt the time-honored stratagem of all who operate diesel engines in the north: they simply did not turn them off; they ran night and day.

Canvas tarps ran down both sides of the cats to try and help the operators stay warm but running a dozer in those conditions was an exhausting, bone-chilling, and often outright dangerous, occupation. Whenever they were pushing timber, which was nearly always, the never-ending danger of a stick or tree being driven into the driver by the moving tracks was a real and constant threat. Carson had several near misses, once the back of the seat on which he sat was impaled by a frozen sapling, missing his body by only inches. Another time, the cat was shut down for a day when a tree somehow dove over the huge blade and into the radiator. On and on it went, week after frozen week. Kirby, the other skinner, was a seasoned hand, having gotten his training on the construction of the Alaska Highway.

The weeks dragged on into late March; first the cold relented a bit, then day by day it grew milder. The frozen roads gradually softened and travel over them, difficult at any time, became nearly impossible. At the last minute, most of the heavy equipment was walked or hauled out of the bush to the nearest place they could be reached by truck and then hauled back into town. Carson came out with the final load and, for the first time in months, slept at the home place. Marta was ecstatic to see him and as always was astonished at how much he had grown and how much older he looked.

In late spring of the same year, Joanna Brennan became Mrs. Russel Grove in a simple ceremony performed at the ranch by the local Anglican minister. She and Russel had both graduated that spring, she with a degree in accounting and he with a civil engineering diploma. Russel's family lived in Medicine Hat, a farming and ranching community in southeastern Alberta. His parents and some of his many siblings attended the wedding, having traveled all the way from Edmonton by bus.

"And what will you do now?" asked Liam. "Are you and Russel gonna stay in Edmonton?"

"We're not too sure yet, Dad. Both of us have lined up jobs for the summer, but they're only temporary. Russ's hoping to find something more permanent, maybe in Edmonton, maybe somewhere else. I want to get my CGA as soon as possible. Working for a few months for a big company like McLeods will give me some hands-on experience first. There seems to be a lot happening in Edmonton right now, but neither of us is that enamored of staying there." Joanna talked on. It was obvious that her self-assuredness had not weakened. She never seemed to have any doubts about anything. Russel was a bit of a mystery to the Brennans because he was so quiet, though when engaged in conversation he spoke calmly and intelligently. The iron discipline and personal strength that had propelled him from a very poor home to university graduation did not reveal itself quickly. He was very polite and formal with Liam and Marta. Liam was secretly surprised that Joanna had chosen him because, at first glance, he was so unimpressive. He was strongly built but a bit overweight and was even slightly shorter than Joanna. He wore dark-rimmed glasses, had short dark brown hair, and the print of his heavy beard showed clearly on the light skin of his face. His hands were impressive though; they were large and powerful looking, the hands of a person who had done some physical work. Neither of them was given to overt displays of affection in the company of others, but it was clear, especially to Marta, that her daughter was deeply in love with this man.

"Russ graduated in the top five percent of his class," said Joanna. "His dean told him he should be able to find a decent paying job wherever he wants to go, right, Russ?"

Russel colored slightly and said, "The opportunities do look pretty good in Edmonton. I've got two interviews next week. One of them is with the City and the other is with a building contractor out at Sherwood. They supposedly have a big housing project to begin in a few months. It sure will be good to have steady work and some income coming in after all those months and years of scrimping at school." He spoke on, with Joanna interjecting from time to time, and Liam and Marta mostly listening.

Carson sat at the same table with them, hesitant as always to enter the conversation, and so consequently, volunteered little, but listened raptly to what was said. Still an adolescent, Carson was becoming physically imposing. Marta could see clearly that he had added some weight to his lean frame through the winter months. His complexion had mostly cleared and his hair was clipped close to his head. His hands, which he seemed a bit self-conscious about, were stained deeply with oil about the quicks of the fingers, which were blunt and calloused. In truth, he felt a bit overwhelmed by the assuredness of his aunt and her new husband and their talk of university and job aspirations. Carson knew he was out of his element here, as he never was among a group of working men. In the camp of the previous winter he had spoken up when the others discussed engines and machinery. At times he had even surprised himself at how easily he had taken part in the conversations. But here. Somehow he did not feel competent to give any opinions in the company of people from a world so far removed from his. When Joanna and Russel departed for Edmonton the following day, he was secretly happy to have the ear of Liam to himself again.

Though Marta lived in constant fear of it, nothing had been heard from or of Leena through the whole of the winter. In the moments when Liam was not too exhausted to listen, Marta had wondered aloud over and over what they should do about Tassy.

"Maybe we should contact the Department of Indian Affairs," Marta proffered. "Maybe they would give us authority over Tassy at least until she reaches the age of consent, whatever age that is."

"I'm not so sure," said Liam, "that anything can be solved by getting the bureaucracy involved. It'd probably just end up with some lawyers wrangling and wasting everyone's time, and they'd end up letting Tassy go back to her mother anyway. Maybe we should just wait a bit and see what happens. Let Leena make the first move."

"Liam, I cannot even bear the thought of Tassy going back with her. If that happens, that child won't have a chance. It'll be as though….as though she were dead." The tears welled up in Marta's eyes.

"Let's just live with it for now," Liam said. "But it's clear that Leena's life is totally out of control. We won't let her ruin that child's life, too."

That summer, Liam and Carson worked together as they never had before. They had a late start, but by some quirk of weather, which held off the spring rains longer than usual, they were able to seed the entire cleared acreage which now amounted to several hundred acres. As had occurred in the past, as more land was cultivated, expensive new equipment was needed. Liam found himself land rich and cash poor. The extensive money earned the previous winter had gone to pay down the massive debt the Brennans had taken on to buy the second dozer. Fuel and parts debts had accumulated through the winter and they had to be paid first. Having paid down the present notes on the capital equipment, Liam found himself borrowing again in May to buy the breaking discs needed and the other equipment required to work down the rough fields. He even had to get credit on the seed and fertilizer used on the fields. Sometimes the weight of the chances he was taking, the debt load assumed, kept him awake at night, something alien to the Liam of the past. Though he had had to pay extensive wages to Kirby, he did not do the same with Carson.

"Carson," he said one day as they bolted harrows together in the yard, "I haven't paid you the wages that you're worth to this operation, but I want to sound you out on something. If you're willing to forgo some of that money now, I want you to be a full partner with me, and I mean completely full partner—in writing. Your grandmother and I are full partners in Outlook Contracting, but if you want to do it, we would like you to be a partner with us. It means that we'll need to change the way the company is written up, but we can do it. If you really want to go ahead with this, it means that any debts that are acquired are as much yours as they are mine and Marta's. But it also means that whenever we make money, one third of it belongs to you. We won't be turning any profits until we get our debts paid off, but if we have a few winters like this last one, I'm convinced we will be able to do okay."

"Grampa, I was gonna ask you about this anyway. You know I want to stay, to be a part of this place—I guess I just didn't know it at first."

"Carson, I want you to think about this for a while, before we actually do it. You're not even twenty years old yet, so I'm not sure it can even be done until you're at least voting age. If you want to do it after you've thought it through—and Marta and I hope you will—as soon as it is legally possible, you can become a full partner with us. And Carson, this means that when we are gone—Marta and I—it will belong entirely to you."

"Grampa...I know that ain't gonna be for a long time."

Liam raised his palm to silence his grandson. "Carson, that time will come. It will probably be a lot sooner than any of us care to believe, and I know that when it does the company will be in good hands—in your hands where it should be. I always wanted my sons to stay here on the place and help it grow into something, but it never seemed to happen. Paul has his own job, his own career and from the way it looks, he'll never be able to get involved around here. If Joanna and Russel come back, they might want to join us, I really can't say now. But I know from the way you handled yourself this winter and the times before it, too, that you're the one to rely on. I just want to say how proud I am of you—Marta too. You're going to be a good man, Carson. Hell, you are already."

This was a long speech for Liam, but it effectively sealed the bond that had grown between grandfather and grandson. It was the kind of praise that Carson was totally unused to but had secretly yearned for. From that day forward, whatever doubts he had held, whatever youthful holding back had been nurtured, these disappeared altogether.

A major concern was the number of cattle the ranch now owned. It was true that they had often turned a dollar when some could be sold: for their upkeep did not cost many dollars, but the labor of calving them, inoculating and branding, and the endless chore of putting up hay in summer and feeding it in winter had it limits. The winter past Liam had often gone for days with only catnaps for sleep because there simply were not enough hours for him to load and feed the hay the cattle required and keep up to the constant needs of the construction far away over rough winter roads.

Marta proved again to be the glue that kept the place running. She pitched hay and drove the tractors—if they could be started and kept running—and when required, she could manage the team of draft horses. True, she never became adept at this, and the huge beasts inspired a fear in her that she couldn't completely master, but she even got the cattle fed alone on those isolated times when Liam just couldn't make it home. She never complained. However, the direction their lives were now taking did not elude her. She wondered in private if the tone of their previous years at the home place had not, for all their cares, been more satisfying ones than what she foresaw ahead. For it was clear that if they continued in their present direction, she was going to see less and less of her husband, be isolated more in some ways than she had ever been.

And there was Tassy. Though Marta could not be sure of her exact age, she felt that it was time to get her started on the rudiments of education. Books and supplies were obtained and correspondence courses began. At first, Tassy seemed overwhelmed by Marta's attempts to teach her reading and simple arithmetic, but once she began to put letters together and see words she caught on quickly. By the end of her first year of home school, Tassy had become an eager and happy learner. She liked to get Liam to hold her while she read to him from her simple primers. "See Spot run. Dick and Jane can go," rang through his head for weeks at a time. Carson found himself surreptitiously borrowing her books, for he knew he was not a strong reader, one of the reasons why he had not been successful in the classroom. Marta fussed over Tassy, trying not to dote too much, very involved in the child's life. Despite her original promises to herself to avoid becoming too attached because of the tenuous position of Tassy at their household, despite her fear that she would be taken away from them, Marta could not help herself. The dark-eyed, raven-haired child, so different from her own, melted her heart.

Paul's career in the oil industry was off to a good start. After a year working out of the Calgary offices of Imperial Oil, he was sent to Saudi Arabia for six months as an on-site geologist. Upon his return, in rapid succession, he married a Calgary divorcee with two small children and was again at work in oilfield geology much closer to home in Alberta's Turner Valley. He wrote short letters home from time to time, always full of optimism about his work and the future of oil exploration in the Peace River country. Liam and Marta had not even met Carolyn or her two young girls after Paul and Carolyn had been married for six months. Paul claimed that there had been no time away from his work, which could certainly be true, for the oil companies were going all out in their search for riches and the leisure time of employees was not a concern. Marta also sensed that Paul might be nervous about his new bride meeting his parents—she was city born and raised—and about the introduction of his two stepchildren into the lives of his extended family. There had been some astonishment on the part of the Brennans at the speed with which Paul's marriage had materialized, but at age twenty-seven, they felt he must know his own mind.

Certainly he appeared to love his work and from all appearances was flourishing in it. Since his early college days, there had never been any doubt where his focus lay; he claimed to have decided that after he had taken his first geology class. Liam found that easy to believe, for Paul had never exhibited any real interest in the ranch and had been eager to go away to school.

Joanna and Russel had both taken jobs in Edmonton, but as to their permanency, it was anyone's guess.

Marta felt her heart beat come up in her throat. A car, a taxi from the look of it, was coming down the long lane from the Hope Road, trailing a cloud of dust behind it.

"Liam, come out here! Hurry!"

Liam emerged from the kitchen in his shirtsleeves just as the car screeched to a halt to the side of the porch steps. As he stepped down next to Marta, who was rigidly standing near the bottom step, the passenger door of the car opened and for a moment, no one emerged. Then a woman awkwardly stepped out, leaving the door open behind her. For a moment, Marta was not even sure that it was Leena. She had not seen or heard from her in more than three years. It was Leena all right, but she had undergone some striking changes. The nice looking young native woman that Marta remembered had vanished. In her place stood a weaving half-coherent shadow, one side of her face horribly swollen, the eye on that side closed to a mere slit. Her lips were cracked and swollen, and when she slurred, "I come for my baby now," her words hissed through broken front teeth. For a moment no one moved; Leena stood hanging onto the door of the cab, struggling to keep her balance.

"No!" Marta heard herself speak. "No, you can't take her now! She belongs here! She needs to be where she can be looked after!"

"I take her now! She belongs to me!" Leena let go of the car door and took two faltering steps toward the porch. As she started to step up, Liam caught her by the arm and held her back, nearly pulling her over sideways.

"Let go!" she shrieked. "I want my baby now! I want my baby!" She began to flail her arms, and Liam had to hold both of them to keep her from hitting him. "Let go! Goddamn! I want my baby!" She started to struggle again and as she lifted her head and shrieked, "I want...." she gazed at the doorway. Tassy stood staring down at the three of them, a mixture of fear and something else registering in her brown face.

"My baby!" Leena pulled loose, rushed up the steps, nearly falling, and knelt in front of the rigid little girl. She threw her arms around the child and hugged her. "I come for you now! You come with me."

Tassy stood still, her face frightened and confused.

"We go now." But as Leena got to her feet, Tassy hung back, pulling out of her grasp. In an instant Liam was on the porch. He pinioned Leena's arms and dragged her sputtering and shrieking down the steps to the open door of the car. He pushed her struggling form into the front seat and held her there.

"You're not fit to take this child! You're a drunken, slobbering mess! Where have you been when your child needed you! I'll tell you where you've been. You've been wallowing in booze and God knows what else in those stinking town beer parlors! You are not fit to raise any child! You're not going to take Tassy back to that! You gave her up long ago when it was just too much trouble to bother with her. She's our child, too! She's not going to be raised by the likes of you! We're the ones that have cared for her, fed and clothed her and loved her—you are not part of her life!"

Liam slammed the door shut, and the sobbing Leena slumped brokenly down in the seat. He walked around to the driver's side of the cab. "And you! Don't ever bring any more of these people on my place again!"

"Hey, I'm just doin' my job. She paid me ahead of time or I'd never have driven clear out here."

"You heard me. Don't ever bring this woman out here again. And make sure no one else from your outfit does either!"

"Okay! Okay! I didn't know she was gonna cause any problems."

"So get her out of here!"

Leena did not look up as the car rattled down the driveway and onto the main road. Marta swept the sobbing Tassy into her arms and carried her back into the house, Liam at her heels.

Later, after the upset, Tassy had fallen asleep. Marta and Liam sat at the kitchen table; Marta's face was anxious and strained.

"Liam, what are we going to do? You know we have no legal right to Tassy. This is going to cause great trouble, I'm sure of it. She's going to report this to the RCMP or child welfare or who knows what else. She's going to try and have her taken away from us, I know it!"

"I can't imagine any judge or any authority for that matter who would give a child over to someone whose life is as out of control as that woman."

"Listen, Liam, a mother has a powerful legal hold on her child—any mother—even one as ruined as Leena. Don't even think for a minute that with a smart lawyer she couldn't get authority over Tassy. It's a fact we have to face."

"We'll get a lawyer," said Liam, "someone who is trained in child custody cases. I just cannot see how anyone could give Tassy back to Leena. If that happens Tassy has no chance whatever. We just can't let it happen!"

"Oh, Liam, the thought of that little girl being sent to live the kind of life she'll have if Leena gets her, I can't even bear to think of it!" Marta put her hands to her face, the tears trickled out between her fingers.

"It's not gonna happen, Marta. I promise you I won't let that happen."

Later, Marta sat by the sleeping Tassy. She laid her hand on the beautiful sleeping face. "I wonder if any of us ever really know the heartbreak we cause others. I wonder if Willie knew. If only things could have been different. If Willie could have lived and..."

"Come on, don't go there now. We've been over this so many times. Sometimes life just isn't fair." Liam took her by the hand, led her out of the room, and softly closed the door.

"So, Tom, how's the outfitting business? You still fleecing those American hunters?"

"Things have gone okay the last couple of years. The hardest part is getting reliable help. The natives are far and away the best guides, and some of them even know the country. The biggest trouble we been having is getting them to show up when they're supposed to and getting them to stay to the end of the season. Sometimes they have their own agenda. I've got three or four of them who've been with me since I started, and you couldn't find better hunters. They really know what they're doing. They don't talk a lot and that sometimes makes it tougher with a certain kind of hunter. Joey Deschutes is my main sheep guide now. A couple of my clients come every year and they insist on him guiding them. His hunters have taken some spectacular rams in the last couple years."

Liam and Tom Curry sat together at a restaurant table in Hudson's Hope. They did not meet often; for obvious reasons, there was always a rope of tension between them. Liam had salved over his surface feelings about the circumstances of Jack's death, but there was a part of him that still blamed Tom, blamed his impatient nature for that terrible day years ago on the flooding Besa River. They saw each other from time to time, more by accident than design. Tom still kept his home in the Hope, though for many months of the year he was far away in the mountains at his hunting territory. He had learned to fly, now had a pilot's license and owned his own Supercub. A few winters past, he had walked a dozer up the frozen creeks and through the mountain passes into his territory, where in the following spring, he had used it to gouge out several landing strips for his plane. After that his guiding business had really taken off.

He no longer had time to do any of the guiding personally; that was handled by his guide employees, most of them natives from the nearby Moberly Lake Reserve. Tom's time was taken up flying hunters and equipment back and forth from the hunting area. His territory was blessed with good numbers of stone sheep, the premier species of big game animal. The price of stone sheep hunts had gone up dramatically, and after some record book rams had been taken in his area, he found he had more American and European trophy hunters clamoring to hunt with him than he had time or resources to guide. It was a heady and frenetic time for outfitters like Tom Curry, who now found themselves commanding fees that would turn some of them into wealthy men. As yet, little thought seemed to be given to the numbers of sheep being killed, but men like Tom could see that it could not go on as it was.

"I think we're killin' too many rams," he told Liam, "but with a sheep hunt worth $6000 a pop, it's hard to get anybody to hold back. I know one thing," said Tom, "if we don't start managing our areas better, don't start limiting the number we kill, we're gonna put ourselves out of business. But it's so damn hard to get anybody to think about that or do anything about it. There is just so much money to be made."

Liam nodded his head. In many ways, he thought, it was no different from what cattlemen were doing to the breaks along the Peace River. Year after year, it was being overgrazed and everyone could see it and it was talked about endlessly among stockmen, but little was being done to change anything. Cattle still ran on the breaks, pretty well unchecked during the warm months. Liam knew that he was as guilty as the next. There was lots of talk about controls but as yet little had been done.

"So how's young Carson workin' out?" asked Tom. "I saw him the other day and I can't get over how he's grown up." He started to say that Carson was a spitting image of Jack, but thought better of it. Tom still felt a deep sense of guilt about Jack. So many times in the intervening years, he had wished he could have that terrible day back. Wished he had not been so driven, so impatient, so blind to what could happen and what did happen. If only....but what was the use? He had to live in the present, not the past.

"I don't know what I'd do without him," said Liam. "He's so focused, so reliable, so different now from the way he used to be."

"Yeah, when he was little, I really wondered about him," said Tom. "I was never able to communicate with him much. He was always your grandson, never really mine..." He stopped and looked at Liam, then dropped his eyes.

"...and Anne?" Liam asked, wondering if he was venturing into troubled waters.

"Well," said Tom, wiping his hand across his forehead. "Actually things could be a lot better. She's had several men in her life now and except for Jack I don't think any of them have been worth much. She's still got two kids at home with her there in Edmonton; oldest girl's married now. I've been after her for years to give up on those dead-end jobs she gets and come back and work for me, but she won't do it. Too stubborn, too proud, I guess, to admit she messed up going down there in the first place. I told her when she left with....Rudi, that she was making a big mistake, but she wouldn't listen." Tom stopped, sighed heavily, tugged at his wide western hat and said, "Carson's quite a hand with machinery, is he?"

"The best," said Liam. "He's got a touch on a dozer or a backhoe that you can't teach—just born with it, I guess. He's a full partner in Outlook, a pretty heavy responsibility for a kid, but he's not your average kid either."

"I can see that," Tom said. "He's one in a million." As always, Tom wanted to say something comforting to Liam about Jack, and as always, could not phrase anything. After they left the restaurant, he watched Liam drive out of sight down the Hope Road toward the home place, thinking as he always did, that things should have turned out differently.

CARSON

I wouldn't mind spending my winters out here if I just didn't have to live in these crappy camps. The first couple of winters wasn't so bad; I guess I was so nervous about my work and concentrated so hard on what I was doing I hardly noticed what shit holes these camps can be. The worst of it is I never seem to get a decent night's sleep. There's always some son-of-a-bitch up drunk and staggering around, carrying on at any hour of the night. I don't know how some of them do it, drunk nearly every night. Up at five o'clock in the morning, and some days spending twelve to fourteen hours in the friggin' cold, laying in trenches, welding, monkey wrenching, when the steel is so cold it burns bare flesh. Muscling pipe and steel parts around.

The food they serve in these places is passable sometimes, but the people looking after meals seem to be a revolving door. One day it's steak, then it's mystery meat for days on end. At least there is never any shortage of food. The nights are the worst: equipment and generators running right outside the walls of the shacks we sleep in. People moaning in their sleep, that is, if they're lucky enough to get to sleep. Some of these guys must drink up most of what they earn before they ever hit town, where the rest of it gets pissed against the walls of the beer joints. Frozen boots and oil soaked clothes everywhere—nobody with time or energy to really ever clean things up. And if they don't do something with the water in the shower room! Hell, it stinks so bad a guy might as well not bother tryna keep clean. Sometimes I really feel the need to get away from here for a few days. It's just the sameness, I guess. One day is pretty much like the next; the only change is what breaks down next. This winter is easier for me in some ways, in others it's worse. True, I don't spend every hour of every working day in the seat of a cat or hoe, but having to keep other guys going, help them fix these everlasting breakdowns and listen to some of them whine about nearly everything. I sometimes wish all I had to do is what I started out doing—just keeping my machine going. But I know it's like Liam says, if we want to make our mark in this business we can't sit still, we got to keep expanding, take on bigger jobs. And, of course, get more machines working.

I sometimes wonder if I was cut out to deal so much with other people. It always has been hard for me to talk to others. And some of these old farts! Most of them are so much older than me; they act like I don't know nothing. Take a guy like Peter over there. Twenty years cat skinning, doing the same thing hour after hour, day in and day out. Sure, he can run a cat better than me, hell, better than any guy here. But that's all he does! He never learned to operate a ditcher, a hoe, anything but his cat. Doesn't have a clue how to read a blueprint, never done anything on the pipe gang. Just sit in the same seat all day, sucking back Camels and pulling levers. He acts like having to listen to me about anything is painful. Liam says just put up with him best way I can because we got to have him. Shows up for work every day, no matter what, hangover, cold, working conditions, don't matter, he never misses work. I guess that has got to be worth something, even putting up with a pain-in-the-ass like him.

This river valley we're working in this winter is way different than the swamps and muskeg flats we been used to. Some of these side hills are so treacherous, even on a monster cat like a D-8. Mud slides in spring that are hard to read with three or four feet of snow packed over them make for really unstable surfaces to move over. The timber here is bigger than anything we've encountered before, too. We used to just push the timber into piles and burn it, but now government requires us to fall these big trees, limb them, cut 'em up to fit on a logging truck and send 'em to the log mills in town. It's a hell of a lot of messing around, but I guess it makes sense. It wouldn't take many of these trees to make enough lumber to build a house. Once the timber's off the lease area and the right of way, the drilling rigs can be hauled in and set up. Sometimes I watch these drills working and I wonder how they ever figured out how to do that. Some of the wells in this area are nearly two miles deep.

The oil and gas is needed, I guess, and the on-site work keeps companies like ours working, keeps people employed, but sometimes I look at what we do to the country, the mess we make of it and wonder if it's worth it all. Liam says that until a few years ago, most of this country had hardly ever seen people except maybe a few Indians moving around in it and a few trappers out here in the winters. Sometimes when I get in the right place and can see the mountains off to the west, it looks so beautiful, so untouched. But 'course, that's just an illusion. What we're doing to this country won't ever be reversed, Liam says, and I think he's right. I guess it would be better if people just let things be sometimes, but they never do. It's so cold around here except during the best days of summer I don't know what other use this country could have other than just being here. From where I'm standing now I can see the road we've been building, snaking up out of the river valley and hear machines running off in the distance. It's only been a few weeks ago I stood in this same place and looked down into the valley. Then you couldn't see one sign of human beings, just the ice-covered river, the cliffs around the far corner and the timbered bluffs. Now in a few days we've changed everything. It must have taken nature hundreds, thousands, hell, maybe millions of years to make this place look like it does, or did, I should say.

I think sometime this country will look like it does down around Edmonton, pretty much cleared with buildings everywhere. But then, I guess it's way too steep and cut up here to ever look like that. I guess I really like it best the way it was in the beginning. But liking it like that doesn't keep it that way. By next week the road will likely be punched right up the valley below me where today it hasn't been touched yet. I like this work, this job, but what I'm saying is I have bad feelings sometimes when I look at what we end up doing to the country. And I don't see any of this changing either. Liam says there's gonna be work out here for years to come. Guess it's better for me than being back in town doing odd jobs, pumping gas, fixing tires, or something. I like the way Liam has given me responsibility and I like being part of something. It's just that sometimes it gets to be kind of overwhelming. I better get moving. Liam's supposed to have that repaired rad into here by noon today. I hope we got the right hoses and connections.

JOANNA

Summer at the ranch is what I miss most. It's not that I don't like Edmonton, I do like it, after a fashion. It's wonderful to have the things you want or need at your fingertips. It's great to have decent roads to travel on, not just muddy tracks like we always had at home when I was growing up. I like being able to go to a movie if we want; heck, it's great just to be able to turn on the lights anytime we want, rather than have to adjust your life to the whims of a generator that can only be operated at certain hours. I kind of like the city lights sometimes, too; it's so different from the quiet of the home place. And yet, sometimes it is the stillness, that dead quiet, that I miss the most, especially at night. In the city, there is noise of some kind all the time. I'll never forget those winter nights standing on the porch in the deep cold, staring up at the stars. It was so calm, so peaceful. Another thing I would hate to go back to is outdoors plumbing. Going to that outhouse in the dead of a winter night was a trial in itself. I was so glad when Dad put an indoor bathroom in the house with running hot and cold water and a flush toilet. You don't miss those things so much if you've never had them, at least that's what Mother says. It changed my mother's life so much.

When I was a child at the ranch, I wanted summers never to end. After those grim winters it was just wonderful even to see something grow again. There's something about the way the trees leaf out along the river. At first as the leaves are just forming, it is such a delicate lime green. Looking up or down the backdrop of the big river with those green hills etched against water and sky, it just takes your breath away. Those islands in the river upstream from the ranch sometimes look like a painting, especially as the leaves are coming on. Dad says people are starting to go up and down the river in warm months in motor boats, something I only saw a few times. He says they sometimes are just families up there to fish or picnic. Things are sure changing fast there. When I was little we hardly even saw traffic on the road in summer, with good reason I guess. The road was always so rutted and after a rain full of mud holes. Now it's graveled and graded regularly.

I miss the green of the growing hay and oat fields. I can't say I miss those darned cows, they were always such a nuisance to have around the buildings, and the mess and stink I don't miss either. It was always such a relief when they were turned out in the hills and breaks for the summer. I guess cleaning up the yards and corrals is not the job it used to be now that they always have those big machines around.

Mother's garden was always a sight to behold. She has always had a green thumb, I guess. She must have learned some of that in the old country when she was a girl. I've never seen such yields of beans, peas, potatoes, and root crops. The cabbages she grows must be as big as they get. And now that they've found the right varieties of corn, tomatoes, and cucumbers, they flourish there too. I wish Russ and I had room in this little place we're renting for a garden, but even if we dug up some of the back yard, which the landlord wouldn't allow anyway, it'd all be shaded by those big trees. It would be wonderful to feel again the satisfaction and security that a garden inspires in me. Of course, here in the city, even if we owned the place, we could never duplicate the wonderful storage of the root cellar at the home place. Dads says the timbers in the roof are getting weak, rotted out, I imagine, by the sod over the top of them. Says that's on his list to fix pretty soon. I wonder how he expects to get it all done. All the work he sets out for himself, I mean.

Since they started that company, Dad has pushed himself so hard. Carson, too. Mother tries not to show that any of it worries her, but I know it does. She's such a rock. She never complains about anything, though her life has been anything but easy. Those early years and some of the later ones, too, they've taken their toll on her. When I saw her at Christmas she looked so tired and this business with Tassy, if she were to lose that child back to the Reserve now, it would kill her. I'm certain of it. Mother says Tassy is going to start school in town this fall, junior high school, I think. Says she's gonna stay in the dormitory and come home weekends. I don't know. I hope Mother's ready for the things that are bound to change. And there are so few native kids in the schools there now, I know Tassy is going to face some problems, some prejudice from the white kids. And being in town could cause other problems, too. Her mother, Tassy's mother I mean, will probably be around there sometimes. It's been a long time since Tassy saw her. I can't imagine how things would be between them, but their meeting is bound to happen. I just hope Mother is ready for all of this. I sometimes wonder, when you lose a child like Mother has, if you're ever the same again. Those times after Jack and Willie died—they were nightmares.

I hope to God I never have to pass through that. I'm saying this, and my child isn't even born yet, but even that is just a few months ahead. I haven't told the folks yet, but I'm going to right now. Russel is so happy. I hope he's thought about me having to quit work and all. We've talked some about leaving Edmonton, maybe going back to British Columbia, closer to my family. Russ's mother is gone now; his father lives in Medicine Hat. Has a town job there now. Anyway we've talked about moving, but that's as far as it has gone. I could probably get a job, even in Fort St. John, as an accountant or office manager. There are lots of little company offices there now, mostly oil and gas stuff. Actually I'm not sure how I could juggle that and look after a baby, we'll just have to see. But there is employment there for sure and maybe a decent job for Russ, too, if we look for it. I've got to pen a letter to the folks now and tell them the good news about the baby. This child is surely going to change life for Russ and me.

LIAM

This morning we got to get started on that cat. Working on these massive, heavy machines is always fraught with difficulty. Sometimes it's even dangerous. But we've got to get the tracks off and replace those rollers before that machine goes off on another job. Carson says he thinks the clutches are almost gone, too. That'll be another couple of days used up and lots of expense in parts. It just seems never to let up. There is always something to fix and usually little time to get it done. If I had to hire a mechanic in town to do these jobs, we'd never be able to handle the bills. Carson's such a natural with mechanics, but he goes so fast I don't know how he remembers how things go back together. I always have to be so methodical, so cautious. But him. He tears into something, the parts just pile up around him and later, sometimes it's weeks, he can put it back together in perfect order and damn fast, too. It's just a gift, I guess. Willie was like that, too.

Carson does need to learn a bit of caution; maybe he has now. Losing the end of that finger this winter needs to be a lesson to him. It's so easy to get hurt with these big buggers. He should be back from town in an hour or so. I've told him he ought to slow down a little on that road; those switchbacks coming up off Bear Flats are as treacherous as ever. Carson always drives with his foot in the gas tank. I got to admit I've never seen anyone handle a cat, a hoe, or even a truck better than him. I just wish he'd learn a bit of caution.

He's filling out now into quite a man. I don't know where he gets that size; the Currys and our side of the family are not really big people. His hands are the size of plates! It's hard to find a pair of boots big enough to fit him, let alone coveralls. He looked like he was stuffed into the cab of the pickup when he left yesterday; his knees were drawn up so high it almost looked comical. Hell, he's well into his twenties now, yet still seems to be growing. I wonder now how I ever got anything done around here without him. He can work two men to death if he wants to.

Mornings like this I look out over this place, all this machinery parked every which way, equipment sheds everywhere you look, fuel tanks, trailers and such. I sometimes have a hard time remembering it the way it was, the way it looked when Marta and I got off that paddle wheeler with a couple of horses, an axe and shovel and damn little else. Those were hard times, difficult years, but taken all in all, good ones. A man forgets a lot of the bad things and really remembers best the good. The way it should be, I guess. Sometimes those early years when we hardly saw another person except each other and the kids, the short desperate summers, the winters with their deep endless cold, sometimes when I look at all of this now, it seems like a foggy dream. There are moments though like this past winter when everything is so...so frenetic and pressured, when a person feels so pushed like something else is in control of his life, times like that leave me wondering if in many ways the old life was more satisfying. Sure, we hardly knew the color of a dollar, and there was endless work to do. I was off on the trapline much of the time in winter and worrying about Marta and the kids too, if I remember right. Those lonely nights spent at line cabins, skinning some critter by candlelight, the walls cracking with the cold, my hands cracked and aching. Do I miss all that? Yes, I guess sometimes I do, though now I'm probably getting too old to handle it. Those hot summer days putting up hay, clearing deadfall and stumps, driving the team in the fields—it was a demanding existence. We had no backup, no one to run to for help when we needed it, and there were times when we did. We had to solve things and rely on each other.

Since that bear thing a few years back, I've never had the strength I felt in those early years. My left wrist is pretty well rigid now and my arm's only half as big around as the other one. I still gasp sometimes when I take my shirt off and have to see myself in the mirror—those huge lumpy purplish scars down my back and side. But I have to remember too how lucky I am to just be alive, never mind some stiff joints or a few scars. If Carson hadn't showed up that day, I doubt I'd be here. I've never liked or trusted bears, more so since that happened.

Anyway, as I was comparing the old with now, there was something about being totally on your own, beholden to nobody, completely self-sufficient, knowing, come hell or high water, deep snow or awful cold, you were in charge, you were going to make it, survive without anybody's help. Way things are now, I lay awake at night worrying about all sorts of things. I never used to do that. Worry about getting work contracts, getting paid by some outfit on the verge of bankruptcy, worry about keeping everything and everybody going. Can we get the parts we need? Can we really fix a thing on our own in the middle of nowhere? Can I make it out there after a big storm? And worst of all, forever worrying about debt. Money looms so large now. Always borrowing more money to get bigger, to buy more machinery, to pay for help and fuel. It never ends. Sometimes it'd be nice to go back to the old days, when all we concerned ourselves with was getting by, surviving.

But I guess that isn't completely accurate either. I always dreamed of making this place into something, even right at the first. Marta and I'd talk about it at night as we lay there, kind of fantasizing, I guess it was.

Never really believing at the core that it could ever happen. Never seeing all the heartache ahead either, thank God. And now...some, much of what I hoped for is happening, and a hell of a lot I would never wish on anyone as well. Life, I guess. Once in a while I go back even further in my mind, back past the war even, back to Ireland and the folks there, to my earliest memories. It seems so long ago now as to only be partly real, like something you read in a book. My father never seemed to make enough to keep things together. I remember moving around a lot...one little shit hole village after another, always the same thing. Father'd get a job, more often than not helping some farmer, get some wages and disappear for a while until he drank it all up, by which time he'd usually been fired from his job and the whole thing would start over again. If it hadn't been for my two older sisters, Ruth and Aral, we'd have been destitute most of the time. And my poor-suffering mother, always so devoted to her Catholicism, her children, and, yes, even to her irascible, inconstant, irresponsible, alcoholic husband. That he only lived a couple of years after I left home, I don't find surprising, but it seems so unfair that my loving mother should follow him to the grave in less than a year.

My middle brother Timothy and I were close as children; we even wrote a few letters to one another after I had left Ireland. When I returned after the war, I learned that he too had immigrated, to the United States, was then living somewhere near the city of Chicago. But I've never heard anything from him, don't really know how to start to find him if he is still living. My sisters are still in Northern Ireland, married to working class chaps. Both had several little ones when I visited and though we said we'd keep in contact, it never happened. I've heard nothing from them in over thirty years.

It is a wonder what happens to us in this life. That I would ever even leave the Emerald Isle never crossed my mind in childhood, let alone make a new life and a new family so far from the land of my birth. I don't regret doing what I did, most things I'd never change, but it has left a hole in my heart to lose contact with my kin. A person should never let that happen. The world is a big place, but not that big. And here I am now more than sixty years old. Should be content to enjoy what's left of my life and what am I doing? Pursuing mammon, devoting every waking hour to chasing the elusive dollar, worrying endlessly about money, bills, contracts, and payments. I wonder sometimes how I got into all of this. What I thought we were going to do was build a wonderful productive ranch, a place where we owed nobody and a place where Marta I could live out our lives in peace, surrounded by our children and their children. Seems it was all just a daydream, totally removed from reality. Why can't we ever be happy with things as they are? Why are we always chasing rainbows? And yet? It is partially the challenge, the challenge of doing something big and, yes, risky, that has held Carson to us. When he first came to us, I didn't think there was a hope in hell of him making anything of his life. Hey, that's got to be him coming round that curve up on the main road now. Sure enough it is and coming like a bat out of hell as usual. When he says he'll be somewhere at a certain time, he always is, mostly he's there ahead of time.

MARTA

It sure seems quiet around here with Liam gone up country so much. I see so little of Carson; he looks different every time I see him. At times it's hard to believe he's the same child that turned up here at the ranch just a few short years ago. I think Jack would be proud of him, the kind of man he's becoming. I worry about him though; he spends so many days and nights in those rough camps. I know there is lots going on there that, well, is a bad example for young guys like Carson. I've not forgotten the language I heard when I rode out to the camp once with Liam. The pictures pasted up inside those buildings are horrible, indecent. I never really knew that women could fall that low. I guess I knew it but that brought it home so forcibly. Don't those men have wives, daughters? How can they look at that kind of thing continually and then behave like a normal person?

Liam says that when some of those guys go to town all of their money is wasted on alcohol and slutty women. It had never even occurred to me that Carson could be doing that, too. I hope not. I don't know if he goes to town with the others or not. I have to wonder when he'd ever have time for it. But I know that women are often blind to what men do.

I often wish I'd gotten to know my own father better. He was a distant figure to me when I was a child—so aloof—so authoritarian with my mother and me, and then the war came, he marched away with the army. I wonder so often what ever became of him. If only we'd ever had some kind of closure. Just another soldier who disappeared during the war and was never heard from again. I used to delude myself with daydreams that he might still be alive somewhere, that he would come back to us, that he could see the good life I have in Canada, but, of course, those are only fairy tale dreams. I know he lies in the ground somewhere on one of those terrible battlefields.

And if only my mother had consented to come to Canada with Liam and me, how different things might have turned out for her, for us. She would have been able to see her grandchildren and know them, take part in their lives. It makes my heart ache to think about how she must have spent her final years, alone and doing for herself. The letter we received, more than six months after her death, said she finally had to be taken into some sort of nursing home as she could no longer take care of herself. It said her mind grew very weak in her final days, she didn't even know who she was. As her child, I should somehow have been able to do something. But she was so far away, a world away! I should have gone home to visit her as I always promised myself I would, but I never could seem to do it. We wrote often enough in the early years, but gradually, even that nearly stopped. There are days when I feel so much sadness over that, but I know I can't dwell on it for it is now part of the past and we must live in the present. When I let my mind think about my sons, the pain becomes a real one in my chest, so terrible it almost suffocates me—I must not go there today!

I don't know if Carson has ever even had a girlfriend, a serious one anyway. He's always been such a loner, most young men look for company with other guys but Carson has always been one to keep to himself. I know that when Liam was hurt and in the hospital, when Carson had to take care of everything here himself—he's been a different person, a better one ever since. I wish he could meet a good girl, but where is that going to happen? I used to wish the same thing for Willie and what happened there? A man won't find a good woman in the beer parlors. And yet—when I look into those beautiful dark eyes of Tassy and sometimes I catch a glimpse of Willie there—maybe God does work in mysterious ways, I don't know. I do know that she is what is left to us of Willie's life, as Carson is of Jack's. At least in that way they still live, are still with us.

Tassy needs to get into the school system now, needs to mix with other young people. I've just about exhausted what I can teach her. God knows she reads as well now as I do, can do arithmetic pretty well, and has even learned a little about history from the books we've got her. But I know she has to learn about the world; we can't keep her from it forever. I think we are going to have to let her board in town, as others her age are doing at the school dormitory there. She can finish her schooling, even graduate from high school. I realize not many natives even go to school, much less finish high school, but I know Tassy has the ability, can do it if she really sets her mind to it. Up to now she hasn't shown much enthusiasm about leaving here to finish school, but I know she thinks about it, worries over it. I'm sure she's just nervous about making that move; fear of the unknown, I guess. She's been so protected here and, yes, so isolated. After all my anxiety about Leena trying to take her back, it has never yet materialized. And Liam even got a lawyer to help us when it happened, we were so sure it would, but it didn't. I wonder what has become of her, of Leena. I felt so horrible about what happened. It was as though we stole her child; I guess that is really what we did do. But we couldn't let her have that sweet little girl to drag through her horrible life. I often wonder where Tassy would be now if we had just let Leena take her. It beggars the imagination to even think about it.

It is strange that we've not heard anything about her now for several years. For a while rumors were always getting back to us that she was going to get the law to help her take Tassy back. We heard some sordid tales about her behavior in town. But maybe they were just that—tales, I mean. I don't know. But it is worrisome, and, yes, a relief, too, that she seems to have dropped out of sight. For a long time, that's all I thought about. Tassy rarely says anything about her. She knows what Leena is, I'm sure of that. I've tried so hard not to be unkind or too judgmental when we speak together about her mother. Tassy realizes now that she is better off with us.

It's going to be hard for her at first, I'm sure, to get used to living away from home. This ranch is really the only home she's ever known. I think she'll be able to adapt to it; I've heard that the people in charge of the student dormitories are strict and fair, I hope so. It's not like we'll be losing her forever; she'll be able to come home at times throughout the school year at holidays and such, and she can still spend summers here at the ranch. I guess it's me that dreads her going away worse than she does. It has helped to fill up my life, having her here. In some ways it's harder having her go than it was when Joanna went off to university. But that was so different. Joanna has always been so strong, so sure of herself. I never worried—not really. I always knew she would take care of herself and do all the right things. And she has. When her baby is born this summer, I know that

Joanna will be a strong and loving mother. You couldn't want a better man than Russel, so focused on his work, and I know he'll be a good father.

Tassy is so different from Joanna though. She is such a loving spirit, so giving and always trying to please. Not that Joanna wasn't or isn't, but Joanna always knew what she wanted and was so strong willed. Perhaps there is some steel in Tassy that we haven't seen, but she is so...so sensitive to others' feelings, and, I fear, so easily hurt. Once she makes some friends at school, I'm sure it will be easier for her. She's coming soon to the age where she'll be noticing boys and with her beautiful face and slim body, I know it won't be long before boys will be after her. I fear it, but I know it is what we all must pass through.

I hope and pray that Tassy's racial background will not be an obstacle for her. I don't know why I'm so anxious about it—many of the men in this country are married to native or part-native women. I guess, truthfully, I'm hoping for a little more for Tassy than some common rig hand or trapper or such. I think she has the potential to be a rather special person, someone above the cut of the ordinary; but maybe that is just the longing and wishful ambition of a mother. But I do have high hopes for her.

Paul and Caroline and their brood sure kept things lively when they were here last fall. I say "brood" because, with Caroline's two girls and now the two boys and another baby on the way, Lord, sometimes it's like a whirlwind to me, the speed at which things move. Little Benjamin and Kelly are such cute boys and so mischievous and full of energy. I was so worried, what with them underfoot everywhere they went on the place. They don't know the first thing about big animals. I was so afraid when they were around the horses. They just walked right under them or behind them. It's a good thing the old team is so gentle and passive.

That river attracted those boys like a magnet. Caroline had to keep them in sight every minute or they were down the banks throwing rocks and playing by the water. It was the same with my own babies when they were little. I love that river, but it has always scared me a bit, too, with its power and immensity, the potential to sweep a small child away in an instant. I never look at that river in flood but what I think of Jack. When he was small, he was as intrigued by the water as Paul's little guys are. And then...

Anyway, it was wonderful to have them here for a few days. Now Paul's in Indonesia, or someplace halfway round the world again. Always with his job. I know Paul loves Caroline and the children but he loves his job just as much, I fear. Six months at a time away from wife and children can't be good for a family. Paul's explained over and over to me that he thinks after he moves up in the company he won't be sent on foreign assignments so much. I hope so. Caroline needs him at home so badly right now. In a few months, there'll be five children—so much stress on a young family with the husband away so much

---

It was during the summer that Liam heard the first faint rumors. He and Ed Wallace walked a stretch of fence that separated the west extremity of the Brennan place from the Wallace property. They made superficial repairs to the fence where it was absolutely required, but it was obvious to Liam that the hodgepodge of rotted posts, poles, and sagging wire would soon need to be replaced altogether. Both of the neighbors had spoken of replacing it with a good four-strand barbed wire fence for the last several years, but Liam never could seem to find the time to do it. He saw now that absolute necessity would soon force his hand. He also knew, having been neighbors with the Wallaces for more than thirty years, that the impetus for this task would have to come from himself. Ed Wallace was not a man to move on anything until it reached crisis proportions. Ed knew that if he waited Liam out, the job would finally be done. Sure, he'd be required to put in some labor, maybe even make a token contribution on the cost of the fence materials, but the drive and most of the labor would come from the Brennan side. And why not? Ed reasoned. Liam was now a wealthy man in his eyes, what with considerable land, cattle, and other valuable resources. And, hell, look at all that machinery he's got. One of those big cats can clear that line out after the old fence is out in no time. Ed would show up to help erect the new fence. He did not intend to exert himself though. "Hell, let the Brennans take care of the grunt work. After all, they're the ones that have the most at stake here. Always so concerned when a few of my cows get onto one of their crops. Besides, I'm a poor man compared to Liam. If he wants a better fence, let him worry about it."

"You hear about that big dam the government's fixin' to put across the river?" asked Ed.

"What?!"

"Yeah, heard it at the Hope last week. They say this new government wants to put a dam across the Peace upstream of the big canyon. I guess they already had a couple of meetings or something about it."

"A dam? Why do they want a dam? For what purpose?"

"I dunno. Some say it's for electric power. They'll be able to run the water over or through big turbines to make electricity."

"Lord, how could that river ever be dammed anyway? It's too big, too wild to back up. I don't even see how it could be done, even if they decide to do it."

"Well, they was able to dam some of the biggest rivers down there in the States. I seen the Columbia River before, I know how big a river that is, and they got a dam up on it now. Mind you, I don't know anybody that's ever seen it yet, but I heard of it."

"I don't know if I like the idea of that or not. I can't even envision it much less have any idea how it'd be done. Hell, I wonder what kind of effect it would have down here, the river level, I mean, if a dam was built way upstream. You say they are wanting to build it above the canyon?"

"That's what I heard, yeah."

"But even up there that canyon is wide, must be at least half a mile, and there's some families living upstream of there at Gold Bar and couple of other places, too. What's going to happen to them, to their places?"

"I got no idea about that. I just heard Court and couple of others jawing about it in the store the other day. Maybe it's just talk anyway. I mean, it don't make much sense to me. Why would even the government want to take on a job like that? Hell, it would cost so much to get it built I don't see how they'd get it paid for trying to peddle electricity. Course, it sure would be nice to get electrical power out here. My goddamn generator's gone down again. Bella's after me to fix it. Shit, that damn thing has never run right since I got it. When it does run though I got to admit it's nice to have electric power, especially lights. Bella says she ain't going back to kerosene lanterns anymore. But that damn generator. Always something goin' wrong with it."

"Ed, do you really think a dam like the one you're telling me about is gonna do you any good? If they were to build that dam, they'd be shipping the power off somewhere else to sell it. Do you think getting electrical power to a handful of stump ranchers along the river will be any kind of priority? The more I think about this, the less I like it. It's gonna change things for us if it's built and I really wonder whether it will be for the better.

I'm used to that river the way it is. Seeing it dammed and changed is worrisome. Government ought to spend some money and develop some decent roads in this country instead of forking out millions to foreign outfits, and that's what it will take to do it," said Liam, "to come in here and dam a river that is best left the way it is."

"Hell, Liam. You know well as I do that the few people livin' up here don't count for nothin' in Victoria or Ottawa. Whether or not this thing happens will be decided by a bunch of politicians that got no interest in a few stump ranchers like you say, no interest in a little bunch of ranchers whose votes won't mean nothin'."

"You know, Ed, this valley has not changed a hell of a lot since I first saw it nearly fifty years ago. Sure we got reliable roads now connecting us to other places, but it's pretty much the way it was when I first came in here on the survey. There's a few farms, yours, mine, and a handful of others scattered along the river flats between here and Taylor Landing, but outside of that and the road, you stand on the edge of that river and you could in most places be looking at it the way its been for thousands of years. And don't believe that if a damn gets put up there in the canyon that it won't change anything down here, because it's bound to. And what about the water flow of the river after they dam it? I would bet it'd fluctuate continually. Could even have some effect on the climate around here."

"Hell, that might not hurt nothin'," said Ed. "Maybe the winters won't freeze your ass off like they always done since I been here."

"Yes, and what happens when we end up getting more summer rain, or maybe hardly any at all? What then? Nearly all the crops we grow here," Liam said, "are adapted to the climate we got now."

"Maybe the Government will have to just buy us out," proffered Ed. A thoughtful look came into his face. "I mean, if they're gonna move in here and mess with everything by putting up a dam, they can damn well buy me out, buy us out," he corrected. "I been slavin' on that place of mine for nearly forty years, now some politician bastards want to mess me up with a dam, they can damn well buy me out," he said righteously. "That land I got and them buildin's has got to be worth a pile."

That Ed's land had hardly changed since Liam could remember, that his 'buildin's' including his house were mostly fallen-down log structures barely improved over the years, was an irony not lost on Liam. Ed blathered on: "If they really are gonna build that dam we better start right now to tell that Government they gotta give us value for all the hard work we put into our places. Hell, place like mine, good bottomland, highly productive, by God, they gonna have to give me a good price."

"My place isn't for sale," Liam said, "at any price. I've spent a working lifetime trying to build it into something. I'm absolutely not gonna be pushed off it now and I'll tell you something else, Ed. If this dam turns out for real, we landowners along this stretch of the river had better side together so that we have some voice, some say in what happens. If we don't hang together, things will be done which I seriously doubt will benefit many of us. Governments like nothing better than to have a free hand with things when people just sit on their hands and say nothing."

"Yeah, I guess so," Ed muttered, but Liam could detect little resolve in his voice.

"I want to know more about this whole thing," Liam said, "and I'm gonna make it a point to find out. It's the same with governments everywhere. You go to sleep on them and don't pay attention the next thing you know they pass some law or decide on some big project where your interests or lives haven't even been considered."

Later in the day after they had left off work on the fence and headed back to their homesteads, Liam was left with the definite impression that Ed Wallace did not really share his sentiments about the dam or about the land, for that matter. It's easy to see why, Liam reasoned. Ed has mainly just been squatting on his place from day one. He never has made any real effort to turn it into something. If he gets a smell of any money or compensation, he'll dump his place in a minute if the chance arises. There are others along the river not too much different either. Maybe I'm getting all upset for nothing. After all, I only even heard about the dam today. Who's to say it isn't just rumor and nothing else. One thing is sure; this area is gonna change fast now no matter what some of us may think or want.

1963

Tassy began grade eight that September in Fort St. John. She was enrolled at the dormitory for students who lived too far from town to be bussed. At first, so many people around at once was overwhelming to her, having spent nearly all of her life in the semi-isolation of the home place. She did not speak up at all in her classes, but she listened and found the lessons the teachers were giving easy and to some degree repetitive, as she and Marta had covered much of the course already in home school. She discovered herself to be a far better reader than most of her peers, but her teachers did not call on her to read orally in class. Most of them thought because she was obviously native that her reading skills would be an embarrassment to her, hence they passed over her in oral reading, ostensibly to save face for her. Her skills in other areas, such as math, were at least average and her extensive reading in Canadian history, carefully overseen by Marta, made social studies relatively simple for her.

Socially, things took another turn. Tassy's clear skin, dark eyes and developing figure did not go unnoticed by the male student population. She quickly found herself the recipient of a fair amount of attention from boys, much of it unwanted and inappropriate. It was bewildering to her, and sometimes quite embarrassing. Some of the girls, who considered themselves rivals for adolescent male attention, reacted to her in predictable fashion. They attempted to ostracize her and whenever possible made snide remarks about her. Inevitably her nativeness became a focus of their attempts to belittle her.

Not all of her female acquaintances took this ploy. At the end of the first semester, she had made some fast friends among the girls in her classes, although others continued to torment her relentlessly. Tassy discussed these things openly with Marta when she came home every second weekend. Upon first hearing what was transpiring between Tassy and some of the girls, Marta voiced her intention to see the principal and discuss it with him. Tassy persuaded her to hold off, realizing with a child's perceptiveness that such intercession by Marta might do more harm than good.

Tassy showed herself soon enough to be no shrinking violet. She began to stand up to those calling her down and answered them back. This seemed to bring a measure of cessation on their part and possibly even a little respect, if not total acceptance. The hazing toned down. There were many students in her school who came from rural backgrounds, many who came from households certainly far less prosperous than her own. The school, in actuality, was a mix of the offspring of town business people, bureaucrats, teachers, and quasi-professionals with an overwhelming number of children from rural households, some of them in near desperate monetary shape. Tassy stood out because she was native, but really for no other reason. She was dressed and outfitted as well as any of them and her preparation for secondary education was deeper than most. Gradually, as the year wore on, she shed some of her initial reluctance to speak in class. Her participation in the oral aspects of class dampened even further those attempts to tread on her. In time, as others clearly saw her intellectual ability, her acceptance, while not totally unanimous, settled in.

The puzzling part of Tassy's life was not really her school experience with whites, which she learned to handle, but her inevitable encounters with natives. Only a mere handful of native students attended the town schools, and in most cases, it was only intermittently. Most of the native families had not yet adjusted to the regularity of white life, especially school attendance. As such, the few other natives enrolled in her school were nearly complete enigmas to Tassy. She rarely saw them and had gotten to know none of them. If anything they seemed to avoid her.

Her first unsettling encounter with local natives occurred just before Christmas holidays sent all the students home for a few days. She was walking back to the dorm in the late afternoon of an overcast December day. She had walked uptown with one of her school friends, the daughter of a local attorney. The girls had bought some school supplies, had a soft drink, and Tassy lingered, looking for Christmas gifts after her friend,

Karla, had left to go home. She was walking west a few blocks from the dorm. She walked past a Chinese restaurant, the pungent smell of its cuisine wafting out onto the sidewalk. She liked the smell and slowed down a bit. In front of her the doors of one of the raucous beer parlors swung open and two young native men of indeterminate age sauntered out onto the walk directly in her path. She took a wide detour around them, passed by them, and continued on. She had gone only a few steps when she felt a hand on her shoulder, which roughly half turned her around. Startled, she stared into the face of a strongly-built native man. "Hey, where you goin? Sure are in a big hurry."

"I'm going back to the dorm," said Tassy in a low, quivering voice.

"Dorm? Where's dorm?" said the man, standing very close to her face, one hand still on her shoulder, the other gesturing widely.

Tassy caught the smell of alcohol and wood smoke. She started to pull away, but the man held onto her coat.

"Hey, where ya goin? Let's have some beer. I got money...see." He pulled a mix of coins and paper bills from a pocket; one of the bills fluttered to the ground but he seemed not to notice. "I got money," he repeated. "C'mon and have some beer."

Tassy tugged away from him and when he held on, she slapped his hand off her coat. She backed a few steps, spun on her heel and walked swiftly away, looking back over her shoulder every few steps. The man stumbled further out into the street but made no attempt to follow her.

"Bitch," he slobbered, "Goddamn Bitch!"

Tassy had to summon all her self-control to keep from running blindly, but she walked steadily toward the dormitory, looking back over her shoulder periodically. This was only the first of a series of encounters which shook Tassy far more than any of her school experiences had.

But one encounter which she both feared and was intrigued by did not occur. Marta had spoken often with Tassy about her mother, had realized that contact between the two would be inevitable given Leena's known penchant for hanging around the town beer joints, only a few blocks from Tassy's school and dormitory. Marta clearly saw that to try to completely shield her granddaughter from her birth mother would never work. Marta had openly talked with Tassy about her partly native background, had tried to show Tassy what problems the native population was trying to cope with in the transition they now found themselves in: one foot in the old band culture, the other in the new ways imposed on them by the white majority. They spoke for hours sometimes about the native situation. Marta tried to impress on Tassy that native behavior seen in town did not represent the lives of the many who still made their living off the land in traditional ways. Most whites never saw these people because they tended to avoid town as much as possible. What they did see were the human wrecks hanging around town, particularly areas around the liquor store and the beer parlors. These native people had cut themselves off from the traditional ways and seemed only to live for alcohol. There were whites in the same situation, but somehow the stereotype of the staggering, incoherent native person seen so often on the streets, was the picture that most white people remembered.

Marta and Tassy spoke of this and also of the life of Tassy's father, Willie. Marta showed Tassy photographs of her father, his few pictures as a child and later of him in his formal military clothing. Tassy was endlessly curious about him and his life, about what he had looked like. Marta mostly emphasized the character of the Willie she remembered before he went off to the war, the Willie of the practical joke, infectious enthusiasm, the mechanical tinkerer, and lover of machinery. She told her of Willie's part along with Liam in the building of the Alaska Highway, let her read the letters Willie had sent home during those months when they labored in every kind of weather to finish the Highway. She showed Tassy books that she had retained from the years when she had home schooled her children. Tassy saw samples of Willie's early writing, even a poem he had written. It made Tassy feel that she belonged, that she indeed was part of this family, her dark eyes and skin notwithstanding.

Tassy did not remember Leena well at all. She had only an impression of a person, someone who had cuddled her at times but one who had also chronically ignored her. She had an impression, though nothing more, of dark scary rooms, of noise and crying, of cold places, of loud aggressive male voices. She seemed to remember riding in cars, looking out the windows, the car always crowded and full of cigarette smoke. She remembered being hungry and crying but no one coming for long periods of time. She tried over and over to remember her mother's face but could not clearly recall it. The smell of smoke-tanned leather immediately triggered memories of these images.

The previous couple of years, Marta had attempted to pick up again her long-ignored religious convictions. She had begun to drive into the Hope on Sunday mornings to attend services at the United Anglican Church there. She found little enthusiasm from Liam and he was content to let her go without him. Marta did take Tassy with her, for she felt that religion, so long dormant in her own life, should be a part of the life of her granddaughter. Tassy went willingly though the services, the formality and ostentations were all totally alien to her. She liked the quiet solemnity of the church, the tall ornately glassed windows, the rich hue of the wood pulpit. The church was never well attended, so the two were able to sit where they wanted, though after a couple of visits they always sat well back on the left side near the windows. Tassy was introduced to Pastor Laughton, who was short and stout with a thick brown beard. She was impressed on her second visit when he remembered her name and shook her hand. She sometimes grew restless if the sermons were too long, but she liked the order of the services and she also relished the chance to wear nice clothing.

Tassy did not see many other children at the services though there was one family with three young boys always in attendance. Marta said they were a German family who had recently taken up farmland in the Farrell Creek area, a few miles from the Hope. The parents of the boys spoke in heavy accents and were very formal in their manners. The boys spoke not at all.

Tassy liked the weekly trips in the car up the now graveled and only moderately bumpy Hudson Hope Road. The views looking up or down the river valley were nothing short of spectacular. Marta, who had only recently learned to drive, drove the heavy eight-cylinder car slowly and cautiously. There were so many deer always moving back and forth across the road that caution in operating a vehicle was imperative unless a bashed-in front end was of no consequence. Moose were a hazard, too, but mostly at night. There had been some serious accidents recently involving moose and vehicles. Tassy and Marta always had a treat of some kind on the trip back to the ranch, whether ice cream, soda pop or candy. The trip became a regular weekly occurrence for the pair, and if Tassy absorbed little in the way of Christian dogma from it, it was another brick in the wall of the deep relationship forming between Tassy and her grandmother.

When several months had passed, Christmas holidays giving way to deep cold in January and February and finally passing into the light madness of March, and still Leena had not appeared, or been heard from, Marta began to wonder what had become of her, for she feared that meeting between

Tassy and Leena more than she had feared anything in her life. To prolong the inevitable was an agony that Marta wanted to end.

One blustery April day, Liam drove down the long lane from the Hope Road to the home place. In the back of the truck he drove was a mishmash of hoses, buckets of oil, a set of hydraulic rams and an oil- and dirt-stained tidy tank. In the front seat opposite Liam were some of the household supplies Marta had asked him to gather while in town. In addition to the cases of canned foodstuffs, oranges and the like, was a stock of week-old newspapers picked up at the confectionery in town. While the Brennans now had a radio and had for some time, there was no newspaper source at the ranch. As both of them enjoyed poring over the written news, it was Liam's habit, whenever in town, to pick up any available newspapers over the previous week or so.

That evening with Liam in the kitchen, after the supper dishes had been cleared away, Marta pored over the newspapers. It was one of the ways of coping with her isolated life at the ranch, where she often did not see a face except for family for long periods. She avidly read the front pages of the successive days of the Alaska Highway News, then turned to the inner pages. Knowing what was going on in the region of the paper's domain helped fill the void left by her lack of interaction with others. In her early years, she had never taken the time to do this; there were always so many demands on her time. Now it was different. With her own children long gone and Tassy away at school, reading had become more important to Marta. She usually read every article on every page of the papers, which only amounted to a few pages anyway. She scanned the obituary column, only half paying attention. The second notice down was a very succinct one.

"Aleena Eklo, 31, of Moberly Lake, late of Dawson Creek, passed away on March 26 of unknown causes. Memorial services were held in the All Saints Catholic Church...."

Marta's eyes started to flick to the next obituary, hesitated and then she sat straight up in her chair as though struck with an electrical current. Her eyes dilated as she reread the notice.

"Liam!" she tried to keep the emotion out of her voice, but it came high and strident. "What did you say was the name of the Indian man that came here?"

Liam was pouring over a parts catalogue. He looked up questioningly. "What?"

"What was the name of the native man?"

"Sorry, Marta, I wasn't paying any attention. Native man, you say. What native man are you talking about?"

"That native man, you know the one with the crooked nose, used to stop in here sometimes. Even had coffee right at this table with you."

"Oh, okay, you mean Noah?"

"Yes, Noah, that's the one I mean. Liam, what was Noah's other name, you know, his last name? I think you mentioned it once."

Liam slid back his chair from the table and put his hand on his chin. "Yes, I did know his name. It's been so long now...Let's see, what was it? Echo or something like that. I haven't seen him in a long time."

"Was it Eklo?"

Liam stared deeply at Marta. "That's it. It was Eklo. Why do you ask?"

Marta slid the open paper across the table. She held her finger on the obituary column. "Read this," she said.

Liam read the column, then read it again very slowly. "So you think...?"

"Liam, that has to be Leena. It all fits. The age is even right, though I'd never have guessed she was so young. You told me once that Noah was part of the Moberly Lake Band."

"Yes, he was a chief of some sort," said Liam. "Told me so himself. But he probably has a lot of relatives there..."

"I think," said Marta interrupting him, "that Leena was probably one of his daughters."

"Or maybe a niece or even a granddaughter," said Liam.

"How long ago was it," Marta asked, "when he was here last?"

"A hell of a long time now," said Liam. "Could have been twenty-five or thirty years. Maybe not that long, I just can't remember."

"How old would he have been then, Liam?"

"Good question. He was definitely older than me, but sometimes those native guys are hard to age. He could have been a lot older, and then maybe not. He was kind of ageless it seemed like, still rode a horse well."

"They can all do that, I think," said Marta. "Do you know if he is still living?"

"No, I don't, but," said Liam, "I have no reason to believe that he isn't."

"We have to find out," Marta said. "We need to know if that woman is really Leena."

"Well, I don't think we should get too excited about it, Marta. There's probably a lot of people by that name around there. Maybe we're getting all worked up over nothing."

"I just believe it's her," said Marta again, her body rigid and her voice quavering slightly. "We need to know. Tassy needs to know."

"And are you hoping that it was her?" asked Liam.

"Liam, I've worried and fretted over this thing since the time Tassy came to live here. I've always been terrified that Leena would have her taken away from us. Never a day in all these years has gone by without me thinking about it. And we've been over this a thousand times, the reasons why I could never stand to see that child go back to her mother. If that is her in the obituary…Liam, maybe it's for the best. Maybe it will be the end of a nightmare for us. But I…we…must know for sure. We've got to find out."

When he stood up to speak at the corner of the table, the men gathered there were surprised at his youthful appearance. "Gentlemen, I've already been introduced by Mr. Atkins, but I'll just tell you my name again. My name is Steve Tramm, and I'm employed by the BC Forestry Service, working out of Fort St. John. One of my responsibilities is overseeing the Government grazing leases let out in this area annually by the Forest Service…" The young man spoke on confidently, his eyes moving over the dozen or so weathered faces around the table. His command of the situation seemed odd for someone so youthful in appearance, but if he was intimidated at all by the demeanor of the generally older men he spoke to, it did not register on his face. While there was no overt hostility detectable in his audience, a definite aura of tension was in the air.

"…and as I said earlier, because of the gravity of the grazing situation along the Peace River and its tributaries, particularly west of the Halfway River, the Forest Service has determined that it is imperative for the ranchers who run livestock during the summer months on crown land along the breaks of the Peace River and any streams flowing into it, that livestock be removed from these areas by the end of September and returned to private land."

"By the end of September! God, man! We've always kept our stock out until late October, even into November most years. What's the big rush all of a sudden, that we got to have our cows off by the end of September?" The agitated voice was that of Hal Goring, a long-time resident of the valley and currently president of the Lower Halfway Cattlemen's Association. Others sitting at the table nodded their heads in agreement, several voicing their objections to the new rules being imposed on them by what they saw as bureaucratic meddling.

"Forestry told us ten years ago," said Bill Atkins, "that we might sometime in the future have to get cattle off before the first snow fell, but they never said anything about taking cattle off this early."

"In the last few years, things have changed dramatically," Tramm went on. "For one thing, the number of cattle is at least twice what it was ten years ago. We've had a series of fairly dry summers and, most serious of all, the hills along the streams in this area are showing serious erosion due mainly to overgrazing the grasses that have always held the soil in check. Another major consideration is that winter habitat for large animals, mainly moose and mule deer, is being adversely affected. Cattle are totally devastating the winter food supply for these animals in their traditional winter areas, which are the very areas we're talking about, the hills and breaks along the Peace River and its tributaries."

That wintering ungulates were finding little winter feed in these areas could hardly be refuted. Most of the ranchers in the room had been plagued in recent winters with heavy infestations of starving deer and moose that ravaged their hay stacks put up to winter their cattle.

"This is a big country," said Hal Goring, "so what if some of the deer die off, there's always gonna be more to take their place. Anyway, far as I'm concerned, we got too many of the buggers to start with. Musta had sixty or seventy hangin' around my yards last winter."

"Yeah, that's right," Maury Hayes interjected. "Maybe we have got too many of 'em. Maybe they got to die back to where they ought to be."

"Numbers of wintering deer can be deceiving," said Tramm. "Some recent studies by Fish and Wildlife have shown that more than half of all the deer we have in the whole upper Peace River area winter along the streams we've been talking about."

"And who's been doing that study?" grumbled Hal. "Bunch of bureaucrats who don't know nothin'! How the hell do they know how many deer there is?"

Finally, Liam, normally reticent to say much at these meetings, spoke up. "Gentlemen, you know that we've all talked about this on our own lots of times. I know I've had conversations with some of you about this same thing. Remember last summer, Hal, when we were talking about it at the rodeo? We keep sayin' this summer range here is going to hell, and we can all see it. Yet we won't, or don't, do anything to change. And, come on, fellows, we do know what the problem is. We're overgrazing, simple as that. I'm guilty of it and so are the rest of you. Maybe I'm more guilty than most because I've been grazing those areas for the longest. We could have done something on our own for years about the problem and we haven't. So, when the problem gets to where it is now, and let's face it, there is a problem and it's a bad one, and the Government finally steps in to do something about it, we sit and bitch."

"Easy for you to say, Brennan." Maury Hayes was growing red in the face. "But those cows are my only income. I haven't got big cats and who knows what all bringin' in money. I got a bunch of calves to sell each fall and that's it. Those cattle got to support my family; I still got a bunch of kids to raise. If Forestry wants to fix this problem, maybe they ought to start with the ones who are causin' most of it." He looked directly at Liam. "Maybe they ought to be sayin' somethin' about how many cows a guy can turn out." There was some truth in Hayes's fulminating. Liam had more cattle each summer on the range than any of the others and the numbers had continued to rise over the past few years.

"Actually," Steve Tramm interrupted, "the numbers of livestock an individual rancher can turn out is going to be dealt with in our next meeting with the Minister of Agriculture. I know that it is in the offing already, and I can pretty well promise that in the very near future the government of BC is going to come up with a system that limits the number of cattle a rancher can summer on crown land."

The meeting ground on into the evening, and at its conclusion, most of the participants left complaining about bureaucratic interference but also feeling inwardly that what had been imposed on them was inevitable. In the minds of a couple of individuals was a smudge of resentment at Liam Brennan, first because he had agreed with the Forestry directives and also because they felt that it was his large numbers of livestock on the range that was the greatest factor in causing the problems. When the others had departed, Liam's downstream neighbor Link Sendol came up and put his hand on Liam's arm. "Liam, I know some of those fellows are upset.

I mean, hell, it is gonna cause them to have to change some things, but I just want you to know that I agree with your stance on this thing. If we don't do something now while there's still time, pretty soon we are gonna wreck the range to where it won't support anything. Some of these guys can't see tomorrow, they only think about now."

"I appreciate knowing that, Link. I'm just sorry that nothing can ever get done around here without it turning into a crisis first. I know that Hal and Maury didn't appreciate me speaking up tonight, but somebody needed to. And I know that they feel like I'm puttin' too many animals out each summer, and that's true, but it's gonna change. I'm either gettin' rid of some of my stock or I'm gonna try to figure out how to truck some of them to some other areas north of here in the summer. I don't know for sure if it can be done or even if it will work, but I'm gonna try something. I just know we can't sit here and keep up with what we've always done in the past. There's more and more of us but the land, at least that part we can run stock over, is shrinking. Things are changing and we got to accept it."

Sweat streamed from the face of the fiddler as he sawed his instrument through another lively dance, his cowboy boots tapping out the rhythm. To the side of him a short balding man strummed rhythm guitar and a good-looking middle-aged lady hammered away on a heavy upright piano, her fingers pounding out the melody sharply. The small dance hall literally vibrated as dancers elbowed their way around the floor in a lively two-step. A pall of cigarette smoke hung over the dancers like a grey blanket. Sometime in the past it had been decreed that no alcoholic beverages could be consumed at the Montney dance, but the yeasty fumes wafting through the enthusiastic crowd indicated that not all were paying attention to rules. The walls on two sides were lined with watchers, women, most of them young and decked out in colorful clothing on one side, males on the other. There was hardly room for more than a score of couples on the floor at any one time, but often there were more than double that number. What, with the loud insistent music and the pounding of feet on the wooden floor, the building literally shook. Dances alternated between waltzes and lively two-steps with polkas thrown in now and then for variation. Few of those in attendance spent much time off the dance floor. Elderly housewives, young, vibrant teenaged girls, stodgy older farmers and ranchers, jeaned and booted local lotharios, all got their turn on dusty floor boards, the enthusiasm electric. Despite the fact that it was several degrees below zero outside, the double back doors were flung wide open and those near the doors stood in a perpetual cloud of steam. In a corner not far from the musicians, a great wood-burning stove, consisting of a pair of 45-gallon drums welded one over the other, along with the sweating bodies provided the necessary warmth. Coats and wraps lay in a great heap in the other front corner, there being no room to hang them up. Despite the open doors and the frigid outside temperature, inside it was a tropical heat wave. Enthusiasm, especially among the younger people, set the tone. Everyone was there to let off steam, shake off some of the winter doldrums. They were there to meet with neighbors and old friends and take part in the infectious merriment. And, of course, the younger among them were there to court and compete.

The winter dances at the Montney Hall were always well attended, giving young and old alike some respite from their often difficult, repetitive, sometimes solitary and in some cases even desperate lives. A bit of a tradition had grown up over many years and local musicians vied for a chance to show their stuff there. The music always had a definite country flavor to it, but that was what those in attendance expected and wanted. It was never a sophisticated affair in any sense. In the early years people had usually come on horseback or by team as evidenced by the still extant hitching rails out back, but now the favored mode of transportation was by automobile, usually pickup truck. Tonight they plugged the snowy parking lot and lined the road on both sides for a considerable distance in both directions from the hall.

Exuberance was not generally frowned upon, in fact, it was encouraged. However, fisticuffs and other forms of mayhem had become so prevalent in previous years that the local burghers had decreed the dances be dry. While most patrons agreed with this, with the exception of the younger rowdier element, it was clearly something that got mostly lip service. John Barley Corn was always an important factor in these dances. And such was the case this evening. A distinct aroma of high test hung in the air, especially around the clot of younger males milling about the doors in the back.

Homer Adkins, a sometime friend and confidant of Carson's, had attended the dances a couple of times in the previous year and had spoken glowingly about the affairs.

"Carson, I'm tellin' ya I never seen so many good-lookin' girls in one place. Hell, it was just crawlin' with 'em. All ya had to do was just dance with one of 'em and pretty soon they was around thick as flies. I mean I can hardly dance anyways, but that don't matter. There was so many people bumpin' into each other on that floor nobody even noticed if you got two left feet. And I like how they play that music so loud and all, makes it easy to sort of get in the mood of the thing. And if you need a little cheer, you can always get a shot out back from somebody, if you follow me. Last time I went, I never got home til damn near sunup. Nearly killed me keepin' up on the pipeline next day, but, geez, it was worth it. Hey, they're havin' another one of them dances next Friday. What say we take it in? We could drive out in my Chev. It might not want to start if it's cold and we stay a while, but there's always somebody'll give you a boost. What say? You wanna have some rippin' and tearin' up there? It'll be a hell of time. What ya say?"

"I don't know," said Carson. "I got to be to work clear up by Jedney next day. That's quite a ways away."

"Come on, Carson. Hell, it won't hurt you to miss a little sleep. You need some excitement worse than you need sleep anyway. You better come, I guarantee you'll have a good time. You never know, you might even get lucky with one of them young squaws around there." He slapped Carson on the shoulder. "So, are we goin'?"

"Sure, why not. What time you want to leave?"

As planned, they drove to Montney in Homer's truck; and because they arrived well after the dance had started, they were forced to park on the side of the road nearly a block from the hall. When they arrived at the back door, a close-packed group of males, mostly young, stood around just outside the door smoking, guffawing in loud voices, some of them sucking not too covertly on small bottles of various elixir. Homer pushed on through to the door and was soon lost in the crowd. Carson hung back. At twenty-two years of age and nearly six and a half feet tall, Carson towered over nearly everyone there. The rest of him was finally catching up with his height. Though still lean, his upper body was filling out, his arms corded and powerful from heavy physical work. His thick-fingered hands stuck out noticeably from his long sleeved pearly-buttoned western shirt.

Carson had never been at ease in crowds, especially if they were strangers or female, so his social skills trailed far behind his physical growth. A person whose size attracted immediate attention could not be left to lose himself in the crowd. At least not for very long. Carson eased into the room and tried to make himself as inconspicuous as possible. He moved a little further from the door to get away from the jostle of the people who kept pushing in and out of the hall.

The band hammered on through a fast two-step, then a polka. Carson was just beginning to relax a little when suddenly Homer appeared beside him with two young ladies.

"Hey, Carson, somebody here wants to meecha!" Both girls looked very young and at the moment a bit embarrassed, too, for their faces flushed a slight red and they continued to smile and banter with each other.

"This here's Roberta," he gestured at a short slender blondie that he held by the wrist, "and this here's her sister Jennifer." The other girl, standing slightly behind her sister, colored a little more, nodded ever so slightly at Carson and said a faint "hi."

"Me and Roberta are gonna have a dance now. Right, Roberta?"

"I guess so," said Roberta. Without further ado they launched off onto the floor in the middle of another lively two-step and were swallowed up in the crowd.

"Would you like to dance?" For a moment Carson stood dumbly, then he realized the girl was speaking to him.

"Oh…uh… well, I'm not a good dancer," he stammered. The girl stood for a second, not sure of herself. She had begun to turn away from him when Carson went on, "But I'd be willing to give 'er a try." For a few seconds they stood awkwardly, kind of surveying each other, then Carson took hold of her hand and drew her out onto the floor, where they immediately bumped into another couple that were literally flying past. Carson took her right hand in his left—her hand felt very warm—and put his right lightly on her waist, her left hand resting on his shoulder. They began to move with the crowd, Carson feeling very awkward and conspicuous. His first thought was to stay in the middle of the milling crowd where his clumsy attempt at dancing would not draw attention. Carson felt even more akward because the girl whom he held was at least a foot shorter than he. They made a superficial effort at conversation but the din in the hall was so loud they gave up and just finished out the dance in silence. It seemed to Carson that the dance lasted an eternity, and when it did end, he made as to move off the dance floor, still holding the girl's hand. Before he could move more than a couple of steps, the band fired up again with a slow twangy waltz, the violin hitting long whiny notes, the guitar player now singing lustily the lines, "...Introduced him to my darlin' and while they were dancin' my friend stole my...." The band ground on and the floor was suddenly even more packed with couples than before, so much so that Carson and his girl could not even get off the floor. Carson abandoned the idea of escape to the crowd along the wall and found himself bumbling along to the slow waltz, ever so fearful that he might step on her toes, which he did a couple of times but only very lightly. This scenario recurred several more times and gradually Carson was getting the distinct impression that the fate always made sure they were in the center of the floor when a dance concluded, so that they were obliged to dance the subsequent one.

He was just beginning to relax a little, encouraged in part because the young lady seemed to be enjoying their sojourn together, and the rhythm of the music was so easy to move to. Then the band took a break and everyone moved off the floor. As they stood by the wall, very near the now-abandoned instruments of the musicians—the players had promised to return shortly—Carson wondered what he should do next. While he dithered, the girl, still keeping hold of his hand, said, "You haven't told me your name."

"My name? Oh! Carson. Carson Brennan."

"My name's Jennifer Nygaard," she said before he could think to say anything more. "That's my sister Roberta over there with your friend. What's his name?"

"Homer," said Carson.

"Right. I've seen him here before. But I don't think I've ever seen you here," she said.

"Good reason for that," said Carson, regaining his tongue. "This is the first time I ever been here."

"I like these dances," said Jennifer. "I've been coming the last few times with Roberta. Before that my folks said I was too young and wouldn't let me come."

"And how old are you?" asked Carson, wondering as he asked if he was venturing into dangerous water.

"Seventeen," she said. "I'm in grade 11 at North Peace Secondary School. My folks have a farm east of here; my Dad drives log truck in the winter. What about you?"

"Well, we live on a ranch on the Peace...."

"No, I mean, how old are you?"

"Twenty-two," said Carson, "last month."

"Did you go to high school in town?" Jennifer kept up a steady banter with Carson, and he could not think of an excuse to break off with her. Just after the band had taken intermission, a punch bowl had been moved into a corner at the right rear of the hall. It sat on a table with a large glass dipper extending into the bowl and stacks of paper cups around it. A couple of older ladies stood guard at the bowl to keep rowdier elements from spiking the watery juice, which in the past had been known to occur. People, males mostly, swarmed now around the table obtaining refreshments for their ladies and themselves. Seeing this, Carson said, "Would you like a drink?"

"I sure would," said Jennifer.

Carson soon found himself jammed into a group hovering around the punch table waiting their turn to dip a couple of paper cups full from the bowl. Again the heady fumes of alcoholic beverage tickled Carson's nose. It seemed to just rise out of the jostling crowd. When Carson finally obtained his two dripping cups, the band had started up again. As he turned to start back where Jennifer waited, he was bumped roughly by someone just behind him. "Watch where you're goin', stupid!" Carson turned in astonishment and found himself staring into the face of a thick-chested, swarthy-looking male, several inches shorter than himself.

"Watch out yourself. You're the one who ran into me."

"Oh, is that right! Maybe you want to make something of it."

"Maybe I do," muttered Carson, who then turned away and carried what remained of the punch to Jennifer, who was now engaged in conversation with Homer and Roberta.

Homer sidled up to Carson and said, "Watch yourself with that twit you were just talking to. He's one of the Sangin brothers who usually make trouble at these dances. There's a whole passel of them, all of them bad news. Give them a wide berth if you can."

"Hell, I never did nothing to him, he just ran into me on purpose."

"Yeah, that sounds about right. That was Davey Sangin, one of the younger ones, but exactly like all the rest of 'em. Now that I think of it, you'd be a natural target for a Sangin. They fancy themselves tough guys, and a big guy, especially a new one, is always a mark for those idiots. They seem to think if they can beat up on some big guy, it makes them look heroic. They're all short of brains, but they are tough. Keep away from them if you can."

Carson gazed thoughtfully back at the milling crowd of males at the rear doors but said nothing. The band resumed playing and Carson found himself whirling Roberta around the floor for a couple of dances, then he and Homer traded partners and he was again guiding Jennifer through the enthused pack on the dance floor.

"So...what kind of work do you do, Carson?" Jennifer asked, during a brief respite in the action.

"Well, dozer work mostly, but I do lots of mechanicing. Sometimes I run other stuff like backhoes and sometimes I drive truck. Just depends on what needs to be done."

"Who...what company do you work for?"

"For a construction company."

"Well, doesn't it have a name?"

"It's called Outlook Contracting; it's a pretty new company."

"Hey, I've seen that name on something," said Jennifer.

"Probably on one of the pickups or maybe it was on a semi. We've got three of 'em now."

"Who owns the company?"

"Well, actually my grandfather and I own it, and my grandmother."

"Wow! You're pretty young to be an owner. Don't you mean your grandparents own the company and you work for them?"

"I mean we own it together; it's partly mine."

The rollicking notes of a polka reverberated through the hall just then, and before Carson could protest, Jennifer had him zigzagging around the floor, other couples moving around them like bumblebees. Carson was concentrating on the steps to the dance; he'd not done too well with it earlier. He felt a sharp jab into his back ribs. He turned his head just in time to catch the alcohol-fueled breath of Davey Sangin as he brushed past in the clutches of a girl Carson hadn't noticed before. He took a few more steps and felt anger rising in his face. He deliberately maneuvered behind Davey and just as the dance was winding down, he drove his right elbow into the back of Davey's neck with enough force to nearly upend him.

Davey whirled around, pushing his dancing partner aside, and bellowed, "You big son-of-a-bitch! You're gonna get it now!"

Carson and Davey flew at each other, both of them swinging their fists, Carson's eyes flashing with anger. But before either of them landed any more than glancing blows, a crowd of onlookers got between them, several men holding onto each of the antagonists.

"Outside!" someone was yelling. "Let 'em go at it outside!"

Carson felt himself being swept in a crush of bodies toward the double door, only a few feet away and next he found himself opposite Davey in a tight-packed circle in the snow-packed yard. "Beat his head in, Davey! Knock the bejesus outa him!" someone was snarling behind him. Carson hardly had time to raise his arms and Davey came at him, swinging wildly with both hands. Carson was not entirely alien to fisticuffs, having had plenty of fights as a child in a tough city neighborhood, but this was his first fight as a grown man. His arms were so much longer than Davey's that he fended off the first wild onslaught by his shorter-armed opponent without being hit except on the arms, but he hadn't yet even swung a blow himself.

Behind him he heard a steady chant of "Kill the bastard, Davey! Kill 'im!" Davey surged forward again breathing heavily. As he swung a wild haymaker, Carson threw his first blow, an overhand right that went over Davey's flailing fists and caught him flush on the forehead. Davey grunted and staggered back a step. Carson then began raining blows from long range on the face of his cursing opponent. Davey threw himself at Carson, who caught him by the collar, flung him back and caught him with a hard right on his temple. Davey sat down abruptly.

"You bastard! Get up and kill 'im, Davey!" Carson stopped and looked over his shoulder at his antagonizer. Quick as a leopard, Davey surged to his feet and lashed out with his foot, catching Carson on the rib cage. A flash of sizzling pain roared through Carson and his breath came in a gasp. Davey circled to his left and again lashed out with his foot. More by reflex than design, Carson caught the foot in mid-air by the trouser bottom, then he grasped it with both hands, and jerked the thrashing Davey off his feet. Davey was snarling and trying to kick with the other foot. Carson suddenly stepped across both of Davey's legs, twisting the foot that he retained hold of. As Davey tried again to kick loose, Carson twisted some more, then threw his weight down onto his opponent twisting the foot as he dropped. There was a loud crack and a horrible shriek from Davey.

"Ahhh, God! You broke my leg, you son-of-a-bitch!"

Several watchers grabbed Carson and pried him off the screaming Davey. It took four strong men to pull Carson away. The sobbing, screeching body of his opponent was carried off by his retainers. One of them, whom Homer later identified as Burr Sangin, kept up a fusillade of dire threats. "You bastard, you'll get yours! You gonna wish you never come around here, I promise you, and I'll be back!" Burr made no attempt to attack Carson but only helped haul the groaning Davey to a car, into which he was dumped, and then it sped away, the back end fishtailing wildly.

Presently the mob in the frozen parking lot dispersed, and the dance continued on, little disturbed by the rather common interruption.

"Maybe we better leave now before the Sangins get back here with reinforcements," suggested Homer.

But Carson, angered to the quick by the attack on him which he knew he'd done nothing to deserve, could not bring himself to depart. He continued to take part in the dances, the deep flush on his face slowly fading, as he stolidly moved around the floor with Jennifer holding tightly to his shoulder. Between dances, Homer spoke again, "That one you clobbered was just Davey, not the biggest or meanest of the Sangins by a long shot. If Witt's anywhere around, he's gonna show up here and then there'll be big trouble."

The five Sangin brothers were all well-known troublemakers around the area. The three older ones, Witt, Burr, and Davey, all had reputations as barroom brawlers and general ne'er-do-wells. There were two younger brothers yet, and although only adolescents, they were exhibiting all of the nasty traits of their older siblings. The Sangin family had come into the region from the blownout prairies more than three decades earlier. What had become of the Sangin boys' father was not generally known, only that several years earlier, he had just taken off and abandoned his family. The mother matriarch was a reclusive figure who had no ken with her neighbors and who had little sympathy from them. She had been accused of theft on a few occasions, but nothing was ever actually proven. Of late, as her sons grew in reputation, the censure of her had become more muted.

"Okay, folks, this one's gonna be the final number of the evening, so grab a partner and kick up yer heels!" The band struck up a fast moving two-step and the crowd, what remained of it, took to the floor with enthusiasm. They had only played a few bars when a commotion even loud enough to be heard over the din of the dance hall erupted at the steaming back entrance.

"Which one? That tall son-of-a-bitch?" A wide-shouldered thickly-built figure stripped above the waist to nothing but an undershirt plowed straight across the floor right through the startled dancers, and made a beeline for Carson. Witt Sangin was a menacing figure at any time, now anger seemed to be radiating from his bull neck and bony face. At twenty-four, he was a veteran of numerous punchups in the bars around the area and not an unknown entity to the RCMP, having cooled his heels several times in the local jail for brawling, public nuisance and other minor offences. He had spent one two-month hiatus at the Prince George Correctional Centre for a vicious assault. Surly at any time, his reputation as a combatant caused most men who knew him to avoid conflict if at all possible. Witt sensed that few men were his physical equals and he made certain that all and sundry understood that. On this occasion, he had the excuse that he was avenging a beating on his brother, so no preliminary antagonism was required.

When Witt was halfway across the floor, Carson let go of Jennifer's hand and took one step toward the human wrecking crew that was bearing down on him. Carson also knew that any reasoning now was long gone. He surprised even himself by what happened next. He thrust out a long straight left jab straight into the outthrust face of Witt Sangin. The blow landed with a loud slapping sound, and though it did no real damage, it brought the raging temper of Witt to a boil. He surged forward swinging madly with his huge fists. Carson attempted to block the blows with his forearms, but this was not a Davey and he was only partially successful, for a looping hook caught him squarely above the eye. He felt himself flying against the legs of a circle of onlookers. He rolled sideways in time to avoid a vicious kick, got quickly to his feet only to absorb a smashing blow on the opposite side of his face. Witt lunged in for the kill attempting to knee Carson in the groin, but as he did so, Carson's long left hand shot out and grabbed him by the throat. As a pit bull would shake a rat, Witt pummeled and kicked Carson, but the hand held like a vice on his throat.

With a muffled roar, Witt smashed into Carson and they both went to the floor among a sea of legs. By now Witt was not getting much air but he smashed savagely at Carson's face and torso. Carson hung onto his grip doggedly and gradually forced Witt far enough from him that his fists could only beat on his arms. Witt's eyes were bulging and his face and neck were a purplish red. They rolled over several times on the floor and as Carson came up, he splayed his long legs out and pinned Witt to the floor. Then, with the full force of his strength and position, he hammered crushing right hands straight into the gargoyle face of his opponent, whose head he held against the floor. Great spatters of blood and gore flew like a foot stomping into a mud puddle. A rattled strangling noise came from Witt's ruined face. Carson struck one last time with all his power, and he felt his knuckles mash out several teeth. Before he could strike again, his arm was held back; several people pinioned him and pulled him off. "Don't let him kill the bastard, though I wouldn't mind if somebody did."

"My God, look at his face!" The partially limp body of Witt was hoisted to his feet and he was half dragged backward toward the door. "Hey, he's gonna have to go to hospital!" Before they could haul him through the doors, Witt seemed to regain his senses. He set his feet and shook off those holding him up. He shook the long greasy hair out of his eyes, spat a great gob of blood and tooth fragments back into the hall and hissed, "This ain't finished, I promise you that!" With that he turned and bolted through the open door, pushing people out of the way as he left, a crimson trail behind him.

Carson stood where he was, in shock from the pummeling he had absorbed before he had choked the fight out of Witt. His new shirt was ripped nearly off him, his face and whole upper torso were spattered with blood, much of it his own. His body felt as though it had been run over by horses, though the adrenalin that pumped through his system still kept the real pain subdued. He started to say something, but his voice came out as a husky squeak.

"Carson, I'd never have believed it! Did you ever bust up that Sangin bastard! God, man, when Witt came in here I thought you were done for. Never knew you had that in you...." Homer prattled on, as did some of the other onlookers, many of them obviously not fond of the Sangins. The band members were putting away their instruments and a couple of guys were swabbing away with rags at the blood splotches on the floor and wall.

Carson became aware of Jennifer again when she said, "I've got to go now. Dad's here to pick us up. Carson, I'll see you again. My Dad's name is Walt; we're gonna have a telephone pretty soon. Call me. I have to leave now. Bye." With that she was gone, leaving Carson to stare after her through eyelids that were nearly swollen shut. He sat down for a few minutes, the adrenalin draining out of him. When he stood again, his whole body seemed to ache and he found himself walking like an old man. He and Homer were among the last to leave and when they had made their way to Homer's frigid truck, they made an unwanted discovery. Every tire on the truck had been slashed; it sat forlornly on its four rims on the frozen road.

They caught a ride to town with one of the last vehicles, and from there to the home place with a fuel truck headed for Hudson's Hope. The sun was just beginning to filter through the heavily-frosted trees around the house when they arrived. Carson started his own truck, got some tools, and they headed back to Fort St. John. The short winter day was long descended to night again before they got the rims to town, had new tires mounted, and retrieved Homer's truck. Carson left straight from there, once the new tires were on the truck and they had finally managed to get it started, heading up the Alaska Highway to the job site where he was now a day overdue.

In addition to his other misadventures, he had not slept for nearly forty-eight hours. For several days afterward his swollen face and blackened eyes were a source of good-natured razzing by his fellows at the job site. "Hey, from the look of your face, you better stick to cat skinnin' and stay out of them bars," one of them laughed. "You get in those shit hole bars and you're guaranteed to get the shit kicked out of you if you hang around long enough and you start runnin' after them tarts."

"Wasn't in a bar," said Carson.

"No! Well, it don't look like you was prayin' with the Mennonite Brethren neither."

"Went to a dance," Carson said. "Got in a scrap."

"I can see that. What dance?"

"Montney dance," said Carson.

"Aha, I coulda guessed that. Last time I was over there couple of guys nearly tore the place down. Other guy look as bad as you?"

"I don't know," said Carson, "probably."

It was weeks before word of what had taken place at the dance hall filtered back to Carson's fellow workers, for Carson said no more about it. After hearing who he had tangled with and the outcome, he was looked at with a new sort of respect. Grousing about the boss's grandson faded off.

The spring following the birth of their first child, a healthy girl, Joanna and Russel returned to the Peace River country. Russel found work with a seismic survey company working out of Fort St. John, and he also got some extra hours with an oil company which was laying out whole blocks of housing in the city limits for its employees.

One of the greatest headaches Liam faced in his company was keeping his increasingly complicated books. Having no training whatsoever in any sort of modern bookkeeping or accounting procedures, the financial end of the business was a frustrating, confusing and sometimes baffling procedure for Liam. Marta, while she had trained herself to handle household records and simple finance, was no help in the debit and credit atmosphere of modern business. As the company began to acquire more employees, payroll and tax records became increasingly complex. Liam hired a series of part-time bookkeepers, but every case proved unsatisfactory, mainly because the part-time employees Liam believed the company required were not prepared to put in the time at the wage offered. Clearly the time for a change to a more sophisticated and workable office was needed.

A small office space was rented in Fort St. John, moving the blizzard of paper-minding out of the Brennan house where it had begun. When the latest bookkeeper quit because her husband was transferred, Liam, Carson and Marta had a long conference. The end result was the moving of Joanna and Russel to Fort St. John and the assuming of the office work by Joanna. She brought her toddler with her to work while she commenced to organize the chaotic paperwork of Outlook Contracting into a functional entity. Joanna was actually well qualified to do this having taken a business degree from university. If moving back to the country of her roots had been a thing she had hoped for, it was a godsend for the family and its new and struggling business venture. Joanna's days were filled with her duties as a mother and wife and taking on a job on top of this gave her the organizational challenge her ambitious spirit required. She and Russel lived as so many young people did, constantly juggling family and job demands while attempting to fit into the life of the community. Their days were full and mostly happy ones.

Weekends were often spent with the Brennans at the home place and these were some of the happiest memories for Liam and Marta. It was not their first experience with family close at hand; that had been going on for a long time. But it was finally a chance to meet and interact with their children and grandchildren in an atmosphere that was not charged with personal or family crisis. Marta loved to cook huge meals composed mainly of the foods procured on the ranch, but artfully and lovingly construed into delicious dishes. The family was fond of great roasts of beef, pork, or even venison, complete with mashed potatoes, gravy, green vegetables and heavy desserts. Marta made pies from the strawberries, raspberries, serviceberries and low bush blueberries she raised or picked locally. Homemade ice cream usually topped off the desserts.

Marta and Tassy, too, were very involved in the life of Joanna's little daughter, Amelia. She was just learning to walk, and the whole family, even Carson when he was home, played and romped with her as she toddled about the house on fat legs. Russel's natural reserve gradually melted away as he found himself part of their close-knit and, in some ways, unusual family. He, Carson, and Liam always spent a part of every visit walking around the extensive yards, looking at livestock sometimes, but mostly focusing on the great machinery always found, though sometimes half disassembled, around the place. As a trained engineer, Russel was keenly interested in the work Liam and Carson were doing with Outlook, and he was always asking questions, usually insightful ones about the ongoing projects. Russel's training had been mostly aimed at industry, but as a former farm boy he still liked to get into the seat of one of the huge dozers and maneuver it around.

Carson remained in the background at these family gatherings, though he took deep satisfaction in his membership. His taciturn nature kept him from initiating conversation, but he spoke readily enough on topics that interested him or in which he felt competence. He was standoffish at first with Russel, awed perhaps by his university education, social acumen and grasp of conversational skills. As he grew older, Carson was sensitive to his own lack of formal education, particularly his meager reading skills. He wished he had taken school more seriously when he had the chance, and in blaming himself for not doing so, he tended to forget much of the conflict in his mother's home which had been a major factor in this. He had periods of time when he thought much about his mother and siblings, but though he thought of writing letters, about all he managed were cards at Christmas and, when he remembered, birthday cards. Though overtly Carson appeared only to live in the present, in his mind he often relived his early life on the streets of Edmonton, of his lack of direction then both from himself and the adults with whom he lived. He marveled at how things had taken on such a different focus for him. He clearly saw that the confidence his grandparents showed in him and their continuing to involve him in the life of the ranch and the company had drawn him out into a wider, more useful life.

It was true that the part he played in the company was restricted to its day-to-day operation. As yet he was not party to the recordkeeping, future planning or the procuring of contracts, though in this last area he indirectly became a factor in the company continuing to obtain work contracts because of the satisfactory work he did in the field. Gradually, he was assuming the mantle of leadership in field operations though figuratively Liam occupied this spot. Carson was rarely away from a job until it was completely finished, so his grasp of the process in on-site oil field work, on which the company focused, deepened. He developed a close working relationship with the half dozen full-time employees and while in most cases he was half their age, he soon gained their grudging respect. Most of them had many years of experience operating large equipment, but few of them were his superior on the job. They joshed and ribbed him about women and his obvious lack of skills in that area, or about his disinterest in partying in town, but gradually they were deferring to his skills in machinery field repair and operation. When word got out of the extent of the damage he had inflicted on his assailants at the dance that past winter, they eyed him with an added respect. He was an imposing physical specimen, anyway, but until then, he had been viewed as an overgrown cub bear.

Contrary to what Jennifer had said to him about her family getting a telephone soon, he was never able to find their name on the list of the few party lines that extended into their part of the countryside. He took to waiting for her in his truck outside the high school on those infrequent occasions when he got to town. If his co-workers at the job site had been more perceptive, they would have noticed that his trips into town for working supplies had gradually increased. On the infrequent times that he met Jennifer coming out of the school, she allowed him to drive her home rather than her riding on the bus as she normally did. On a couple of occasions they stopped at one of the town's diners for lunch and coffee, thereby turning heads and initiating rumors that got back to Jennifer's parents, for she had not told them anything about Carson for fear that they would interfere. Her parents, her father in particular, had high hopes for his daughters, especially Jennifer because she was a bright and gifted student. It was expected that she would be the first in the family to go on to post-secondary learning and hence a better life. This was intensified because her only other sibling except Roberta, an older brother, had disappointed the family when he dropped out of high school in grade ten to work in the oilfields. Knowing this, Jennifer had sworn her sister to secrecy concerning Carson and when in due time her father got wind of the meeting with Carson and their continuing tryst, he was not pleased. This was due in large part because his information was second and third hand, and the brawl at the dance hall had been embellished in the frequent retelling. Consequently, the picture he had of Carson was that of a troublemaker and common brawler.

This was the way things sat when one late spring afternoon, Carson's pickup drove into the Nygaard farmyard with Jennifer ensconced in the seat beside him. Walt Nygaard had just arrived ahead of them in his logging truck. It was the first time he had been at home when Carson drove Jennifer out to the farm. Walt stood, steely-eyed, beside his truck and watched the approaching pickup. Jennifer eased away from Carson as she saw her father standing there. Her apprehension grew as she could tell by his stance that her father was not happy. Carson drove the truck up nearly beside Walt and killed the engine. He started to roll the window down, thought better of it, opened the door and got out of the truck. He took a couple of steps to where Walt was, put out his hand and said, "Hello, my name's Carson Brennan."

Walt had been building himself up to be very stern with this suitor of his daughter, whom he had seen in his imagination as an adolescent male that he would cow, sternly reprimand, and run off, hopefully for good. The towering figure he now saw before him did not fit into the mold he had created in his mind. He found himself extending his own hand though he had not intended to do so. It was taken by a mallet-sized mitt and firmly shaken. Some of Walt's rehearsed paternal indignation leaked out of him as he looked up into the serious face of Carson Brennan. Instead of speaking to Carson, he directed his remarks to Jennifer, who had gotten out of the truck and stood beside him. "So how come you didn't take the bus? Are you getting too important for that now?"

Jennifer refused to take the bait. She replied, "Carson asked me if he could drive me home today when school was out and I said yes. There's nothing wrong with that, is there? Bob's been driving Roberta around for a long time and I haven't heard anybody saying anything about that."

"That's different. Roberta's older."

"Yes. Dad, one year, and Bob's been driving Roberta home from town for a lot longer than that."

"Well, I don't like it. Kids driving on these bad roads all the time when it isn't necessary. It's just asking for trouble."

"Mr. Nygaard," Carson said, looking slightly down at him, "Jennifer and I like to be together sometimes. I've had plenty of experience driving. I do it nearly every day. If there was any way to do it, I would have called ahead of time and asked if it was all right for us to see each other, if it was okay for me to drive her home from town. I guess that's what I'm asking now. Would you mind if Jennifer and I saw each other? I don't get a lot of time away from my work, so it's not like I'm gonna be around all the time."

Despite his initial misgivings and his resolve to set this young guy straight and outright tell him to stay away from his daughter, Walt Nygaard hesitated. In truth, he was disarmed by everything about Carson Brennan. First, there was his commanding physical presence—it was obvious that this was no snot-nosed teenager. Secondly, he spoke up clearly and honestly about his intentions, his manner totally bereft of any obsequious declarations nor any bluster either. And it was also evident that he was gainfully employed in honest work. Walt heard himself asking, "Who do you work for?"

"Actually," Carson said, "you might say I work for myself, but that isn't really true either. My grandparents and I own an on-site oil field construction company called Outlook Contracting. I work for the company. Right now we're doing some work for High Tower about thirty five miles northeast of here."

There was a long pause. Walt considered what he had just heard and weighed it against some of the idle talk he'd heard about Carson. "And, you know, Jennifer's mother and I have high hopes for her schooling after she graduates next spring. We've kinda been preparing for that for a long time. I just want you to be aware of that." There was another long pregnant pause.

"Jennifer's told me about that, and I wouldn't be the one to interfere with her plans. It's just that I'd like to see her when I can and maybe do some things with her."

"Like going to wild dances?" asked Walt, looking directly into Carson's eyes.

"Mr. Nygaard, I don't know what people have said about what happened at that dance last winter, but I want you to know that I didn't start any of that—it was forced on me; I had to defend myself, that's all."

Walt took a deep breath and shrugged his shoulders. "No, I guess you can't say anything against a man's standing up for himself. I know a few things about those Sangin guys myself. But I do want you to know that I don't want my daughter involved whatsoever in that kind of thing, and we don't hold with the drinking that goes on at some of those places."

"Mr. Nygaard..."

"Call me Walt if you want."

"Walt, I don't drink myself and I wouldn't be trying to get Jennifer to either. I can promise you that there'll be no drinking when I'm with her."

Walt realized that he'd already given his tacit permission for Carson to continue seeing Jennifer, and he wondered what had become of the paternal rectitude he had so carefully rehearsed in his mind. Fact was, he liked what he saw in this young man; it was a far cry from the callow adolescent he had expected. But even then, after Carson had driven off on a positive note, he rehearsed again with Jennifer the family expectations of her. Jennifer had been nervous about Carson's inevitable meeting with her father. She felt that, all in all, things were turning out better than she had expected.

"Mr. Hilgar, can I talk to you for a minute?"

"Sure, Tassy. Still having trouble with those signed numbers?"

"Yes, I sure am, Mr. Hilgar, and I'm still a bit confused with the equations that we did yesterday."

Tassy had completed two years at North Peace Secondary School and was now almost through her grade ten year. The transition from home schooling to public school had been fraught with many difficulties, most of them totally predictable. At the beginning of her first year, she had been nearly overwhelmed by the whole experience. Unused to so many people being around her at a time, she had great difficulty focusing on what the teachers were doing and saying. Everything was new—and frightening. The impersonal nature of the public school classroom was the first thing she struggled with. She was used to poring over lessons, Marta often at her side and discussing each part of the lessons with her. In fact, it was Marta who now missed the camaraderie with her granddaughter much more than she had foreseen.

Another great challenge for Tassy was adapting to being in a room with up to thirty other adolescents who were approximately the same age. Many of them already knew each other, whereas she was nearly a total stranger to all of them. Two other factors entered in as well. First, she was part native in a school which, at that time, had few natives in it, and secondly, her striking appearance called attention to her, attention that in the beginning at least she wanted desperately to avoid. What she strove to do in those early months was to hide in anonymity, to melt into the group, trying not to stand out or be noticed in any way. In this, she was partially successful. She quickly found her "sea legs" and taught herself to focus. She worked hard at ignoring distractions in the classroom, and there were many. A good percentage of her peers did not share her dedication to learning, preferring rather to distract themselves and others with poor behavior.

After nearly three years at NPSS, Tassy had changed a good deal from the way she was when she had begun. She had made a few very good friends—she was never really outgoing—had earned the grudging respect of those classmates who valued their marks with her steady dedication to her studies, and had learned to defuse some of the female antagonism she experienced because of her appearance. Males were attracted to her, but she gave none of them any real encouragement. She learned to interact with them, and in some cases, even developed arms length friendships, but at age fifteen, she had never yet had a date with a boy or any sort of amorous relationship. Her teachers generally liked her. She did not speak up much in class, preferring to listen to others blather, but she could and did respond intelligently when called upon. She quickly showed that her best subjects were those whose foundation was reading: hence, she excelled in history, English and social studies. Her performance in mathematics and the sciences were less stellar. She often stayed after class to go over math difficulties and sometimes even came in before school for extra tutoring. She took no part in any extracurricular activities, though she did enjoy watching hockey and basketball. There was a dorm basketball league, even for girls, but she lacked the self-confidence to put on gym clothing and compete openly. The truth was, she was learning how to compete academically, and though there was little overt evidence of it, she took great pride in getting a high mark in class.

By the middle of her grade ten year, the number of natives attending high school in Fort St. John, was still miniscule; but even then, there was a slight increase over previous years. Most of them did not do well in their studies because they lacked basic skills; many were very poor attenders. Tassy, at first, tried to become friends with some of them, particularly the ones at the dorm, but generally they gave her a cold shoulder. This was extremely confusing to her, but she gradually saw that she was resented among the native school population for the very reasons that made her a good student. Natives were not supposed to experience academic success but rather just go through the motions of the white culture and fall back into their own. While the white student population was mostly indifferent to Tassy's academic success, in the native quarter her successes were viewed with jealousy and suspicion.

One afternoon as she went into the library to retrieve a binder that she had left earlier in the day, she found scrawled across the front of it in bright red felt marker: "Tassy is a white man's bitch." She stared at it for a moment, then stuffed the binder into her schoolbag. She went to her room at the dorm, locked the door, and cried. Finally, she took the binder cover off and threw it into a trashcan. She did not tell anyone about it, not even Karla or any other of her close-knit group of friends.

The following weekend, when she was home, she told Marta about it. And then she sat at the kitchen table, looking out through the window at the fields beyond, which were greening up now with the first burst of spring growth. A tear, then another, trickled down her light brown cheeks.

"There now, Sweetheart, don't cry, please don't. You know, Tassy, we've talked so many times about all of this. We knew your going into town to finish school would be hard for you, for me too, and that you'd have to learn how to get through the aggravation that you'd face, the unkindness and thoughtless actions of people who don't know you. We knew all of that before you even started. Do you remember our long conversations about it?"

"Yes, I do remember," Tassy said, "but I was so excited to go, the adventure and newness of it, I guess I really didn't understand what you were saying, not really. Then I didn't know how people can be, how mean, how hurtful. Gramma, I don't know who wrote that on my book, but whoever it is, it's hard for me not to hate them. Because that, that which they wrote, is so wrong, it isn't me."

"Of course, it isn't you," Marta said, "but I don't want you to fall to their level, to learn to hate. Whoever wrote that, Tassy, is far below you and to hate back is to be like that person is. Some people always resent it if another person does something with himself and rather than try to bring themselves up to that person's level, it is easier to try and pull the other person down to theirs. You know what I'm saying?"

"Gramma, I've tried so hard to be nice to everybody and not offend a soul. I never talk badly about people, even ones who have tried to hurt me. I've tried to treat everyone the same, just like we've talked about so often. And yet...some of them just won't leave me alone. And if I try to be friends with them, when one of them is alone with me, it almost works out. Then later, when that person is back with their other friends, they side against me, try to make fun of me or call me down for something. It's like they hate me for no reason. And the native kids...no matter how I try to be friends with them, they just ignore me, go out of their way to leave me out of their group. Sometimes it just seems like I can't win. Like it's all just not worth it, not worth the trouble." She wiped her face with her hand and sniffed loudly. "Sometimes I feel like just telling all of them, whites and natives too, to go to hell!"

"Tassy, you know better than to talk like that! You can't feel sorry for yourself. And you know you've made some good friends too, don't you? You've spoken so often about them, about Karla and Rita and..."

"Oh, Gramma, I know that's true. I have made some great friends. You know when I stayed at Karla's place, her family, they are such nice people. You couldn't ask for better. Oh...I'm sorry, Gramma, it's just that being a half...being native is so hard sometimes."

"Tassy, you are native, but you're also white, too. And nothing can ever change that. And you're my granddaughter and nothing will ever change that either." She put her arms around Tassy and hugged her. "And nothing can change the fact that you are a beautiful girl, Tassy, and I know you're as beautiful inside as you are on the outside. And I don't ever want that to change. So try to ignore the hurtful things that others do to you and look for the good. It's the only path that will bring you happiness, I know that."

"I know that, too, Gramma, just like they say in the sermons at Church. I'm so sorry for behaving like this, for speaking badly. I won't do it again."

"Tassy, I'm glad that we can talk together. I want it to always be like that. Life is so much easier when you have people in your life that you trust to tell the truth to."

"Gramma, do you really think that was my mother in that newspaper notice, that obituary, last year? I've thought about it over and over. For the longest time I thought, fantasized I guess, about meeting her. Something inside me wanted it and yet I was so afraid of it, too. And now, if that really was her that died, well, somehow I feel so empty about it, let down, I guess. And there is another part of me that is relieved, relieved that I won't have to face her, to face up to who she is, what she is."

"We haven't been able to find out, not positively, if that really was Leena. But I felt when I read it and still feel, that it was Leena, that it was your mother, who died. But I promise you, Tassy, that I'm going to double my efforts to find out, and I'm going to see to it that your grandfather does, too. This is something that has been let go too long, and it must be settled. But one thing is certain, either way it doesn't change anything between us, between you and this family. You are a part of the Brennan family and you always will be."

As the lime colors of spring slowly gave way to darker green on the poplars, as the last vestiges of winter ice melted, even in the deeply shaded south banks of the big river, as the robins and other songbirds returned and the dust on the main road grew deeper, Liam sensed some changes that he had not noticed before. Boat traffic on the river had gradually been increasing for many years, when the ice was out, of course. Most of this traffic was just people going past on their way to the wonderful trout and grayling fishing to be had just downstream of the Peace Canyon, slightly west of the hamlet of Hudson's Hope. The fishing was most active in mid-spring after the big ice jams had cleared off the river. And there was a continuing flotilla of pleasure boats right through the summer months, mostly weekend picnickers and their families, many of whom spent nearly every weekend on the river, creating well used campgrounds along the south bank and on some of the larger islands. Liam had grown used to seeing their jet boats, full of camping gear and often children too in their bright red life jackets. But lately, particularly this summer, Liam was seeing something different. He was seeing long narrow jet boats usually with just two or three men in them plying the river in both directions and not just on the weekends. The boats were stopping often, and people were getting off and walking around on the shore. Sometimes they seemed to anchor in places for a time and through his field glasses Liam could see men sticking poles down into the water, pulling them back out while others wrote something in a notebook. This continued all through the early summer. Although they were always too far away to see much detail through binoculars, Liam could see that often the men had various sorts of insignias sewn on the sleeves of their shirts. Sometimes it almost looked like they could be wearing a kind of uniform.

Traffic on the Hope Road seemed to be up a few notches as well. Large flatbed trucks hauling bull-dozers and sometimes log skidders rumbled by, just often enough to get Liam's attention. Invariably the loads were headed west toward Hudson's Hope, not much going the opposite way. Through the previous winter, Liam had heard constant talk, much of it, he thought, just idle rumors and speculation about a huge dam the British Columbia Hydro Authority was preparing to build, somewhere above the wild canyon which was only a few miles upstream from the home place.

Liam had been troubled when the first rumors began to circulate several years earlier, and his consternation had deepened as it became clear that the dam was actually going to be built. There had been sporadic public meetings, sometimes with Hydro authorities present, and despite the assurances that no great changes would be wrought on personal property or the environment, many people, Liam among them, felt otherwise. At the public meetings, protests and misgivings by residents of the area were dealt with by promises of studies and bureaucratic reassurance that all would be well. Most of the results of the promised studies, such as water drops in the river, never seemed to be made public. The authorities tended to focus on the advantages the dam would create, namely, the need for a gigantic work force to construct the dam itself, the huge network of lines needed to carry the power to distant places, and the ongoing employees required to operate the dam after it was built.

This, of course, did not fall on deaf ears, for the entire region was starved for providers of steady employment. For years, until the advent of oil exploration only a decade or so earlier, the only steady employment for the majority of work seekers was in the agricultural sector. These tended to be low paying and seasonal, to say nothing of the long hours and difficult conditions under which casual help, for that's what they were, worked.

The oil companies had and were still changing that picture and along with a steadily increasing logging sector providing job opportunities that had been non-existent only a few short years in the past. And now, the prospect of a huge project to last, some said, for several years, loomed opportunistically on the horizon. Anyone who wanted work would have a job, so the story went, and at superb wages as well. The glossy picture of prosperity for everyone painted so glowingly by proponents of the dam project muted to a great degree the opposing minority's objections. And so the juggernaut rolled forward, the apprehension of the few notwithstanding.

As one of the first settlers in the immediate area, Liam clearly remembered the valley as it had been, saw it as it was now, and worried over its future. He, more than most, was anxious that the core of the river valley remain at least in some places as he had seen it in the beginning. Roads, farms, and fences had changed much of the valley anyway, some of it regrettably, Liam knew, because of himself, but in his mind he clearly saw that a mammoth project like this dam would in one fell stroke render the surrounding country changed forever.

And in this he was torn by other considerations: as the co-owner of one of the bigger lines of operating machinery in the immediate area, he was in an enviable position to benefit monetarily by the dam's construction. He saw clearly the serious money that Outlook Contracting could expect to pull in if he just covered over his doubts and threw his hat into the ring. In fact, this very morning he tinkered about the equipment yard awaiting someone's arrival. The person for whom he waited was an official with B.C. Hydro, charged with issuing contracts for timber salvage in the huge area upriver from the dam that would, after its construction, be inundated by the gargantuan lake created by damming the river. Liam had been in that valley only a few times despite the ranch's proximity to it, it being only about twenty or thirty miles away. He remembered the beautiful stretches of the river there, uninhabited save for a handful of homesteader families who had been there, some of them even longer than he had been at the home place. The river ran through a broad valley whose densely timbered slopes seemed to stretch away into infinity, the great spine of the Rockies behind etched in white and purple in the clear sky.

Just then a white truck with B.C. Power Authority printed across the driver's door pulled into the yard. A thickly-built middle-aged man with short cropped grey hair got out of the driver's side and extended his hand. "Hello," he said formally, "I'm Ian Horvold, with the B.C. Power Authority, and this," he nodded at the other man who had also gotten out and stood next to him, "is Nelson Pierce. He'll be our pilot today."

As had been prearranged, the three men drove to an area west of Hudson's Hope called Beryl Prairie. There was an airstrip there, a small hangar and several small aircraft. The craft they were to fly in was a four-seat Piper Comanche which they pushed out of the hangar and onto the narrow strip. As Pierce started up the engine and went through his pre-flight routine, Liam observed the man more closely. Nelson Pierce was a small man, thin, wiry-looking and very short. He had dark brown hair combed back off his forehead and he wore wire-framed glasses. He didn't look to Liam to weigh more than 130 pounds.

"Don't worry, Liam," Horvold was saying. "I've been flying a lot with Nelson over the past year, and I can assure you he is a first-rate pilot. We've been flying for weeks over the country southwest of here, trying to get a good handle on where the shoreline of the reservoir will extend. Today though we'll concentrate on the area in the main river valley directly behind the dam site."

They took off into a slight east headwind. The powerful plane roared down the runway, lifted off just before the strip terminated, passed just over a dense stand of spruce and powered up into a flawless blue sky. When they were several hundred feet above the timbered terrain, Pierce made a gradual bank to the right, the nose of the plane still tilted slightly up. Liam was sitting opposite the pilot, Horvold occupied one of the rear seats directly behind him. Horvold spoke into Liam's ear as the magnificent panorama of the great mountains spread out before them, extending north and south, seemingly into infinity. As the plane gained elevation, Liam could see that the mountains visible when one looked west from ground level, the ones that he had been seeing for so many years were but the eastern most sentinels of several chains of mountains extending one behind the other as far as he could see until they disappeared in the mists of the western sky. On a day so clear and cloudless as this one, it was an awesome sight. The great snow-covered peaks sawed into the sky. It looked for all the world like a sea of mountains undulating off as far as the eye could see. There was no evidence of human intervention at all. The mountainsides on either side of the river valley that they were following showed no signs of logging scars or roads. But Liam knew now that was slated to change shortly. A few minutes up the valley, they flew over a cleared flat on the north side of the river, snake fence clearly setting off the small fields from the wall of forest. The plane roared over a cluster of small buildings set back off the fields against the northwestern edge of the clearing. Liam could clearly see the log house with stone chimney coming up through the middle of it. He could also see some animals near the buildings, horses it looked like. He wasn't sure, but he thought he could see chimney smoke. The whole operation sat back less then one hundred yards from the river which flowed swiftly past, held in by high banks on both sides.

"And what about this place?" asked Liam as he turned his head and spoke into Horvold's ear to be heard above the roar of the engine.

"What's that?"

"What happens to the people who own that place we just flew over? What happens to them when the dam starts backing the water into this valley?"

"Oh, well, B.C. Hydro has been empowered by the provincial government to buy them out, compensate them for their holdings, possibly help relocate them elsewhere. It's going to be several years before that actually happens, after the dam has been totally constructed. It will undoubtedly take several years before the waters behind the dam find their maximum height and begin to establish a shoreline. So people like those back there aren't being pressured to move just yet."

Liam pondered that as the plane soared on up the river valley. In his mind's eye, he saw the labor, the years of sacrifice and toil it took to carve out a place like that from wilderness. The isolation, the everlasting cares that went with pioneering. And to end in what? The bottom of a manmade lake, submerged and forgotten? As though the lives spent to hack out this enclave of hope had never even existed? In his memory he saw his own place as it had once been. How would he feel now if he knew it was destined to end in grey oblivion, drowned out and forgotten? And who is to say, he mused to himself, that that very thing won't happen to us when some distant group of bureaucrats decides that more dams further down the Peace would serve some political agenda?

The plane powered up the river valley passing two more homesteads similar to the first. At the last he definitely saw smoke rising from the chimney and then he saw very close to the log house what looked like a woman and two children. They were waving as the plane passed over them. The pilot rocked the wings then roared on until Liam could see that the river they were following was formed by two rivers coming from opposite directions. Then he spotted what looked like some kind of settlement on the north tributary, just up from its confluence with the stream coming in from the south.

"That's Finlay Forks," yelled Horvold into Liam's ear. "The rising water is supposed to stop right about there. It's an Indian settlement." Horvold shouted something into the pilot's ear and the plane began a wide turn to the left, and gradually began to parallel their outward path but considerably further west. In less than an hour, they were back at the landing strip.

———

"But you're convinced that this dam is going to go ahead after all the objections of the people in this valley?" Marta asked. "It seemed like a couple of years ago you and most of the neighbors were sure it would never happen."

"I know, Marta, but now it looks different. There's been so much activity in the area this summer and yesterday Ian said the government is buying out the private landholders who live up the valley behind where they say they'll build the dam. He took me back there to look at possible timber salvage and at places where they want to knock down the brush and trees whether they're salvaged or not."

"Don't you think they listened to us at those meetings? It seemed like they took our concerns seriously, they promised to do studies of all kinds. We must have gone to half a dozen meetings with those government people, and I can't remember them ever saying outright that the dam was going to really happen. They said the government had proposed studies to look at the viability of a dam."

"I think that was just bureaucratese. I think they knew from the very beginning," Liam said, "long before we had any of those meetings that this thing was on, that it was going ahead come hell or high water. I don't believe that they'll let the objections of a few private landholders along this river get in their way. Whether we like it or hate it is irrelevant to them. I think we've lost the battle and there's damned little we can do about it." Liam sat at the kitchen table with his arms resting on it, a half-empty coffee cup next to him.

"Have you thought about what that Hydro guy was saying?" Marta asked. "He was proposing to hire our company to work in that salvage operation, wasn't he?"

"Yes, of course he was. He knows nothing about our fight to try and keep the dam out, probably not interested anyway. He's just doing a job. And, Marta, it would be a tremendous job for us, one that will last a couple of years, maybe more. And yet...I feel so mixed about this. I never wanted to see that dam built in the first place. I've been one of the loudest in condemning it, and I still hate the very thought of it being there. But, Marta, they're gonna build it anyway, that much is clear to me now; and how we feel about it won't matter, it's just a fact of life, I guess. Those work contracts are going to be let out to someone, if it isn't us, it'll be somebody else. We can sit here and be sickened by the whole thing and have nothing to do with it, and will they care? Will anything be changed? We can watch that work go elsewhere, as it surely will, or we can stop complaining and get on with it. Somebody is going to do well with all that government work. It's going to be done anyway. Is there any real sense in us staying out of it? Tell me what you think, Marta."

"It looks to me like we've just got to accept it," said Marta. "The work is going to be done anyway. I guess there's really no use in our staying out of it."

"Sometimes I wonder why everything always has to change," Liam said, looking up into her face. "When we settled here, I never in my wildest dreams foresaw how it all would go."

"I know, Liam. I didn't either. When our children were small, I guess there really wasn't much time anyway to look very far ahead. We've lived through some sad times here, Liam, and some good ones, too; but I guess all in all, I'd do it over again. We should have known that things couldn't stay the way they used to be. It's just not the way of things, I guess. The world moves on and we can fight it or accept it; it's our choice. But, of course, nothing is ever accomplished by fighting change. Liam, if you think we should do it, let's go ahead with that job. As you say, it's going to get done anyway. We might as well be involved. And it sure would be a boost to our company. But maybe the job's too big. Do you think we have the resources to handle it?"

"Well, we're not going to be the only company involved," Liam said. "We will have to decide what's within the scope of our resources to accomplish. For certain, we'll only be able to do a given amount of work up there even if it is two or more years."

Their conversation lasted well into the night. Liam felt a hollowness in his chest despite their reasoning and despite Marta's support in the decision to go ahead. He and Carson had spoken often about the problems, but it was clear to Liam that Carson did not feel as deeply as he on this issue. To him, it was a great opportunity to improve the fortunes of Outlook Contracting. Carson was far more concerned about the logistics of the job than ruminating over the morality of it.

LIAM AGAIN

I remember pretty well now how it happened, though for a while the whole thing was fuzzy in my head. This time we had a different pilot, the young fellow Pierce was off flying somewhere else, so that day we went up with a guy named Snider, Ward Snider it was. We were in a different plane, too. This one seemed to have longer, wider wings, and Horvold said it would be able to fly at a slower speed without the worry of it stalling. The engine seemed to have plenty of power, and it was maybe even noisier than the one we'd been flying in previously.

It was the fourth trip we'd made out there in as many days, and this time, there were big fluffy grey-white clouds rolling over from the west; but they didn't really look threatening and the winds were slight. The last three trips before this, the sky had been as clear and blue as you could want, the kind of extended good weather that in this country doesn't happen too often. So far it had been a relatively dry summer, some of the ranchers, myself included, were starting to worry a little about the scant rain we'd had. Anyway, Horvold wanted the pilot to get down really low and try to fly around the area of the projected northwestern shoreline of the lake. Obviously, Horvold's superiors were dithering about what was to be done with the timber, and there was a hell of a lot of it that was destined to go under water after the lake behind the dam formed. At first, during the earlier trips I'd made with Horvold, it seemed like the plan had been to build rough roads into the best stands of timber, log them off, and haul it where it could be milled into lumber. Now the plans seemed to be morphing into something else. Ian said that the powers that be were now realizing what an undertaking that would be. They also were coming to grips with what the costs might be to make those roads and move the timber, which, he said, would be astronomical. Also, he said they were wondering about the time frame. Was there really enough time to construct all those roads and get the timber out of the area in the time that remained before the dam construction would be finished and the lake formed? At any rate, Ian didn't seem to know just yet what the final decision on that would be. I kept arguing that if this whole area was going to end up at the bottom of the lake, then the time ought to be taken, even if it meant holding back on the dam for a few years. I mean, some of those timber stands were magnificent, and they were vast. Ian said that wasn't how governments operated. He said once the plans were finalized and the money slotted, it had to go ahead, no matter what. Personally, I thought that didn't make a hell of a lot of sense, particularly in this case where they would waste so much, but then what did I know? Now Ian was talking like what they might end up doing was just move in with big bull-dozers and push down the timber stands so they wouldn't just be sticking up out of the water. I couldn't comprehend what kind of lake that was going to be with all the timber and brush floating around in it. I wondered, though I didn't exactly say it to Ian, if these government bastards really knew what the hell they were doing here. Anyway enough about that for now.

We'd been flying for a couple of hours maybe. We'd swung way over to the northwest, then we gradually turned back and were flying southeast opposite the way we'd come but much further south. The clouds to the west of us definitely were thickening and getting blacker. It looked like rain couldn't be far off, though none had fallen yet. I remember we'd just passed over a small tributary of the big river, and Ian was talking to the pilot, telling him to drop down and follow that stream back to the Peace, which from the elevation we were at didn't look all that far away. Just then a loud noise started coming from the engine, then another one even louder. By the time I figured out what had happened, I smelled smoke. I looked out the window over my right shoulder and I could see we were leaving a trail of thick black smoke. I looked at the pilot and what I saw didn't inspire confidence. His face had gone very pale. I glanced back at Ian and he just had a startled look on his face, I didn't think it looked like he was scared. The engine must have stopped right after those noises, I don't remember for sure. I looked out and I could see that the propeller was just windmilling, it wasn't really under power then. It was clear to me that something major had happened to the engine though I can't remember any of us saying it. What I do remember is Snider saying, "We've got to put down someplace. I've lost power completely."

I've been scared a few times in my life, that day on the Somme when I was looking down the bore of that German rifle and that time with the bear, but in those cases things happened very fast, I didn't really have time to think about it. This time maybe was a little different. We were still pretty high up in the air, but anybody could see we were losing elevation, and fast. The pilot's face was still chalk-white and I could see why. We were just coasting now, no power at all, and there looked to be absolutely no place where the plane could possibly land. That time I felt real fear, maybe the worst I've ever felt in my life. It was almost like somebody had me by the throat, my breath was just coming in gasps. But I have got to hand it to that pilot. He seemed to pull himself together then, and I'm sure I owe my life to what he did in the next thirty seconds. The color came back into his face, and as we nosed down, a few hundred feet from the treetops that were passing under us, he said, "Over there," and nodded his head to his left. For a second I couldn't see anything in front or below us except big trees. He began to swing the plane to the left, and then just ahead I could see what looked like an opening in the timber, but it sure wasn't very big and it was very close. The plane dove down hard, still swinging to the left. We must have just brushed over those last trees and the clearing was right in front of us. The plane nosed down really hard then, and I could see we were going to go right past that opening if we didn't drop quick. Then I knew we were going to hit hard. I don't remember if anybody said anything, but I figured it was over for all of us. The trees of the far side of the clearing were coming toward us fast, but they didn't look like big trees. The wing on the pilot's side hit first, and there was a terrific roar; I threw my hands up in front of my face. The next thing I remember was I was half hanging out of the plane, still in my seat belt and everything was very quiet. The smell of fuel was everywhere, almost overpowering. I don't know how much time had passed since we hit, maybe only a few seconds. I put my hand to my face and it came away covered in blood. I got my seat belt off and I had to hold myself back from falling right into the instrument panel or what was left of it. My side of the plane was at least six or seven feet in the air; the pilot's side was torn almost off the plane and was nearly at ground level. I had fuel all over me, it must have soaked everything in the plane and I was terrified of fire. I don't know why it didn't happen. As I got down out of the fuselage to the ground, I kept wondering why I was having so much trouble until I looked at my arm, my left arm, the bad one, the one that I had injured so bad in the bear fight. It was broken again a few inches above the wrist. The hand was canted off at a bad angle. The bone was clearly broken in half and displaced, but it hadn't broken through the skin. Right then I don't think I felt any pain at all. I'm sure I was still pretty much in shock. I got out on the ground and moved around to the pilot's side. It was then that I saw the pilot, and in one look, I realized he was gone. A tree had hit right where he sat. The whole side of his head was crushed. His body was hanging out of the shattered fuselage, only held there by his seat belt. I got his belt lose and eased his body down to the ground under what was left of the cockpit. I checked for breathing or a pulse and could not find any. I don't believe I expected to, the whole side of his head and face were pulverized.

Then I heard a groan or cry or something from the back of the plane and remembered Ian. For a second I couldn't even see him because the front seats of the plane had been rammed back so far, they had just kind of piled up on top of him. Then I could see his face pushed way down in a corner, his body and legs wedged into an impossibly tiny area. With the terrible fear of fire still uppermost in my mind, I started to try and get him out of the wreck. I was having to do everything with just my right hand, the other was just hanging by my side, absolutely useless. I didn't think about it at the time, but it must have been some kind of miracle that neither of my legs were broken. My pants were torn and I was scraped and bruised real bad, but the bones were not broken or displaced. I pried what was left of the door off on the same side as the pilot; it just fell off with a hard tug. I reached in and got hold of Ian's hand and tried to pull him loose; he yelled out in pain.

"Ian! Ian! Can you hear me? Can you talk?"

"I hear you," he moaned. He seemed to be coming to. He grabbed my extended hand and tried to pull himself up out of the corner he was wedged in. There was blood all over him, he was sticky with it. I leaned in and got my good arm under his shoulders and around his chest. I set my feet and pulled as hard as I could. He kept gasping and crying out, but I pulled him so he was sitting up, but his legs were still kind of folded under him. He put his arm around my neck and I pulled as hard as I could. He sort of slid out of the wreck and onto the ground. He was screaming the whole time. I think he passed out again for a minute or so. But I was so fearful of the fuel catching fire that I dragged him a few feet away from the plane. Looking back now, I doubt it was far enough to save him had it caught fire, but I just couldn't do any more until I caught my breath. He started to come around again, groaning and crying out the whole time.

"Ian, we've got to move back from this plane before it catches fire. You've got to help me!" It was then that I could see that he wasn't going to be able to do much. His right leg was broken below the knee and bent at about forty-five degrees to the side. The other leg didn't look right either, and it was a few minutes later that I discovered it was broken, too, but the break was just above the knee. It looked pretty horrible, because the blood was building up under the skin to a huge purplish bag. I got hold of him by the hand and skidded him a few more feet away from the plane, but I had to stop again, my breath was just coming in big gasps. He was in horrible pain, and I just tried to lay him down on his back, but there was no real level ground. He was just kind of jammed into some brush. He had a big gash across the one side of his face that extended right into the hairline at the temple. My hands were so slippery with blood—both mine and his—that I was having trouble gripping anything. I just sort of sat down beside him, maybe I passed out for a while, I'm not sure. What I remember next was that it had clouded over and light rain was falling. I could see lightening flickering way off to the west and there were long rumbling claps of thunder. It was really socking in then and cloud cover got lower. The rain was gradually increasing.

We could have sat there a couple of hours, maybe more. By now our clothes were soaking through and I was getting very cold. Ian seemed to go in and out of consciousness. He was in such pain that it was better for him when he wasn't conscious. He kept gasping out in pain, and it was difficult to listen to. And the terrible thing was there was absolutely nothing I could do for him. It had been a warm summer day when we took off, so none of us had so much as a jacket to keep warm with. These northern rains are always cold when they last very long, even in mid-summer. As I sat there shivering with cold, it was hard to remember that up until the crash it had been pleasantly warm. My own body was hurting now, really bad, the shock of the crash and the immediate time afterward had worn off. The throbbing in my arm was increasing, and I could feel my heartbeat in it. Everything was being made worse by the shaking of our bodies from the soaking cold rain. Then I began to wonder how we were going to get out of there or if we even were. I've since learned that planes are supposed to file a flight plan when they operate, but I had no idea if Snider had done that. I thought that probably he hadn't bothered; we'd been doing this everyday for several days.

By then my arm was hurting me so much I knew I had to do something. It was bent outward at a pretty bad angle from the break. I got up on my feet and searched around until I found a couple of stout sticks about a foot long. Now I find it hard to believe what I did next. I put my left hand into the crotch of a low tree and pulled back until my arm was straighter than it had been, then I sat down on the ground and put the sticks down either side of my arm and wrapped my belt around it as tight as I could get it, doing it with one hand. I'm telling this straightforward, but in reality, I was crying out in pain the whole time. And it took a long time to do it, too. I don't even know if it did that much good, it had to be reset later in the hospital, but it didn't look quite as bad. I don't think it did anything for the pain.

It must have been getting very late in the day by then. I don't really remember. But summer days in this country are almost eighteen hours long; it only gets really dark for about three hours. The rain was still falling, if anything harder than it had been. From the shape Ian was in, I knew I had to do something for him, but what? Both of us were completely soaked now and shaking with the cold. I decided to try to build some kind of shelter over him right where he was. I knew I couldn't move him then anyway. It's awful how pain and cold can take the heart right out of you even when you know you've got to act. I don't think I've ever had too many hours harder than the next ones. I got up and looked around and could see nothing to make any kind of shelter out of. I thought once of trying to drag Ian to a grove of big spruce where we'd be mostly out of the rain, but they were at least seventy yards away, totally out of the question. Finally I started picking up pieces of the plane that had torn off it. I managed to drag a chunk of wing material and prop it over him and then I pulled some more off the wreck. I ended up dragging all the loose pieces of the wreck that I could move and just piling them over and around Ian. It wasn't very effective, the rain dripped through, but it was slightly better than nothing at all. Besides, it made me feel like I was doing something to help the situation, though in reality, it amounted to little. I slid in under the pile and pulled myself up beside Ian to try and warm him a bit with my own body.

That's how we spent that first night. The darkness only could have lasted a few hours, but it seemed like it would never end. Ian was conscious now, most of the time anyway, and I've never seen a man in such pain. I guess I did in the War but that was a long time ago. The bleeding around his face had stopped, but the rain had washed down his neck so that his clothing was saturated with it. I remember I kept saying, "Ian, hold on! We'll get out of this!" though I don't think then I really believed it.

When light came, it was still raining steadily and no end seemed in sight. I kept listening for the sound of aircraft, but never heard any. I realized they probably couldn't be flying in this storm, certainly not low enough to see below this dense cloud cover. I got up and walked around the crash site. It's amazing how a forest can cover everything over with its leaf canopy. When the plane had stopped, it was into the edge of the timber again, and I wondered how hard it would be to see from the air even if the sky was clear.

Somehow we got through another day and then another night. When morning came, the rain had slowed to a drizzle, but it hadn't stopped completely. The mosquitoes started up then, or at least I noticed them for the first time since the wreck. Pretty soon there were clouds of them around us, biting every inch of exposed skin. If I've ever been more miserable than I felt that day, I can't recall it. I made Ian a swatter out of the sleeve of Snider's shirt, so he could do something for himself to keep some of those mosquitoes off. I felt so terribly sorry for him and so much anguish that I couldn't do more to help him or ease his pain. I found a coffee cup under the seat in the plane and was able to dip some water out of a depression so he could at least have a drink.

It must have been toward the end of that third day that I finally made up my mind to try and find my way out of there and get help. I really didn't know how much longer Ian could last, but I felt like I just couldn't wait here any longer. Late that day the cloud cover lifted some, and I thought I heard an airplane far off on two different occasions, but I could never see anything.

It was one thing to decide to find a way out of there and another to do it. Before I left, I covered the body of the dead pilot with some leaves and rubbish. The body was swelling by then and there was a definite smell. I stomped the ground down as level as I could so Ian could at least lie back on the ground without roots and brush sticking him in the back and did the best I could to make him a shelter to protect him from the sun, which we hadn't seen now for three days. The rain had stopped falling, but the sky was still heavily clouded over. The mosquitoes were now around us by the millions. They were such a distraction. It was hard to even think. I knew Ian was terrified that I was going but he knew I had to do it. If he was going to get out of there alive, something had to happen soon. Twice early that morning we heard planes far off in the distance but still could never see them.

My plan, which I explained to Ian, was to move back north a ways and find that stream we passed over in the last few seconds or so the plane was in the air, and follow it down to the Peace, where I hoped to hail a boat. There was a fair amount of boat traffic downstream of the big rapids, as boats were also being used in the preliminary surveys of the area to be backed up behind the dam. Then we'd have to come back with a rescue party to take Ian out and Snider's body, too. I think both of us knew how next to impossible that sounded, but there were no other options. Perhaps a helicopter, if any could be gotten on short notice. It didn't sound realistic to me, but I couldn't see alternatives.

I struck out about mid-day in what I believed retraced the back path of the plane in those final moments we were in the air. Clouds of mosquitoes tormented my every step. I had to just shut out of my mind the torture that Ian had to be going though at the crash site.

The clearing in which we had attempted to land was, I discovered, a muskeg swamp. If the plane had come down there, we might have been in worse shape than we were, but then at least there were no big trees. The clearing was surprisingly tiny and in a very short time, I was back in a very dense forest trying to stay on the course I had decided on and not end up going in circles, which was my greatest fear. I kept hoping the sun would come out so I could orient myself by it, but for the longest time, it didn't. After I'd been out for an hour or so, I again thought I heard a plane but never saw anything due to the dense forest. It sounded as though it were way off to the north of where I was. It also confused my thinking some, too, for I wondered if I should go back to the wreck and wait there as I originally thought to do. I delayed for a while, tormented by indecision and mosquitoes. Finally I decided the best course was to follow through with what I'd started. Besides, I was now a fair distance from the wreck and finding it again in this trackless bush might not be that easy. Then I got lucky. The sun finally broke through the clouds and blue sky began to show, at least as much of it as I could see through the trees. I figured I was still pretty much on course from the angle of the sun and the time of day. I ran onto the edge of a sluggish stream a short time after that. There wasn't much current at first, but there was enough to convince me that it had to flow toward the big river. I really had no idea if it was the one I had seen from the air just before we went down. Knowing how streams can meander all over the place, I hated to have to stick to the edge but didn't have enough confidence of my direction to leave it and strike out cross country. Most of the time the walking was very difficult. There was blowdown timber everywhere, making walking extremely slow. The whole area was thick in rose bush and they were sticking into my legs through my thin pants at every step. The mosquitoes were so thick they were just a cloud, flying into my eyes, up my nose, into my mouth.

Now the hunger that I had been repressing for three days became intense. I would have eaten almost anything had I been able to find it. But I couldn't even find any berries, though I didn't deviate from my course to look for them. My stomach was growling and my legs felt weak. I would have given anything for a piece of bread.

It got noticeably warmer, first, because of my exertion and, second, because the sun was out now. I kept doggedly on, knowing I couldn't afford to stop and rest, trying to blot out the pain in my left arm.

It was sometime very late in the afternoon when I stumbled onto them: A grizzly sow with that year's cubs watching me from the opposite bank of the creek as I stumbled out into the relative open of the now steep stream bank. As soon as I saw them, I froze; a tingle of fear ran down my spine like an electric current. They had seen me before I saw them. All three were standing rock still, looking at me across the stream. They were close enough that I could clearly see the guard hairs on the sow's neck standing straight up. She stared intently at me for a few seconds and, for an instant, I though she was going to come after me. Then one of the cubs bolted away into the timber, then the other. She hesitated, then let out a deep "ruff" and ran after them. I waited for quite a while; I could feel my heart hammering in my chest, and I was breathing like I was climbing a steep hill. Bears are so unpredictable anyway, and after my ordeal with that boar at the trapping cabin a few years earlier, I was really nervous. Finally I set off again, but for the next hour or so, I caught myself starting from every shadow or forest sound.

The stream was picking up some momentum by then and was also picking up volume from little rivulets that kept joining it. It was getting late now and I was very tired. I listened for planes whenever I could but never heard anything. By ten o'clock, it was getting fairly dark in the timber, but I kept on. Then I began to hear something that sounded kind of like a hum. At first I thought I was imagining it, but I kept hearing something. Then I realized what it was: the sound of running water, big water. But how far away? Air currents can project sound great distances. I kept going even though by then I knew I was on the edge of exhaustion, I couldn't keep it up much longer. It was then past midnight and under the trees I was having a hard time to find my footing even though my eyes had adjusted to the darkness. The water had stopped dripping off the vegetation, but my clothing was soaked with sweat and dew. I started to feel light-headed and very weak. The hum I'd heard hours before I could hear clearly now and it sounded very close. The stream began to widen into a floodplain, studded with boulders and piles of logs thrust up in the spring runoff.

I pushed through a heavy stand of willows and cottonwoods and then I saw it. The great river running just below the bank I was on like a great living thing, flashing in the light of the clear night sky. The bank where I stood dropped nearly straight down to the water, the banks undercut by times of high water. I figured, though in the quasi-darkness it was hard to tell for sure, that the bank was at least sixteen feet above the river. I remember sitting down right where I emerged to rest for what I thought would be a few minutes; I was too exhausted to go on without a brief halt. The next thing I remember was sitting up and it was full daylight. I looked at my watch and it was 4:30 a.m. I must have been sitting there asleep for maybe three hours. I pulled myself to my feet; I felt very weak despite my rest and I knew I had to eat something soon or I couldn't keep on. I started to walk downstream, trying to clear my head, trying to summon the energy to continue. After a few minutes it seemed like the current of the water was moving faster, and when I looked carefully at it, I could see clearly that it was. Also there was increasing noise and within a few hundred feet, I could see why. I was right at the head of some very rough-looking rapids. Moving aways further along the bank, I could see high vertical cliffs ahead of me on both sides of the river. The river seemed to elbow to the right suddenly, and I could see that the water was constricting into a narrow channel with a sound almost like distant thunder. This must have accounted for the humming noise I'd been hearing even though I had been far away on the tributary. Massive boulders stuck up in places out of the boiling water and huge standing waves showed there were others just beneath the surface.

For a few minutes I almost lost heart. I felt so sick and weak and looking at what lay ahead, I realized I'd have to go up over those bluffs the river had sawed through, and at that point, I couldn't even see where those rapids ended. It was clear that no boats were going to be coming up these rapids, at least not power boats. I had read somewhere that the old voyageurs had pulled canoes up these waters with long ropes, though looking at the boiling cauldron in front of me I couldn't even imagine how they did it. I only knew that if I was going to find help, I'd have to get downstream of those awful rapids; nothing mechanical would be coming above them. For a few minutes I almost gave up.

Once I began to pull up the rock bluff that lay in front of me, I discovered that if I stayed right at the very edge of the drop, I could avoid the worst of the blowdown timber that seemed to wall off my progress everywhere else. It was also very clear that a single misstep would send me over the edge to certain death in the furious water below. But it was my only option. By then I didn't have the power to get through the blowdown just a few feet to my right. There was a strong breeze in that canyon and for a while at least the mosquito plague abated.

It could have been a mile, I'm not sure, maybe it was a lot less, but it was an eternity for me. Looking back on it, I was past sixty years of age, my left arm was useless, I'd had no food whatsoever for three and a half days, and my strength was nearly completely gone. I think I was starting to hallucinate some: I kept seeing people who were not there. One of them was my deceased son, Jack. I kept seeing him just ahead of me and he seemed to be beckoning me to keep moving forward. There were others, I can't remember now who they were.

I seemed to snap back into reality, and I was looking down into a great pool at the foot of the rapids. Downstream a hundred yards maybe, a powerboat was moored to a clump of trees hanging off the bank and out over the water. There were people on the narrow beach beside the boat. They were loading barrels and other things into the boat. For a second I thought I was still hallucinating. I squeezed my eyes shut and opened them; the boat was still there. It was real! I started to yell, but I must not have been able to make much noise, because they didn't seem to hear me. I started toward them, down the steep bluff, moving back from the rocky edge. I caught my foot on a log or something and fell face first into a pile of dead trees. It must have made a loud noise, or maybe I cried out, I'm not sure. When I pulled myself to my feet, there were two guys staring in my direction. I waved and shouted again, and for a minute they just stood and stared. Then they started walking toward me.

"You know, Marta, most of my life it seems like I haven't been particularly lucky. But I was lucky for sure that time. If those guys in that boat hadn't had a radio and there hadn't been a helicopter at Chetwynd—most of the time there isn't—we'd never have gotten Horvold out of there in time to save his life. I'm pretty sure even a few more hours might have been too long. When they set that chopper down next to the wreck, I didn't really think we'd find him alive. That chopper pilot had a hell of a time getting down anyway through all that brush and timber. I didn't think we'd even be able to land at first, but we did and only about fifty yards from the wreck!"

"But, Liam, you said you were totally gone, exhausted, when you found the boat. How on earth did you keep going for another ten hours?"

"That doctor at Chetwynd. They had phoned ahead to tell him they were bringing me in. Anyway, he gave me a couple of shots. Must have been mostly painkillers. It held me up for the rest of the ordeal. I knew I had to go back on the helicopter; they'd have never found the wreck in time, maybe not at all. After all, search aircraft had failed to find it in two days of searching. It was really tough to see from the air if you didn't know exactly where to look. I'll never forget the smell, when we set down and got over to the where the plane was. That pilot's body was bloated to two or three times its normal size. Never have I smelled anything like it before. It was really warm by the time we got back there. Ian was right where I'd left him and at first sight, I thought he was gone. His face was monstrously swollen, a reddish black color from all the insect torment. So were his hands. There was still dried blood all over him. Both his legs were swollen beyond belief. The first thing the medics did was cut off his trousers so they could look at the damage to his legs. I'm telling you, they looked awful. I wondered then if they could save them even if he survived. He was delirious and totally incoherent, but when they gave him water, he guzzled it until they made him stop. His eyelids were totally caked shut with dried blood, but his face was so swollen I doubt if he could have seen anything anyway. Those two medics knew their stuff. They gave him some injections, got him onto a canvas stretcher and carried him to the helicopter. After they got him in there, they hung a bottle near him and had some kind of liquid running into him through a needle they had put in his arm. After that, the medics and the pilot rolled poor Snider's body into a huge canvas sack and tied it shut. Even then you could smell it some through the material. They loaded his body in the back of the helicopter and we got ready to lift off. It was pretty spooky. The pilot had to zigzag back and forth as we rose up to miss all the trees that were in the way. It didn't take as long as you'd think to get to Fort St. John."

"Why didn't you go to Chetwynd? Surely it was a lot closer."

"It was," Liam said, "but I guess they'd decided that it would be easier to airlift Ian out of Fort St. John where they had a bigger airport. When we got there, they took him straight off the chopper and onto another plane and flew him directly to Edmonton."

"You looked more tired than I've ever seen you," Marta said, "when I met you there at the airport. And your arm seemed twice the size it should have been."

"They splinted it, the medics on the chopper that is, before we headed out to get Ian. After they got Ian sent off to Edmonton, one of them drove me back into Fort St. John to the hospital. I didn't really want to stay there but the doctors took one look at me and put me in a bed. They must have given me something to put me out. I don't really remember. But the next day when I woke up my arm was in a cast and I had one of these needles running stuff into my veins out of a bottle suspended over the bed. It looked just like what the medics did with Ian. Just like what I had that other time in Edmonton."

"The doctor says you've got to keep that cast on for quite a while yet, Liam, so don't start thinking about getting it off right away so you can get back to work."

"Well, my arm feels pretty good now and this cast itches something awful. Besides the bone must have knitted back together by this time; hell, it's been nearly eight weeks. What good is it now?"

"Listen, Liam, you're going to follow that doctor's orders. Remember he said he had to put some steel pins in there to get everything back together. It's not like it's the first time you hurt it. After that bear thing, you were lucky it healed like it did. And now this. I want you to be patient and do what they told you. Liam, you are lucky to be alive, so a few extra weeks to let everything heal properly is not too much to endure. Liam, I was so terrified when they came and said the plane was missing. And when they couldn't even find it after days of searching. I didn't give up hope because I know you're a survivor and if you had a chance you'd get back; but I have to tell you I was severely tested. I never slept or ate from the time they told me you were missing until I got that message from Chetwynd. I'm just so glad your life was spared again, and you came back to us."

"Marta, I'm a very lucky man because I had you to come back to, you and the rest of the family. We've had a great life together, Marta, and I'm not ready for it to end yet. And I made a vow that if I got out of that mess alive, I was going to do some of the things we've talked about so much and never done. Like building you the house you've been wanting and I've been putting off."

"Oh, Liam, the house we've got is all right. It has seen us through a lot of years. It's sound and warm and it's home. I guess we don't need anything more."

"Yes," Liam said, "we do need something more. You deserve a real house, one with smooth sides, not just logs on every wall like this one. I promised you before we ever came here that one day I'd build you a good house, like what you were used to in the old country, and I've never come through. But this last incident convinced me that we don't have unlimited time to realize our dreams. I could have just as easily been dead, but I'm not."

"This log house," said Marta, "has served us well, something we built with our own hands without help from a single soul. If I don't get another, it won't matter. I'll still be contented with it."

"No," said Liam. "I want to build that house we always talked about. And what I can't do, we'll hire done. We've got the resources and the money to do it now if we want to. What else could we spend it on?"

"If you really want to, okay," said Marta. "I guess it would be pretty exciting to live in a house with lots of room, a big kitchen that is separate from the living room, lots of bedrooms for when the kids come to visit, lots of windows, a house where the wires are hidden away in the walls, not just stapled to the logs."

Marta and Liam talked on and on about the home they would build. For Marta, it would be the realization of a long-held dream, something she'd fantasized about for decades, but she had never really pressed Liam about it. The old house had served well, she mused, but it was time to move on.

"Ladies and Gentlemen, the next event is one you've been waiting for, the grandaddy of all rodeo competitions. I'm talking, of course, about the saddle bronc riding. This event pits big tough broncy horses against the skill of the cowboy who must stay in the saddle for eight seconds with only the buckrein to hold on to...." The announcer carried on in a powerful baritone, his voice obviously practiced in his craft. It rose, fell and droned at times, but he kept up a constant patter.

Tassy and Karla hung back timidly at first from the high fence separating the arena and its contestants from the spectators. Mingled smells of tobacco smoke, manure, and frying hamburgers made a powerful and heady mix of aromas that wafted on the warm summer air. There had been recent rains, but the dirt of the arena had been churned and trampled by livestock until dust rose in a haze from the feet of animals and humans alike. It was a clear July day, a blue sky with heavy cloud hanging on the western horizon that promised showers later in the afternoon. But with the present excitement of the rodeo crowd, no one seemed concerned.

Tassy was spending a few days in town with her close friend Karla and her family. She had hoped to find a summer job of some sort, but as yet she hadn't even had time to look. In September she would be starting her final year of high school, and she and Marta had agreed that it was time for her to be earning some money of her own. In fact, Tassy had been pestering Marta to get a summer job for several years now, and at last Marta had relented. Before, she had always insisted that there was plenty of work for Tassy at the ranch, which there was. Marta clearly saw that Tassy would soon be leaving home on her own and the Brennans couldn't keep her protected at the home place forever. And, after all, she needed to acquire some employment skills. At age sixteen, Tassy was a very good student, did well in her school studies, but apart from the many tasks she had been given at home, had never really had a job. Or a real boss.

There was a colorful collection of northern humanity gathered this day at what then was one of the biggest social events of the year, the annual Fort St. John rodeo. Mingled with the curious townfolk were oil field hands, farm families, ranch operators, and a goodly number of natives from the many reserves scattered through the area. Added to this mix were fractious adolescent males intent on an afternoon of surreptitious boozing and ogling the plentiful female population. Their female counterparts strode about in tight fitting jeans, sometimes topped with western hats and boots. The actual contestants in the rodeo events were a curious mixture of farm lads mostly entered to impress the girls, young outfitter guides and wranglers escaped from their guiding duties for a day or two, plus a few serious contestants both native and non. All milled about the chutes, clad in traditional leather chaps, spurred boots, and western hats of individual bent. Some of the hats, more often the native ones, sported hawk or eagle feathers stuck into the hatband and poking off the back of the rim. A constant commotion issued from the heavy wooden bucking chutes as animals were run into them from a series of alleys and small holding pens directly behind. On a roofed stand, a few feet above the chutes, the rodeo announcer was ensconced with a couple of assistants. Although the rodeo was supposed to adhere to a tight time frame, there were constant delays in the action: a bull took out a section of the arena fence and it had to be repaired; horses had to be re-rigged or re-saddled to suit their riders; an ambulance was brought in to gather up a contestant who had been injured, and on it went. But few seemed to mind; most hardly noticed. It was the heraldry that mattered, the unfolding of the timeless western pageant of man versus beast, so easily understood and admired by the western psyche. Time was not a major concern—unless, of course, rain intervened.

Tassy and Karla hung back a little, intimidated a bit by the brassiness of the women and the bravado of the males. But the sounds, the smells, and the devil-may-care attitude was infectious, carnival-like. They edged toward the hamburger stand and found themselves at the back of a noisy crowd of revelers enveloped in a pungent cloud of cigarette smoke. Everyone seemed happy and there was a noticeable absence of normal decorum. A couple of guys they knew from school sidled up and engaged them in loud garbled conversation. Their glassy eyes and loud slurred speech betrayed them as quickly as the reek of alcohol from their persons. The girls edged away and into the pack waiting at the hamburger stand. At last they were waited on by the beleaguered servers, took their burgers and pop and looked for a place to sit in the moiling wooden stands set just back from the arena fence. They sat down quickly when a couple to the side of them got up and moved off.

"Okay, folks, here we go! Your first saddle bronc contestant coming out of chute No. 1 is...Spence Morgan from Baldonnel, BC, on a horse called Big George." The gate on the near chute sprung open revealing a large-boned rangy-looking pinto, a cowboy sitting in the saddle, hat pulled down nearly over his eyes. For an instant the animal seemed not to notice the gate was open, then he sprang out, broke into a terrified run, and after covering about two-thirds the distance across the arena, ducked his head and took a long crow hop. The young neophyte on his back hung on during the initial run but was rocketed high over the horse's neck at the first jump, landing unceremoniously on his back in the churned dust. He immediately jumped to his feet oblivious to the poor showing he had made. He trotted back to the chutes with a wide smile on his face, his pinned-on line number flapping on his back. Several of his fellows darted out to slap him on the shoulder, gesticulating and guffawing. The young rider was kicking the dirt with his feet but was obviously quite pleased with himself

"Let's give that young man a big hand," blathered the announcer. "All he's gonna get today is what you give him." The crowd applauded lustily with loud cheers and whistles. With varying degrees of ineptitude the next half dozen riders performed, only one staying on for the required eight seconds, and that because the horse did little more than gallop the perimeter of the arena.

"Our next rider, well known around the Peace Country, is making a name for himself this year, having won money at the Calgary Stampede and several places in between. I'm speaking, of course, of Royce Eklo of Moberly Lake. He's drawn a big buckskin horse today called Powder River...."

At the sound of the man's name, Tassy sat up and began to pay more attention. Before, she had been too distracted by the antics of the noisy crowd to pay close attention to what was happening in the arena. There was a loud smashing sound of hooves on wood and the chute gate shot open. Almost simultaneously the powerful buckskin leaped high into the air, almost brushing off the cowboy's hat on the overhead bracing. Ducking his head far between his front legs, the squealing horse took several twisting jumps, traveling only a few feet into the arena but very high into the air. This rider was very different from his inept predecessors. His spurs moved back and forth from the horse's shoulder to right behind the saddle in rhythm with the horse's frantic leaps. The horse grew even more intent, his back feet kicking high above the rider's head, his front feet hitting the earth and driving forward in powerful jolts. For the first time during the whole of that event, people were paying attention. This man could ride! The buckskin whipped around and came down the length of the chute, scattering the cluster of spectators and hangers-on. Each high twisting jump brought the legs of the rider within inches of the chute gates. And as the horse jumped high, daylight could be seen between the saddle and the rider's behind, but he never really seemed in danger of being "piled." The eight-second buzzer rang and the crowd applauded wildly; the two pickup men moved in and tried to get on either side of the still firing bronc. The cowboy now had one hand tightly gripping the saddle horn and was finally grabbed out of the saddle by a burly pickup man who eased him to the ground as the bronc continued to buck furiously around the arena. The crowd was on their feet cheering and stomping. The slender native cowboy doffed his hat gaily at the crowd and walked stiff-leggedly back to the chutes to the expressed admiration of his peers.

"Uh...could you talk to me...just for a minute?" Tassy had finally caught up to the young native cowboy when he finally walked out of the arena and behind the holding pens. Tassy had been biding her time looking for a chance to talk to him. She'd been far too shy to go into the arena or behind the chutes where he had been milling about with other contestants. It was evident that not all his female admirers, and there appeared to be no shortage, were loathe to pursue him openly. Several girls, mostly native but not all, had flirted shamelessly with him while Tassy waited her chance.

At Tassy's voice, Royce turned around, looked her up and down and put on his best smile. "Hey, how ya doin?" he said, pushing his hat back off his forehead. He had perfect white teeth Tassy noted. She also was not oblivious to his slender cowboy figure or his hawk-like but very handsome face. Taken all in all, he was definitely a pretty dashing figure. And he was well aware of it. In fact, he was used to being the center of attention for admiring females. He liked what he saw, for Tassy herself, was used to turning heads.

For a few seconds, they stood, Royce sort of appraising her, Tassy trying to find her tongue.

"Your name...your last name?"

"Eklo, Royce Eklo. You gotta tell me your name." He moved closer to her. He put his right hand behind her neck. Tassy stiffened and stepped slightly back, lifting his hand off her neck and dropping it.

"Hey, honey, what ya say we get together for a drink maybe, soon as I'm done. Still got a bull to ride first."

Tassy looked carefully at him and said, "My name is Tassy Brennan. Actually my real name is Patricia, but everyone calls me Tassy."

"Tassy, hey great! I like it better than Patricia...suits you better. Where you from anyways? Don't remember ever seein' you around. You live at one of the reserves or what?"

"No, actually I live near Lynx Creek on the Peace, on the Hope Road."

"Oh, yeah?" he said quizzically.

"I live with my family there, actually my grandparents."

"What, your folks, your parents, that is, they're not around?"

"Both my parents are dead," Tassy said, looking him up and down but her body language tacitly discouraging him from touching her again.

"Oh, too bad. You miss 'em, I guess."

"That's really what I wanted to talk to you about," Tassy said.

Roy's smile faded a bit and slight look of puzzlement replaced it. "You wanted to talk to me about...what?"

"Well," she stuttered, "well, my mother's name was Eklo, at least as far as I know."

"Yeah? It was Eklo?" Royce looked even more flummoxed.

"And..and...as far as I know...I think she was from Moberly Lake."

"What was her name? Her first name?"

"Her name was Leena, Leena Eklo."

Royce stepped back slightly and looked hard at Tassy. "But Leena's dead. Been dead a long time I guess...long time...too much booze, I guess."

"You knew her?" Tassy asked in a quiet voice.

"Yeah, I knew her. Leena was my sister. Lots older than me though. Can't remember her much. Been dead quite a while. Noah, that's my pa, he knows. He'll know how long it's been since she died."

"I know it's been a long time," said Tassy. "I can't even remember her very well."

"So...if Leena's your mom...who's your dad?"

"Was," said Tassy. "My father was Willy Brennan."

"Don't know them Brennans, I guess," Royce said. He seemed to be losing interest in the conversation. "Georgina lives with my other sister Melba now, with her old man and their bunch. Pretty wild buncha kids, I guess. Always gettin' in trouble and stuff."

"Georgina?"

"Yeah, you know, Leena's other girl."

"Leena has another daughter?"

"Sure. You don't know her? Younger. About thirteen or fourteen. Somewhere round there, I guess. Ain't seen any of Melba's bunch for a while now."

"Where do they live? Do they live around here?"

"Sure. Still livin' at the reserve. Jimmy, her old man, he's got a job in Chetwynd at the mill."

Tassy spied Karla a few yards away, motioning her to come. "I gotta go now." Tassy said, "but I want to talk again sometime. Can we do that?"

"Sure, you bet. Anytime," said Royce, pulling at his hat. He eyed Tassy thoughtfully as she moved away from him. "Sure too bad," he muttered as he watched her striking figure walk away. "Sure too bad she's a relative."

"And he says Leena had another child, a daughter; her name's Georgina. Royce said she lives with another of Leena's sisters at Moberly Lake."

The car wound slowly along the river road from Hudson's Hope to the home place. It was a late August Sunday, overcast and slightly windy. The first signs of fall were starting to appear on the hillsides and the wooded riverbank. Poplar in places were gradually turning from a very dark green to brownish yellows, though greens and the blue of the clear running river still dominated. The heavily grazed hillsides on their left looked very dry, cattle trails visible everywhere, even on the steepest slopes. Marta and Tassy were returning from their near weekly trip to the sparsely attended Anglican Church at Hudson's Hope. It was the only time when either of them ever dressed formally or wore dresses. Sunday had become a special time for them, a time to visit and for Tassy, at least, a time to confide. Both of them looked forward to these trips, as much for the social event it had become as for the spiritual interlude Marta had originally intended. In truth, Marta, who had been raised a Catholic, did not delve beneath the surface of the Anglican doctrine and though she detected considerable difference in what she heard at the Anglican Church from the Catholicism of her youth, she did not trouble over it. It was enough, she felt, to recognize the hand of a creator in all things and to abide by a moral code which she believed was extant in the teachings of most religions. She had never been able to arouse much interest in church participation in Liam, himself also of Catholic background. He had told her many times he'd had his fill of the church as a child and wanted no part of it now. To him it was a part of the old he'd shucked off when he had left Ireland for good. He did not discourage Marta's rekindled religious participation though he secretly wondered that she had chosen a protestant church.

"What do you think Georgina's like, Gramma? I mean...do you think she knows about me? I wonder how old she is exactly. Does she go to school?"

"Well, I'm sure she must go to school," Marta said. "It's the law now. But then I really don't know whether any attempt is being made to get natives to comply."

"Have you ever gone there, to Moberly Lake, I mean?" Tassy asked. It was clear that this new piece of knowledge about her deceased mother and her unseen and unknown relatives, so close by but never seen, was weighing on her consciousness.

"Yes, I've been there a couple of times. The road to Chetwynd goes right through Moberly Lake, or did the last time I was there."

"What did it look like there? Do they live in houses just like us? Did you meet any of the people?"

"No, I didn't meet anyone there. I don't really remember ever stopping at all. As for the houses, there looked to be some good ones and quite a few that were in very poor shape. You know, Tassy, sometimes native people don't look at things quite the same as we do, as whites do. Some of them have just really started to live all the time in one place, in one house, so they maybe don't pay as much attention to appearances, to keeping it looking neat or repaired. Things like that. They're still learning to live a new way. It's probably been hard for many of them. This country was a lot different, not so very long ago. It's changed a great deal even since your grandfather and I came here. You'd hardly have recognized it from the way it is now."

Tassy listened, hanging on Marta's every word, trying to garner a picture and an understanding from her grandmother's edited description of native life. She knew that Marta always tried to soften the reality of things for her; she knew Marta never overtly criticized anyone's lifestyle, that she always defended natives even when others, including most of the people she knew, found their lives insufferable. Tassy knew far more about natives, about their susceptibility to the vices of the white culture than she let on to Marta. Her years at school had not been wasted in that regard.

"Gramma, I want to ask you something, and I hope it won't upset you, but I've got to do it. I know that I'm part of our family, the Brennan family; we've talked about this so many times. But I'm also part of them. I'm also part of the natives, part of my mother, of her family, of the Eklos. I just feel like I need to know them. You know...meet them and...I don't know…I just need to do it…to know who I am. I…I have a sister there and a family, too…people I don't even know, but I feel like I need to. Can you understand that? I don't want to upset you or make you feel bad about it, it's just there, that's all."

Marta pulled the car to the side of the road, stopped it and turned off the engine. She stared out across the valley, across the river to the hills beyond. She was silent for a very long time. Finally she turned, took Tassy's hand in hers, and spoke thoughtfully.

"Sweetheart, you know Liam and I have never kept anything from you. We've always been up front about your birth mother, about Willie, your father…we've done that from the time we felt you could understand. But there's something I have to tell you now, that we've kind of left out or glossed over. After your mother, Leena, left you with us that last time and then came for you to take you back with her again,…well, we refused to let her take you back. In truth, Tassy, we took you away from her, from your own mother. And even now I'm not sorry…we felt like we had no choice, that we had to do it for your good to save you from the kind of life you'd have had with your mother. Tassy, we did that because Leena was lost… lost to the world that you and I live in. And from what we know of her life after that, we did the right thing. I'm sure her very early death was a result of alcohol, though we have never really been told. So…so what I'm saying is, I'm not very confident that your mother's family doesn't harbor some anger against the Brennans for, maybe in their eyes, stealing you away from them. In short, myself and maybe even you, may not be welcome there, at the reserve, I mean. It's hard to know how we are seen by them. They may want nothing to do with us…with you. You have to be prepared for that if you go ahead and try to make contact with them. I'm not telling you not to do it, but you have to prepare yourself for almost anything, maybe to be rebuffed altogether. And what you're going to see there at the reserve may be a shock to you. I'd say it's going to be troubling, at the least. I know those people have mainly got us to thank for it, but I'm afraid alcohol is ruining a lot of their lives."

The rest of the trip back to the ranch was taken mostly in silence; both Marta and Tassy lost in their own thoughts, not sure what more there was to be said. As they turned off the main road onto the long lane to the house, Tassy finally spoke.

"Gramma, please don't be hurt or upset by anything we talked about today. I just want you to know how happy I've been to be part of the family, part of this place. And I am so very grateful to you and Grampa for all that you've done for me. I'm going to say that the things you did, when I was a little child, well, I know now that you did the right thing for me, and I love you for it."

Marta parked the car next to the house and the two of them got out and held each other in a long embrace.

"So when we gonna have some dinner around here?" came a theatrical voice.

They looked up and Liam was standing on the porch looking down at them.

"We're gonna have a great dinner right away," said Tassy as she climbed the steps and hugged Liam. "We're gonna have roast beef, gravy, mashed potatoes, turnips, all the things you like the best!" Tassy left Liam standing there and skipped through the door and into the kitchen.

"You must've had a good trip," said Liam, raising an eyebrow at Marta.

"We did," said Marta, putting her arm around his waist. "We surely did."

"You looked like you were frowning when you got out of the car."

"I'll tell you about it later. Let me help Tassy get dinner going."

Construction on the house was to have begun in early summer of that year. Liam had intended to start when the last frost was out of the ground, but there had been continual demands on his time. Carson was far away most of that summer on a big site east of Fort Nelson. Liam had been kept constantly busy keeping the parts and fuel moving to the job site and helping Joanna with the paper trail. There was another job going as well, but not so far away. It was an on-site job involving a compressor station in the Halfway Valley. Carson and Liam had selected Kirby to oversee and foreman that project, but there had been the usual problems with equipment breakdowns and roads in very poor condition. Normally little oil field work was done in the temperate months, the companies preferring to wait for freezeup and avoid the problems of constantly wet terrain and boggy, near impassable roads. This year, for whatever reason, there was no lull when breakup came. Most of the crews stayed in the bush and slogged on, many of the workers complaining bitterly, as summer was their time to do other things. Many of them were farmers and ranchers, so much of the construction had to be done without their experienced hands, greenhorns and men of lesser experience filling in. This exacerbated an already difficult situation and the poor ground conditions teamed with inexperienced help culminated in added headaches for men like Liam and Carson. Through the months of July and August, Carson had not been home at all, and Liam only intermittently.

A few days earlier, Ian Horvold had visited Liam and Marta at the ranch. He had only partially recovered from his terrible ordeal of the previous summer, and he still was on crutches. It had taken the expertise of the best surgeons in the country and several operations to save his shattered legs. His once portly frame was down considerably from what it had been before the wreck and his face was still pale and gaunt. He was just returning to work when he stopped at the ranch and spent a day with the Brennans. It had not been lost on him that he owed his life to Liam's clearheaded actions and toughness after their harrowing accident, and he was effusive in his praise and admiration of Liam's help.

Earlier Liam had accepted contracts to begin piling timber as soon as possible. The building of the dam seemed imminent at that point and the two spent several hours in discussing the construction timetable. Already, equipment was being erected on the dam site and a mammoth conveyer belt being set up to move material where it could be used in the dam itself. Much of the titanic earthmoving work had been let to huge international companies, but there was work for a myriad of smaller operations like Outlook Contracting. Horvold said the time frame for the dam's construction was in the neighborhood of five years from start to finish.

When Ian had gone, Liam saddled one of his horses and took a ride ostensibly to check his yearlings that were summering on crown land adjacent to the ranch—the older cows, as Liam had promised, were now summering in the '98 country many miles northeast—but he paid only cursory attention to the cattle. Today his mind was on the building of the dam, a project so immense that it beggared his imagination. He still was riddled with self-doubt about his and his company's participation in an event that he detested with every fiber of his being. But there was really no compromise: the dam project, only a few years ago unthinkable, was going forward. And he and everyone else who protested it had found themselves beaten. It was going to happen, it was happening—and there was no going back, it was going to be done. And, he reasoned for the thousandth time, he could stand on the sidelines and wring his hands and later accept the inevitable or he could see that his little operation—and in comparison to the international conglomerates involved, it was little—got some of the action, some of the spoils. Was it so wrong, he wondered, or could he have done more to prevent it? But the thought was ridiculous; no individual or even group could stand before the will of the province. He was doing now the only thing a prudent person could do. But the dichotomy of his position would not give him any solace. He wondered idly how he would be seen by his neighbors and peers. A Judas? A hypocrite? That many of them were lining up to do the same as he, did not salve his conscience. It had, after all, been he who first sounded the alarm over the dam construction, he who had been the strongest, most persistent voice of opposition. And now what had he done? Caved in to the inevitable and was now prepared to help it come to pass.

Pushing his horse to climb higher on the steep gully-riddled hillside, he saw a doe and two fawns watching him casually from across a narrow ravine. He stopped the winded horse, its sides now wet, sweat dripping off its belly. Gazing off to the southwest across the great river, he was mesmerized for the thousandth time by the drama of the great mountain ranges that slashed across the entire skyline north to south. Their white summits were clearly outlined against the clear blue behind them. It was a pity, he thought, that those ranges couldn't be seen from the home place only two miles or so below him. The great river valley with its densely timbered south bank walled off this panorama from river bottom height at the ranch.

This time of year the water flow in the river was gradually dropping after the high water months of mid-summer. Sandbars and spits were visible above water now where they hadn't been a few weeks ago. Looking upstream he could see the familiar densely timbered islands that pocked the main river channel. He could just see a silver boat tied up in the lee end of the nearest island. Most likely sport fishermen who were becoming more prevalent as the years flowed by. Liam mused on the contradictions he saw: he who had lived beside this great watercourse for nearly half a century had yet to wet a fishing line in its waters. Actually, he amended, that wasn't totally true. He vaguely remembered setting trotlines in the deep holes upstream of the flat in those far away days when he and Marta had gone months at a time without seeing any human visitors. But that had been totally removed from any semblance of sport fishing, not like the boaters he saw these days who kept only certain species and hurled the rest back like so much offal. The fishing they'd done then had been totally in earnest, and failure to catch something—any kind of fish was welcome—might mean a meal of potatoes and stewed vegetables bereft of the flesh of fish or fowl. Hell, there had been times in the genesis of their life here when they didn't even have that. He dimly remembered once eating the last scraps of flour in a batch of biscuits not knowing clearly where the next meal might come from. Framed against the plenty of their current lives, it all seemed so far away as to be only imagined, but he knew it had been so.

He urged the slightly revitalized horse further up the hillside. The convex slope began to level away now to the fringes of the as yet primordial forest that lay on the plateau above. Looking up river, from any height on these rutted hills paralleling the north side of the river had always been one of Liam's favorite vistas. He never seemed to tire of it; it always seemed new and slightly different from previous sightings.

"God never made a more beautiful, more perfect place," he heard himself utter out loud. He was a bit surprised at himself, for though he had a deep reverence for the sublime in nature, he was not given to poetic utterance. He halted the horse again on a fairly flat indentation created by lounging cattle. For a moment he just wanted to soak in some of the deep peacefulness of the moment.

It was one of those rare late summer afternoons when the weather seemed perfection. A very light breeze blew up from the valley, light fluffy cumulous clouds drifted calmly overhead in a brilliantly blue sky. The sun seemed warm but not hot. On a day like this, it was hard to imagine how this place would be again in a few months. In his mind's eye he saw the black and white of the coming winter landscape, the dried out streaks of grasses edged against the snow-choked timber, the stark leafless deciduous trees plastered willy nilly with the evergreen conifers. The great moving river stopped as though in death, sheathed in four feet of ice and shrouded by the same everlasting white blanket that covered the rest of the world. The terrible coming cold, cold that numbed and struck like a blow that sucked the life out of all living…he willed himself away from this grey vision. This was not the time to be worrying about the vagaries of the ever-revolving seasons. It was a beautiful day—best to leave off thinking beyond it.

Horse and rider were almost in the deep timber of the plateau when a great grey-brown shape lumbered up out of the deep ravine they were paralleling. The saddle horse snorted and shied a bit from the huge bull moose, though it had seen enough of them in its life not to be very alarmed. Liam was slightly awed, as he always was by these great creatures. It amazed him, this animal composed of parts seemingly just thrown together—great bulbous nose on a long narrow muzzle, huge mule-like ears, humped, heavily-haired shoulders behind a ridiculously short neck, the whole discordant figure of a narrow but extremely deep hearted body mounted on heavy, impossibly long legs. How could anything composed of these ugly parts end up in something that, taken as a whole, had a beauty, a grace of its own? The great bull stopped and stared back; everything in its profile personified power. The bull eyed them mildly for a long moment, then it walked a few steps toward the heavy timber, finally breaking into a trot as it disappeared into the trees. Liam watched impassively from his saddle, then as the horse leveled off just before the thicker timber, he realized he was intercepting the old trail that ran north to his trapline.

As he struck the trail, Liam reined in his mount for a moment. He hadn't even thought about going over to the old line cabin when he had left the house. From here it was about a three-hour ride, most of it through heavy timber skirting the numerous ravines that cut through the land. He got off the horse, stretched his legs and tried to decide if he wanted to spend the time it would take to ride over to the cabin. A month earlier there would have been no decision, unless he needed to go there: the insect pests would have made the ride miserable. But today with the dryer weather of late summer, the mosquitoes and black flies would be past their zenith. And, he mused, he hadn't actually been over there himself for nearly three years. With the multiplication of duties coming from his construction business, he had reluctantly seen that he could not devote any time to running his trapline—not if he really meant to prosper in business. So the trapline had been let to a fellow from Hudson's Hope who had operated it for the past three winters. Liam received little rent from the line; the man claimed that fur had been scarce and prices not particularly good. Liam thought back over the many years he had trapped up here. Once he'd learned the business, he had never really had poor years. He also remembered being careful of overtrapping an area. He had operated the line almost like a farm: always harvesting some pelts but never taking too many. It seemed to have worked, for he had enjoyed a long run of good years.

Liam remounted and started the none-too-enthused horse up the trail. He thought back on those many years he had moved up and down this trail. The money he'd gotten out of his fur had never been much; compared with his income now, it seemed paltry, but he had not forgotten how much they'd relied on the tiny income in those years when it was nearly their only cash money.

The trail seemed more closed in than he remembered. That the old burn through which it ran was growing up was plain. What was also plain to Liam was that virtually no brush had been cut off this trail since he'd run the line himself. From what he could see, none at all. Small stumps from trees he had cut more than 40 years ago could still be seen if he looked closely. Liam hadn't forgotten the time and heavy labor he had put in to cut this trail, where none had been there before except the stretches that had been earlier game trails. It was clear that animals, wild and domestic alike, used the trail now, for tracks of all kinds were stamped into the dried mud. Liam thought of the heavy packs he'd carried on his back on snowshoes, labor that was later done by his packhorses. He remembered driving dog teams along this trail in times of deep snow. That had always been a tricky and tenuous job, as the dogs were so irascible and hard to keep working together. He found himself recalling those days with some fondness, though at the time he had always been in dead earnest, so focused and serious. He remembered times snow-shoeing into the main line cabin and back to the home place in the same day though even then when he had been in his physical prime, it had taxed all of his energy to do it. The very thought of even attempting it now was preposterous to him: he knew he'd be hard pressed today to snowshoe one way with no pack at all, a luxury he never had in those bygone times.

A couple of times the calm old horse shied slightly from a grouse flying up under its feet, but apart from that, he plodded steadily onward with little attention from Liam. Liam was content to let the horse move at his own pace, for he was reliving some of his past as they went along. He stopped the horse once to stare down into a small creek bottom that paralleled this stretch of the trail. He thought back to the many times he'd been down along that creek making sets for lynx, marten, and, where there were dams along the creek, beaver. That had always been hard slogging in the heavy snow of winter and he in heavy clothing. He was happy today just to think about it, glad that he was up here on the trail.

His mind wandered back to a recent meeting he'd had in Hudson's Hope. He'd been there at the only hardware store in town and was just going out the door when he'd almost run into a wizened native man coming the other way. Liam had excused himself, then he looked more carefully at the old fellow and it came to him. The old man was Noah Eklo.

"Noah! How are you?" he had said, wondering what kind of response he'd get.

Noah had stopped, looked him up and down and replied, "Okay, kes not too bad." The old man was clad in cowboy hat, jeans, and moccasins inside low rubbers, conventional daily wear for many men, native and white alike. His long grey-white hair was still done up in pigtails that hung under his black hat and down the front of his stooped shoulders. Liam thought of him as he had been on their first meeting at the home flat so very long ago now. He had been fairly tall and well built, Liam remembered. It was hard to equate him with this thin stooped old man with the deeply lined cheeks and trembling hands, but the rest, the high thin nose, broken and pushed to one side, were the same and the deep-set, piercing black eyes that peered out from under the heavy brows were what Liam remembered. That much was unchanged.

"So Noah, how are things?" asked Liam, trying to think of a conversational direction. "You still living down at Moberly Lake? How's your family?" Liam wondered why he had said that, for visions of another time were flashing through his memory: of standing in the mud of the home place, Marta holding the wailing Tassy and he forbidding a native woman to take her back. Had he tread into deep water with old Noah? Was he inured against Liam because of it? Looking into that implacable, seamed, brown face, it was hard to know.

"Yeah, at the Lake. Don't ride no more. Too old now for horse. Both my wives, they die. No wife now, but lots of kids, lots grandkids, too, I kes."

Liam was somewhat heartened by the old man's response. Was he friendly? Did he even know about Tassy? Maybe he had forgotten about her even if he ever did know. But he had to know...

"My son Royce top rider. Rides good. Rides in rodeo...good every place, even long way from here."

"Yes, I've heard about him," said Liam, feeling a little easier now. Maybe he wasn't going to have trouble with Noah over the thing with Tassy. "I've never seen him ride myself, but Carson says he's the best in the country right now."

"Royce make money at that Stampede they got. Makes good rides there...."

For a few minutes Liam stood on the wooden sidewalk conversing with old Noah. He was about to conclude that Noah had forgotten about Tassy or maybe never knew about her in the first place—Noah had given no sign or said anything to suggest he did. They talked on for a few minutes and Liam decided that it was time to go.

"Well, Noah, good to see you again. You take care now."

"Yes," said Noah. "You take care now that girl you got from Leena." The old man turned slowly, pulled the store door open and entered without another word. Liam had stood rigid for a moment, brought up short by this last revelation. So, he did know, knew all along. But he had said nothing about him or his family trying to take her back. He hadn't seemed hostile but not particularly amicable either, but then he never was. This unfathomable old man, a specter from Liam and Marta's first days in this country. And now tied to them by blood.

Liam's mind wandered back and forth from the distant past to the immediate past to the present. It was wonderful, unknowable, the way that people and events became tangled and intertwined in the web of life. Noah, who'd have ever thought that summer day when he first rode onto the flat, who could have foreseen that his and our lives would ever intersect like this....?

The horse moved leisurely on, and Liam realized they were nearing the line cabin. Then he pulled back on the reins, stopping and listening. Somewhere off to his right, not very far away he thought he could hear an engine. For a minute he couldn't hear it. "Must be hearing things," he muttered. Then he heard it again and something else besides. It was the sound of breaking timber. Then it dawned on him. Somewhere very near here, a dozer was pushing down timber. Clearing land, clear out here! Could that really be? But it had to. Whole damn country's changing! Land being cleared, everywhere, even way in the hell out here! Liam held the horse in and sat pondering. He couldn't see what was happening but he'd done enough clearing himself that he didn't have to, he knew the sounds all right. None of what was being cleared was anywhere near his own land. He'd always assumed that this was crown land and always would be, yet he was deeply troubled by it. It was another block in the great wall of change that seemed to be engulfing the area, engulfing the life he had known here, had thought would always be. And with the revulsion he felt for what he saw and heard, he knew very clearly that he himself was one of the greatest agents of change. Yes, he thought with a deep sense of guilt, he had wrought as much change on this heretofore pristine land as the next guy, hell, more than most! He rode on hearing from time to time the revving and falling of the engine, the splintering crash of heavy iron on trees.

They were suddenly in a clearing and there it sat, brown and weathered with time, but otherwise just as he'd remembered it. Somehow though, it seemed even smaller than his mental picture of it. The pine slab roof still looked to be sound. He noted someone had actually installed a crude glass pane in the side window; before, it had been covered with polyethylene when covered at all. He halted his mount, stepped down, loosened the cinch slightly and tied him to a thin tree. The short hitching rail he'd put up long ago was now fallen to the ground, the spikes that had once held it still embedded in the trees. He looked around and was not totally happy with what he saw. The immediate area around the cabin was strewn with empty tin cans, partially rusted, some still with their labels on. Only a few feet from the door, a burned-out drum heater sat rusting in the sparse grass. Pieces of black plastic and other flotsam lay scattered about the premises. On three of the outside walls of the cabin hung many leghold traps of various sizes, suspended from large nails driven into the logs. A large wash basin with deeply chipped enamel hung there as well. Liam stood looking around the cabin seeing what was there and some things that were not. His mind raced back across the years he had known this spot so intimately. He dimly remembered cutting the logs with an axe and painstakingly putting the building together. In his memory, he saw himself and his two small sons putting on that roof...No, he wouldn't go there.

He stepped to the cabin door, still hung on its rawhide hinges, the bullet-shattered outside planks sheathed over now with a thin veneer of plywood. He lifted the heavy latch and pulled open the door and took one step inside the musty interior. Then he turned and looked back and down. Yes, they were still there—four powder-burned holes on the inside of the door. Yes, it had actually happened right here where he was standing. It wasn't just a long ago nightmare. He took a deep breath, his heart was racing. He moved into the center of the cabin and looked about. The low ceiling almost, but not quite, touching the top of his head; there was something vaguely claustrophobic about it—he remembered that, too. The heavy plank shelves nailed to the walls were empty, as they should have been. Leaving food here, even canned stuff, through the summer months only invited pests. A partially empty cardboard box of salt sat on the edge of one shelf, an assortment of empty tobacco tins next to it, filled with a collection of metal odds and sods. The pole bunk, painstakingly built into the corner, lay empty, even the straw-filled mattress was gone. A wood-burning drum heater, a newer replica of the one rusting outside, sat in the opposite corner, the door ajar and the interior still plugged with last winter's ashes. That was about it, he thought; he turned and started to walk back outside, then he halted, considered for a time, then sat down heavily on the poles of the bunk. He pulled paper and rollings from a shirt pocket, absently rolled a soggy cigarette, lit it with a paper match, took a long drag and exhaled the fragrant blue smoke. He thought back on the hundreds of times he'd done exactly the same thing in exactly the same place. He took another deep drag and sat with his back against the log wall, staring absently out through the open door of the cabin and beginning to relax a bit. He looked at the misshapen cigarette between his fingers and thought again of Marta's long campaign to get him to quit. He'd cut back a lot, sometimes even went weeks without a smoke, but never seemed to be able to completely bid tobacco farewell. When he had smoked it down to a tiny stub, he dropped it on the hard packed floor and ground it out under his feet. "Well," he mused, "I've managed to waste most of this day, better be heading back."

After walking outside, he dropped the latch that held the door shut, stepped back, looked around like someone expecting a long absence, remounted and started home, never stopping to look back. He halted the horse often and listened, but he couldn't hear the dozer running. Somehow he felt better.

He felt such anger that his heavy hands were clenching the steering wheel like a vice; he was actually so infuriated he literally shook with it. He pressed the accelerator as though he would drive it through the floorboard with his foot. The truck rocketed down the long straightaway, passing several other vehicles as though they were standing still. Carson knew he'd better get control before he killed himself and someone else besides. He took deep breaths, exhaling fiercely, barely under control.

The evening had started out innocently enough. On one of the rare Friday nights when he was not working in camp far from town, Carson and Jennifer had attended a movie at the Lido, the only theater in the community. Jennifer was still in her last year of high school, and even though it was not a weeknight with school the next day, her parents were adamant that she be home by midnight. Carson intended to comply with this, for he was still viewed with some ambivalence in the Nygaard household. He and Jennifer had dated half a dozen times or so, and he was scrupulously prompt both to pick her up and get her home under her parents' curfew. This night they had traveled to town in his newer model pickup truck, which he had taken care to shine up both inside and out. It was one of the few extravagances Carson indulged himself with. Its jet back paint and shiny chrome mirrors certainly set it apart from most of the rigs on the road.

Upon arriving in town, they had parked just adjacent to the theater on the street between it and the post office. Across the street, even at this early hour, the noise from the Frontier, a notorious beer parlor, was already heating up. There was lots of loud conversation, the clatter of beer glasses along with the stench of stale beer fumes drifting out into the mid-fall evening. As they were even a bit early, it was not necessary to wait in line at the door, as it sometimes was, so they went in and seated themselves. The movie itself was not inspired: a John Wayne western of some sort, but no matter. The young couple was just happy to be spending an evening together. They held hands and sat as close as the rickety seats allowed. When the movie ended, they left through the side door with most of the other patrons. Carson was slightly annoyed by the gum-pocked floor and packs of noisy children, but it was the price you paid to see a movie.

Their intention was to dine on hamburgers at a local drive-in, then Carson would drive Jennifer home on time, thereby maybe getting himself in her parents' good graces. He would then go straight back up the Alaska Highway to the construction camp he'd been living in all spring.

Things didn't happen quite that way. While they were still several steps from his truck, Carson saw that something was terribly wrong. He pulled up in shock. The beautiful chrome mirrors on both sides of the vehicle had been pried completely off, the supports ripping a ragged hole in both doors, the glass broken out of the mirrors and the supports twisted like pretzels. Horror turned to indignation and then to hot wrath in a few seconds. Who had done this? Carson turned and stared across the street, his face twisted in anger. Standing in the well-lit doorway of the frontier were two beefy figures; they were watching him intently. Suddenly, they turned and ducked inside. The Sangins! It had to be them! Carson started across the street in a red rage. He was halfway across the street when he remembered

Jennifer. She was standing stiffly by the truck and she looked frightened. Carson's mind raced. Another brawl with Jennifer at his side was not in the cards, not if he wanted to stay in the good graces of the Nygaards, not if he wanted to continue to see their daughter.

He had taken Jennifer straight home—all prior plans forgotten. As they drove back to her place, he fought to control himself. He was not given much to conversation at any time; now he was speechless in his fury. He hardly spoke; he did not curse or threaten. But just the same, Jennifer was frightened—the anger oozed out of him like sweat. She didn't really know what to say either. As he let her out and walked her to her door, she put her hand on his arm, pulled him around, and looked into his steely eyes. "Carson...please be careful...please don't get into trouble...don't get hurt." He surprised them both by kissing her lightly on the lips—he'd never even done that before—and retreated back to his truck without a word.

Once out onto the road again, he let loose of the iron control he'd held himself under for the past hour. The closer he got to town, the more his feelings raged. It never even crossed his mind that he might need help in what he intended. He drove the last few blocks comprising the main street at far too high a speed. If any policemen had been near, he'd never have made it back to the Frontier. As it was, he was later deeply troubled by what happened next. As he drove his truck the last block to the brightly lit Frontier, something frightening seemed to take hold of him. Instead of stopping at the curb and racing inside to confront vandals as he had seen himself doing, he drove diagonally through the intersection and straight through the swinging doors of the Frontier. He was extremely fortunate that at that moment no one was coming or going, for they would have received serious injury or death. A thunderous explosion of breaking wood and glass rocked the foyer and beer parlor of the Frontier. The grill of the truck struck a pillar just inside, only feet from some of the screaming patrons, and stopped.

Carson hurled himself out the door and into the smoky den. Directly in front of him, Witt Sangin was pulling himself up out of his chair, a stunned look on his face. Carson lunged forward, sweeping up a barstool in his right hand. Before Witt could even raise his arms in defense, Carson whipped the stool up and brought it down on Witt's head. If Carson had not pulled back at the last instant, Witt probably would not have survived the blow. As it was, the stool shattered like matchwood and Witt dropped, senseless, to the floor. At the same time Burr Sangin was attempting to get out of his chair, skidding it back from the table, not able to get his balance. As though it had been rehearsed, Carson swept up a chair with his free hand, tipped the table over with his other, and lurched toward Burr.

"Hey, it wasn't me...." Burr did not complete the sentence before Carson swung the chair in a sweeping horizontal motion straight into his face. Burr only managed to raise his arms to fend off the blow when he was propelled violently backward against the wall. He slumped down, hugging his right arm to his chest. "My arm! You son-of-a-bitch..." Again he did not get to finish his words. Carson kicked with his pointed-toed boots, catching Burr in the rib cage. A loud high-pitched scream escaped his contorted face as he lay convulsed against the paneled wall.

Carson saw movement on his right, turned and looked straight into the eyes of Davey Sangin. Davey stood rock still for a long second, the fear clearly outlined in his eyes, then he spun around and ran pell-mell out the rear doors. The room was alive with the sounds of chairs being tipped over and of glass breaking. The hall bouncer elbowed his way through the stunned throng, only to be rewarded with a smashing backhand that sent him rocketing backward into the upset tables and broken glass. Behind the bar, one of the barkeeps was frantically dialing the telephone. Most of the patrons, to whom fisticuffs and violence were daily occurrences, moved back but did not leave, fascinated by this new wrinkle, when they thought they had seen it all.

The bouncer, a husky thickset native was back on his feet and moving toward Carson menacingly.

"Stay there!" Carson raised his left hand and pointed it straight at the wary bouncer, who despite his reputation as a mean scrapper, stopped in mid-stride. The sight of this veritable giant and what he had just witnessed was giving him, if not fear, second thoughts. At that moment, three uniformed RCMP officers rushed into the room via the shattered foyer. All of them held heavy billy clubs and were carrying sidearms.

"Stay where you are! You're under arrest!" said the largest of the trio though all of them were big men. He stepped forward as though expecting Carson to respond with violence, but he did not. The officer raised his club menacingly.

"I'll come," said Carson. "Leave off."

The officer moved quickly behind Carson, grabbed both his wrists, pulled them behind his back and snapped on a pair of cuffs. He continued to hold Carson tightly by his forearms now pulled behind him. One of the other officers went to the telephone and summoned an ambulance, which arrived quickly. Two white-frocked attendants appeared with a stretcher and tried to get Witt onto it. Witt was truly frightening to look at. Blood still poured from an ugly gash on the top of his head, soaking his black hair and shirt, puddling in the floorboards under him. His face, that part which wasn't covered with blood, looked waxy, his eyes half open. One of the attendants got down on his knees and put his ear close to Witt's face. "This one's seriously hurt," he said to the nearest officer. "I can barely hear him breathing. Skull's probably fractured, concussion, for sure." Another attendant appeared and the three of them got the inert Witt onto the stretcher and carried him to the waiting ambulance outside, the red flashing light on its top garishly lighting the street.

Carson was now breathing normally, though still taking deep breaths.

"Who's gonna get this goddamned truck out of my bar?" rasped the proprietor, who had come down into the bar from upstairs.

"Take these things off me and I'll back it out of here," said Carson, looking at the nearest officer.

"You'll be doing nothing of the sort," said the officer. "Send for a tow truck," he said to the agitated owner.

"So who's payin' for that?" the proprietor whined, "and what about all the damage this bastard's done? Who pays for that, I'm askin?"

"It'll be looked into," replied the officer.

"I'll see that things get fixed," said Carson. All noise in the room subsided. This was something new—someone actually offering to pay for damages, rather than having it wrung out of him by the judge.

The ambulance attendants were back. They gathered up the moaning Burr Sangin and half carried him to the ambulance, his body bent over and him wincing and crying out with every step.

The fascinated collection of bar flies, not quite believing what they'd just seen and heard, still hung around the edges of the room, backed up two and three deep, staring and mumbling animatedly to one another.

"Never thought I'd see those assholes get what they had comin."

"I wouldn't a cared if he'd killed all three of 'em. They been runnin' roughshod over everybody for a long time. Got exactly what they deserved."

The talk went on; few, it seemed, had any sympathy or anything good to say for the Sangins. None of them had any idea who Carson was, so infrequent were his visits to town.

The bulky constable held onto Carson's handcuffed arm and pushed him out of the chaotic room, onto the street and through the heavy wire back door of the paddy wagon. No one spoke as the wagon rolled the few blocks to the town jail, the red light still flashing vigorously.

"The defendant will please rise."

It had been six days since the debacle at the Frontier and it had not been a happy time for Carson Brennan. For forty-eight hours, Witt Sangin had not even regained consciousness and, for that time, his life seemed hung in the balance. When he finally did waken, he pulled the IV and other medical paraphernalia from his arm and was just wobbling out into the hallway intending to leave, when he was intercepted by a gaggle of agitated nurses, and shortly two RCMP constables, who pulled him back to his hospital cot. His skull had been fractured, and despite being on his feet, he was only partially in control of his senses, which was portentous for Carson, for in the first hours after the melee, it was thought that Witt might even die. But, no, upon waking, Witt had to be threatened with all manner of dire consequences, even a strap around his chest to hold him in bed, if he tried to leave. He raged, argued, and even condescended to beg, but to no avail. One constable was even posted outside his room to see that he complied. Burr's broken arm had been set and cast, his broken ribs taped; he had been sent home but was presently occupying a stool at the Condill Hotel taproom.

Having cooled his heels in the city lockup for a few days, Carson was now deeply penitent about what had happened. He promised himself, and later his grandparents, over and over that he would never allow himself to lose control like that again. He had talked to Jennifer once and that only by telephone; her parents, having got wind of the dustup at the Frontier, had forbidden her to see Carson—permanently. The several hundred dollars worth of damage done to the premises of the Frontier, Liam had consented to cover, an act for which Carson was deeply grateful. Carson's smashed truck now sat at a local auto repair, awaiting further orders. For a couple of days the town had buzzed with reports of the fight at the Frontier; but already after less than a week, it had been partially forgotten, superseded by other beer hall mayhem: just another Friday night at the "Fort."

"Carson L. Brennan, as a magistrate of her Majesty's Court, it is my duty to find you guilty of the following charges: Assault with the intention of bodily harm, destruction of private property, operating a vehicle in an unsafe and perilous manner, endangering the lives of innocent bystanders and causing a disturbance in a public place." The judge stopped, removed his glasses, and looked down sternly at Carson, who refused to meet his stare but looked at the floor between his feet.

"Mr. Brennan, what you did last Friday night is absolutely unconscionable and completely unacceptable in a civilized society. You not only endangered the lives of the people in that establishment, which you turned into a shambles, but you injured and brought close to death a fellow human being and seriously hurt another. Do you have anything to say for yourself before I pronounce sentence?"

Carson raised his head, took a deep breath, paused, looked down again.

"No sir," he said in a near whisper.

"I have heard from your counsel the reasons why you claim you instigated this debacle, and I am not totally unacquainted with the plaintiffs. I have also heard of your life and the exemplary use you have heretofore put your working life to; however, as a judge in a civilized country I cannot overlook or condone your actions in any sense. So it is my duty to impose upon you the following sentence: Two months incarceration at the Northern Correctional Institute in Prince George and suspension of your driver's license for the period of six months." The judge dropped his gavel loudly, stood slowly and strode from the courtroom.

Carson's defense lawyer grasped his hand and offered to appeal, but Carson shook his head. Liam and Marta were at his side; both of them put their arms around him, Marta's eyes wet with tears. Liam looked disconsolately at the wall but said little. It was not a totally unexpected sentence, but when given, it still sent tremors of shock through the whole Brennan family. The bailiff came forward, and after a few words with his grandparents, Carson was led away.

When Liam and Marta embarked on the construction of the new house, they were innocent of the turmoil they were getting into. Just deciding on its location was an event in itself and was the opening volley of a campaign that inexplicably found the two of them at loggerheads. Marta had suggested that the house should sit much nearer the road than the present one, and thereby eliminate, at least to some degree, the long lane they had always had from the Hudson Hope Road. Also, it would set the house apart from the unseemly sprawl of the equipment sheds and livestock yards that lay just behind the log house. Liam countered with the argument that setting the house a couple of hundred yards from the equipment and stock made no sense because that was where he spent most of his time on the home place and that distance from the house would render things unhandy. They eventually settled on a compromise: the new house would stand adjacent to the old one, across the lane from the main road. A fence would be erected behind it to partially camouflage the collection of buildings and sheds between the house and the river. Liam had promised to straighten up the equipment yard and remove anything necessary to make the whole view more eye appealing.

Ground was broken with Carson digging out the soil for a basement with one of the heavy backhoes owned by Outlook Contracting. Liam marveled at his touch with the great machine; the walls were straight and true to the markers the two of them had set up with a transit earlier. Footings were constructed and leveled and a cement truck brought in from Fort St. John to fill them. A local contractor had been engaged to erect the cement basement walls, which went up without a hitch. A framing crew set about as soon as the cement forms were removed and the long awaited house began to take shape. Marta spent hours watching the proceedings out of her kitchen window, though she rarely ventured over to the actual construction site. She noticed that Tassy, now home for the summer, seemed to spend an inordinate amount of time watching the framers and conversing with them. She found herself comparing the rapid rise of her new house with the building of the one she now occupied. It had taken a whole summer for her and Liam just to get the walls up and the roof on. Every log had been skidded out of the nearby forest by horse team the summer before building started, debarked with endless hours of toil and set on planks off the ground to season. They had had no chainsaws or power tools; everything had to be shaped and fitted with nothing more technological than an axe or adze. It had become very apparent to them after the house was up and they'd moved in that it would have been better had they had the luxury of time—which they did not—to let the logs season a year or more longer. In those first years, they'd had constant trouble with doorframes separating and windows compressing and sometimes spaces appearing between the logs, which they had chinked again and again with moss and clay. This day, she and Tassy watched as three workmen put the complete set of roof trusses up in a single day.

"Gramma, we're sure gonna have a lot more room over there, eh?"

"Liam says the house will have three bedrooms on the main floor, two in the upstairs, and more if we want when the basement gets finished."

"Well, Gramma, you've waited a long time for this. Now we won't have so many things stuffed into just a few rooms, a place to hang up clothes in every room, it kinda seems like a dream even yet."

"It does to me, too," said Marta. "We talked about this new house, your grandfather and me, for so long I guess I gradually came to feel that it was just a fantasy, a dream, not something that was ever going to happen. And now that its becoming real right before our eyes, I'm starting to think a lot about what it's going to mean to leave this old one forever. I've spent so much time here now; it seems like the only home I've ever known, though, of course, that isn't true. We had a good house back in the old country, too, but I've been gone from there now for so very long, it is hard for me to really remember it as it was."

"Was it bigger than this house?" asked Tassy.

"Well, I'm not sure it was. It may even have been smaller, but it was arranged differently. Of course, it was not built of logs as this one is, but the rooms had very high ceilings, and in those times virtually nobody had electricity or indoor plumbing. The climate was very different there as I have told you so often before. We had lots of rain sometimes, but the winters were never so long or as fierce as here."

"What color was your house there?" asked Tassy. "Were the houses even painted?"

"It must have been painted sometime because I remember it as a grey-green sort of shade; I don't remember it ever being painted when I was a girl. I do remember how hot and stuffy the house got in summer and how cold it sometimes got in winter. Before the war, stove fuel was hard to get. After the war got going it was virtually impossible to get any coal."

"You burned coal, not wood?"

"We burned coal when we could get it. Wood was not available, not like here where you can cut firewood almost anywhere."

"Wow, I'd sure hate to have to use an outhouse," Tassy sighed. "It would be awful to have to go out there in the winter, anytime, I guess."

"Sweetheart, you don't remember it, I guess, but we never had indoor plumbing until after you came to live with us."

"How did you stand it?" Tassy asked, a scowl on her face.

"When you know nothing else, Tassy, you don't know that what you've got is a hardship. But I must say it didn't take me long to learn to love indoor plumbing."

"Grampa says the new house will have a bathroom upstairs and downstairs, with a shower and all. Geez, I can't believe it!"

"Incidentally," Marta inserted, "I see you talking a lot to that one young fellow who is helping with the building. Do you know him?"

"Which one do you mean?" said Tassy, not meeting Marta's eyes.

"The one you've been talking to half the time."

"Oh, you mean Loren," Tassy said in an offhanded way.

"Oh, it's Loren, is it. So who is Loren?"

"Loren, you know, Loren, from the church."

"Ahh," said Marta as one to whom things were now growing clearer. "Part of that German family who usually sit in front of us. The one you've been gaga about for a long time."

"Oh, Gramma, it isn't really much, I guess, but I do kind of like him."

Before the roof could be finished, a heavy rainstorm blew in and pelted down for the best part of a week. The new building stood forlornly in the weather for a few days; the trusses reminded Marta of the rib cage of a dead animal sticking up into the sky. The subfloor of the building was partially protected by canvas tarps that Liam and Carson spread over them when it appeared that this was going to be a soaker. Great puddles appeared, as they always did on the lane road; the river ran clear at first but darkened with mud and debris as the storm continued.

Liam came and went continuously and Carson as well. For the past year in all seasons except for the few weeks of breakup, they had four huge dozers working back in the trench, which would be covered over by the waters behind the dam once it was completed. Liam and Carson were kept on the run, hauling fuel and parts to the machines. Carson had spent nearly ten months operating one of the dozers himself and supervising the other three. Now that he had his driver's license back, Liam had taken him off his machine as it was becoming too much for Liam to keep the supply line open by himself. The past winter he had done that, but he spent so many hours on the road and so many nights away from home that Marta had pressed him to hire another operator so Carson could help him. That had been done, but now they were operating so far up the trench that even with the two of them working together it was a stretch for them to keep up.

Carson did not elaborate to his grandparents or anyone else for that matter on his two-month sojourn at the correctional center. Liam had heard a few faint rumors through the past winter that indicated to him it likely was not a peaceful interlude. It had gotten back to Liam that Carson had been compelled to assert himself physically with some of the inmates but that after an initial confrontation, he had been left strictly alone. Liam had pondered that. He found it hard to imagine that there were those who would care to arouse the wrath of his grandson. Carson never spoke of it and Liam decided to let sleeping dogs lie.

The months Carson spent in camp had been calm and uneventful but even that changed with the coming of spring. In mid-May after Jennifer Nygaard's graduation from high school, she and Carson eloped and were married in the Alberta town of Grande Prairie. Marta and Liam had seen it coming but were still jolted by the rapidity of it. When Jennifer's parents had forbidden her to see Carson after his sentencing, the obvious occurred; it was like, Liam said, waving a red flag in front of a bull. It had only drawn them together. They corresponded constantly while he was in Prince George, and after he returned, Carson spent many sleepless nights, driving all the way from his work site, many hours away, to meet her clandestinely in town. It seemed to Liam that after the initial parental uproar over the elopement that the two had somehow negotiated a peace with the Nygaards. At least he thought so, though Carson said little to him of it. And if Carson was not seen as a jewel of a son-in-law to Jennifer's parents, at least, he had managed to negotiate an uneasy truce.

Carson now commuted from Fort St. John each day where he and Jennifer kept a small rented house. She had already found employment in the office of one of the oil companies. He had brought Jennifer to the home place a few times lately and the Brennans, particularly Marta, had tried ever so hard to make her feel welcome and at ease. Jennifer was not a closed vessel like Carson, but she was shy and quiet, slow to open up to strangers. Marta saw that and secretly felt good about it, for she sensed that when Jennifer grew to know her in-laws, she would become a strong and loving member of the Brennan clan. It was clear that she knew Tassy well, and Marta could only wonder what part Tassy may have played in those winter trysts before the marriage. Marta guessed that when Tassy wished her to know more, she would. As it was, when the young couple were at the ranch, Marta could see that they were much like young lovers in all times. Marta could see it in Jennifer's eyes when she and Carson were together. As for Carson, he was a far harder book to read, but his deference to her and his protectiveness of her feelings were apparent. Marta privately found herself shaking her head over the rapidity of the whole affair, for she had thought at one time that Carson's withdrawn persona would forebear his ever having a close relationship, much less marrying. And now events had happily, at least for the present, sorted themselves out.

Construction of the dam had now begun in earnest. Huge machines tore at the river canyon walls where the dam would stand, cutting out multi tons of intrusive stone right down to bedrock. The whole of the river had been diverted to one side and roared through massive steel culverts, enabling the building to proceed in the riverbed itself. Great tunnels were being cut through solid rock, which when finished would pull the waters through the great turbines that would in time be set in place. Viewed from the nearby hills that overlooked the dam site, it resembled nothing quite so much as a giant anthill. The machines and men moving to and fro below were almost insect-like in their actions and accompanied by a constant mechanical cacophony. More and more men and machines were being brought into play now that construction was fully underway. The great conveyer belt that would shortly be moving fill for the structure stretched like a great serpent along the river and then was lost as it disappeared into the timber on the north bank. It would move untold tons of gravel and rock for several miles, fed on the supply end by massive bull-dozers gouging the material out of pre-selected sites in the river valley itself.

The hamlet of Hudson's Hope, born of the fur trade more than a hundred years earlier, was undergoing severe growing pains, growing from a sleepy little village hugging the high north bank of the Peace River to a trailer house metropolis, sprawling all around the old core. With the infusion of all sorts of new residents, came a tidal wave of change. The few established merchants, namely, store owners and gas station operators with a few eateries, found their business skyrocketing. In a few months, the local schools, bursting their seams found it necessary to create all manner of semi-permanent classrooms which, like most of the new housing, were composed mainly of cheap pre-fabs and even trailers. So great was the need of housing that during the first warm months, workers found themselves housed in canvas tents or lean-to's.

The need for after-hour diversion for the hordes of workers created a clutch of noisy bars, replete with all of the annoyances of their kind. Violence and rowdiness became common around the liquor dispensing establishments at night. The local RCMP detachment needed an infusion of extra personnel to keep the lid on. Drunkenness, nuisance, and domestic violence shot up sharply. And, as always, the native contingent suffered from the easy acquisition of booze. In short, Hudson's Hope during the days of the WAC Bennett Dam construction was a typical boomtown with all of a boomtown's opportunities and annoyances.

Deep in the trench, where the lake would lie, work was also grinding on. It was becoming clear that much of the vast area, all of it timbered to some degree, would just be going under the water as it stood. Great swatches of timber were leveled, some of it hauled laboriously out to the log mills, some of it piled by dozer and burned, most of it left where it fell. The dimensions of the great man-made lake would be staggering, with a shoreline many hundreds of miles long, drowning out small streams altogether, reaching into distant valleys and around and through mountain ranges. The scope of Williston Lake was truly mind-boggling.

In some areas where timber was not extremely heavy, great cables were stretched between massive bull-dozers and then dragged by them over the terrain, flattening the trees, their root systems thrust up out of the ground like huge upended toadstools. Passage on foot through these horizontal jungles was next to impossible.

Of the fate of untold and unmeasured legions of wildlife displaced by the usurpation of their habitat, no one could guess, though common wisdom had it that they would be absorbed into the surrounding unmolested areas. Many, including biologists and knowledgeable local hunters, were dubious, for it seemed unlikely that uprooted and displaced moose, deer, and bear plus untold numbers of small species could blend into surrounding areas already at their maximum sustainable numbers. Local hunters and lovers of wildlife in general found their reservations about what lay ahead for the wildlife of the area drowned out by the flurry of activity and problems inherent in the mammoth building project. For the moment, the dam's creation held center stage; other problems would later be addressed. When it was too late to change anything, some thought.

※※※

For the hundredth time Tassy asked herself why she was doing this. Wasn't it enough that she was a loved and appreciated member of the Brennan clan, included in the very heart of all things family, educated in the best manner available, consulted about important matters, doted over by loving grandparents, included in intimate family gatherings, with aunts, uncles, and constantly increasing numbers of young cousins? Hadn't she made Marta and Liam beam with pride at her high school graduation where she had received academic honors? And most of all, wasn't she a confidant of Marta, especially in the last few years? With her grandmother she shared a deep trust; she knew she could discuss anything with Marta, reveal her inner feelings, fears, and hopes and know that Marta would respond in total honesty. She knew that what passed between them would never go further unless she wished it. Theirs was a friendship that transcended age and blood. She had never had a friend like her grandmother even among the many close friendships she had developed at school. It was often uncanny, Tassy mused, how Marta knew what she was thinking, knew what to say to her.

So why was she doing this, carefully hiding it from her grandmother, from all of the Brennans? She took a deep breath, clenching and unclenching her hands on the steering wheel, the beauty of the surrounding countryside passing by her window unnoticed. She had seen herself doing this over and over in her imagination, and later each time it happened she chastised herself for even imagining it. And now it was actually happening. But it wasn't too late, she could still turn around and go back. But she didn't. Something drove her, something had been driving her for a long time now.

When she first got the idea, she couldn't even remember now. Probably it had started with that conversation she'd had at the rodeo with Royce. The part where she'd learned about the existence of Georgina. Georgina, her half sister, that she had never met or seen, but whom she had thought and wondered about continually ever since. She had told Marta about her and had wondered aloud in her presence what she should do. Shouldn't she somehow try to meet her, reach out to her? Marta had for once seemed perplexed, unsure of what Tassy should do. She had, at Tassy's continued absorption in the matter, even offered to drive her to Moberly Lake herself so that the two sisters could meet. Marta did this with great reservations knowing enough of the reserve there to be nervous of it. She had implored Tassy not to go there by herself, had once even asked her to promise she wouldn't. This was not really like Marta, but Tassy understood rightly why her grandmother would react this way. She knew deep within herself that it was only out of a sense of responsibility, of love and devotion that she felt compelled to warn Tassy off.

And now here she was, doing the very thing that flew in the face of what her grandmother had wanted. She was, on this pleasant summer morning, driving alone and unknown to anyone but herself to Moberly Lake to seek out the other side of her family roots. That was the way she explained it to herself, though if she allowed herself to ponder it, as she had been doing since she left the ranch earlier, it was hard to make real sense of it. Was she betraying her grandmother? She hoped not, but somehow, someway, something within her drove her to reach out to her unknown native family.

When she passed the sign that announced the reserve, her stomach was twisting in nervous knots, and it was all she could do to keep from stopping the car, turning around and fleeing back to the safety of the home place. But she did not. A small store with a Coca-Cola sign and some gas pumps out front caught her attention. She pulled into the rough, mud hole-pocked driveway and turned off the car, got out nervously, and went into the store. For a moment she thought there must be no one around, for she seemed alone in the interior. Then just as she was about to leave, a stocky native woman, who appeared to be middle-aged, clamored in the back door, slamming it behind her.

Tassy hesitated, pushing down the urge for flight. She had rehearsed to herself what she would say but now was not quite able to find her tongue.

"You want somethin'?" queried the no-nonsense-looking woman, coming forward heavily to stand behind the cash register.

"I...ah, y...yes...actually I do need something," stammered Tassy, deeply intimidated by the tough-looking exterior of the storekeeper.

"Well, what is it? I ain't got all day. You need gas, groceries, what?"

"Ah...no...I don't need to buy anything. I just wondered if you knew where...where Jimmy and Melba live?"

"Jimmy and Melba? Lepeau? Jimmy Lepeau? Yeah, I know where Jimmy and Melba live. You can see their place from here. Come out." The woman moved laboriously from behind the counter, walked out through the screen door, motioning Tassy to follow her. She stepped out onto the muddied gravel near the door, looked back at Tassy and pointed. "That's Jimmy's place, that white house there back in them trees. See it?" She continued pointing at a white building set well back off the road on the Lake side, partially obscured by poplar trees.

"Yes...I see it," said Tassy

"Well, now you know," said the woman and she trudged back inside, oblivious to the mud that had collected on her shoes. Once inside she turned and saw Tassy, who had come back to the door, but did not re-enter.

"What? You ain't from around here?" the woman asked.

"No, actually, I'm from over by Hudson's Hope."

"Yeah, I know that place. What is it you want with them Lepeaus?" she asked straight forwardly as though anyone's business was common business.

"W...Well," stammered Tassy, "I just wanted to talk to them is all."

"Seems like long ways to come just to talk," replied the woman. "You know them?"

"Well, I guess you could say I do," said Tassy, finally able to find her voice.

"Listen, when you go down there, you tell that Melba them fuckin' kids hers better stay away from here. Keep stealin' stuff outa this store. Caught two of the little bastards in here yesterday, stealin' candy and other stuff. I've told Melba over 'n over but don't do no good. Them kids always around here causin' trouble. And tell Melba she better be paying some of her credit bill, too. Ain't paid a fuckin' cent since last winter. What the hell. I can't keep givin' credit if they don't pay. I got to pay my bills, too. Those damn people never seem to worry 'bout nothin' 'specially payin' their debts."

Tassy stood stalk still, her mouth partially open. She could think of nothing to say, shocked at this candid outburst from a total stranger.

"Thanks," said Tassy finally. She turned and hurried toward her car. The woman followed her back out the door. She halted a few steps from the car.

"You never told me what your name is," she said.

"Tassy. Tassy Brennan." She got quickly into the car, closed the door and started the engine, heading quickly out onto the road before the woman could say any more. She only had to drive a few hundred feet before turning into the driveway of the Lapeau establishment.

She was not encouraged by what she saw. As she drove the car slowly into the cluttered yard, a pair of mongrel dogs came racing out to meet her, barking furiously. Another dog emerged from under the partially fallen porch and trotted out to join his companions. They swarmed menacingly around the car, keeping up a crescendo of yapping. A rusted engine sagged on a chain from an improvised tripod of poplar trees a few steps from the front door, which appeared to be partially open. To either side of the house and extending back into the woods behind it was a sequence of broken down cars and pickups in various stages of disassembly. The battered body of a pickup sat on three concrete blocks a few feet back from the muddy driveway, one of the wheels resting on the ground near an upturned block. Next to the porch itself, a snow machine sat ignominiously in the mud, its ripped plastic seat exposing the yellow foam underneath. The steps to the porch leaned crazily to the left, and a hole in the porch itself just outside the door revealed a missing board. A flotsam of broken plastic toys, children's shoes, empty cans, and chewed bones lay strewn about in every direction. Piles of dog shit made any attempt to reach the house hazardous.

Tassy stopped the car, leaving it running, wondering what to do next. The dogs continued their deafening cacophony, now standing just below the driver's window, the scruffy fur on their necks and shoulders standing up. Tassy stayed put, watching for someone to emerge from the door of the house, not daring to get out and place herself at the mercy of the fierce-looking dogs. A couple of minutes went by and nothing.

Then just as she had put the car into reverse and was beginning to back up, the door moved a bit and a brown face peered around the side of it. Finally, a child, a boy of perhaps seven or eight, opened the door further and stepped out onto the porch. He was not wearing any shoes. Tassy stopped, changed gears, and drove back slowly toward the house, wondering all the time why she was doing this. She put her head out the car window and said "Hello" as loudly as she could. No response. The child stood half obscured by the door.

"Hi," shouted Tassy again. Again, no audible response, but the child moved slightly away from the door.

"I'm Tassy," she said as clearly as she could, wondering how she must sound. When she looked again there were two figures in the doorway, the latest one even smaller than the first and clad only in a grimy tee shirt and underpants. Tassy decided she had to risk getting out of the car. She opened the door tentatively and put her feet on the ground. Two of the dogs rushed up sniffing loudly, running noses around her trouser legs. The third dog moved back a few steps and continued to menace her, barking and then growling deep in its throat. Tassy stood up and closed the door behind her. Her throat felt tight with apprehension. The dogs whined and circled her, tails wagging but continuing to bark intermittently.

"Nice dog," she said, but when she tried to touch them, they slunk back away from her. The growling dog, the one Tassy was deeply afraid of, circled behind her. She turned to face it, half frozen with fright.

"Rover, get away!"

She glanced up and saw the larger child now off the porch with a stick in his hand, advancing toward her. He struck the growling dog with the club and sent it kiyiing to the back of the house.

Tassy looked at him, forced a smile and said, "Hi. Is your Mom home?" The child stared at her impassively. "Is Melba here?" asked Tassy again, trying to keep her voice even.

"She ain't here," muttered the child.

"Is she at work or gone to town?" asked Tassy. The child seemed loathe to meet her eyes. He merely shrugged his shoulders. Tassy straightened her back. "Is Georgina living here? Is she at home?"

"She sleepin'," said the boy.

Tassy considered this communication. It flashed through her mind that one o'clock in the afternoon was a strange time to be in bed.

"Do you think I could talk to her? Do you think she'd mind?"

"Dunno," muttered the child again.

"Could I come inside and talk to her?" asked Tassy, wondering why she was even asking.

"Guess so," the boy proffered. He turned around and plodded back through the muddy clay to the porch. He made no effort to clean his bare feet of the mud that clung to them and walked straight into the house through the still open door. Tassy followed him up the steps, avoided the gaping hole in the entry and stepped inside the shaded interior.

A sour smell composed, she thought, of rotten food and unchanged diapers permeated the interior. For some reason, probably just training,

Tassy reached down and slipped off her shoes, holding them in her hand. The floor under her feet felt rough and gritty; obviously sweeping it was not a priority. She glanced about her. A kitchen sink was adjacent to the door on the left wall, the curtainless window above it so smudged with film and dirt that it only let in a quasi-murky light. In the sink, on the counter next to it, on the table that rested a few feet away, on every horizontal surface, sat piles of unwashed pots, pans, plates, cups, and food-smeared silverware. A once white refrigerator stood just next to the door she had entered, the handle smeared nearly black with handprints. On the opposite side of the door were piled cardboard cases of empty beer bottles, some of which had tipped over, the bottles sticking half out of the cases. The only sound in the room at first was the hum of a multitude of flies which flew about the room constantly lighting on exposed skin. Tassy found herself slapping at her face and arms. Both the boys stood looking at her, with little apparent interest. She looked into another room that opened off this one. A shabby davenport festooned with pieces of clothing seemed the only furnishing except a decrepit-looking television that sat on the floor in the far corner. As she focused on the litter on the floor, she spied yet another child, this one only an infant sitting up in some blankets staring out at her in silent nakedness.

Tassy tried to compose herself, to think of what to do or say. She was struggling with this when she heard movement in the hallway, which had two or three closed doors opening off it. One of the doors opened and a girl emerged. She was barefoot, clad only in jeans and absently buttoning a long-sleeved western shirt over her front. It was obvious that she wore nothing under it. She lifted her head as though just noticing Tassy, still only one step inside the door that remained open. She offered no comment but stared impassively at Tassy, her eyes seemingly unfocused.

"Hello. My name's Tassy Brennan. Patricia actually, but I've always been called Tassy." Tassy was mortified by the sound of her own voice, it sounded so hollow, so unsure even to her. But what to say? The girl stopped, looked, Tassy thought, sullenly at her, but remained silent.

"I thought I should come and see you," Tassy said, aware that her voice was quavering. "Ah...Royce told me about you....about Leena...and Melba."

The girl cocked her head, her heavy black hair falling and partially obscuring her face. "Yeah?" she lisped. She didn't even sound like it interested her. Does she even know what I'm talking about, thought Tassy.

"Your name's Georgina? Right?"

The girl nodded almost imperceptibly.

"As I said, I ah...heard about you from Royce last summer. You see... Leena...Leena was my mother...too." She stopped, the words seemed caught in her throat.

Georgina raised her eyes a bit, blinked a couple of times and said, "What'd ya say your name is?"

"My name is Tassy Brennan. You see, I was raised...am still living with my father's parents, Liam and Marta Brennan."

Georgina eyed her vacantly. "Yeah, where's that at?"

"You mean where do I live?" asked Tassy. "I live on the Hope Road, a few miles from Hudson's Hope."

"Don't know that place," Georgina replied, absently scratching under her shirt.

"Do you ever go to Hudson's Hope?" asked Tassy, wondering where this conversation was going.

Georgina replied, a slight look of irritation or maybe even scorn in her petulant face, "Sure, I go there alla time, maybe even today. Lotsa men that place," she said as though an afterthought. "Sure, goin' down there today with Sally. These kids can watch the baby, I guess. Melba sposed to be here pretty soon, I think."

"Oh, is that Melba's baby?" Tassy asked nodding at the silent child looking out at them from the other room.

"She's mine," said Georgina flatly. "Melba got a whole herd of her own."

"Yours? Your baby?" said Tassy incredulously.

"Sure. She's almost a year now. Sure a pain in the ass, too, nobody want to watch her when I ain't here. Sometimes Melba but these fuckin' kids hers won't do nothin'." At that the baby began to whimper and flap her arms up and down, still sitting up on the discolored linoleum floor.

"What's her name?" asked Tassy for want of anything else to say.

"Randa," replied Georgina, but said no more.

"Randa. That's a nice sounding name," Tassy said.

Georgina shrugged, "Good as any I guess."

"The baby's father...I mean...does he live here?" asked Tassy, thinking that this was a bad question but unable to hold back her shocked curiosity.

"Dunno, might be one of them Desjarlais or maybe one of them guys from down at the Hope. Dunno." The baby's whimpers were now giving way to persistent wailing, but Georgina seemed not to notice. The two boys had disappeared somewhere.

Tassy closed her eyes very hard, then re-opened them. "Georgina, how old are you?" she asked, tipping her head to one side as she spoke.

"Fifteen, pretty soon sixteen, I guess," Georgina replied absently.

Tassy changed tack. "Did you know Leena very well? I mean, what was she like?"

"Not too good, I guess. Always gone. Drunk too much. After while didn't see her no more."

"What did she die of?" asked Tassy, determined now to carry through with her inquiry into her mother's short life.

"Hell, I dunno, too much drinkin', I guess. Been a long time ago."

"Is her grave...is her grave here...on the reserve?"

"Her grave? Dunno. Dunno nothin' bout where it is." Georgina brushed her straight hair out of her eyes. She spoke this time with an edge in her voice. "Why? Why you askin' all these questions? You don't live here anyways. Whata you care about here? It's not your place. You livin' with them white people. This place is for us, not your place."

Tassy was stung by Georgina's barely concealed hostility, by her indifference, but most of all by her clear rejection of her attempt at friendship. The wailing infant now lay back on her filthy blankets, obviously fouled with her own waste, shrieking so loudly the room seemed to echo with it. Georgina seemed not to notice. She turned her back on Tassy, went into one of the rooms and returned with a lit cigarette between her fingers.

"Anyways," she said, not looking at Tassy, "got to get ready. Sally comin' to get me. Can't talk no more. Gota get ready to go."

At that moment, as if on cue, an older model car of some sort, wheezed into the driveway, blue smoke pouring from under it. There was a series of loud honks on the horn, but no one got out of it.

Georgina appeared again, clad now in a light jacket and some kind of boots. "So...I gotta go now." She motioned at the door, meaning for Tassy to leave.

"B...but the baby? What about the baby?" asked Tassy, her face pressed into a questioning scowl.

"Melba fix her up pretty soon, I think," said Georgina, who brushed past her, out the door, down the decrepit steps and across the littered yard to the car. She opened the door, got in and immediately the car shot back toward the road, chunks of half-dry mud flying from its tires. It disappeared in a cloud of blue smoke, heading east.

Tassy stood in shock for a moment, her shoes still in her hand. She became aware that the baby had stopped screaming. She looked up to see one of the small boys putting some sort of food—it looked like candy—into the child's fist. She suckled loudly, still whimpering and hiccupping.

Tassy drove back the way she had come, her mind a vacuum. Tears were running down her cheeks, but she clenched her teeth to keep from sobbing. A few miles from the reserve she veered the car into a turnout and stopped; the motor still running, she sat limply behind the wheel. She sat, trying to come to grips with what had happened, to make some sense of it, if there was any. The well she had been holding back broke and she shook with her sobbing. She had never felt so utterly rejected in her life. Finally she put the car in gear and drove slowly back to the home place.

It was the first time all of the Brennans had been together in a long time. Paul, noisy and full of himself, along with Carolyn and the boys and new baby—all of them had recently returned from Indonesia where Paul had been overseeing a giant oil refinery complex for Imperial Oil. On Paul's previous assignments to Saudi Arabia and Tunisia, he had gone by himself, leaving Carolyn and the kids in Calgary; but this time his management status had made it possible to take family with him. They had spent eighteen months there, all of them deeply tanned and seemingly healthy. The two boys were noisy and rambunctious, maybe a little out of control Liam thought. Carolyn was quiet and smiling, saying little, letting Paul take the lead in family interaction, which he was happy to do.

Paul's rise in the oil industry, if not meteoric, had been steady. He was now moving into senior management and the excess flesh on him showed that he took little time for outside pursuits.

"I'll be involved in those North Sea projects for the next couple of years, probably based out of Edinburgh or Aberdeen. Still trying to decide if Carolyn and the kids will come with me. Might be better for the kids' schooling if they don't keep being uprooted and moved constantly. We'll see. Carolyn and I are still talking about it. If I land a senior management post, there are excellent family accommodations that go with it, but we're not even sure of the posting yet, so we'll just have to wait and see." Paul rambled on about his work, his young family, the places he'd been, and his undying enthusiasm for the oil industry. "Studies show," he said, "that here in northern BC and Alberta, we're sitting on some of the largest natural gas deposits in North America, maybe even the world. The oil industry is going to boom here before long and the development we've seen up until now will seem like peanuts." He held forth for a long time on the coming of the oil bonanza and the opportunities it presented. Carson, as always, listened but volunteered little. Privately, he saw Paul as a bit of a blowhard, but it was not his nature to speak up. Paul seemed to think that Outlook Contracting was just dozing along. Did he really think they were just sitting on their hands or what?

"Well," Liam interjected, "we've managed to keep busy, especially with this dam project and the on-site oil work we get. The country is booming enough for me already. I'm not looking forward to more oil expansion all that much. It seems to me that things are being changed around here fast enough as it is. More expansion just brings more people and, in the long run, more problems."

"Dad, you're not going to fight progress," said Paul. "You guys might as well make your minds up about that. There's going to be a lot of work and big money to be made, so you might as well be in on it...." Paul talked on.

It occurred to Carson that Paul must think himself the only person ever to have an original thought. Hell, he and Liam and often Marta talked about these things all the time. Paul seemed so taken with his own observations that he was oblivious. No question about his knowledge in his field, but sometimes his endless enthusiasm bordered on boorishness. Paul always touched cords of slight resentment in Carson, if only because of his opinionated manner and unabashed self-confidence. Inwardly, Carson wished he was better at expressing himself; he always seemed to allow others to guide conversation and dominate, to say what they felt, what they thought, how they saw things.

After a gargantuan midday meal in the new kitchen/dining room, the whole clan toured the new house, gawking and marveling at its spaciousness, its modern conveniences and the quality of workmanship. The older children, Paul and Carolyn's boys and Joanna's daughters, were soon tearing up and down the stairs, both upstairs and in the basement. Eventually, Joanna shooed them out of the house to play outside.

Liam and Carson originally had intended to do much of the framing and rough work, but things had not worked out that way. They were kept away from the home place by the ever-increasing demands of their work, so much that in the end Liam had hired a reputable builder out of Fort St. John to complete the job. And, as far as any of the family could tell, the work had been done well. The spacious but not ostentatious living room was dominated by a huge stone fireplace enclosable in glass doors and equipped with fans to move the air through the house. This was not the only heat source though; a forced air system had registers in every room, the heat produced by a compact oil furnace located in the basement. The kitchen, which was Marta's dream realized at last, had cupboards covering three of the interior walls, an electric range and oven, the latest in refrigerators, enclosed overhead lights, a large window over a double sink with a side door opening onto the deck which circled the entire house, the roof extending over it. The kitchen floor was composed of lino squares in intricate design. The walls were painted a plain white to enhance the light that Marta had so missed in her log kitchen. There was one large bedroom on the ground floor with its own bathroom, three bedrooms upstairs, and two more in the full basement as well as a huge storage and work area. Now that the house was completed and the family moved in, Marta wondered how she had ever lived so long without its conveniences. Liam was pleased with the building, too, but wondered privately how they had underestimated the cost so drastically; the overrun had amounted to nearly half again what they had projected. No matter, it was done, and Marta was elated with it; he could ask no more.

Outside, the spacious lawns planned for had yet to be planted; at this late date in fall, they would be better postponed until spring. The fence around the grounds that Liam had promised as a site compromise had only just been started. A rectangle of seven foot treated posts stuck up from the ground like topless trees. A gigantic granite boulder, dug out of Turtle Mountain and hauled to the ranch by dump truck, rested a few feet from the side of the house, there only to provide what Marta called "decoration."

The male members of the family and most of the older children repaired to the stables, a couple of gentle old horses were saddled and the ecstatic children allowed to ride.

"Ronnie! Ronnie! Take the slack out of your reins," coached Paul. "That's it!

That's it! Now tap him slightly with your heels to make him go. No! Don't kick him! Just tap him a bit with your heels." And so it went. Soon the two old geldings were walking slowly round and round the yard between the buildings, around machinery, often three or even four children on their backs. They moved off smartly when the child holding the reins knew the drill, but as soon as the men took their attention away, the old fellows stopped to crop grass, oblivious to the shrieking children on their backs.

Later yet, fishing poles and rigging were fetched from the cars and everyone trooped down to the river edge to fish. In truth, the only one of the adult males interested in fishing was Russel; the rest, Paul, Liam and Carson, were content to oversee the kids, untangle their lines, fix the reels, and bait hooks, all the time talking of other things. They moved off upriver by a gravel bank jutting out into the channel and forming a deep hole, the waters moving round and round in a great eddy. Here they actually began to catch a few fish, nearly all of them white fish or suckers, but the grandchildren were elated, though the smaller ones quickly lost interest and had to be watched over carefully as they romped along the bank. Liam felt a deep peace in all of this; it was one of the visions he'd always harbored—family communing together in simple enjoyments.

At the kitchen in the new house, Joanna, Marta, Tassy, Carolyn, Jennifer and the babies sat around the great walnut dining table and visited. Joanna had to keep a handle on herself to avoid dominating discussion as she knew she was prone to do.

"So, Tassy, what have you got planned for yourself now that secondary school is finished?" Joanna inquired. "Mom tells me you're a gifted student."

Tassy's light brown face colored slightly. "Oh, Gramma has a tendency to exaggerate," she gushed. "I'm okay in school, but I couldn't claim to be gifted."

"Now, Tassy," Marta interjected, "you take credit where credit is due. She isn't telling you that she was in the top five academic students in grade 12. We've got the certificate to prove it."

"Well," Tassy said, "I did well in most of my subjects, but I'm still kind of weak in math."

"Math is an important skill," proffered Joanna, "especially if you've got any aspirations about working in a business. In the office we use math continuously. Of course, what the business world mainly does is use arithmetic or business math, the kind you use in payroll calculations, for example."

"I don't have much problem with that kind of math," volunteered Jennifer. "The stuff that gave me trouble was algebra and like that."

"That's the kind of math, I meant," said Tassy.

"Of course," said Marta in a chiding voice, "Tassy has other demands on her time now, what with a steady boyfriend and all."

"Oh, Gramma," Tassy said, her face blushing, but still smiling, "it's not steady or anything. I've only gone on a couple of dates with him."

"A boyfriend?" said Joanna. "Well, come on, Tassy, out with it. Who is this wonderful person?"

"Well," Tassy said obviously embarrassed but still pleased with the attention, "his name is Loren Rutmar. His family only emigrated here a few years ago from Germany. Loren was born there, but says he doesn't remember much about it. He was in high school with me, has a very large family, lots of brothers. Lives out in the Beryl Prairie area. They have a farm there. Loren says he doesn't want to farm though. He's more interested in machinery and things like that. Says maybe he'll get a trade as a machinist or something."

"How did you get to know him?" asked Joanna.

Before Tassy could respond Marta said, "We met the Rutmars at the church in Hudson's Hope. Very nice people. The parents still struggle with English and I guess, like lots of others, they're struggling to make a living off farming. I like Loren, he's a very nice young man, quite serious he seems, but there's nothing wrong with that."

The women talked on and on into the early evening, content in one another's company, Jennifer and Carolyn as new members, becoming more confident in their new familial surroundings.

Finally Paul and the rest of the males trouped back to the house; he was carrying Ronnie, who had skinned his elbows in a fall while playing wild games with the others.

He was obviously tired and cranky now, for he was wailing loudly, dirty tear streaks running down his face. Carolyn took him up on her lap and the wails subsided into snivels.

"Big day?" Carolyn said.

"I guess so," said Paul.

Witt slipped out of the Frontier just before the 1 a.m. closing time, taking the back entrance. He got into the seat of the battered Chev, started it up and moved off down the back alley, then onto 100th Avenue, heading west. He took care to stay within the speed limit; he didn't want any trouble with the cops this night. He turned right onto the Alaska Highway, moved northwest out of town through the hamlet of Charlie Lake, headed up the Highway toward Mile 95.

In the trunk of the car were stowed various articles that Witt intended to employ once he reached his destination far out on the 95 Road past the Halfway Reserve. The previous night as Witt sat drinking in the Frontier with some truck drivers, he happened onto an interesting bit of information. Two of the drivers had just returned from the 95 Road that afternoon where they had hauled two heavy dozers belonging to Outlook Contracting. Outlook was to start in a few days to construct several miles of oil road that would intersect the main 95 Road. Equipment was being moved there in anticipation of this. At present, several large pieces of Outlook's equipment sat in a gravel pit alongside the main road.

Witt pondered this, and later that night he settled on a plan of action. For over two years, ever since the Sangins' ignominious episode with Carson Brennan, Witt and his brothers had been ruminating, drinking, and festering, trying to figure out some way to take their revenge. All of them by that time understood the danger and really the futility of confronting Carson in any kind of stand up fight. All of them had received broken bones in previous attempts, that and a severe loss of face at the drinking establishments among their own elements. Well, it was an eye for an eye, and if they could not pound him to a bloody pulp with their fists, as they would have done with most others, well, then there were other ways to make him hurt. Let's see how he feels when he finds them big machines ain't runnin' so good. Witt relished the very thought. A little sugar in the fuel tanks should fix that up nicely. A few rifle rounds through the block wouldn't hurt either, but he rejected that as noisy and far too obvious. No, a few pounds of sugar funneled into those fuel tanks would leave no signs if he was careful and would end up costing Outlook Contracting and the Brennans plenty before they realized anything was wrong. And eventually they'd figure it out, but let 'em try and prove anything. It wasn't the kind of retribution Witt wanted by a long shot, but for now, until something better came up, it would suffice.

For once, Witt had actually planned things in advance. He hadn't taken anyone into his confidence. His brothers would have been eager allies, but for a change, both of them were employed and living in camp some hours distant. No, he'd take care of business by himself this time. Witt had, however, already miscalculated in at least two areas. The first was the amount of alcohol he'd consumed whiling away the evening until he planned to proceed, and the second was the time it was going to take to drive to the scene of the crime. Witt realized that later when, after an hour's driving, he was still far from his objective. His solution was elementary: he'd drive faster.

The first rain drops began to spatter off the windshield just as he reached the Upper Halfway turnoff at Mile 95. From there out to the gravel pit where his objective lay were more than thirty miles of dirt road, shored up in the worst places with rough pit run gravel. It was a rough drive under any circumstances, and now the steadily increasing rain introduced yet another factor into the equation. The surface dirt on the road changed in minutes from blinding dust to greasy, slippery, gumbo. After only a couple of miles, Witt found the car fishtailing and skidding continuously when he tried to make faster time. The road, like most other established roads in the area, was crowned in the middle, sloping away to both sides. This was to keep water from ponding up, to keep it running off the road into the ditch on either side. This worked admirably with the water; it also had the unnerving effect of causing vehicles to slide away from the middle toward the ditch as well. The only way to counter this was to try to keep the car exactly in the middle of the road where the forces of gravity would pull at it equally from both sides. The wetter the road got the more difficult this became. It was made doubly difficult for Witt, first, because he was driving far too fast for the conditions, and second, because the booze he'd soaked up made the split second reaction required impossible.

After he had progressed a few miles down the road, the rain now falling steadily, he should have considered turning back, but his befuddled brain refused to process the message. To hell with it, he'd keep going and do like he'd planned. Besides, there were few places he could turn around. He knew the gravel pit would provide that service and, anyway, by that time the rain would probably be over. He did not concern himself about the trip back; that was too far away to worry about.

A few miles further, the slope began the long descent to the Halfway River valley, beginning with some wide sweeping turns which gradually sharpened into hairpin S turns, the banks falling away sharply below the narrow shoulder of the road. Once he started downhill, Witt found it increasingly difficult to keep the car in the middle of the road. He took a long draught from the beer bottle he held between his knees and glanced at his watch. Almost 3 a.m. He'd have to move it if he was going to do as he had planned and then get out of there before daylight brought others down the road. This area being open range, cows blundered into the road, watching his lights stupidly as he approached, moving barely in time to avoid a collision. Witt cursed loudly at them out the window as he swerved past.

The car dropped rapidly down a steep hill, Witt fighting to keep it on the road. He rocketed over a narrow bridge just avoiding sideswiping it with the fishtailing rear of the car. The road leveled out a bit; Witt laughed, opened the window, and flung out an empty bottle. As he fumbled with his right arm over the seat behind him for another beer, fate took a hand in the proceedings. The road took a downhill abrupt turn to the left, and Witt realized instantly the car was not going to make it. He flung his arm up over the seat and gave the wheel a savage turn and at the same time unconsciously slammed down the brakes. The car shot sideways off the right side of the road, the wheels catching the soggy bank and sending it into a spinning roll. It was only saved from plunging even further into the heavy timber by a deep ditch put in to carry water away from the road in rainy weather. The car came to rest abruptly on its top, both doors splayed open and gouged into the banks of the soggy ditch.

Witt awoke with rain spattering on his face. There was no sound but that of rain falling on trees. He automatically attempted to sit up and found that impossible. He was pinned by most of his lower body by the top of the car and the crumpled door which held him as though he were in a vice. He strained and twisted, but although he freed his arms, the rest of him lay jammed into the narrow waterway of the ditch, which had saved him from being crushed, but now held him prisoner below the inverted automobile.

In few minutes his head cleared and he realized then his predicament. There was no way he could even start to lift the weight of the car which bore him down. He hurt everywhere but had no idea of the extent of his injuries. He struggled mightily for some minutes trying to wiggle out from under the car body but to no avail. A wave of claustrophobia hit him and he screeched and tore at the ground but could not even start to free himself.

He lay back, gasping for air and trying to think. Maybe someone would come by soon, see his skid marks, look over the edge, see the wreck and figure out how to get him out. Truckers, ranchers, and natives traveled this road constantly, but not, he reflected, at 3 a.m. How long? How long was he going to be trapped before someone came? He shut his eyes, gritted his teeth and sank back.

It was then he made a chilling discovery. The water in the bottom of the ditch where he lay like a rat in a trap seemed to be rising. He twisted his head and felt water running down his neck and into his clothes. A shiver of fear shot through him. What if this water kept rising? It was easy to figure out that it often did during rainstorms and what if nobody came... before... This thought sent him convulsing into a fit of terror, tearing at the mud around him but succeeding none at all in freeing himself. His legs, far under the car, felt numb. And flat on his back as he was, they were absolutely useless to him. By pressing with his elbows he could raise his head and shoulders up out of the water altogether for a while, but fatigue kept forcing him to lie back. No doubt about it now, the water was definitely rising. How in the hell had he ever gotten himself into this mess? Twice in the next half-hour, he thought he could hear an engine far off in the distance. Was it just imagination? He found himself pulling up on his elbows and screaming with all his strength. Help! Help! He kept it up for a long while, then was forced to lie back into the deepening water, gasping and spent. That no one in an automobile would likely hear him even if it sat idling on the road above him was lost in the wave of fear into which he sank.

"Must be about an hour yet before light," Carson said to Kirby, sitting opposite him in the heavy one-ton truck. "What ya think? Should we wait here for daylight or just run 'er the way she is?"

"Waitin' for daylight ain't gonna change anything," Kirby replied. "The road from here on in will be a sewer, always is when it rains. Why can't those damned road guys put some gravel on this bitch of a road?"

"Wanna chain up?" asked Carson. The truck sat just off the turnoff from the Alaska Highway, rain drumming off the hood. "I sure hate the thought of rollin' around in that mud."

"Well, we won't go anywhere if we don't chain, but in the ditch," said Kirby. "Let's get at it."

Both of them got out into the soggy darkness. A plastic tarp was thrust down behind each tire in turn and the heavy chains put on, accompanied by a constant patter of cursing.

"Son of a bitch! I was gonna untangle these damned chains after last winter and forgot about it," Kirby growled.

"What the hell's the matter with these hooks?" Carson retorted. "They seem seized up. Hand me a hammer. I'll bust 'em loose."

Finally the chains were secured and bungee-corded to keep them tight. The two washed the mud off their hands in ditch puddles. They got back in and started tenuously down the nearly impassable road. Outlook Contracting had one of the few four wheel drives in the country at that time. On this dreary morning it made the difference between crawling slowly down the desperately slippery road and sliding off into the water-filled ditch.

"How long before we start on that road?" asked Kirby.

"Don't know for sure," replied Carson. "Liam thought we'd be started already but the oil company hasn't given the go-ahead yet. Probably still dickin' around with permits. Now this damn rain. If it keeps up for long, it'll just make another delay."

"Gonna have to rain a bunch to have any effect on cuttin' that grade. All that scrub timber we gotta move is my big concern," said Kirby. "Rain or no, we ought to be gettin' after it soon."

"Well, you know well as I do, the paper pushers got to give us the go-ahead," said Carson. "Not a damn thing we can do before they say so. Man, this road's a mess. You'd think long as this one's been used, it wouldn't turn to loon shit every time it rains a few drops."

"More'n a few drops this time," Kirby noted. "Looks like it could keep it up for a while. Blacker'n hell down in the valley there. Watch this bridge comin' up; it's narrow as hell and right on a turn at the bottom of this hill."

"Yeah, I remember it from when we were out here couple of winters ago. Another marvel of engineering: bridge set right on a turn. Why the hell did they have to make it one lane anyway? You get a big rig on it, there ain't hardly even room for it by itself."

"Looks like the last guy down this road was tryna use the whole thing," observed Kirby. "Tracks runnin' back and forth to the edge on both sides."

"Coulda been one of them guys from the Reserve," observed Carson. "They ain't always in the best of shape on their way home. Likely we'll get to pull him out of the ditch before we're there."

"Lucky us," muttered Kirby.

"I'd kick er up a notch," Carson said, "but everytime I do, this heap wants to dive over on one side of the crown. We're just gonna have to take our time, take er slow and easy."

They eased down a steep hill, crossed the bridge at the foot of it, and started across a series of winding turns.

"Hey, what the hell was that?" growled Kirby.

"What was what?" responded Carson.

"Back there. It looked like somethin' had gone right over the edge."

"Hell, I didn't even see it. Whataya think? Should we stop?"

"Probably just what you said a minute ago, one of those Reserve guys with a belly full of beer. If they're down in that timber, don't know how we're gonna pull em out anyway."

Carson eased the truck to a sliding stop. "Well, what the hell. I guess we better look. Never know when it'll be us in the ditch. Can you see anything?"

"Back up if you can, but keep away from the edge," advised Kirby.

"Hope nobody comes smokin' around that hill behind us," noted Carson. "Be near impossible to keep from hittin' us."

The truck backed a few yards, keeping away from the muddy shoulder. When the rear of the truck began slipping to the side, Carson stopped. Both Carson and Kirby got out, the truck left idling, the brake on as well as the signal lights.

"Look," pointed Kirby. "There's an outfit down in there upside down." Both peered into the half darkness, rain pelting off their clothes.

"Think there's anybody still down there?"

"Dunno," replied Carson, "Coulda just left er and headed off for home if it was one of the natives."

"Or," said Kirby turning to look at Carson, "they could maybe be trapped inside."

"Or under it," muttered Carson.

"Hey, did you hear that?" Kirby asked.

"Hear what?"

"Listen!" Then they both heard it at once.

Someone was calling out in a hoarse whisper. "Help! Help! Help me!"

Both men, without further comment, clambered down the muddy bank, clinging to bushes to keep their footing in the slippery clay.

"Somebody's partly under here," said Carson, standing over the mud-encrusted upper torso of a figure sticking out from under the inverted car. Muddy water rushed over Carson's boots as he looked down; it swirled around a face totally plastered in mud, the eyes staring up wildly, the rushing water nearly even with the mouth and nose.

"Put somethin' under....under my head, I can't hold it up no more...anything! A stick! Anything!"

Carson stared down for a moment, then reached down, put his hand under the bedraggled head and lifted it slightly.

"Looks like he's caught under from his chest back. This hole must be all that kept it from mashin' him," said Kirby.

"We gotta do somethin' here pretty quick, or his head'll be under water," replied Carson, an edge of urgency in his voice.

"Can we? Do you think we can lift this car up enough to drag him out?" queried Kirby.

"Let's give it a try," Carson said. He released the sopping head and stepped ahead to help Kirby. Immediately the face began to sputter and gasp.

"Carson, wait a minute," said Kirby, "He's drownin'!"

Carson darted back and again lifted up on the man's head, this time only able to barely keep it above the water.

"Hell, it's risin'. We gotta do somethin' quick!" growled Kirby.

"I'll hold him up, see if you can lift it up enough for me to drag him out," Carson shot back.

Kirby bent down, grasped the hood of the car and lifted up, grunting and struggling, his feet slipping and seeking purchase in the viscous mud. Nothing. The wreck remained where it was.

"Hell," Kirby panted, "I can't do it. I just can't lift this heavy piece of shit!"

"Come over here," Carson said. "Hold up his head."

Kirby wallowed through the rising water, bent over and held the inert head. "Hell, he's goin' under! Can't hardly keep his face up!"

Carson moved forward, grasped the car bottom and lifted with all the strength he could muster. Mud and water sucked it down, but it lifted a couple of inches. "Pull on his arms!" he gasped between clenched teeth.

Kirby got his hands under the shoulders and wrenched backwards, pulling the mud-encrusted body from under the upturned roof, tearing a long shallow rip in the man's thigh, but freeing him from a watery grave. The sodden Witt muttered unintelligibly but could do little to help the other two as they wrestled his heavy form up the steep bank, both Carson and the nearly-spent Kirby gasping for breath, their clothes now soaked completely through and plastered with mud. They got Witt into the cab, managed to turn the truck around a few hundred yards further down the road and slogged up their back trail toward the Highway and ultimately the hospital.

Hours later as the two of them drove toward the home place, the trip to the gravel pit postponed, Kirby asked absently, "You got any idea who that was?"

"Yeah, I know who he was." Carson said.

"Well, who was it? You know him?" asked Kirby only half interested.

"Yeah, I know him. Just a guy I know."

By the time they had lived in Fort St. John for five years, Russel and Joanna's family had grown to five. Their three children, two daughters and a son, were like stair steps, all of them blonde, fair, lively and noisy. Joanna now divided her time between the Outlook office, which she oversaw, and her many duties at home. There was now a receptionist who looked after the front desk and the telephone, so that Joanna could focus on the company's books. As Outlook's business in the field had multiplied so had the avalanche of paper. Still, Joanna found time to be involved in the community. The previous year she had co-chaired the annual Heart Foundation Drive and was presently being urged to let her name stand in the local municipal elections. Her intelligence, ambition, and natural charisma did not go unnoticed. She was at once outspoken but fair-minded. Joanna had been opinionated and strong-minded all of her life, qualities that took her to the foreground of every group she was a part of. Russel, naturally less inclined to human interaction than his wife, would have been satisfied to see her consumed with the two worlds of work and family, but by now he knew her well enough to realize this was not to be. Joanna must always be involved in a multifaceted life. The two of them had made the transition from university life to that of work and living in a different environment, and though their lives were often frenetic with all they gave themselves to do, they were happy. Russel's surveying job kept him moving about the country continually; he spent most nights at home but some of them were spent by necessity in camps far from town. Even on those occasions when he could not make it home, he spoke with Joanna on the radiophone when he could.

JOANNA AGAIN

Russel just phoned to let me know he won't be able to get home tonight like we had originally thought. That makes it three nights in a row he's been stuck out there. I wish he had a job where he could be home with us every night; I know it's hard on the kids when he's gone, it's hard on me, too. If he stays on with surveying, it's not likely to change either. So many of the jobs for men in this country, the good paying ones anyway, take them away from home a lot. It's the price you pay to live here, I guess. I didn't see that so clearly when Russel and I came back here. Everything has worked out so well for us in most ways. We're close to family, we're doing okay financially, and I know Russel loves his work; it's just these constant little separations that make it less than ideal.

Amelia loves kindergarten and has a good teacher. She's going to be ready for grade one next fall. I've made a lot of friends since we came back. The town is growing so fast there are lots of young people like us moving in all the time, and there are quite a few people living here yet that I went to high school with. There are so many things that need to be done in this community, and I've let myself get pretty involved, but then somebody has to do it. I'm still trying to make up my mind if I want to run for city council. It's not like I don't have enough to do, what with the office and the kids and everything, but I do like to be involved. I think I'm happiest when I've got all I can possibly do.

There is one thing, I was going to say it's a small thing, but it seems to be growing into something bigger, a thing that is bothering me. For the longest time I thought it was just my imagination, something that got into my mind because I'm home alone with the kids so often—kind of a "fraidy cat" thing women get into sometimes. But it doesn't really stand the test of reason. I know myself well enough to know there's no fear in me about being alone. I mean, I spent great amounts of time alone as a kid at the ranch, admittedly only a few times at night, but I know I'm no shrinking violet. I know I am capable of taking care of myself. But lately, just these last couple of weeks, I've become sure of it: somebody is watching, watching this house, or me, which I'm not sure, but somebody who doesn't want to be seen is hanging around here. I've had intimations of this for a while, but this afternoon I believe I've confirmed it.

I came home at midday, something I don't often do. Fall is just turning into winter and yesterday, we had a skiff of snow. This house we're renting has a garage, not attached to the house, but set back diagonally on the back corner of the lot next to the lane that runs down the whole block behind all of the houses. I went back to the garage, looking for something I wanted. We've never used it for what it was intended, which is parking our car. I rummaged around inside, and when I came out of the side door, I saw something that, most of the time, I wouldn't even have noticed. Right at the corner of the garage, the one next to the fire lane and the part you don't see from the house, well, someone had been standing there in the dusting of snow, just standing there in one place, but whoever it was had been shifting around because the snow was pounded down, like he had been standing there for quite a while. I'm saying "he" because the footprints were large. I wear a size eight and they were lots bigger than mine. And whoever it was stood there long enough to smoke at least two cigarettes, for the butts were stubbed out in the snow by the prints. Anyway, finding that brought me up short, and at first, I wondered why anybody would be standing out there in the first place. I thought maybe it was just kids, you know, sneaking out somewhere for a smoke, but I don't think so. There was only one set of prints, and besides, that would sure be a cold place to be standing, exposed as it is to the wind. I became convinced when I stood in those prints and looked around the corner over the top of the chest high stack of boards Russel has stacked out there. Facing that way, as the maker of those prints had obviously done, made a little chill run down my back. For looking as he had done, he'd be looking through our patio window, straight into the living room and down the hall to our bedroom, and if it was dark, there's no way you'd ever know anyone was there.

I went into the house, turned on all the lights, the hallway, bedroom, all of them, and left the bedroom door open. Then I came back out and stood there again. If the door were even partially open, aided by the big mirror on the opposite wall, you could see right into mine and Russ's bedroom! For a minute what I happened on scared the hell out of me. But I have to say that it did not totally catch me unaware. As I said earlier, I've had this sensation, I don't know, call it intuition or maybe premonition, I don't know what it was, but I have sensed something for a while now. I'm wondering now how long it's been going on—I mean him, whoever, standing out there in the dark, looking at us in this house! I mean, this is the first snow; has it been going on all fall or summer even? The feelings I had at that moment were pretty overwhelming. Who was this sicko? What did he want? Is he just a peeping Tom or someone thinking something more sinister? And, of course, the next thought was for my kids. What kind of threat might he pose to them? At any rate, all of this was swirling around in my head like a storm as I hurried back in the back door of the house and pulled the shabby drapes over the patio window. Those crappy drapes, which we haven't had the money to replace, were part of the reason they were usually left undrawn.

There's something about making a discovery like that that makes everything look different to you; things you hardly paid any attention to now seem frightening, spooky. I know I sure didn't like how it made me feel, unlike anything I'd ever felt before in my life. I rushed into the kitchen, picked up the telephone directory, found the RCMP number and started to dial it. About halfway through dialing, I hesitated, then stopped and hung up the phone. Why I didn't finish, I'm not totally sure, but I guess it had to do with a lot of things. First of all, I had to think about what would happen as soon as I notified the police. They'd undoubtedly send someone over here to talk to me, then they'd go around the neighborhood asking questions and, you know what, all it would do is cause a commotion for me, for Russ, for the kids and for the neighbors. And the worst thing is they wouldn't catch the guy anyway. I've got a friend, lives out in Aneofield and something like this was happening to her a while ago. The cops spent months investigating, prowling around, driving up and down her back alley, and ultimately the word got out, just causing her a lot of personal embarrassment because, of course, no one was ever caught or charged. She told me later that she got the impression that some thought she was just imagining things or maybe even making them up. But if she had the same sense I had this afternoon, the scary sense of having your private life violated, then this thing is for real.

I sat down at the kitchen table, the phone directory still in my hand, and I tried to think. Whoever this is, it's got to be somebody that lives close by, somebody who noticed something, then later went back again.

Is the person a teenager, old, middle-aged? It spun around in my head. One thing is for sure. If he keeps coming back to that one place, that one corner, it would be easy to wait on him and catch him. Catch him...and then what? That was the part that drew a blank in my head. Would you call the cops after you had the person in tow? But likely they'd just go tearing off, if you confronted them, especially if it was dark, which it would be. But not if you put a gun to his head. For a minute I was even shocked at myself for thinking it. But then we're not dealing with a normal situation to begin with. In my mind the use of force is justified when someone could be threatening you or your family. And at what point do I involve Russel? Actually, I've come very near to confiding to him on several occasions that I felt someone was watching this house, but I had no tangible proof and I knew it would just make him anxious, especially every time he had to be away at night. And up until now, I wasn't even sure myself that it wasn't a figment of my own imagination. But now I know and what to do?

Carson remembered the shoes when he was half a block past the repair shop, so he had to circle north then west and come down 100th Avenue again, hoping there'd be some place to park on the main street. For once he was lucky, for a car pulled away from the curb just as he drove up. He'd been forgetting to pick up these repaired shoes every day for the last week. The ones he'd had to wear while his better work shoes were being re-soled were already worn-out past help. It was a late afternoon in autumn, the light fading fast though it was barely past 6 p.m. Carson was still spending some nights at the work camp, but these days he made it in at night far more often than he had in the past. He and Jennifer were going to be first time parents and though it was still months away, he fussed and doted over her, calling faithfully on the radiophone whenever he couldn't make it in. Work was going well, but as always, demanding of his time. Work on the mammoth dam was now going full out, the land clearing behind it was winding down. Other projects, log road building and on-site oil field work, were quickly picking up the slack; no doubt, Outlook Contracting was looking at another frenetic winter.

Carson eased out of the cab of the truck and noticed idly that he was parked directly in front of the Condill Hotel. Not that it mattered to him; he never went in there anyway or for that matter to any of the noisy watering holes that lined the main street in this part of town. He walked directly across the busy street, not bothering with the crosswalk at the traffic light a hundred feet or so away. Most people didn't. This was especially true of the patrons of the beer parlors located on either side. Several had been run down by automobiles over the past few years, some ending in fatalities. Carson entered the repair shop, exchanged a few remarks with the grizzled proprietor, paid for the work and left, the pair of size 14 work shoes clutched in his left hand. He stood for a moment at the curb as a huge Halliburton truck thundered past. He thought he heard someone call out to him but thought it was just the truck noise. Just as he was stepping off the curb and into the street, he heard it again.

"Brennan!" He halted and looked up the street. A wide-shouldered, hulking figure advanced out of the failing light. Carson recognized Witt Sangin instantly. Many things flashed through his mind in a millisecond. Did Witt want trouble? Probably. And if so, what was his own course of action going to be? Carson had no fear of Witt, having dispatched him a couple of times already. But he was extremely concerned of any more consequences. The two months spent at Prince George, if nothing else, had shown Carson that it was unwise to ever let his temper rule the situation. It had been a bitter lesson, but it had not gone unlearned. Also, he had other things to consider. Family things. His standing with his wife's family was delicate at best. The previous dustup at the Frontier with the Sangins, Carson's incarceration and then later his and Jennifer's elopement had left him estranged in the eyes of the Nygaard family to say the least. He was just now getting back on speaking terms with Jennifer's father and had not even advanced to that point yet with her mother. These thoughts were poisoning his mind as he stopped, turned and faced Witt.

The small black eyes boring from under heavy brows and a week's growth of beard framing his bony face, his long black hair greased and pulled back out of his eyes, Witt Sangin could only be described in one word: menacing. He halted a few feet from Carson, and for a long moment each stared into the face of the other. Carson stood, still holding the boots in his left hand, his right hanging at his side in a half-formed fist. Carson's face betrayed no emotion, but his large body seemed rigid, or rather, coiled, like a heavy spring. Witt continued to stare into Carson's face for what seemed an eternity. Then he muttered a single word, "Thanks."

Carson's lips parted slightly as the import of the word rang through his mental circuitry. And he heard himself answer almost tonelessly, "That's okay."

Carson relaxed slightly, some of the pent up tension draining out of his shoulders. Finally he slowly raised his right hand and extended it to Witt. "Peace?"

Witt blinked rapidly a couple of times, then extended his own hand and grasped Carson's lightly. "Okay," he said.

Carson nodded slightly, turned, stepped off the curb and crossed the street to his truck. Witt watched him for a second, spun on his heel and retreated the way he had come into the gathering darkness.

Several times in the weeks following her discovery, Joanna was sorely tempted to tell Russel what she had found, but each time she held back. She could not have said exactly why. But she did contrive a plan.

Russel, unlike the men she had grown up around, had never had any connection with hunting and, for that reason, until very recently had never even owned a gun. But a year or so previously, he had struck up a friendship with some fellows at work who often hunted waterfowl in the numerous marshes around the countryside. In the course of his friendship with them, Russel had gone duck shooting a few times, using a borrowed firearm and had been inspired to buy a gun of his own in due course. That had been over a year in the past, and so far this fall, he had been so busy at work, he had never found time to hunt again. If the truth were known, Russel, only marginally interested in shooting sports and egged on by his enthusiastic friends, had quickly lost interest anyway. But the gun, a pump-action twelve gauge shotgun, still stood in the bedroom closet, a couple of boxes of shells on the shelf above.

Joanna began to carefully monitor the neighborhood for unusual or suspicious-looking characters, and found none. She watched the streets around their home as she drove to and from work. For the first time, she paid attention to the foot traffic about the immediate neighborhood and she noticed vehicles that came and went up and down the street in front of the house. But not once did she see anything that she could put her hand on as being overtly suspicious. She saw the same people pass the house over and over, most of them children and teenagers going to and coming from school.

She began to check the one place that had alerted her to the idea that someone had the house under surveillance—the half-concealed corner by their garage. She did not walk out there, for there were now a couple of inches of snow and to do so would possibly alert the perpetrator. Instead, she drove the family car down the fire lane that ran adjacent to the garage and conducted her observations from inside the car, which she could drive within a few feet of the spot where she'd first seen the footprints. As there was occasional traffic down the fire lane, at least in the daylight hours, this did not give her away. She took to driving there every morning as she left the house. If the children wondered why their mother was taking a new route to the babysitter and Amelia's kindergarten class, they never said so.

Several days after her initial discovery, with Russel stuck in camp for several days, Joanna drove past the garage. It was a frosty November morning. The previous day there had been a dusting of snow, but this morning the skies were robin egg blue. She drove slowly past the spot and nearly stalled the car in her astonishment. There, clearly imprinted in the new snow as they had been before, were the large footprints. Joanna's heart pounded in her chest, her breath came in short gasps. So here it was, it hadn't gone away; it hadn't been a one-time thing; she hadn't just imagined it. She fought the impulse to stop the car and investigate more carefully, but she drove slowly on by, delivered her children to their destinations and repaired to her work. When she arrived home that evening, she set in motion a routine that she followed for several nights. She fed the kids their supper, allowed them to play for a bit in the basement, read to them for their allotted half hour and put them in bed. They usually fell asleep within minutes.

The first time she did it, she wondered at her own actions, her own temerity. When she had checked the kids several times and determined they were asleep, she left via the front entrance, locking the door behind her—all of the doors in the house were locked—descended the steps, turned left, and, shielded from the garage by the house itself, moved until she was behind the tall fence that separated the front yard from the back and moved quietly in the snow until she stood at the back entrance to the garage. There, it was an easy matter to let herself inside. She needed no light for she had carefully plotted out her course in advance. Once inside she moved to the side door of the garage which, virtually never used and always kept locked in the past, opened onto the fire lane only a few feet behind the intruder's footprints. In her hands she carried Russ's now loaded shotgun, a round previously run into the firing chamber so as to make no noise. She eased the side door back just a crack for that was all that was needed to determine if anyone was outside—there wasn't. She eased the door closed again, leaned sideways slightly, letting her shoulder rest against some shelving. The cold in the building was considerable, but she had anticipated it; she wore warm winter boots and a heavy down coat. On her head was perched one of Russel's fur caps. She stood this way, not moving for the better part of an hour. She moved the door ever so little every once in a while to check—nothing.

The dark silence gave her ample time to reflect on what she was doing. Did this really make any sense? Why hadn't she told Russel? Because... because it wouldn't have solved the problem, probably would make it worse. She thought through again for the hundredth time her course of action. But was she justified? Of course, she was. Whoever this miscreant was posed a threat to her and to her family. Right? If the person did not have bad intentions, then why was he skulking around her house at night trying to look into it? Is window peeking a crime, she wondered? If it isn't, it sure ought to be. But how would this be looked at if it ever ended up in a courtroom? Am I encouraging this? She found these thoughts running through her mind over and over as she waited silently in the darkened garage. After waiting for an hour or more and still no sign of anyone outside, she slipped back out of the garage, into the house, closed the drapes, checked on her sleeping children, turned out the lights and retreated to her bed to turn in uneasy slumber through the remainder of the night.

Joanna was not a person given to starting and abandoning projects at random. Once she targeted an objective, usually after considerable deliberation, she pursued it relentlessly, with all the force of her powerful character. It had been the same since childhood, whether it be the competitive atmosphere of the classroom, the esoteric skills of the chessboard or selection, pursuit and capture of a mate, Joanna was accustomed to seeing things through to a conclusion, prepared to stay the course. Generally she initiated action only after reflection, but once underway, she tended not to be hampered by self-doubt.

For the next four nights in succession, she stuck to the routine she had established. She fed her children, read to and entertained them, put them to bed, and took up her vigil at the garage. And was rewarded with nothing. In four trips, she heard or saw no one. Russel returned from camp and for the next ten days life fell back into a familiar routine. Around the first week of December, Russel's company began a project in the Boundary Lake area, many miles east over as yet very bad roads. Russel began by driving home every night but soon was forced to cut his trips home to one night in three. Neither he nor Joanna liked the arrangement, but the very long hours on the job and the trying roads were very hard on Russel; besides, the job was to be completed by Christmas, so they just lived with the situation as temporary.

On the morning following Russel's first of two nights spent at camp, the footprints were there again. Her resolve reinforced, Joanna was at the garage the following night. This time things were different.

She had been sitting on the chair she had placed near the side door after that first night when she'd had to stand on the concrete floor for a long hour. The shotgun rested across her knees. Firearms held no mystique or fear for Joanna. She had been raised with guns. Liam had used them routinely through her childhood to put meat on the table. She had seen him dispatch several deer with his rifle, most of them a stone's throw from the house. In her teens she had shot deer herself and once a moose that wandered into the feed yard. She knew guns as the tools they were, and she knew they were not playthings. She clearly understood that a gun in the hands of a competent erased any advantage an opponent might have in strength or gender. With this in mind, she settled back into the chair, her gloved hands clutching the grip of the shotgun. Fifty minutes or more passed without a sound, save the rustling of mice in the cardboard boxes stacked on the floor. Her mind wandered, but her resolve to wait at least an hour held her.

There was the slightest whispering of sound that seemed at first to come from inside the building. She tensed, her stomach tightened into a knot; she felt herself trembling slightly. Then she heard it clearly; something, someone was moving just outside the door. She saw a tiny glimmer of light and for a second thought a car was coming down the fire lane. Just as quickly the faint glow died. Then she knew: whoever stood outside had lit a cigarette. She smelled it ever so faintly as the smoke drifted through the crack of the door. She sat frozen in the chair, heart pounding fiercely in her temples. Minutes passed. This was why she was here. Did she have the strength to follow through? For a time, she was tempted to just sit and stay silent, let this spook or whatever it was, smoke his cigarettes, get his fill of looking and vanish. Finally she found herself shifting the heavy gun so that she held it vertically with her right hand, willing herself not to bump it against the door. She rose from the chair in a slow, measured movement, feeling her knees popping slightly from their long stillness. She reached across her body, clutching the knob and pulling the door open slightly. For a second she could see little, then as her night vision resettled, she saw standing no more than two strides away a figure outlined slightly by the faint town light. She stood rock still, almost holding her breath. The figure moved slightly and her heart was in her throat! There was a slight rustle of clothing and then an illumination as a match was struck and a face illuminated. Lighting another cigarette! In an instant Joanna pulled the door open, stepped across the sill and took a long stride straight behind the figure; it's face still framed in match light. She rammed the barrel into the small of the back and snarled, "Stand still! If you move, I'll shoot! I mean it!"

The man, for it was a man, half turned around in an automatic response movement, and Joanna pushed the gun more forcibly into his back and thumbed the safety off with a clearly audible click. The man froze and a shudder ran through him. His forward route of escape was blocked by the woodpile he looked over; to escape he'd have to move backward a step and then go right.

"Lift up your hands!" commanded Joanna. "Lift them high! Now! Now!"

The man responded jerkily, his whole body was shuddering convulsively.

"Now, lie down slowly, face down, and don't think I won't shoot you if you try anything! Do it!" She shifted the force of the gun barrel up between his shoulders as he sunk down to his knees. She pushed the muzzle right against his back as he lay down prone in the snow.

"Keep your arms out in front of your face!"

She could hear his rapid and very loud breathing like an athlete that has just run a race. She pulled the powerful flashlight from her pocket and shone it on the back of the man's head.

"Turn your head," she said between clenched teeth. "I want to see your face!" She reinforced this by pressing the muzzle of the shotgun under his ear. She shone the light down into the terrified eyes, the nostrils dilating and closing as he took deep rapid breaths. She realized at first glance that she had seen this face before, it took only a few seconds to pull it from very recent memory. This was a face she'd seen at the company Christmas party only a few days before!

"What's your name?" she demanded. "I want your name now!"

The figure mumbled something unintelligible.

"Your name, now!"

"Bill Jones. My name's Bill. Bill Jones," he sputtered.

"You're lying. I know where I saw you—at the Mansell company party—so you better tell the truth. I know your name's not Jones. You work with my husband!"

"Oh God! Please!" he whined.

"I want your real name now!" She pressed the muzzle ever tighter into his neck.

"It's Howard, isn't it?" she said, pressing even harder with the shotgun. "Now give me your real last name!"

He closed his eyes and swallowed several times. "Howard...Howard Komec," he whispered.

"Now you explain why you've been hiding here and staring into my house."

"I wasn't," he panted. "I was just passing down the back lane. I stopped to have a smoke."

"You're lying! You were standing there for over twenty minutes, time enough to light two cigarettes."

"I...it...it was the first time. I don't know why, I just stopped."

"If you don't quit lying, I might just as well shoot and then call the cops. You've been leaving footprints right there where you were standing ever since the first snow and who knows how long before that, so don't try to tell me tonight was the first time."

"Oh God, please...please. I'll never do it again. Never, I swear." His eyes were now running tears, he was actually whimpering like a frightened puppy.

"Your wife would be pretty interested in knowing about all this," said Joanna. "I'll bet she'd be really proud of you."

Komec said nothing only clenched his eyes shut tightly, his body still trembling violently.

"Get up off that ground," Joanna hissed through clenched teeth, retreating back a step, but keeping the gun leveled at his face. "You get away from here and don't ever, ever come around my house again. If you ever do, I swear to God I'll see you ruined. I'll bring the police in and the first move will be phoning your wife. And worst of all, Mr. Komec," she sneered, "I'll let my husband in on this. He'll pound you to a bloody pulp!"

She said this emphatically, wondering herself how true it was. But no matter! She wanted to terrorize and humiliate this dirt bag. "Now get out of here and don't forget for an instant what I've said." She motioned with the muzzle toward the lane and then repeated it when he remained paralyzed in his tracks. "Move!"

Komec took a couple of jerky backward steps, almost fell, recovered and then moved hesitantly away down the fire lane. After he had gone a few paces, he broke into a trot and then a frenzied lurching run. Joanna looked at the print of his figure in the snow at her feet. It was completely soaked. She stayed where she was long after he was out of sight in the shadows. Her legs felt strangely weak, as though they could barely hold her up. She found herself breathing as though she'd just climbed a steep hill.

She closed the open door, walked around the garage along the fence, unlocked the front door, stepped inside and leaned against the door. She felt exhausted and fought back the impelling need to weep. She unloaded the gun, put it back in the closet. She did not even go to bed that night, for she knew sleep was impossible. She drank several cups of coffee, sitting at the dining room table, found herself going over and over what had happened. She awoke just before dawn, still sitting in her chair, her face buried in her arms against the tabletop.

The entire family assembled that year at Christmas in the new house at the home place. Marta, Tassy, Joanna and Carolyn and Jennifer, too, spent the whole Christmas day creating a mammoth dinner. The five of them spent hours together in the new kitchen, interrupted from time to time by children playing on the stairs, in the living room; there were a few squabbles over toys. Liam had erected a bushy blue spruce Christmas tree in the corner next to the patio door; it was decorated with long strands of tinsel, striped red and white candy canes, various gew gaws that the children had made, a spiraling band of red, green, and blue lights, and was topped with a glittery silver-white angel. Presents had been opened long before light and a blizzard of wrapping paper, cardboard boxes, children's books and toys lay scattered in chaotic splendor across the carpeted floor.

This was the one time of year that the male members of the family felt no compulsion to be about work outside the house. Liam and Carson had risen, even before the children, and fed the stock, which these days, comprised only a dozen horses and fifty two-year old replacement heifers. The two hundred or so of Liam's stock cows were being wintered many miles away at Flatrock, having been contracted out to a rancher there until they were to be returned to the home place just before calving began in mid-March. With their ever-increasing and ever-pressing construction work, neither Liam nor Carson had any time for the husbandry required to mind wintering cattle. Two more locals would be hired to take care of the calving once the stock was back at the ranch. Truth was, it was costing what little profit there was in the stock to have them cared for by others, but Liam had spent so many years building his herd, that he had not been able to bring himself to get rid of them. He saw very clearly that there was far more profit to be made in oil field construction, but the life of a gentleman rancher had been a part of Liam's dream from the beginning. He still lived life on the land in his mind and heart, if not totally in substance.

Carson sat among the Brennan men as an equal among equals. Taciturn as always, he seldom initiated discussion but took part more willingly and more easily than in the past. His impending fatherhood sat well upon him, and he accepted Paul and Russel's ribbing and joking in good humor. When discussion inevitably turned to work, Paul, as always, was dispenser of advice and business acumen to the others.

"Hell, Carson, if you keep on spending your winters glued to the seat of a cat and backhoe, you're gonna wear yourself out before your time. You know what? You and Dad need to hire all of your hands-on help and move back into a supervisor-advisory role. Hell, you can afford to do it if you hire the right people. That's the key. The right employees. Right, Russel?"

"Yeah, I guess so," Russel reflected, "but you still got to keep in touch with the daily things the employees are doing. At Mansell, the boss, the real boss, the owner of the company, the guy who started it and ran it successfully for years, well, he works in the office all the time now. Actually, he doesn't come in a lot of the time, and as far as I'm concerned, it's hurting the business. He's got a few guys now who are not pulling their weight, are being unproductive a lot of the time and nobody's doing much about it."

"What! You don't have a foreman or a boss?" asked Paul.

"Yes, we do , but he's too laid back to be very effective as far as I can tell," said Russel. "And we've also got a couple of employees there who are not very motivated. They take a lot longer to get some jobs done than they need. And they've learned that there are no reprisals for slacking off, though, actually just this past week, the company got lucky. One of the worst slackers, for some unknown reason, just quit, pulled up stakes and is moving his family to some place in Alberta, I'm not sure where. I feel sorry for his wife and six kids, is all. If his potential employers over there bother to check up on his work history, he could find it hard to get hired. It's a mystery to everybody at work as to why he decided to quit, but, be that as it may, Mansell is fortunate to be rid of him. I just hope whoever his replacement is will be more of an asset to the company..."

Liam sat ensconsed in a large armchair, taking sporadic part in the ebb and flow of the conversation, but allowing his attention to be deflected by ongoing interaction with his grandchildren. He wrestled, romped, and played with them on the floor to their shrieking delight, read to them and was read to. Liam sometimes felt his age, especially on cold winter mornings, but he seemed blessed with continual good health. His steel-grey hair was still thick and his lined cheeks brushed with pink below the crowfeet around the corners of his eyes. His large hands remained calloused though not to the hoof-like quality they had once been. He was one of those fortunates who never seem to gain weight no matter how much they indulge themselves at the table. While Marta had been fighting a mostly losing battle with the bulge for years, Liam remained pretty well as he had always been, wiry and lean.

Paul looked much like what he was, a business executive, employed by a multinational oil conglomerate. His days were increasing spent, wearing a hard hat, deeply involved in the production management end of his company. He continued his steady rise through the ranks of middle management, his focus always on the next step. After the Christmas holiday, he, Carolyn and the children would be flying to Aberdeen for a year and a half, possibly longer, where Paul's company was heavily involved in off-shore drilling. Paul had just returned from there, having spent six months away from his family who had remained behind in Calgary. Carolyn was happy to be going with her husband, but she privately worried over the many changes that would be inevitable and, of course, about the children adapting to ever-changing circumstances. Carolyn was not a particularly social person, and she foresaw having to change with the rising status of her husband; she secretly agonized over it. As always, Paul forged ahead, supremely confident in his own abilities, understanding his talent for organization and team cooperation. When he experienced moments of self doubt, they were never allowed to surface; he always projected a demeanor of optimism and enthusiasm, sometimes to the point of irritation to people like Carson who, while not a great visionary, saw the world through the lens of the hands-on worker. Paul was concerned with the ideas and general picture, Carson with the reality and the day-to-day details.

That Christmas was a wonderful time for Marta. A deep communion with her family was something she had always wanted and so rarely realized in the past. Tassy noticed that she tired more easily than she remembered, but she put it down to the long hours Marta had spent preparing for everyone, cooking the meals, accommodating and attempting to make everyone comfortable. She seemed to be relishing her role as family matriarch. She tried to cook everyone's favorite dish; she pampered and indulged the grandchildren. By the end of Christmas day, Tassy saw that Marta was very tired, though she was trying very hard to shrug it off. Tassy, and Joanna, who was also aware of Marta's fatigue, tried to get her to relent in the kitchen, let them take over, but she would have none of it. By the end of the week, when everyone had departed, Marta was visibly exhausted, but she had gloried in having the whole family around her. She professed to Tassy that she didn't care how tired it had made her, it was worth every second of it.

Snow fell almost unceasingly during the middle weeks of January that winter. The skies, often very clear and blue at that time of year, were mainly overcast, dark and brooding. Dry gritty snow continued to fall day after day, piling up on the south facing slopes above the Hudson Hope Road, on the road itself, in the fields and on the long lane connecting the Brennan home place with the Hope Road. The yards behind the house were choked with snow. Liam pushed it here and there with a dozer to keep it from plugging the yards altogether. His trips to distant work sites became continual battles with horrific road conditions. He spent more nights away from home than he wished. Tassy, employed in Fort St. John, stayed at Joanna and Russel's during the week but spent most weekends with Marta at the ranch. Fridays, she rode home with Loren on his way to the Rutmar homestead in Beryl Prairie. Loren's family continued to struggle with their homestead, his many siblings dispersing to jobs here and there, his German parents gradually acquiring better English skills. Loren was more than happy to give Tassy a ride; in fact it was one of the highlights of his week. They often saw each other several times during the week, as Loren was employed in town, too. Joanna kept Marta informed on what she perceived as a hot romance that was developing with Tassy and Loren.

"Come on, Gramma, you know I'm old enough now to handle things. I'm an adult, I'm eighteen years old, a high school graduate, and holding down a full-time job. There's nothing wrong with going out to movies or things now and then."

"Joanna tells me it's pretty well every night you're out with Loren," countered Marta. "If he's spending all that time with you, how is he to progress in his mechanics courses you've been telling me about?"

"But, Gramma, Loren's been getting just about straight 100% scores on his tests; he's right at the top of his group. Anyway, Gramma, forgive me for saying it, but Joanna is trying to mind my business too much. Geez, you'd think she was my mother or something."

"Well, she's always been like that," Marta said, "always in charge, always looking at everything that goes on around her and, of course, giving her read on things."

"You know I love her like she was my mother," Tassy said, putting her hand on Marta's arm, "but she does exaggerate things sometimes. I mean, no one was giving her advice when she was going out with Russel, she wouldn't have stood for it. I just wish she'd show a little more confidence in me, that's all. She hasn't really twigged on the idea yet that I'm a grown person now, not a child that needs her constant monitoring."

"So," Marta said, looking across the kitchen table at Tassy, "have you and Loren made any plans, I mean, long-term ones?"

"Well," Tassy said, meeting her eyes, "I know he wants to marry me though he's never actually said it yet. But he talks about the future and I'm always in the pictures he paints along with him."

"And what will you say if he asks you...when he asks you?" Marta corrected.

"Right now, well, I'm not sure. But I do like him a lot."

"He's a nice young man. I thought so the first time we met him and his family at Church," Marta allowed. "But remember, Tassy, that if you marry Loren you're becoming a part of his family. And you know they're very European, very German. They have traditions and so on that are quite different from ours."

"I've been at his house a couple of times," Tassy admitted. "Yes, they are different from us. His parents still speak German in the home, but they are very nice. Hard working people, too. Loren's younger brothers are so shy, but they've gone out of their way to be nice to me. The only thing I had any trouble with was the food. They have so many dishes I'd never even seen before. It'd take some getting used to if I had to eat that all the time...."

The two of them talked on into the night. Both of them noticed that the wind outside was up now, even more than it had been an hour or two earlier.

"The wind was blowing snow around so hard Loren could hardly see the road, and it was drifting, too. There's so much snow anyway, and now it's blowing all over the place. There were even little drifts right on the road," Tassy said. "I hope he didn't have any trouble getting on out to his folks' place, that's still another thirty miles or so. He's a good driver though; he'll make it."

Tassy got up from the table, went to the front door, opened it and peered outside, the howl of the rising wind very audible now, snow blasting in through the open door. She closed it abruptly, a look of awe on her face. "I can't ever remember the wind blowing like this before, ever," she said, "and it's so cold to start with."

"Liam fed up all the livestock before he left this afternoon. He said they'd be all right until tomorrow," said Marta, rising from her chair to stand beside Tassy, staring out into the blackness through the front window, windblown snow flying by, held almost horizontal by the driving wind.

"I don't expect he'll be back now until sometime tomorrow. You and I will need to put some feed out for the cattle but we won't have to worry about it until daylight."

Tassy moved to the huge cast-iron stove that sat ensconced on slate slabs in the opening between the kitchen and the dining room. Long ago the Brennans had realized that in this cold country fireplaces could not provide constant heat and so in the new home a massive stove had replaced it, surrounded by a wall of beautifully-laid field stone. Built into the stone wall was a ledge which could be loaded with enough wood to supply the stove for long periods. From this stack Tassy selected a huge half log, opened the stove door and cast it in.

"We might as well keep the stove burning hot all night," Tassy said. "I can feel the cold sucking the heat out of the house right now. Gramma, can you ever remember a wind this bad?" she asked a bit incredulously.

"Well, you know this river valley is pretty protected against wind most of the time," Marta replied, "except when it comes out of the east, like it is tonight. An east wind in winter is always a very cold wind. It just blows upriver with not much to break it up. That's especially true since so much of the timber has been taken off to create farmland east of us."

Both of them stood beside the stove now, listening to the keening of the wind in the eaves. It shrieked and whined like a living thing.

"Those poor cattle," Tassy said. "How do they ever stand nights like this?"

"They have got some shelter," Marta offered. "They have the sheds and windbreaks that Liam built years ago. As long as they can get some relief from the wind, they'll be all right no matter how much it snows or how much the temperature drops."

"Is it ever cold!" said Tassy again. "I can feel it right through the walls. I'm gonna check the thermometer on the back porch." She walked through the kitchen, opened the door; the roar of the wind spat at her as she shone a flashlight on the thermometer attached to a pillar on the porch. She rushed back inside slamming the door behind her, hugging her arms across her chest and hunching her shoulders. "It's minus 31," she said, shuddering. "How can it blow like this and still be so cold, too? Do you think Grampa is okay?"

"It doesn't help to get worked up over it," Marta said. "I know your grandfather will look after himself. I can't even begin to count the nights like this in the old house when I stood shivering around the stove half crazy with worry about him. But you can't do anything about it but trust his judgment, I guess. He always came out of it all right. Couple of times had frostbitten toes and fingers, but never anything really bad."

"I sure hope Loren got home all right and isn't stuck in a drift someplace. But," Tassy added, "the wind was nowhere near this bad when he left here."

"I'm sure he's okay, Tassy. Let's not worry ourselves anymore than we can help it," Marta said. "It just doesn't do any good, and we can't do anything about it right now. I'm so tired I've got to sleep. This storm will likely blow over by daylight. Then we'll have to get out and feed the stock.

That's going to take some energy so I've got to rest. Please turn the lights out when you go to bed."

Long after Marta had gone to her bedroom, Tassy sat at the kitchen table, listening to the maniacal wind screaming around the house. She was used to the cold winters here, but wind like this, so powerful combined with the numbing cold, struck a note of fear in her. Everything about this storm told her that it was not usual but different and possibly deadly.

Around midnight, just before she lay down on the davenport—she did not go to her bed—she checked the temperature again. This time she put on a heavy coat just to venture the few feet to the thermometer. It read exactly minus 40. Combined with the terrible wind it cut through even the heavy coat. Her face went numb instantly. She scurried back inside, filled the stove, damped it back then lay down fully clothed, pulling a wool comforter over her. Sleep was a long time coming and when it did, it was fretful and uneasy. Sometime in the night, she thought it was between 2 or 3 a.m., she heard Marta get up and she saw the bathroom light go on. When she woke again, the light was out. She knew her grandmother had not been feeling quite herself lately. She had seen it in her face though Marta was not given to complaint no matter how bad she felt. Tassy closed her eyes and slept.

When she woke again it was still pitch dark and deadly quiet in the house, save for the creaking of the walls in the terrible cold outside. She sat up and stared across the room at the illuminated hands of the clock on the wall. It was 6:30 a.m. She rose and turned the light switch—nothing happened. She paused, tried again, and again the light did not come on. She walked across the room and tried the light switch for the front porch, again with the same result. The power, for reasons unknown, was off. She opened the back door and stared out into the blackness. The wind was not so strong as it had been earlier, but it still seared her face like a frozen blowtorch. She was astounded at what she saw—or didn't see. The porch steps had disappeared under a huge shelved drift that ran right across the back of the house. How deep it was she could not really fathom in the quasi-darkness but it had to be deep enough to obliterate all of the steps. She drew back and closed the door, stood leaning against it, shivering. The electricity was off—so the oil furnace in the basement could not be functioning—the stove had to be kept going. Had it gone out in the night? She moved to the stove door, opened it slowly and peered in. A faint bed of coals still glowed though all of the wood she had put in earlier seemed used up. She took some smaller pieces and arranged them in the stove's interior so that there was air between them and the glowing embers. She closed the door and opened the draft all the way. She realized then how cold it was in the house. It took a minute or so of fumbling to find her coat and even after she put it on she did not feel particularly warm.

After a time, the wood in the stove blazed up, she could hear it popping. She opened the door, the flaming interior reflected fantastically on the adjacent walls. She put in more wood, bigger pieces then and left the door slightly ajar to provide some light. She moved off into the kitchen and fumbled around in some drawers where she knew her grandmother kept candles. She found a handful of long slender ones but could not find any matches. She returned and poked a candle into the stove long enough to light the wick. She found her flashlight, put it in her coat pocket but held onto the candle. She glanced at the clock again—still not quite 7 o'clock. It was unusual for Marta to sleep past this hour and Tassy thought to wake her, then held off, remembering how tired Marta had been the previous night. Let her sleep if she wants, thought Tassy. There's nothing to be done anyway.

She wondered what had happened to the electrical power. It had only been a few years since the light plant had been discarded, after electricity had become available when the line was brought along the road from the Hope. Probably a tree over the lines, she thought. As hard as the wind had been blowing all night, there could be several trees down. Who knows when anybody can get out to fix the problem. How long before daylight? At this time of year, not much before 9 o'clock, she thought. She went into the kitchen to set a pot of coffee on the electrical stove, realizing as she did it that she was wasting her time. She picked up the pot, took it into the next room and set it on top of the massive wood burner. She glanced at the candle still held in her hand, the reflections moving in ghostly shadows on the walls. People used to live like this all the time, she thought. Every day of their lives in winter anyway, they got up in darkness and had to mess with candles and lanterns, couldn't just throw a switch like she'd been used to doing all of her life. Gramma and Grampa never had electricity in the old house until they'd lived there for many years. Lord! How did they stand to live like that? How did anybody stand to live that way? For a few seconds she had a fleeting glimpse backward into the lives of her living predecessors, lives lived in hard and primitive conditions, so different from her own life and yet so close to it in time. For a few moments she could at least partially understand what it meant to pioneer, to settle in wild, primitive places and to build a life there with nothing but hand labor and natural materials, where every necessity had to be hewed out by backbreaking toil and long suffering patience. Deprived of the power that made life so much easier than it had been for her grandparents, Tassy was able to appreciate more clearly what they had accomplished in the long years before electricity had lifted some of the burdens from their hands.

She stood close to the stove, which now roared as the additional wood caught. She closed the door but was hesitant to leave the aura of warmth around it. It was certainly cold, even in the house. What the temperature had fallen to outside she could not even guess. Again she wondered about Marta. Was she warm enough? Maybe she should open the door to her room so that what warmth there was could penetrate there. She tiptoed quietly down the hallway, grasped the doorknob and pushed it so that it stood about half open. She was tempted to call out to her but held off. Let her rest; she had seemed so tired last night.

Tassy moved back to the stove and idly watched the coffeepot first blow steam, then finally come to a slow boil. She waited until she judged it was fit to drink, got a cup from the kitchen and stood sipping, shifting her weight slowly from one foot to the other.

Then with a twinge of anxiety, she remembered the stock, horses and cattle that would be needing feed so very badly in this awful cold. And it would have to be done soon.

First, she put on a pair of Liam's heavy winter coveralls, then a wool sweater over that, followed by her own winter coat, a wool toque and lined leather mitts. She finished with wool socks inside of felt-lined boots. She realized she had so much clothing on that physical work would be badly impaired, but she also knew what it was going to be like outside. She took a deep breath and slipped out the porch entrance, closing the door as quietly as she could behind her. She was expecting the cold to hit her like a blow and she was not disappointed. For a few seconds she just stood to give her eyes a chance to adjust to the light, or the lack of it. It was actually fairly easy to see once her eyes got used to it. The wind had died down, but there was still a strong breeze from downriver that seared her face whenever she had to face into it. She started to kick her way through the drifted-in steps, retreated and held her flashlight to the thermometer on the pillar. The scale only went to minus 60 and the red line was stuck right at the bottom. No wonder she had thought it was so cold. It was! She could not remember ever seeing the thermometer bottomed out like that before.

After she had forced her way through the drifts, some of them waist high, the dog came floundering out to meet her from the shelter of the equipment shed where he always stayed at night. He fell in at her heels as she pushed on to the feeding sheds. She could hear the cattle milling around over the frozen ground even before she could see them. At least here they'd had some shelter from the terrible wind. There were fifty or more of them crowded inside the roofed-over feeding area. The vapor from their breathing turned the air murky with steam. They kept up a steady lowing as she began to fork hay off the stack and into the mangers. They jostled and pushed and shoved each other trying to get at the hay that was so slow in being spread for them. It was much darker inside the shed, so Tassy tried to hold the flashlight and the pitchfork handle in the same hand. It kept falling into the hay and she was forced to lay it down near the edge of the manger and make do with the tiny bit of light it cast. Though she had covered herself in so many clothes, she was not over warm at first. The cold was so deep, so penetrating that it frightened her a bit. She kept doggedly on, not able to move much hay, as it was tightly packed and difficult to tear loose. The cattle pushed and milled in a frenzy to get at the feed, their feet keeping up a steady clatter on the frozen floor. By the time she had put hay the full length of the manager, most of what she had put down at the start had disappeared. She went back over the whole length again, finally taking off the coat as she felt the sweat beginning to form under her clothes. She was breathing hard and her arms and wrists ached. Still, her fingertips were so cold she could feel nothing in them.

Leaving the cattle shed, she crossed the yard to the horse shelter, where she forked over as much hay as she could dig out to the rime-encrusted horses. Some of them had so much ice around their eyes and nostrils she wondered how they could function. The dominant ones bit and kicked as they forced their way to the front, the yearlings and smaller horses, milling at the periphery. Here was the law of the jungle: the strongest took as much as they could, the weaker getting the crumbs. Tassy spread the hay as best she could so that all of them would at least get some feed. By the time she was finished, her inner clothing was damp with sweat. Pulling on her coat, she slipped the hood over her toque and slogged through the drifted feed yards back toward the house. It was noticeably lighter now, a rosy glow shone on the top of the hills to the southeast. She saw that the wind had moved the snow willy nilly. In some places, the drifts were nearly four feet deep, in other places the frozen ground was exposed. The dog clung to her heels. When she arrived at the house, she went in, got some scraps from the kitchen and tossed them to him, closing the door quickly, knowing he'd retreat to the shelter of the equipment shed when it was evident nothing more was forthcoming.

Tassy had half expected to be greeted by her grandmother, but everything was still quiet in the house. A tiny alarm of apprehension went off in her head. It was totally unlike Marta to be in bed when others were up and around. Besides, it was Marta who had reminded Tassy that they would have to take care of the stock at dawn.

"Gramma," she called out softly down the hallway toward the half open door of the bedroom. "Gramma, are you up?" She could hear no reply. She listened intently for a few seconds, the called again. "Gramma, Gramma, are you all right?" Silence. She walked softly to the door, pulled it completely open and stared into the half light of the bedroom. "Gramma."

The figure in the bed stirred slightly. Tassy walked to the bedside and put her head close to her grandmother's. "Gramma?"

Marta's eyes were open and her lips moved slightly, but no sound came from them.

"Gramma!" Tassy said in a quavering voice. "What is it?"

Marta seemed to stir slightly, her eyes locked on Tassy's, and her lips moved slightly but no sound escaped them.

Tassy put her hand under Marta's head and lifted it. "Has something happened, Gramma? Can you say anything?"

Marta's eyes moved back and forth, she seemed to be breathing deeply as though making some great effort, her mouth continued to move. Tassy put her ear only inches from Marta's moving lips, then she could hear her faint but clearly discernible whisper,

"Liam, get Liam. I can't move—find Liam!"

Tassy laid Marta's head back on the pillow and stood rigid with fright. What should she do?

"Gramma, I'll get you something to drink." She darted to the now half light kitchen, fumbled in the cupboard and found a glass, which she half filled with water. She took it back to Marta's room, propped her up as best she could and put the glass to her lips. Marta closed her eyes and took a mouthful of water. She seemed to struggle, trying to swallow it, but it trickled from the corners of her mouth and ran down her neck into her bedclothes. Tassy held the glass to her mouth again with the same result. It was clear now to Tassy that something was terribly wrong, her grandmother could not even swallow. Marta seemed to strengthen slightly then sank back on the pillow, but her eyes blinked open. Her lips were moving again. Tassy bent over her, her ear close to Marta's face.

"Find Liam! Get your grandfather!"

Tassy heard it clearly again. She stood up. Her mind raced. She touched Marta's hand and found it stone cold.

"Gramma, I'm going to pull your blankets up over your arms so you won't be cold." She propped Marta's head up with more pillows, then pulled the bedding up over her arms and close to her chin.

Tassy filled the stove with the largest pieces of wood she could find, damped it back and stood rigidly before it, her mind racing, trying to understand what had happened to Marta and, most of all, considering what she should do.

"Find Liam!" Her grandmother's words flashed back and forth through her mind. But how? Her own car was here parked beside the house but hadn't been started in several days. She knew enough of mechanics to realize that on a day like this, nothing was going to run anyway.

The telephone! She raced to the hallway, picked it up. The familiar buzz or the sound of someone talking on the party line was missing. There was no sound at all. It was completely dead. She pushed the receiver button several times. Nothing. Whatever had knocked out the electricity must have taken out the phone lines, too.

She rushed back into Marta's room and put her hand to Marta's face. "Gramma, the phone is dead and it's way too cold for a car to run, but I'm going to get some help. I don't know how yet, but I'll think of something. Just try to rest and keep warm."

She looked down into the grey eyes, which stared up her, blinking as though to confirm understanding. Tassy fussed over her, trying to make her comfortable and warm. She spoke as she moved around as much to dispel some of the frightened confusion she was feeling as to comfort her grandmother.

"I know whatever has happened has something to do with how tired you've been lately, it has to. Maybe it will be better after you get some rest," she said though not believing it herself. "I'll find Grampa for you and he'll know what to do. I'll figure out some way to get hold of him." She leaned over and kissed Marta's forehead. "Just try to rest."

She went back into the kitchen and paced back and forth, through the whole of the lower house except Marta's room. Hudson's Hope was twenty miles, more than that to Fort St. John. Was the road blown in? It had to be after a storm like this. And the temperature! She'd never seen cold like this before in her whole life! Then what? What to do?

She put on her coat, boots and toque again and went outside on the porch. It was full daylight now, though the sun still sat behind the hill to the southeast. The sky above her looked to be clear blue, but a heavy ice fog made objects more than a few hundred feet away blurry, after that they were blotted out altogether. It was becoming nearly still now, but the cold was intense. It clawed at her nose and cheeks though they were half hidden in the coat's hood. She descended the porch steps and pushed out into the lane, facing north down the long lane that connected the home place with the Hope Road. She walked several steps in ankle deep snow then ran abruptly into a waist deep drift that lay crossways across the lane, extending into the field on both sides. She pushed a few feet into it and stared ahead. It seemed to go on far enough that she could not discern where it ended, if it ended at all. She stood for a minute or so listening but not really expecting to hear anything moving on the road which lay a few hundred yards ahead of her, all but invisible now in the murky ice fog. A deep silence lay over the valley except for the faint, far off bawling of cattle. Her body was now beginning to shake with cold. She retraced her steps to the house, went inside, stood leaning against the door as she took off her coat and boots. Her mind was as unclear as the fog-shrouded flats outside. What should she do? Even if she could find some way to get out to find help, should she leave Marta here alone and helpless? But what could she do for her even when she was here? She went back into the bedroom and laid her hand against Marta's cheek. The grey eyes opened and looked up at her.

"Don't worry, Gramma. I'm gonna get you some help, I know it. Can I get you anything? Something to drink or eat?" She heard her own voice and felt foolish even saying it. She said, "Gramma, I'll put my ear by your face. Tell me if there is anything I can do for you."

She listened intently and she heard faintly, "No, nothing now."

The day wore on slowly. Tassy paced back and forth through the house, her anxiety growing ever stronger. She knew Liam would be concerned because of the storm, was probably even trying to reach them, but how could he? The roads everywhere must be choked with snow, the horrific cold killing every attempt at automated movement. She thought of the neighbors, the Wallaces. But they were several miles up road and what would be the circumstances there? The same as here, no doubt, maybe even worse. Those people never seemed prepared for anything. How could she move, get to town for help? It was clear to her that nothing mechanical would be coming or going down the roads until they could be plowed out. Her mind flickered to the horses in the stockyard. She shuddered at even the thought of trying to ride in conditions like this. She had ridden much in her earlier years on the ranch though little lately. There were a couple of older horses she believed she could manage. Were they even here?

All Liam could do was follow slowly behind the grader trying to control his exasperation! And they could do nothing but stay behind it; without its huge bulk pushing the drifts aside a truck wouldn't move five feet down the road. Carson sat at his side, the heater going full tilt. He fidgeted with the door handle, the seat covers, the zipper on his greasy coveralls. They had been driving directly behind the grader for the past two hours and both passengers were pent up and impatient, yet they knew clearly they had at least another hour before they would reach the lane connecting the Hope Road with the home place. An hour earlier they had helped the grader operator put his chains on as the drifts grew ever deeper.

"Liam, I don't know if we did the right thing, shutting everything down, we're already way behind on this job and High Tower is phoning every day to see if the road is almost finished. They always want everything done yesterday, but never seem to appreciate how hard it is to make a passable road through country like that."

"I couldn't see doing anything else," Liam replied. "Francis broke his dozer blade twice yesterday. It's just too cold, Carson. Hell, it took more time to weld everything back together than we worked. These welders don't work for nothing either. I was surprised the fuel lines didn't freeze up, I've seen it happen before in cold snaps."

"Ever see it as cold as this?" queried Carson.

"I guess I have," said Liam, "but right now I can't remember it. When it gets like this, you've just got to stop and wait for a weather change."

"I wonder how long we got to keep all that equipment running, sucking up fuel and just sitting there?"

"Well, if we turn any of it off for more than an hour or two, we might spend a hell of a lot of time getting them going again even when it warms up."

"Guess if we get too pressed for time, we can bring that other dozer over off that Farrell Creek job," Carson mused, "but there's another big buck spent getting it hauled over."

"No use worrying over any of that now," Liam said in a tired voice. "We'll worry about that when it happens. But I know one thing: if we try to keep going out there in these temperatures, we'll lose more than we gain. Right now I'm more concerned about getting home. I hope Marta and Tassy have been able to get the stock fed with no big problems."

"All they had to do was fork it into the managers," Carson reminded him. "It's not like they got to get anything running to do it."

"I hope," Liam replied, "that they've kept the stove in the house stoked. From what we've heard that wind has knocked out power all over the country."

"Musta took out the phone line, too," Carson said, "I tried to call over and over last night and today, too, but the lines are dead."

"I wondered when we got rid of the old generator last year if it'd ever come to something like this. When we had that, it didn't matter if the power lines were down."

"Yeah," Carson reminded him, "but remember what a pain it was getting to be to keep it running. It was just plain wore out."

"We'd have had to replace it for sure," Liam said, "but at times like this, it would have sure come in handy."

"If we could keep it running," Carson said.

"We'd a been able to keep it running long as the shed door was kept closed," Liam replied. "It was a lot better after we insulated it."

"I don't know. I'm cold...hey, what's that?"

"What's what?" Liam responded.

"What the hell is somebody doing riding a horse down this blown-in road on a day like this?"

Liam peered ahead, trying to see around the plodding grader.

"That horse sure looks like...hell, it is...it's Ranger. I'd know that bald face anywhere," said Carson.

"What the hell is that guy doing on him out here?" fumed Liam

"That's no guy...Grampa, it's Tassy!"

The big black gelding was blowing furiously, steamed breath blowing geyser-like from its dilated nostrils. He was sidestepping nervously now, perilously close to the fence as the roaring, grinding grader lumbered toward it. The driver stopped the machine.

Carson was out of the truck, plunging through the drift on the side of the grader, Liam at his heels. The swaddled figure astride the big horse—lathered around the saddle blanket and between his front legs despite the cold—seemed at first not to notice what was happening. Tassy looked up dazedly just as Carson caught the bridle reins and stopped the horse. She was clad in an oversized pair of insulated coveralls, huge leather mitts, pack boots, her face covered except for her eyes by a heavy scarf wound around her face. A billed fur cap was pulled down over her ears, the earflaps poking outward. Her black hair stuck out in long strands from under the cap. Her feet were at least six inches above the flapping stirrups, though Liam could see that the heavy boots would never have fitted into them even if they'd been the right length. Carson lifted her as easily as a doll from the saddle, Liam holding the reins of the gasping horse. He stood her in the snow at the horse's feet.

"What's going on?" Liam asked. "What are you doing out here?"

Tassy pulled her scarf back from her covered mouth, but her face was so rigid she could only sputter unintelligibly.

"Carson, get her to the truck. I'll look after the horse. And hurry up, she looks nearly frozen."

The grader operator peered down from his machine, the door half-open. Liam waved his arm for him to continue. The grader engine ratched up and it groaned forth. The tired horse rolled his eyes but remained still. Liam took the bridle off, pulled a piece of rope from the truck, tied a bowline around the horse's neck and tethered him to the back. He loosened the cinch slightly, but left the saddle on.

Carson lifted Tassy into the seat, seeing that she could hardly move her legs or arms. Liam got back into the seat, Tassy wedged between the two men, the heater blasting out maximum warmth. Liam loosened the top of her coveralls so she could move her head more easily and unwound the half-frozen scarf from her face. Tassy was taking deep breaths, but she still seemed dazed. Liam pulled the mitts from her hands, which felt like ice. He held them with his large work-scared hands wrapped around them.

"Grampa, my feet! My feet are hurting awful!"

"Carson, help her get her boots off. We better do something for those feet right now." Carson opened the door, stepped out and quickly unlaced and pulled off the heavy pack boots.

"Tassy, I've got to rub your feet with some snow. I know it's going to hurt, but it's all I know to do now. I don't want you to get frostbite." Liam walked around to the passenger side, turned Tassy sideways in the seat, pulled off her wool socks and began rubbing her bare feet with handfuls of snow. She bore this ordeal for a few moments, tears running out of the corners of her eyes, then she began crying out.

"Oh, Grampa...oh, please...please, stop...my feet hurt so much!"

Liam continued rubbing for a few seconds, grabbed her scarf and dried her feet as best he could.

"Carson, drive this thing, and I'll work on her feet. Don't go too fast, you still got Ranger tied on!"

The truck moved forward again, Carson at the wheel, Liam rubbing Tassy's icy feet which he held in his lap.

"Tassy, sweetheart, can you tell us now, tell us why you are out here, why you left the house."

Tassy sat grimacing in pain, hunched against Carson. She blinked her eyes, tears still trickling from their corners. She sniffled loudly, still breathing as though she had just run a long race. "Gramma...something's wrong! I don't know what it is. She can't talk now—only whisper. She's been like that since last night. It's like...it's like she can't move. She kept whispering to get you, over and over. Oh, Grampa, I'm so afraid for her! I didn't know what to do. I tried to phone you but the line was dead. The power is out, too."

"Where is she? Where is Marta?" asked Liam.

"She's in her bed. She seemed okay when she went to bed last night. Something happened to her in the night...I don't know what it is."

"You had heat in the house?"

"Yes, the stove is clear full of wood and damped down. That was the way I left it."

It was after dark when the truck followed the rumbling grader down the long lane to the house, the horse still plodding resolutely behind it. Carson waved to the grader operator, then followed Liam and Tassy to the house, the three of them kicking through the drifts and not bothering with their boots when they got there. Liam went directly to the bedroom, Tassy and Carson at his heels.

"Marta...Marta!" Liam took her hand. He felt its iciness.

Marta lay as Tassy had left her, her head tipped back slightly, her eyes partially open. Liam bent over, laid her hand to her side and put his ear to her mouth and then to her chest. He repeated this. He slowly straightened up, his eyes and face blank. "She's gone," he said.

A clear June Sunday, warm wind blowing downriver. His seventy-something body restless, feeling the need to move, to accomplish, Liam poked about in the large double-doored machinery shop behind the old house. Greasy tools, rags, half empty pails of lubricants were strewn about; a huge dozer squatted in the middle of it all, its tracks off, radiator shield removed and leaning against the engine frame. Liam walked around through the mess, looking absently at the disassembled parts, hoses and piles of bolts. Carson and his help were going through the yearly ritual of repairing and servicing the company's working assets, though owing to the Sabbath, none of them were here today.

Liam walked to the wide doors and peered out upstream; he could hear Carson and the children he'd taken fishing a little way upriver. He wondered idly if they were actually doing any fishing, they were making so much noise and running up and down the river banks horseplaying. He could just see the tops of some of their heads, but he could sure hear them. He smiled to himself when he thought about Carson, how domestic he could be, how much he liked keeping the kids entertained. He had his hands full with his and Joanna's today. It wouldn't be so long before Tassy's Simon would be out there, too. Today, Simon was being entertained in the swings behind the new house by Joanna's Amelia.

Liam stood in the shop doorway a while, soaking up the warm sunshine, not really paying much attention to his surroundings. He wandered out toward the stock barns, looking at everything and nothing in particular. They'd need to be getting a new roof on some of these buildings before long. Somewhere on the barn roof ahead of him, a piece of metal roofing scrolled up off the roof surface, torn loose sometime recently by wind. The stockyards were pretty dry now. Great piles of manure were pushed up in the center of the corrals, awaiting hauling onto the nearby fields. The smell was not so noticeable today as the breeze swept it down the valley. It'd be good to get it hauled out soon so Joanna could quit grousing about it. Liam wandered slowly on, fouling his clean shoes in a seam of drying mud, but he seemed not to notice. A clutch of his horses grazed in the east pasture far off downriver, he could just barely see them. None of the cows were here now, trucked off a couple of weeks ago to summer pasture fifty miles northeast. It was a relief to be rid of them for a while. During spring calving time they had required endless attention. At Liam's heels trailed Tippy, his mongrel dog. There had been any number of Tippys down through the years, all of them related, none exactly alike but all bearing the same name. This particular Tippy was black and various shades of grey, its squat shape testament to some kind of shepherd blood.

Liam wondered absently if dinner was nearly ready; probably not or somebody would be calling him. These Sunday family dinners, started years before by Marta, had become an entrenched family ritual. Half the Sundays in a year were spent here by the Brennans, at least the ones close enough to attend. Paul, Carolyn and family were rarely seen though they came with their growing band of children every other summer. Presently they resided in Tulsa, Oklahoma, where Paul continued his rise up the corporate ladder. They were expected sometime next month, unforeseen problems not withstanding.

Liam found his feet carrying him in the oft-repeated direction past the machinery and stock buildings and along the strongly fenced edge of the large garden now cultivated and cared for by Joanna and her growing brood. Liam remembered as he always did when he went out there that long ago time when he and Marta had first broke ground. It looked so different now, but then again, he thought, it hasn't changed all that much, just the surroundings. If a person looked behind him toward the river, the scene did not seem much changed at all. But the whole place had an aura of permanence that had been missing then. Everywhere Liam looked, he saw the print of his own hand: the buildings, the fences, the cleared fields, the old house, a dovetailed corner of which he could just see through the jumble of stock buildings. He had put his mark on everything here, everything, that is, except the great river behind him.

He turned around and looked at it, the south bank just visible from where he stood. But then, he thought, I've even helped to change that, too. He thought of the low river levels now as the dam held back the waters in the great reservoir behind it. He thought of the peculiar and faintly disconcerting fact that the river no longer even froze, no matter the temperature, its waters somehow heated by the dam he'd helped to create. His own culpability as an agent of change settled onto him as it always did when he allowed himself to think about it.

He turned back to look at the old house; did it really look as shabby as Joanna said it did? He thought of their conversation of the summer following Marta's death.

He had gotten up one morning; it was about this time of year, too, he remembered. He'd spent another near-sleepless night in the new house, most of it drinking coffee at the huge new kitchen table, listening absently to the radio but mostly just staring at the walls. Those months had been so hard and, in many ways, confusing for him. That was the only time in his life he'd ever taken any kind of medicine. That stuff was supposed to make him sleep better; it hadn't, he remembered. He had never, prior to Marta's death, thought much about life without her. And it had happened so suddenly, no one could have seen it coming. He reasoned as he sat there or paced through those long nights, that separation of loved ones by death was part of the natural order of things. How many times had he learned that even before this? But it hadn't made the abrupt jolt of her passing any easier. It was like part of his life was severed from him.

It was a morning after one of the long soul-searching nights, the sun just coming up and a promise of a clear calm day. Liam had left the new house, wandered around the place, not much different than he was doing now, except that nobody was around. He found himself at the door of the old log house. It was much as he and Marta had left it when they moved into the new one. The grass around the house was still kept clipped, for what purpose he knew not. He hadn't, to his memory at that time anyway, actually set foot in it since the move.

He stood in front of the door for a long moment, then grasped the heavy, slightly rusted door handle and swung the door open. The kitchen into which he stepped had a slightly musty smell, but it wasn't as bad as he'd expected. He gazed at the log walls, brownish-grey with age and use. He noted the incongruity of the electrical wiring strung from room to room high upon the logs, the plastic covered outlets notched back into the logs just above floor level.

The worn linoleum covered floor creaked slightly as he walked diagonally across the kitchen and peered into the two floor-level rooms that opened off the kitchen. He started to climb the stairs to the bedrooms in the loft and then stopped; he stepped back down as a wave of memories flooded over him. He raised his hand to his face and found it wet. For a long time he stood and looked at the walls around him turning now and then to face another part of the house. Had they really spent more than forty years of their lives in this house? Somehow it didn't seem that long—and yet? If he forced himself to, he could faintly remember every hour of labor he and Marta had put in to build and render livable this structure. His two oldest children had been born in this very house; in his mind's eye he saw himself and two small boys plastering wet clay into the spaces between the logs. He fumbled for a time in his shirt pocket, remembering finally that he no longer carried rollings, the smoking habit finally extinguished—he hoped. He cast about for a place to sit and rest his knees and there was none: not a stick of furniture remained. He walked to the kitchen window; the battered old sink was still where they'd left it. He leaned on the edge of the counter and gazed out the window at the new house directly opposite, a long stone's throw away. He stood quietly, motionless, for many minutes, thinking deeply.

"Dad, I just can't believe this! Why on earth would you even consider it? All the planning, all the work you and Mother went through and now you don't even want to live in it? What can possibly be wrong with this house? You've got everything in it that a person could ever want! And the thought of moving back into that old log thing—well, it beggars the imagination! It doesn't even have central heating, just that ancient wood stove. How will you be comfortable with that?"

"Joanna, do you remember all the years you lived there? Was it ever cold? Were you so uncomfortable?"

"But, Dad, that was before I even knew about modern housing, carpeted floors, windows that open and close, bathrooms with showers. Honestly, I'm actually worried about you that you'd even consider leaving all of that to go back to something as...as primitive as that old house! And the waste! You spent all of that money to build this place just to...to reject it? Dad, this makes no sense!"

"It's not going to be wasted, Jo, I've thought about that, too. What would be wrong with you, Russel and the kids moving in here? Hell, you've said yourself that your place in town is far too small; the kids need more room...."

And the conversation had gone on for days, actually weeks. Finally, in gradual capitulation, Liam prevailed over his strong-willed daughter. But it was not accomplished without addressing many complications. The rest of the family had to be considered, solicited and listened to, for they all had a stake in this.

It was obvious that Paul would have no objections; he was never coming back here to live. Loren and Tassy, just beginning their married lives, were both employed in Fort St. John and living in a small, but nice, rented house there. Carson was the biggest consideration, but objections from him never materialized. He and Jennifer were happy where they were. He'd always commuted to the home place since his marriage, and anyway, most of the time he was away on jobs far from either place. Liam was secretly a little disconcerted about Carson's keeping his space from the ranch, but then he told himself, it wasn't really surprising. Carson had always been a loner, his own person, though still integrated implicitly into the family orbit. That he'd want to be slightly separated from the nucleus was consistent.

The biggest obstacle was Russel's work. Living at the ranch made it necessary for him to commute distances he'd not otherwise have faced. In the end, he and Joanna consoled themselves with the idea that the environment the home place provided for their children overrode resulting annoyances. When Joanna, Russel and their brood finally moved to the new house, it was with the understanding that they would pay for it as they could, the proceeds to be divided among the other members at a later date. Joanna, with her accountant's efficiency, had finalized the legalities within the company framework.

It had taken the better part of a summer to accomplish it, and, of course, Joanna would never allow Liam to move back into the log house without what she considered making it livable. Workmen were brought in and the interior walls were meticulously sanded with power tools, the old wiring removed, the logs grooved, then the wiring put back with split doweling concealing it; then the whole thing covered with a clear lacquer. The kitchen floor was resurfaced, the old kitchen sink replaced, carpeting put into the bedrooms both upstairs and down, and a shower painstakingly installed over the bathtub. Liam, who had always used the tub, thought this a needless expense, but Joanna, as usual, prevailed.

Liam remained immoveable on one item: the exterior of the house was not modified nor anything added to its weathered surface but a coat of linseed oil. Joanna balked at this. "Dad, it looks so old fashioned, so shabby!" But Liam would not budge. He moved his and Marta's old bed back in and his few personal items. The house was furnished, too sparsely Joanna said, with simple furniture that Liam picked out.

It was a comfort to have Joanna and her family near, though Liam wondered if he'd ever said it. And now this Sunday afternoon as Liam poked around the place as was often his wont while the women put together the usual considerable Sunday fare and the children romped, he found himself on the little knoll, looking south just above the vista of the great river that he and Marta had always loved. His stiffened knees were starting to bother him again, but he ignored them and moved on, his mind not focused on anything in particular. He came to the edge of a white wooden fence, the only fence on the place that was never allowed to fall into disrepair. He leaned against the gate and looked into the small enclosure: the cluster of pines that had never been molested, still looked vigorous inside the fence. His eyes fell on the three grave markers, as they always did on these trips, the one for Marta and the two for their lost sons, though one lay here only in spirit.

Liam's mind slipped back to that grey winter day when he and Carson assisted by a backhoe, trucked here from a job miles away, had torn through the iron soil to create Marta's final resting place. He saw himself and the family, even Paul, summoned from half a world away, his eyes dark with fatigue, as they stood around the site, the Anglican pastor presiding. It seemed long ago and yet it was not, only a few years. The grass around the graves was clipped, and as always at this time of year, had glass containers of flowers from the beds around the new house. For the thousandth time, he wondered, had he given her the life she really wanted? The one he had so glowingly painted for her in far away Europe. Had she really loved it as he did, or had she just endured all those difficult years in the beginning for him? For he had wondered so often, even in that far off time, if she was truly happy here. He hoped so. Sometimes life was a great puzzle, unclear, much like the aneurysm that had taken her.

"Grampa! Grampa!" Liam stood up and looked over his shoulder. Five year old Nancy, one of Joanna's, ran across the field toward him. "Grampa, dinner's ready. Mum says to come now!" As she said this, she tripped and fell almost at Liam's feet. He picked her up in his arms as she puckered up and started to cry, "Grampa, my leg hurts!"

Liam sat her down and rubbed her scuffed knees. "Nancy, sweetheart, you need to be more careful. Don't try to run so fast!"

The child sniffled a minute, leaning her head against his thigh. When the tears stopped, they started back toward the house, the child holding his lumpy, scarred hand.

"Grampa, why do you always go here?"

"Oh, I don't know, guess because it's a place I like."

"Mum says Gramma Marta's there. Will I get to be there, too, when I die?"

"Well, I don't know, Nancy, that's a long way off, I'd think! That's a nice dress you're wearing."

"Mum's gonna be mad when she sees I got it dirty already."

"Maybe we just won't tell her, what do you think?"

"I...Grampa, why are your fingers all funny?"

"Well, just grew that way, I guess."

"Liam! Nancy! Come on! We're waiting on you!"

Liam looked up to see Joanna framed against the back door. He and Nancy trudged hand in hand toward the house.

About the Author

JERRY SECRIST was born in California and grew up in Utah where he lived with his parents and siblings in a small farming community. He attended Utah State University and received a Bachelor of Science Degree in English Education in 1968. While teaching English and Journalism in Moses Lake, Washington, he became personally acquainted with British Columbia's Peace River Country when he helped a friend haul farm machinery to the land where he was homesteading. In due course, he convinced his wife that they should move there. He was intrigued with the modern pioneer lifestyle that had and was still developing there and he wanted to be a part of it. In 1971, he and his wife with their small family moved to the community of Fort St. John, where he taught high school. They made many life-long friendships in those first months.

Jerry's many friends and acquaintances in the agricultural sector taught him to appreciate the challenges and difficulties of farming and ranching in a new and raw environment. As he witnessed their lives and taught their children in school, he marveled at their stoicism and pioneer spirit, many still living without the comforts of electricity or indoor plumbing. Pioneering was only two generations back in his own family background in the western U.S. and he vowed that when he had the time he would write their collective story.

Jerry retired from teaching in 1999. He and his wife live in Charlie Lake where he raises and trains horses. He spends his summers in the mountains of the beautiful Peace River Country.